THE PRIDE
OF THE
TREVALLIONS

Carola Salisbury

THE PRIDE OF THE TREVALLIONS

0272

DOUBLEDAY & COMPANY, INC.
GARDEN CITY, NEW YORK
1975

All of the characters in this book are fictitious, and any resemblance to actual persons, living or dead, is purely coincidental.

Library of Congress Cataloging in Publication Data
Salisbury, Carola.
    The pride of the Trevallions.
    I. Title.
PZ4.S1678Pr3 [PR6069.A46]   823'.9'14
ISBN 0-385-06742-9
Library of Congress Catalog Card Number 74-9462

To B—, without whose continuous
and clamorous support this book
could never have been written.

THE PRIDE
OF THE
TREVALLIONS

CHAPTER 1

One afternoon, quite late, I stood in the old garden of Mallion and looked around me at the ivy-girt battlements that I
have loved—and hated—so well.

The wind, coming in from the sea, brought with it the
tumbled clouds that stole the last of daylight and made white
waves in the wrinkled water below me, beneath the great walls.
Gulls swooped low over the stark stone islet offshore: the islet
among the treacherous rocks where—legend tells—the wreckers
used to hang lanterns, to lure in the ships to their doom. The
cries of the gulls came up to me, and they were like the
despairing cries of drowning sailors.

When the clouds had moved across the last of the blueness,
and Mallion was enfolded in shadow, a great heaviness fell
upon my spirit. The castle, which had looked so strong and
benign in the wintry sunlight, took on a dark grimness that
seemed to echo its violent, strife-torn past. I tried to throw
off my sudden disquiet—but it was no use. The light continued
to fade, and the malaise increased in my heart.

Now the castle was a dark and shapeless bulk looming above
me; a giant monument to the wild and tragic Trevallions who
had built it in their pride and had defended it, down the
ages, with their blood and their arrogance. The very walls
seemed to threaten me. It was not only that I heard the

rustling of the ivy; the castle was a living and speaking thing. I had only lately come to know this; the Trevallions had always known it.

The spirits of five centuries of Trevallions looked down on me—the stranger, the interloper, the nobody. No wonder I despaired. How could I have thought, I asked myself, that I should ever be accepted here?

As if in answer to my question, it seemed that the menace turned to mockery, and they were laughing at me, the spirits of Castle Mallion; mirthless, scorning laughter that jarred in my ears, so that I pressed my hands to my ears to shut it out. Then I seemed to see their faces—the dark, proud faces that looked down from the long rows of portraits in the Great Gallery—their arrogant lips twisted with soundless, hate-filled mirth.

I turned and ran—anywhere—to get away from them. The thickets plucked at my skirts as I plunged through the neglected garden, past the decaying statuary, all overhung with ivy.

And, all the time, I kept my hands pressed to my ears—lest I should truly hear what, in my heart, I knew to be a fantasy of my overwrought mind.

* * *

I can pinpoint the date when it really all began. A firm of tea importers in Kingston had sent a calendar to the plantation, and my father had given it to me to hang in my room. The morning of that unforgettable day, I wrote on the calendar, in a careful roundhand: *Tonight is the night of the Ball*. And the date was May 15, 1859.

We had been in Jamaica, my father and I, since the end of the Crimean War four years previously. He was an ex-soldier. My mother had passed away when I was ten. She—a gentlewoman who had been cast off by her family when she married a common soldier—had, herself, educated me far beyond my station in life. On her death, I was taken into the charitable care of the Reverend and Mrs Smithers of St Martin's, Kennington, who had looked after me and educated me as a child of their own while Father was away in the Crimea. They, too, were now both dead.

Father, a corporal of horse, had taken his discharge when the awful war had ended. A corporal's slender pension would never have kept us, but Father had served with Lieutenant Piers Trevallion. What was more, he had ridden with the lieutenant in the terrible charge at Balaklava. A man who had carried his wounded officer from the field of battle, and who had dressed his hurts and brought him to a place of safety, need have no fear for the future welfare of his motherless daughter and himself—not when the man he had served was a Trevallion. Though Piers Trevallion had later died of his wounds, his two younger brothers were quick to show their gratitude. A few days after my fourteenth birthday, Father and I boarded the transatlantic packet at Liverpool on the first part of our journey to Jamaica, where he was to be the bailiff at Roswithiel.

Roswithiel—which was the name of the Trevallion family's sugar plantation on the island—was, apart from my stay with the Smitherses, the first real home I had ever known. Before that, my memories were of Army barrack life and seedy lodging houses.

That May morning—which began like any other morning—heralded the beginning of yet another new life for me. Yet there was nothing very special to show it—only that it was to be the night of the ball.

My father laughed at me when he saw my writing on the tea importer's calendar.

"Lord love us, Joanna! What's it to you, lass, that they're having a rout at the big house? There's none of the young swells of Kingston or Montego Bay as would give you so much as a glance, and it'd break your heart with envy to see laces and fineries that the pampered little she-parakeets will be wearing."

"Nothing to stop me from watching from afar," I replied pertly. I had had a lot of arguments with my father recently, and it was quite obvious that he had completely fallen into local custom, and was now taking rum with his breakfast coffee every morning. His linen was none too clean, either, though I had laid out a fresh shirt and necktie for him the evening before.

"Let it be from afar, then," he said. "And don't get any ideas in your head about sneaking into the house and watching the goings-on from the top of the stairwell with the servants. Your white face would stand out from amongst those blacks like a golden guinea in a coal scuttle, and it's me who'd be on the carpet before Mr Benedict in the morning."

"Surely Mr Benedict wouldn't bother to do that," I said wonderingly. "He scarcely knows I'm alive."

"There's not much that escapes his eye," said Father. "What's more, he's got the uncertain temper that makes him dangerous. I've known horses like that. It's all in the breeding. Too finely bred by half. I remember when we were trans- porting the regimental horses out to the Crimea . . ."

By now, my father was well away with his Army reminis- cences, and I shut my mind to him. I thought of the three Trevallion brothers: Piers who was dead, and Benedict and Saul who were both very much alive at Roswithiel—though their paths scarcely crossed mine.

Piers Trevallion's face I knew from the one and only time when I had set foot in the big house. This had happened two years before, when my father had been summoned to give an account of the state of the sugar crop to Mr Benedict who was in bed with fever. Plantation business was always transacted in the office, and on this special occasion Father had yielded to my pleas to allow me to go with him, so that I could see the inside of the fabulous Roswithiel mansion.

Father left me in the hall, under a huge and glittering chandelier. A Negro butler in white gloves took charge of me while Father was upstairs, and it was he who showed me the picture over the great fireplace and said that was the elder Trevallion brother who had perished of his wounds after the charge at Balaklava. To the day I die, I shall remember that lean and beautiful face looking down at me from under the unruly mop of careless black curls; the deep-blue eyes that seemed to be filled with some private laughter. As much as

4

one can fall in love with a painting of a dead hussar, I fell in love with the portrait of Piers. I was sixteen at the time.

Saul Trevallion, the second brother and successor to the vast estates in the West Indies and the family castle in Cornwall, was a gross caricature of the face and figure in the portrait. He had the dark good looks, but his cheeks were puffy and his eyes pouched. It was common gossip that he had a bad reputation with women, and that he drank heavily. The evil showed in his face.

The younger brother, Benedict, was Piers with a dark shadow of melancholy cast over his face, so that the eyes were haunted with a strange sadness and the mouth forever turned down in bitterness. Two deep indentations between the brows —as if someone had drawn two fingertips in soft clay—betrayed him, also, as a man of savage temper.

These were the Trevallions, the last of an ancient line. Both were unmarried, as Piers had been. Their invalid mother, so we were told, lived alone in Castle Mallion, in far-off Cornwall. They seldom visited her, but preferred to live their lives of unfettered luxury in the tropical sun of Jamaica.

Though I hardly ever saw them, and feared them both, the brothers filled me with a strange fascination. They were the great ones who ordered my present existence and my father's. At their whim, we had been taken from poverty and brought to live in their own private kingdom in the tropics. Their hold over us was complete: at another whim, we could be thrown back to poverty in England, or be made to eke out some sort of existence in the steamy slums of Kingston.

Twenty-five years had gone by since the slaves were freed in the British West Indies, but the whipping block still stood —a mute reminder of an evil past—in the courtyard of the plantation. To me, it was a symbol of the power that still remained with the Trevallions: the crushing power of wealth, of influence, of birth.

My father and I were very close to the source of this power. A low garden wall separated our modest bailiff's house from the lawn of the mansion. Simply by standing on a stool, I could peer across to the carriage drive that stopped at the foot of the marble steps beneath the tall white columns that fronted the great house. So near to all that splendour; but we might as well have been living in a different world.

But that night—that May night—there was to be a grand ball at Roswithiel mansion, and all the youth and beauty and wealth of the island would be there.

And Joanna Goodacre, I told myself with determination, was going to see as much of the glamour and excitement as she could.

* * *

The whole day was full of preparations for the ball. The field hands had been up, as usual, since before dawn, but no work had been done among the sugar cane. Instead, long lines of Negroes were to be seen carrying great baskets of flowers up the long drive to the mansion, which was soon aflame with colour. Hibiscus and bougainvillaea, jasmine and scarlet rhododendron heads were banked against the tall columns, till the mansion looked like some great white wedding cake rising up from a bride's bouquet. The house servants placed long tables on the lawn, under the eucalyptus trees. They laid them with white linen cloths and swags of flowers along the edges, then they covered them with dishes of exotic foods, till one could no longer see the tablecloths for the blaze of silver, of green, saffron, and reds. And all through the long afternoon, Negro footmen in powdered wigs stood by the tables and fanned away the flies with palm leaves. I watched all this from my vantage point of the garden wall.

I spent all day at the wall, and missed no detail of the preparations, or the comings-and-goings. And anyone with half an eye would have been aware that the whole complicated business of arranging for the ball revolved round the commanding figure of a woman in a black silk dress.

This was Mayana. I was not to know it then—how could I have guessed?—that Mayana was destined to play such a vital role in my life.

Long years have passed, and many tears have dried, but I can still see her as she was on that May day at Roswithiel with her little boy by her side. She was one of the most beautiful women I have ever known. A mulatress—part white, part Negro, part Indian—it was as if the essence of physical perfection in all those three races were joined together in Mayana. Though young—she could not have been more than twenty-five—she was housekeeper at the Roswithiel mansion, and she ruled the small army of black servants with a rod of iron. Even my father, who had nothing but contempt for coloured people, always spoke of Mayana with respect. Yet how she performed her duties so ably remains a mystery to me to this day. For Mayana was a deaf-mute.

Her affliction made no difference. She stood on the steps of the mansion, her splendid body rising from the black crinoline, her blue-black hair drawn back into a chignon. She had only to snap her fingers and point, and a basket of flowers was rearranged, or a silver dish of food placed in a particular spot. Her control was perfect.

Her little boy was a mystery to me. Whenever I asked about him, my father dismissed him as a love child and changed the subject. He never left Mayana's side. That May day in Jamaica, he would have been about four; a pretty, milky-skinned boy in a sailor's suit.

In the late afternoon, the Trevallion brothers came out on to the steps, and Mayana greeted them with a deep curtsey. Even from a distance, the difference between the two men was very marked. Saul, the older, was putting on weight, and he walked with a pompous man's swagger. Mr Benedict had a lean, catlike grace about him. It was he who spoke to Mayana, no doubt asking her how the arrangements were going; she replied with a sweep of her hand that indicated the banks of blooms and the laden tables. Mr Benedict nodded with satisfaction. When they turned to go back into the house, the younger brother paused to pat the head of the little boy in the sailor's suit.

Tropical darkness began to fall. Lights went on in the windows of the great house, and the footmen hung lanterns among the branches of the eucalyptus trees.

The time had come, I decided, to put my daring plan into action.

* * *

Father had gone out for the evening. Drinking with his cronies in the town. He would come riding back in the early hours and swear loudly at the stable lad who had waited up for him. Then go reeling off to bed. It suited my plan.

Up in my bedroom, I changed out of my sprigged muslin dress, for what use is a crinoline when you want to go creeping about among rhododendron bushes? I put on the breeches, shirt and short jacket that I had borrowed (with dire threats of unspecified punishment if he so much as breathed a word of the transaction to anyone) from the stable lad. My mane of unruly chestnut hair, I piled up on the crown of my head and covered with a spotted handkerchief. Then, stockingless and barefoot, I examined myself in the long mirror—and liked what I saw.

I have never prided myself on being a beauty. My nose is too long and my mouth too large. At seventeen, I told myself I was too tall and gawky by half. But I made a splendid boy in patched and worn breeches. And the handkerchief was the finishing touch. I looked the regular pirate captain's cabin boy.

The sound of an orchestra came out of the velvety darkness as I crept out of our back door, across the garden to the low wall, scrambled over it, and dropped on to the forbidden lawn of Roswithiel mansion.

It was my intention to get so close as to be almost a part of the most alluring and enchanting event of Jamaica's social year. I had decided this long before my father's warning to keep my distance. The garden wall was fine enough for watching the comings-and-goings, but it only commanded a view of the carriage drive and the buffet tables on the lawn. The most sparkling part of the gay proceedings—the dancing —would take place, I knew, at the rear of the house, on the terrace above the water gardens, near the two great ornamental fountains. That was where I wanted to be. And all I had to do was crawl there. On my hands and knees, if necessary, through

8

the rhododendron bushes that stretched all the way, to within inches of the terrace.

The bushes offered better cover than I had expected, and were well out of the loom of the lights from the house and lawn. I was able to move quite quickly, at a crouch, and still peer over the tops of the scented blooms.

The guests were arriving fast. There was a long line of carriages in the drive, and footmen with blazing flambeaux were marshalling them to the great portico, where a red carpet swept up the steps to the door. All this passed from my sight as I circled the mansion. And then the terrace came into view.

The events of the years between have never erased the memory of that magical and enchanting scene.

The terrace was ablaze with light, with colour, and with sound. A thousand pinpoints of candlelight came from silver candelabra held by bewigged black footmen lining the sweeping curve of the terrace. The light shone on the banks of flowers and on the white shoulders of women. It was caught by the rich folds of silks and satins, and by the white shirt-fronts of the men. It was reflected, in a million diamond droplets, from the two fountains that rose from their marble bowls into the velvety night sky.

The orchestra was playing a waltz, and perhaps a score of couples were dancing in the open space between the fountains. The rest milled about on the terrace, their laughter rising above the sound of the flutes and violins.

I remember, so vividly, how I stood rooted to the spot by the sheer shock and delight at the magnificence of it all. Hidden there among the bushes in my rough lad's clothes, I think, at that moment, I would have given half my life to have been able to take my place in that brilliant throng; with my hair dressed with diamonds, my shoulders bare, and the candlelight bringing out the sheen of my satins. And with some fine, handsome beau to pay court to me. Not one of the chinless sprigs from one of the great plantation families, nor some drawling ass in military scarlet; but someone whom I could look up to, someone strong-willed, poised, mature . . .

I crept nearer the scene.

9

The tall rhododendron bushes ended at the very edge of the terrace, and it was there that I took my place—where the very leaves and flowers were damp with spray from the fountains, and each fitful zephyr sent a fine flurry of moisture against my cheek. There, peering out through the greenery, I could have reached out my hand and touched the whirling skirts of those whose partners danced them to the limit of the terrace, where the spray was flying—and there were many who braved the dampness, for coolness' sake, throwing back their heads and laughing as the gleaming droplets rained down on them.

The night drew on. I had no sensation of the passing of time, though I became aware that more and more guests were coming out of the French windows on to the terrace, and that the ball was becoming more hectic and noisy. Girls with faces flushed with champagne waltzed close past my hiding place, laughing up into the eyes of their beaux. The music grew louder, more abandoned. The waltz gave place to the polonaise and the tarantella, and the schottische—a kind of polka which, I knew, was all the rage in Kingston that year. Some of them danced well, some badly: quite a few of the younger men had soon taken so much rum, or champagne—or both—that their partners were almost having to support them, and they stumbled in their turns.

And then—I saw Benedict Trevallion.

He was in a tail coat of hunting scarlet, with snow-white breeches and gleaming hessian boots. He came out of the dancing throng with a lovely blonde in his arms. I didn't recognise her, but took her to be a daughter of a plantation owner, or a society girl from Kingston or Montego Bay. She danced like a dream and I found myself hating her for that —not to mention for her magnolia-like beauty, her dress, and her jewellery.

Benedict Trevallion's dark good looks complemented her fairness in every way. They were like a pair of sharply contrasted carriage horses put together in harness for the sake of a stunning effect. In no time at all, the others had all stopped dancing and were leaving a wide space for them. The music increased in tempo. The hessian boots fairly flew. Round and round spun the hem of the girl's pink satin dress.

Round and round, with their gazes locked, each to each.

I felt my cheeks flame with excitement, and could scarcely stop myself from joining in when the watching throng began to clap in time to the rapid beat. Never in my life, before or since, have I been caught up in such a wave of heady intoxication. My jealous resentment of the girl forgotten, I willed her to respond even more nimbly to her partner's lead. Not that she needed support from me, or any other. She was like thistledown in his arms. Her step never faltered.

He was quite merciless to her. There was no pause in his wild turning. And, all the time, he looked down on her with a grin of savage exultation.

"Enough's enough, Trevallion. You'll kill the gel!"

"Poppycock!" came the countercry. "Dance her off her feet, Trevallion. Show the little beauty who's master!"

The end—when it came—had a dramatic suddenness. Benedict Trevallion raised his hand in a signal to the orchestra conductor, who immediately responded by ordering the music to a close with a mighty drumbeat and a clash of cymbals.

The heels of the gleaming hessian boots came together with a resounding click of finality. The dance was finished. The pink satin skirt billowed, and was still.

In the shocked silence that followed the sudden cessation of sound and movement, the blonde sagged, fainted clean away, and would have fallen—but for Benedict Trevallion's supporting arms.

"By jove, I was right. He's done for her!"

"Loosen her stays!" came a tipsy roar. "Fetch a damned doctor!"

The tall figure in the scarlet coat swept the senseless girl right off her feet, high in his arms.

"Where's he taking her?"

"To the fountain! The feller's going to revive the little beauty with a cold tub!"

Holding his limp burden high, Benedict Trevallion stepped right over the edge of the ornamental bowl and into the thigh-deep, foam-flecked water. They were both instantly soaked to the skin by the descending cascade.

I stared, dry-mouthed with awe, and saw the girl recover with a scream—which she instantly turned into a peal of laughter when she saw the reason for her plight.

A cheer went up from the watchers as the blonde wound her slender arms round her partner's neck and laughed into his face. He let the lower part of her body slip from his grasp and into the water, and they stood together amid the torrent, locked in an embrace. As their lips met, his hands came up behind her, plucked away the pins that bound her golden hair. It tumbled down about her waist.

I don't know how long they stood there, shut off from all reality in their private world of cascading water, lips locked in their act of unbridled passion; I only know that I suddenly became aware that someone was standing near to me.

I looked sidelong: it was the beautiful deaf-mute, Mayana.

She stood by the edge of the terrace, close to the bushes. So close to me that I could quite easily have touched her. No one else saw her, for no one else had eyes for anyone but the dark man and the blonde girl in the fountain; and she was entirely unaware of my presence—indeed, I doubt if she had a thought for anyone in Creation, save the object of her hatred.

For what I saw, on the flawless face of the lovely mulatress, was such hatred and detestation as I never hope to see again on the face of a fellow human being: a primeval loathing that, nevertheless, carried with it a hint of inner heartbreak.

And, surely, it was directed towards Benedict Trevallion; for who would waste that sort of hatred on that stupid creature in the wet satin dress?

* * *

Immediately after the episode of the fountain, the scene on the terrace changed. Benedict Trevallion helped his partner out of the bowl, then turned curtly on his heel and went into the house. It was as if he had suddenly soured of the situation, and wanted only to put on some dry clothes. The blonde was

12

led away, giggling, by a severe-looking matron who could have been her mother. The orchestra took a rest for refreshment. Most of those who had been dancing drifted round to the front lawn and the buffet tables.

Mayana had disappeared almost without my noticing.

I wondered about her. If, as I supposed, her fury had been sparked off by jealousy, then what was her relationship with Benedict?

I had heard tell that many men in the 'Trevallions' position were in the habit of taking coloured women for their mistresses. Such a thing would scarcely cause a raised eyebrow in Jamaica—provided it was done with discretion.

Was this what Mayana was to Benedict? If so, it could account for her reaction. What, then, of her little boy—he whom my father contemptuously dismissed as a love child?

It was all too puzzling. And, besides, it was getting late. I resolved to put the matter out of my mind for the time being and get myself out of the grounds of Roswithiel mansion as carefully as I had got myself in.

Fate had decided otherwise.

* * *

The first intimation I had of any danger was the double-double blare of a hunting horn, coming from the kennels, which lay beyond the coachhouse and stable block at the far side of the mansion. Quietly engaged in treading my way back through the rhododendrons, I gave no thought to the sound—for the Trevallions were hunting-mad, and there was the blowing of horns at the slightest pretext around Roswithiel —till it was repeated, this time nearer, and accompanied by raucous cries and drunken laughter:

"Gone away! Gone away! So-ho!"

"Tally-ho, Tally-ho! Slip the hounds! Slip 'em, I say!"

Pausing, I looked back across the lawn—and saw it all; saw the bestial scene in all its grim clarity.

Skittering across the lawn was a large ginger cat. I knew it well, for, though it lived in the kitchen quarters of the big house, it was not averse to cadging scraps at our door. In hot

13

pursuit were half a dozen of the ball guests, all in the scarlet tail coats that showed them to be members of the Trevallion Fox Hunt. Saul Trevallion was well to the fore, and moving quickly for a man of his bulky condition—though, perhaps this was because he was being half-dragged along by two foxhounds that he had leashed in his hands. I saw, by his flushed countenance and wild eyes, that he was both drunk and dangerous.

I realised immediately what had happened: inflamed by drink, and casting around for some form of brutal amusement, Saul Trevallion and some of his cronies had fetched two hounds from the hunt kennels. To go hunting. They had chanced upon the ginger cat—and now they were hounding it to its death. Twenty-five years ago, before the emancipation, a Negro child would have served them just as well.

"Dammit, slip those hounds, Saul, before the brute reaches cover!"

Saul Trevallion obeyed the last shouted injunction, and the two hounds streaked away from the men, baying wildly. The hunters whooped with excitement to see them fan out and close with their quarry from both flanks.

"Seize him, Lightning! Kill, Trinket!"

The cat saw its danger and swerved wildly. Now it was heading straight for the bushes where I crouched, and it had, perhaps, ten strides to make before it might find some measure of safety among the thickets and the trees beyond.

Only—it was not going to reach the rhododendrons: the nearest hound was outpacing it, and closing in, jaws gaping, for the kill.

An instant later—with no thought for anything but to save that terrified creature from being rent to pieces before my very eyes—I broke cover and ran towards it, hands extended.

It leapt into my arms and clung there, yowling. The hounds slewed to a halt at my feet, baying terrifyingly and rearing up to strike at the trembling creature in my grasp, their tough claws lacerating my arms.

"Dammit, who's this brat? Give the jackanapes a cut with your whip, somebody!" The scarlet coats crowded about me.

Scarlet, angry faces and mouths that gaped and drooled with fury, like those of their hounds.

"Put that confounded cat down, you young scoundrel. What d'you mean by it, hey?" The voice of Saul Trevallion himself.

Someone wrenched me by the shoulder and spun me round, so that the cat slipped from my grasp. In the instant, it dived into the bushes and was gone. The hounds paid it no attention—it was I who was now the hunters' quarry.

"Who is the brat?" cried Trevallion. "Turn his face towards the moonlight and let's see his jib, dammit!"

One of them grabbed for my head, seizing a handful of the handkerchief and the hair beneath. I screamed out with pain and instinctively pulled away. The handkerchief came off, and my hair, freed of its binding, fell about my shoulders.

"What the deuce! It's no brat—it's a gel!"

"What's this?" cried Saul Trevallion. "By gad, you're right!"

He took me roughly by the shoulders and spun me round to face him. I caught the sour and sickly stench of island rum on his hot breath.

"Bless me, it's Goodacre's filly."

"Never mind who she is," said another, in a slurred voice. "Let's have a bit of fun with her, hey?"

"Leave her be!" Trevallion struck down his companion's arm and leered into my face. "This little morsel of womanflesh is for me. Devil take it, I've fed and stabled her, haven't I? And, by gad, she's advanced real proudly. Haven't seen her about for a while, and never realised we had such a little beauty ripe and ready for the picking. Come to the master, my pippin-cheeked Aphrodite."

He was very strong, and there was no resisting his grasp about my waist and shoulders.

"Please, sir, let me go," I pleaded. "I won't set foot in the grounds again, I swear it."

"Come as often as it takes your fancy, my pretty. Now—let's have a kiss, for a start."

His mouth descended to meet mine. I turned my head away, sickened by his brutal passion and the bestial smell of him.

It was no use. Roughly, he took my chin in his hand and forced me back to face him.

Blinded by tears, I cried out that I would tell my father. This brought a round of drunken laughter from the watching company, and Saul Trevallion made a brutal comment to his friends:

"Do you hear the wench? Ha! Wait till I see that scoundrel Goodacre in the morning. I'll horsewhip the dog for daring to hide away this proud-stepping little morsel. And I'll have him send her round to me every afternoon for a bit of sport —or it'll be the worse for him."

Again, his hateful lips advanced to mine. I closed my eyes and willed myself to be elsewhere—anywhere—when the moment came that I should have to be filthied by his lust.

"Stop! Take your hands off her! Leave her be!"

The commanding voice rang out, deep and clear. Saul Trevallion gave a muffled curse and relaxed his grip on me. In a trice, I pulled away from him, and looked round to see who was my rescuer.

It was Benedict Trevallion. The younger brother came striding across the lawn towards us. He had changed into a black tail coat. His face was dark and angry in the moonlight.

"Who in the blazes d'you think you're addressing?" demanded Saul Trevallion.

"You!" snapped the other.

"By all that's holy, I'm master here—and I won't have you forget it!" shouted the elder Trevallion.

Benedict brushed straight past his brother and put a hand on my shoulder.

"Go back home," he said to me, his voice cold and impersonal, as a master addresses a servant. "Go back home the way you came, and don't come here again. Do you understand?"

I faltered: "Yes, Mr Benedict."

"Then be gone with you!"

But Saul Trevallion was not so easily to be put down. He

16

stood between me and the wall, and his hand reached out to bar my path.

"I'm master of Roswithiel," he growled slurringly, "and I say the damn' little slut stays right here."

"Go home, girl!" snapped Benedict. So saying, he struck down his brother's arm.

I ran.

"You'll be sorry for this, my fine sprig," cried the elder brother. "I'll not be preached to and made a fool of by the likes o' you, dammit! I'll take whatever wench I fancy, and not ask your leave."

When I reached the wall, panting, and hauled myself over it, the two were quarrelling bitterly and loudly.

* .* *

"Lordy me, Miss Joanna! What I done with that bitty sharp little knife as I used to cut vegetables?"

I gave a guilty start as our cook Rososa questioned me from the sink, where she was busy preparing sweet potatoes.

"You ain't had that bitty sharp little knife for somethin', Miss Joanna?" There was a hard shrewdness about Rososa that sometimes didn't quite square with her habitual amiability, and I wondered if she suspected anything. But, of course she couldn't. It was just my guilty mind.

I replied: "No, Rososa." But I was careful to cross my fingers.

"I don't know where it coulda gone."

"Perhaps it'll turn up," I said helpfully.

I knew well enough where the knife was: hidden in a drawer in my room, freshly honed to a fine point and ready for use.

Two days had passed since the night of the Roswithiel Ball; two days in which I had lived in a constant state of terror at the consequences of my conduct on that night. On the morning after, I had wakened early, expecting swift retribution. The fact that it had not come had done nothing to lessen my fears; by the second day, I was now in a far worse state of dreadful anticipation.

I had many hideous images of what might happen to me.

17

The worst—by far the worst—was that the evil and ogreish Saul Trevallion would call upon my father, horsewhip in hand, and force him to send me to the mansion every afternoon for—as he had put it—a little bit of sport. In my partial innocence, I had only the sketchiest notion of what horrors this might entail; but I had the hideous memory of his slack lips descending upon mine, and his fetid breath upon me.

I had quickly resolved that, rather than be subjected to any more of his forced attentions, I should kill myself. The hazard, I told myself, was quite great. He had boasted that my father would disobey him at his peril; no one knew better than I that we owed our livelihood, our home, the food we ate, and the very clothes we stood up in, to the whim of the Trevallions. Father's feelings for me fell well short of the love of a father for his only child. His position as nominal bailiff on one of the finest plantations on the island was a sinecure, and he knew it. He lived the sort of gentleman's life that was beyond the dreams of any ex-corporal of horse, with servants, money, and drink to spare.

In my heart, I knew that, if Saul Trevallion carried out his threat and made his demand upon my father, he would probably be obeyed.

Which was why Rososa was missing her bitty sharp little knife: I had taken it and hidden it—so that I could kill myself, if Saul Trevallion came for me!

"Miss Joanna! I thought you was s'posed to be watchin' that saucepan. Lordy me, you just done stood there an' watched it boil over!"

Rososa's great bulk moved nimbly across the kitchen. She brushed past me and took the big iron saucepan off the stove.

"I'm sorry, Rososa," I said.

Suddenly—and typically—she was all sympathy and compassion.

"What's wrong with you, chile? You ain't been yourself these last days. You ain't sickenin'?"

"I—I've been rather tired," I said feebly. "It's the heat. It makes me tired."

She took my chin in her big, pink-palmed hand and looked into my eyes. She shook her head, and I dropped my gaze.

"You lyin' to me, chile. You ain't bein' straight with ole Rososa. What is it? Tell now. You havin' trouble with your daddy?"

The kindly black cook knew well enough of the differences between Father and me. She knew how neglectful he was. And she knew—every servant on the plantation knew—about his heavy drinking. I had lain awake till dawn on the night of the ball, and had heard him come home—the whole house must have heard him come home—at first light.

"It's your daddy, ain't it, chile?" she repeated.

Before I had time to frame an answer, there came a clattering of a horse's hooves from the yard outside, and a shouted order:

"Take Mister Trevallion's horse! Jump to it, you damned black brat!" My father's voice.

I felt every hair of my scalp prickle with terror, and a cold finger coursed right down my spine. My worst fears had come true: the ogre of Roswithiel had come to make his claim on me; the sharp knife that lay upstairs in my drawer would soon —given that I had the courage to do it—be sheathed in my shrinking flesh.

Rososa was at the window and looking out into the yard. "It's Mister Benedict," she said. "Mercy! I do declare he gets to look more haggard-hungry every time I clap eyes on him. That butter-yaller trollop Mayana ain't feedin' him, an' that's for sure."

"Mr Benedict!" I cried, hope flaring feebly in my heart. "Then it's not Mr Saul?"

It was Benedict Trevallion, right enough. He was dismounting from a big black hunter whose head was being held by the stable lad that Father had summoned. Father was giving a swaggering military salute—which was coldly ignored. Mr Trevallion looked angry. I knew instinctively that his anger concerned—and had been aroused by—me.

I was peering over Rososa's massive shoulder. "He's coming in!" I cried.

19

"No, he ain't," said the cook. "He's gonna walk your daddy up an' down."

Benedict Trevallion had tossed his riding whip to the stable lad. Hands clasped behind his back, he was striding up the yard, away from the house, with my father trotting at his heels and trying to catch up. Father was red-faced and scared-looking, and he was doing all the talking at the moment: I knew from his blustering manner that he was offering excuses —and making a bad job of it.

When they reached the far end of the yard, Benedict Trevallion turned on his heel and faced my father, whose words seemed to die on his lips as he met the other's flat, contemptuous stare.

In that moment, I felt truly compassionate towards my father. I sensed what was coming. It came quickly.

Benedict Trevallion pointed to the house—our house and began what was—for Rososa and me—a soundless tirade that quickly reduced Father to a state of shrinking collapse, like a worn-out doll whose stuffing is slowly dribbling out of its feet. I would have given a lot to have heard some of it.

"Lordy me!" breathed Rososa. "I dunno what Mister Benedict's a-sayin' to your daddy, chile, but it sure is pilin' the burden o' years on to your daddy's life!"

I knew—from Benedict Trevallion's gesture towards our house, if from nothing else—what it was all about. He was telling Father about what had happened on the night of the ball; how I had ventured into the forbidden grounds and caused trouble between him and his brother.

He was putting the blame on my father's shoulders, for not looking after his wayward daughter. Next, he would lay down the law, and order him, on pain of instant dismissal from his sinecure, to keep me in check in future.

Yes, this was the part . . .

Another point towards the house (and I shrank lower behind Rososa's shoulder), then he shouted something close to Father's frightened face, punctuating each word with a stab of his finger towards Father's shrinking middle. I could imagine the words:

"*Keep your ill-bred offspring away from the mansion and grounds,*" I seemed to hear him cry. "*Or, by Heaven, I'll give her to Mr Saul myself, and let him make what sport with her he will!*"

Father's mouth fell open; his eyes glazed.

"*Understand?*"

Father swallowed, and nodded vigorously.

Benedict Trevallion cast him one last, contemptuous glance, and walked back to where the stable lad was holding his horse. He took the reins, brusquely refused the lad's offer of a leg-up, swung into the saddle, and clattered out of the yard without a backward glance.

"Lordy me!" cried Rososa.

I exhaled a long, shuddering breath.

"Back to work, the both of us," said Rososa, giving me a push. "Yo' daddy's comin' right in here, an' if he thinks we've been a-watchin' all that, he ain't gonna like it at all, chile."

I was industriously stirring the saucepan when my father came into the kitchen and threw himself down on a ladderback chair without a word. I stole a glance out of the corner of my eye: his face had an unaccustomed greyness about the cheekbones, and he looked all of his forty-nine years, and more.

"Your favourite for dinner," I said, casting my net carefully. "Pork stew with black-eyed peas, sweet potatoes, and green bananas."

No reply.

"Miss Joanna done helped me herself," supplied Rososa, whose eyes were also rolling cautiously in Father's direction.

He sat hunched in the chair for a very long time, looking down at his hand, that rested on the kitchen table, with a slightly surprised air, as if unable to accept that it was his own. At the end of it, both Rososa and I had given up any pretence of detachment, and were openly staring at him.

Presently, he let out a shuddering breath, and looked across at me. The expression on his face was like that on the face of a man who is gazing at a familiar scene suddenly turned unfamiliar.

"Are you . . . happy enough here, lass?" he asked huskily.

"Yes. Of course, Father," I replied, puzzled.

He nodded, then his glance dropped away. He got to his feet slowly and went towards the door. With his hand on the latch, a thought seemed to strike him. He turned again.

"If . . . if you wasn't happy . . ." he began.

"Yes, Father?" I said.

"If you wasn't happy. If you wasn't happy, you'd tell me, like?"

Bemused, I replied: "Yes, of course, Father."

This seemed to satisfy him. He went out into the yard.

"Well, I do declare," whispered Rososa. "Whatever it was as Mister Trevallion done said to yo' daddy, it sure changed him, the way I ain't never seen a body changed afore."

I privately agreed. Nor was that the end of it. For many long weeks afterwards, Father's attitude to me was quite different from what it had ever been: there was a new considerateness, even respect. Fully a month went by, furthermore, before he went out on one of his nightly drinking bouts with his friends in the town.

It did not last, of course. A leopard does not change his spots, nor a corporal of horse the ingrained habits of a lifetime. In the end, I was back with his coarse, barrack-room tongue and his neglect.

But sometimes—months afterwards—I would look up from my needlework, or from my dinner plate, and see him eyeing me covertly; eyeing me with an expression of wonder and mystification—as if he could not credit it: that he had produced the seventeen-year-old he saw before him.

And it all stemmed from his short encounter with Benedict Trevallion that day in the stable yard.

I teased my mind in speculations about what had been said during that encounter; but there were wispy young saplings in our garden at Roswithiel plantation that would grow straight and tall to the sky, before I had the answer.

* * *

Rososa, like her father and mother before her, had been born a slave of the Trevallion family. She often talked to me about

22

those bad old days, sometimes with a note of nostalgia in her voice.

She had known the brothers, Piers, Benedict, and Saul from their cradles—and Piers had been her favourite. Such a lovely natured little boy he had been, said Rososa; and tears came into her eyes and poured down her black cheeks when she spoke of his death in the war. The plantation, she said, would have been a very different—and happier—place, if Mister Piers had lived to be the master. Remembering the laughing-eyed hussar in the painting, I could not but agree with her.

Rososa had only contempt for Saul—contempt mixed with fear, and I echoed her feelings exactly.

There remained Benedict, and Rososa was not to be drawn on her opinion of the younger brother. I always gathered that she had quite liked him as a child, but that the way he had turned out in later life had cost him her affection. A violent and tricky temper he had, said Rososa. I, who had seen him berating my father, shared her opinion.

She disliked Mayana, always referring to her as "that Mayana," or "that high-yaller baggage," or some such. Whether this dislike stemmed from the envy of a woman of dark colour for one who could almost pass for white, I never did discover. And when I tried to probe her about Mayana's child, she would merely sniff, or mutter some disparaging epithet—and change the subject.

It seemed strange to me that Rososa could have felt any nostalgia for the days of her slavery—till I came to realise that slavery had also meant a kind of security that she and her people no longer possessed. Now she worked for us, my father and me, for a wage—and a miserable wage at that. My father could dismiss her at a moment's notice and she would probably starve. Before the emancipation, slave though she was, she could look forward to a lifetime of being fed, clothed, and housed.

The emancipation had led to a great deal of discontent. My father always said that the island was like a powder keg that only needed a spark to blow it apart. The planters had received compensation from the British government of nineteen pounds for every freed slave; but they were left with a shortage of labour, because the more enterprising among their former unpaid workers left the plantations and moved to the hills, where they set up smallholdings of their own.

On the one hand were the planters, who felt that they had been cheated of their birthright of prosperity, and on the other were the freed slaves, badly paid and insecure.

On several occasions, I was rudely brought into contact with the dark forces of hatred and resentment that lay just beneath the surface in that outwardly languid and sun-blessed island. One day, about six months after the episode of the ball, I went with Father to Kingston. Somewhere along the way, in a dusty lane shaded by high bamboo trees, we came upon a group of Roswithiel plantation workers who, angered at having had some of their meagre pay stopped for no very good reason, had walked out of the cane fields. When my father, with his usual coarseness and lack of tact, ordered them to go back to work on pain of whippings all round, they became ugly. I was never so frightened in my life, to see those hate-filled black faces closing in our carriage, and I am sure things would have gone badly for us both, if my father had not belatedly realised the virtue of discretion and whipped up the horses.

It was with this background of unease—the shadowy menace just out of sight and hearing—that the months went by in Jamaica. The seasons came and went. The great rains swelled the mature sugar canes that dominated the life of the island; twenty feet high in their full splendour, and coloured in all hues from white, through yellow to deep green, purple, red, and violet.

I kept myself apart. Never again did I peer over the wall into the grounds of the big house. Whenever I saw either of the two Trevallion brothers—which was not often, and always from afar—I invariably looked the other way.

Two years went by, and the night of the Roswithiel ball— the one at which I had been an uninvited observer—seemed like an isolated event in my life: something unique and unrepeatable.

It was no such thing. I was not to know it then, but that

night was the beginning of everything; nothing after that night was ever the same again.

* * *

It was October and rain. Jamaica was dripping green, with low clouds that swept like cannon smoke over Jim Crow mountains. The stable lad told me that it was the tail end of a hurricane that had passed us thataway—pointing to the northeast. This accounted for the oppressive heat that came with the rain. It was the heat that I found hardest to bear: any effort was too much, and I simply sat and watched the rain stream down the window panes. The roof of Roswithiel mansion, usually visible over the garden wall, was lost in the greyish mist that rose from the humid earth. The more delicate of the flowering bushes had lost their blooms, but the bright heads of the sturdy hydrangeas still swayed defiantly in the downpour. I felt unaccountably depressed. Only the hydrangeas gave me heart.

It was on a Monday that the rain slackened and died, and the roof of the mansion appeared above the wall for the first time in a week. Monday was the day that my father went on a ride of inspection of the outlying cane fields. It was almost the only bothersome part of his job; the rest of his time was spent in the plantation office, where he kept a supply of rum for his cronies who dropped in for a chat. The real supervising of the plantation was done by the overseers, a tough breed of men who, in the bad old days, had imposed their will with the whip and the branding iron.

Sometimes he went alone on his Monday ride of inspection, sometimes with one or the other of the Trevallion brothers. It was with this in mind that I watched him, that fateful day, over his breakfast.

In the two years since the memorable Roswithiel ball, Father had matched my growing-up by deteriorating far beyond the looks of a man of his age. I remember my mother telling me, before she died at the beginning of the war, what a dashing figure of a man he had made as a young trooper. I thanked Heaven that she was spared the sight of what four unaccustomed years of gentlemanly living had done to what had remained of the clean-limbed hussar who had stolen her heart all those years ago.

Though barely seven o'clock, the morning was already stiflingly hot and steamy, so he was breakfasting just as he had rolled out of bed ten minutes before: unshaven and unbrushed, in a long-sleeved undershirt that revealed the pitiful sag of his muscles and the rolls of flesh at his waistline. The undershirt was stained with his night's sweat.

Quenching my revulsion, I forced myself to watch him cramming food in his mouth and washing it down with scalding hot coffee. He had been out on the town most of the night, and his eyes were red-rimmed and watery. When he spoke, it was only to growl a complaint:

"The damn' coffee's thin as gruel. Tell that black baggage to make another pot with a bit of strength in it."

"Yes, Father," I said, and I called the maid Hannah.

"And bring some more meat. Plenty of it. There's not enough meat here for a man what's to be in the saddle all day."

"Very good, Father," I murmured, and I instructed the girl accordingly.

He forked in another haunch of cold pork and wiped his greasy mouth on his sleeve. Then he picked up the black bottle of rum that stood by his elbow and poured a stiff dose of the deep amber liquid into his coffee cup.

"What are you looking at me like that for?" I had thought him to be bemused with drink and sleeplessness, but his eyes were quick and cunning, suddenly flashing at me over the rim of his cup.

"Nothing, Father. But . . ."

"But what? What is it, gal? You've got something to say—say it."

"Well, it's only that . . ."

"Yes?"

He said the word very quietly and rose to his feet as he did so, his eyes never leaving me. His hands dropped to his waist, to the buckle of the thick leather cavalryman's belt that encircled his paunchy middle.

"Father . . ." I drew a shuddering breath as he came towards me, round the corner of the table.

"You was goin' to say something, lass. Let's hear you say it." His voice was low and menacing.

I suddenly determined to say my piece, no matter what. After all, I was nearly twenty and a woman. The woman of the house, and his only relation. Someone had to tell him.

"I wondered whether you were going out today on your own," I said. "Or with one of the Trevallions."

"Why was you wondering that, pray?" He stopped beside me, and his hands, on the buckle of the belt, were on a level with my eyes.

"Well, it makes a difference, doesn't it?" I said.

"Does it?" he said flatly. "Why?"

He was playing cat-and-mouse with me, and I was suddenly angered. I looked up at him, saw him staring narrowly down at me, challenging me to say the words that teetered on my tongue.

I said slowly and deliberately: "Because, if you're going out on your own, it doesn't much matter what condition you're in; but, for all our sakes, I think you'd better leave the bottle alone if you're going out with one of your employers!"

The angry blood darkened his cheeks, and his thick fingers unsnapped the buckle of the belt.

"By God, I'll mark you for that, you whey-faced . . ."

I sat very still, looking up at him and trying to will my heart to stop pounding and my lower lip to stop its treacherous trembling.

"Do that," I said, in a voice that sounded strangely unfamiliar to my ears. "What are you waiting for—*brave corporal?*"

The heavy belt was unloosed and the end of it coiled round his right fist. He raised his arm on high above me; the cruel buckle hung in the air. I forced my eyes to stay open—looking at him.

There was silence: a moment of eternity.

And then: "You've no right to talk to me like that!" he cried petulantly. "I'm your father, ain't I? Don't I deserve some respect?"

He threw the belt on the table and strode across the room. When he reached the window, he turned round and regarded me, gesturing wildly with his hands.

"I mean, what respect do you give me, eh? I've taken care of you, haven't I? Brought you out here, to live like a lady. There's not many fathers you could say that of. Not many who'd be burdened with a bit of a gal. I've done all right by you, my lass, and don't you forget it."

His voice took on a new note:

"And don't you think," he said, "that, just because I go to the bottle a bit now and again, them Trevallions would ever throw us out of this place. I've got this job for life. *For life!*"

Now he was the boastful old soldier again—a more familiar posture for him than the whining and misunderstood father-of-family.

"For what I did for their brother, the lieutenant," he cried. "By thunder, my gal, do you know what a cavalry charge is like, hey? The screamin', the fear, the takin'-off of heads. It's hell, I tell you. I could have got out of it without risking my own skin to save him. After the charge was over, it was every man for himself. I had my horse, still, and not a scratch on either of us. I could have ridden right back, and no one would have said a word against it. Instead of that, I dismounted and picked him up, the lieutenant. Put him across my saddle and led him back on foot. They know what they owe me, and they'll never get rid of me. Never!"

I took a very deep breath, and said: "That's as may be, Father, but let me tell you this: If you so much as threaten to lay a hand on me again, I shall leave this place. Forever."

"Will you now, my fine daughter," he said. "Then you may go to hell as soon as you like!"

With that, he picked up the rum bottle and, placing it to his lips, he took a long deliberate swallow. That done, he wiped his mouth on the sleeve of his undershirt, eyeing me malevolently the while. But I could see that my threat had found its mark: I had shaken and frightened him: stripped the mask from the braggard and revealed the empty, posturing creature within.

"I think it's time you went about your day's business, Father," I said coolly.

He stomped out of the room without another word. Minutes later, I heard him crossing the yard; heard him curse the stable lad who was waiting with his horse. Then came the sound of the horse's hooves clattering out and down the drive.

I smiled to myself and nibbled at another oatcake. This day, I had scored a notable victory over Father. Between us, I said to myself, Benedict Trevallion and I had given him plenty to think about.

* * *

I had planned to go into Kingston in the afternoon, to buy some materials for a dress that one of the plantation seamstresses was to make up for me: I had told the groom to have the carriage ready to drive me in at three. But, by midday, the mist had closed down again, and with it came a fine, drenching rain. I cancelled the carriage—and gave a wry thought for my father, who might be out in it, at the farthest-flung end of the estate, with no shelter for miles. Serve him right, and I hoped that Saul Trevallion was sharing his discomfort.

All that long afternoon, then, I sat in the window seat of my little bedroom, reading Mr Charles Dickens's *A Tale of Two Cities*, a romance about the French Revolution, which was appearing in the periodical *All the Year Round*, to which I subscribed, and which was sent out to me from England— though not with any regularity, and often, as on this occasion, more than a year after publication.

While the rain drenched down in the dripping green world outside, I lost myself in Mr Dickens's tremendous story as it swelled towards its climax. It seemed to me that Sydney Carton was being carried—by his secret love for Lucy, and by his own wayward nature—towards some nameless and dreadful fate. It was around five-thirty o'clock, and the rain had not slackened all the afternoon, that I turned over the page to find the end of the instalment—with Carton's fate still nameless and unresolved. I cried out with disappointment. It might be another three months before I received another packet of issues from the publisher.

In that instant, a tremendous lightning flash burned the scene outside my window to a horrifying whiteness. Blinded, I recoiled—and my ears were instantly affronted by a deafening peal of thunder from immediately overhead.

The storm which had gathered immediately above Roswithiel unleashed itself with savage fury. A tremendous wind scoured through the garden, flattening the long grass, uprooting bushes and bowling them along before it. I heard a scream from the kitchen. Then my casement window burst open, jarring back upon its hinges and threatening to dash itself to pieces on the outside wall. I struggled to close it, and my hair was instantly taken and soaked by the wind and the rain that poured into the room. I had just managed to get it shut when the maid Hannah burst into my room without knocking.

"Miss Joanna! Miss Joanna!" she wailed. "They's some men a-comin' up the drive!"

"What men are these, Hannah?" I demanded.

"Men from the plantation, Miss Joanna," she replied. "They's all lookin' mighty angry, and I's scared, Miss Joanna."

"Don't be a silly girl." I pushed past her and went downstairs—just as there came a heavy knock on the front door. It echoed hollowly through the house, and then died, and the noise of the wind took over again.

"Is anyone in?" shouted a voice—a voice that stirred a chord of memory in my mind.

"Yes," I cried. "I'm coming, I'm coming."

We seldom used the front door, and usually kept it bolted— the more so since there had been murmurings of trouble from the plantation workers. My fingers were all thumbs with my haste to move the heavy bolts, and I was made all the more nervous and fumbling by another heavy hammering on the other side and by another impatient cry.

"Come on, wench! Get this confounded door open!"

I knew, then, who stood at the porch of our house. And with the knowledge, my spirit grew strangely calm, and my will directed my hands to complete their task.

I unlatched the door and swung it open: Benedict Trevallion stood within touching distance, with his surprised eyes staring down at me.

"So it's you?" he breathed. "I'm sorry. I had thought it was one of your women."

I was too overawed to reply. My sole desire was to find the will to wrench my gaze away from the imprisoning stare of those disconcerting sea-blue eyes: but I knew there was not enough strength in me for it.

He was bareheaded. The rain had plastered his thick curls closely to his temples. His face was streaked with red mud from the roads, and his boots and clothing were the same. He had ridden far on that night of tempest. Why, I asked my astonished heart, had his journey brought him to our door?

I was soon to be answered. There were dark figures moving about in the yard. Men were shouting to one another above the roar of the wind. Benedict Trevallion seemed suddenly to be aware of them. He glanced back over his shoulder for a moment, then laid a hand on my arm.

"Let's go inside and shut the door," he said. "There's something I have to tell you."

I stepped back into the hall, and it was he who slammed the door against the wind. He turned to regard me again; I saw the marks of strain in his face and was suddenly frightened.

"What is it?" I said. "What's happened?"

"There's been trouble."

"Trouble?" I was puzzled.

"My brother . . . and your father. They have been set upon by a mob of rioters. I came straight to tell you."

To my mind sprang the vision of Father as he had been that morning; surly, unkempt, and more than a little drunk; but brutishly alive and invulnerable. So now he had been set upon and hit over the head; beaten, no doubt, with his own whip, with which he was so fond of threatening the plantation workers. I saw him reduced to a week in bed: frowsty and demanding, with me dancing attendance on him day and night.

Only—it was not to be like that at all . . .

"Is he hurt?" I asked Benedict Trevallion.

"Hurt?" The indentations between his brows deepened, and he looked about him, as if for the reassurance of a familiar

31

face. There was no one but Hannah, who stared, wild-eyed, from the foot of the stair.

At that moment, the door was opened again. The wind took it and sent it crashing back against the wainscotting. There was a sudden confusion of driving rain and darkness, with men struggling to carry something over the threshold. Something long, heavy, and swaithed in dark cloth.

"Get out!" shouted Benedict Trevallion. "Don't bring it in here! I told you to take it to the barn!"

I recognised two of the men as white overseers. The others were blacks. They all looked in fear and confusion towards their master. The thing they were carrying was a hurdle from a fence, and it was barely narrow enough to get in through the door. In their haste to retreat, they brought it in sharp contact with the wall.

It tipped slightly: a limp hand and arm slipped from under the dark shroud and hung, swaying.

"Father!" I screamed.

"No!" cried Benedict Trevallion. "Stay here!"

And his arm was round me like a band of steel, so that I was unable to take more than a step towards the group at the door, who were now backing away into the darkness again with their burden.

My captor was holding my head, now, pulling it towards him, pressing my face against the rough, wet broadcloth of his riding coat.

"You mustn't see it," he grated in my ear. "What those black devils have done to the both of them isn't a pretty sight. Thank God it was all over quickly."

I won enough freedom to peer over the top of his broad shoulder: in time to see the scared face of the white overseer who pulled the door shut against the restraining wind.

I saw the telltale red splashes on the holystoned step, and on the polished woodwork of our threshold.

And then I fainted in the arms of Benedict Trevallion.

* * *

I came to with the aromatic scent of wood smoke in my nostrils, and with a pleasing sense of warmth and well being, a heady languorousness that had no place in the world of reality.

Half opening my eyes, I could see a pattern of firelight dancing on a white-panelled wall; opening them a little farther brought into my vision the edge of a richly carved pine bookcase, with row upon row of tooled leather in reds and blues and golds. Looking higher, I saw the lower part of a crystal candelabra that hung from a ceiling so lofty as to be outside my vision—unless I moved my head. And something—some impulse of self-preservation—told me not to move my head, not if I wished to keep my privacy.

Someone was in this room—this elegant and alien room—with me.

I examined my situation. As well as I could make out, I was lying on a sofa or a daybed, with a shawl draped over me; the shawl was silky on my hand, and the cushions of the sofa suave and cosseting to my head and body. The bookcase was immediately opposite, and the fireplace was somewhere over on my left. It was nighttime: the room was lit only by the flickering fire, and by a small amount of candlelight—not from the hanging candelabra, but again from my left.

My mind slowly probed the problem till the idea crystalised and took shape: the idea that the unknown someone who shared my silence was also somewhere over on my left, in the area of the candlelight and the fire's warmth. After this, I strained my every sense in the direction where I supposed my companion to be.

Yes. There it was: above the drumming of my own heartbeats, I distinctly caught the rhythm of someone breathing. What was more, it soon became obvious, from the direction of the sound, that I had only to turn my head the merest fraction to bring whoever it was into my vision.

I was right. The tiniest movement, and I strained my eyes—to see Mayana.

The beautiful deaf-mute was sitting in a low chair between me and the large marble fireplace that dominated all that side of the room. Her lovely head was bowed over a small circular embroidery frame, and her slender fingers worked the needle and thread with an easy, unhurried elegance.

It was then, and only then, that my bemused mind took in the awesome and frightening fact that I must be—I had to be—in the forbidden confines of the Roswithiel mansion!

I had hardly come to grips with this than Mayana got to the end of her piece of thread. She lifted the embroidery frame and nipped off the end of coloured silk with her marvellously white teeth.

In that moment, her huge eyes flashed up—and met mine.

She gave no sign of surprise or acknowledgement; but merely rose gracefully to her feet and crossed the room, passing quite close to me, so that the rustle of her skirts sounded loud in my ears. I heard the room door open and close quietly, and then the tap-tap of her footfalls down a corridor outside, fading away into silence.

Very soon, other footfalls approached from the direction in which the mulatress had gone: the booted footfalls of a man. And I never had any doubt about who it would be.

"Are you feeling better, then? Mayana informed me that you were conscious." Benedict Trevallion came into the room and strode up to where I was lying. He was wearing a short black jacket, and there was a stock knotted loosely round his neck: it looked startlingly white against his bronze skin.

"I feel sleepy . . . rather dizzy," I replied.

"We managed to get a draught of laudanum between your lips," he said. "Thought it best if you had some sleep, to help lessen the shock."

"The shock?" I asked, bemused.

His face was quite expressionless. "The shock of hearing about your father," he said.

And then it all came back to me.

"He's dead, isn't he—they killed him?"

"Yes. And my brother, too."

"But . . . how?" I felt no grief; only a dreadful sense of deprivation; Father had been alive and in rude health only that morning; it was unthinkable that I should never see him again.

"They were ambushed. It happened on the road to the northern fields," said Benedict Trevallion. "They had no one with them, and no weapons. A market woman found their

34

bodies and brought them by cart to the nearest plantation house. I rode there with the men as soon as I got the news, but, of course, there was nothing I could do"—he paused for a moment—"we've buried them already. It was best. It had to be done, quickly, you understand."

I nodded. I was past taking it all in.

He crossed to the window, beyond the great pine bookcase, and pulled open the shutters that had kept out the night. The rain had stopped and the moon was out. There was something else in the sky: a lurid redness beyond the dark trees, far off.

"The blacks are burning sugar warehouses," he said savagely. And, though his back was turned to me, I could well picture the expression on his dark face, with the deep lines of anger between his brows. "Not Roswithiel property—not yet. But it will come to it, unless the confounded government does something about the situation, and quickly . . ."

He turned and strode the length of the room, hands clasped behind his back, shoulders hunched, deep in angry thought. I lay and watched him as he paced to and fro, from the fireplace to the window, and back again. Despite the numbness of my drugged mind, it occurred to me to wonder what were his feelings about the death of his brother. I called to mind the anger that had flared between them, on my account, on the night of the Roswithiel ball. There could scarcely have been much love lost between them, or such words would never have been spoken . . .

He broke in on my thoughts: "It's not the blacks' fault, poor devils. We're all in it together, plantation owners and labourers. When those fools in London got rid of slavery, they knocked the props from under us all . . ." His voice was harsh and swift, and, though he was speaking aloud, what he said seemed to be meant not for my ears, but for his own, as if he was trying to convince himself . . . "the end of slavery would have destroyed the Athens of Pericles and the Rome of Caesar Augustus. It will destroy Jamaica! And now there's talk of fetching in cheap labour from India, to bring the blacks to heel. Well, I'll not stay here to see the end of it!"

He paused in his striding up and down, and regarded me

as if for the first time. I felt myself shrinking under his brooding gaze. I might have been a piece of furniture that he was contemplating buying—or a slave at the auction block.

"Do you have any relations?" he demanded.

I shook my head.

"No one in England who'd give you a home?"

"No."

"Your mother, I take it, is dead?"

"Yes. She passed away before the war."

"Who, then, looked after you when Corporal Goodacre was in the Crimea?"

I told him about the Reverend Smithers and his wife.

"So you could be said to be alone in the world." It was a flat statement of fact, without evasion or pity.

I nodded miserably.

"Well, I'll tell you this, young Joanna Goodacre," he said. "I'm shaking the dust of this confounded island from my boots. I'm going back to England, where, among other things, I must convey to my mother the sad news of her second son's untimely departure to the bosom of Abraham. You may stay here at Roswithiel if you please, and take your chance that the mob will burn down the bailiff's house and you with it—unless they cut you to pieces with their machetes, the way they did my brother and the corporal. On the other hand, you can leave Roswithiel and starve to death in the stews of Kingston. On the other hand . . ."

I looked up at him, numb with uncertainty and fear.

"On the other hand," he went on, "you are perfectly at liberty to accompany us to England."

"To . . . England?" I faltered.

"Yes," he said, with a wintry smile. "To Castle Mallion, the family seat of the Trevallions. It is in Cornwall. Were you ever in Cornwall, young Joanna Goodacre?" . . . and when I shook my head in baffled reply . . . "I think you will find much in Cornwall, and in Castle Mallion, to amuse you. You will, of course, be provided for and given some suitably genteel employment around the establishment. They tell me that you have been educated to a standard well above your station, and I must say you strike me as a young person of some refinement. Well, that's settled then."

"But . . ." I began.

He looked at me in surprise, one eyebrow raised.

"Do you, perhaps, have some other solution to your problem?" he demanded. "I mean, something other than a slow death in the stews, or a swift one at the hands of a rioting mob?"

It was then that the last vestiges of the drug they had given me seemed to slip away from my mind, leaving it naked, unprotected, and vulnerable. All at once, the true fact of my father's sudden and hideous death was borne in on me. I remembered his past, occasional kindnesses; the rough tenderness with which he had often treated me when I was younger.

I bowed my head from the tall, frightening man who loomed over me, and burying my face in my hands, I gave way to my grief.

Later, much later, I looked up to see that Mayana had reentered the room. Benedict Trevallion was explaining matters to the deaf-mute. This he did by gesturing with his hands towards me as he spoke. Her eyes never left him, and her own lips seemed to shape the sounds in unison with his. She understood all.

"We will leave for England immediately, Mayana," he said. "The four of us: you, me, the child, and Joanna. Joanna, here, has no doubt in her mind that this is the best course for her to take."

I was too overcome to say anything, not that Benedict Trevallion waited to hear if I had any comment to make; he turned on his heel and strode out of the room, leaving me alone with the beautiful mulatress.

I searched Mayana's face, but it was entirely expressionless. Whatever her thoughts about my accompanying them to England, she was not communicating them to me. She may, or may not, have been Benedict Trevallion's mistress, but she showed no signs of regarding me as a possible rival.

Three days later, we set sail for England together.

CHAPTER 2

We came at length to a wild and beautiful Western land where the granite rocks join with the sea. A land beyond the civilisation of teeming, smoke-ridden towns: though even the new highways of steel were snaking towards it, for this was the great Railway Age. We journeyed most of the way from Southampton by train, and two travelling carriages met us at the station. One carriage was for us, the other for our luggage—I say "our" luggage, but most of it was Benedict Trevallion's; I had only a trunk and Father's capacious carpetbag, while Mayana's gear and that of her little boy was carried in an old teak chest.

We were driven through narrow lanes lined with high, stone walls that kept their secrets of what lay beyond. It was October, but the memory of summer still lay upon the land. The trees were all the shades of red from flame to russet brown, but they carried all their leaves, and there was a heady languor in the air, and the scent of flowers.

As we neared the coast, gulls swooped in the narrow valleys between the heights. There were stone towers on some of the hills, and these puzzled me, till Benedict Trevallion told the little boy that they were tin mines. Tin, he said, had once been the glory and lifeblood of Cornwall, and Cornishmen had wrested it from their red earth since before the Romans ever came.

He spoke often to the boy. I never saw him so relaxed, or smile so much, as when he was with Mayana's child, who was named Jackie. On shipboard, when Jackie had been ill during the rough, midocean passage, he could not have shown more concern if the child had been his own: inventing diversions for him, reading to him. And, on the last stage of the voyage, during the run up the Channel to Southampton, when the weather was glorious, they walked hand-in-hand together on the decks—the tall, bronzed man in the white Panama hat and the little boy in the sailor suit.

For my part, I was never able to get close to Jackie. I found him a sweet and appealing little lad, and often tried to ingratiate myself; but he was painfully shy, and I had the suspicion that Mayana influenced him to keep me at bay. Her attitude to me was to treat me, so far as she was able, as if I never existed. Benedict Trevallion seldom spoke to her (or to me either, for that matter), but when he did, she paid him all attention, watching the movements of his mouth and copying them herself. Most of the time, she simply looked beautiful and inscrutable, unbending only for Jackie. With him, she was all tenderness, and it was the tenderness of a pantheress for her cub. She would hold him to her with a savage possessiveness, stroking his magnolia skin and smoothing back his raven curls. I had the impression, at these moments, that anyone who ever sought to take the child from her would unleash a pantheress upon himself; a spitting, clawing creature of the wilds.

Yes, we were an ill-assorted party, the four of us who had travelled together from the far-off sunblest island in the Caribbean. Benedict Trevallion—when he was not amusing the child —remained sunk in a brooding silence. Perhaps he sometimes thought of the last of his brothers whom he had left behind in the family mausoleum in the little churchyard close by the plantation. I went there before I left Jamaica, to pay my last respects to Father. It was a place of sunlight, shadows, and whispering cypress trees. The Trevallion mausoleum stood out from the rest. In it were interred all those members of the family who had passed away in the island since the Trevallions first came there in the seventeenth century. My father's last resting place was a humble mound that lay—fittingly—within the shadow of the great mausoleum. Someone, presumably at the orders of the surviving brother, had placed a wooden cross at his head, carrying his name, military rank, and the date of his death.

My own feelings towards Benedict Trevallion were confused. I still saw him as I had always seen the Trevallions: as a source of power that could command my life and my happiness. And the fact that Benedict had imposed his will upon me at a time when I was confused by shock and horror only served to increase this sense of being a mere puppet under his control, to be done with as he willed.

And yet, and yet . . .

I could not help thinking of the night of the ball, when he had saved me from his brutish brother's hateful attentions. That he had done it out of regard for the good name of the Trevallions, and not through any squeamishness about my feelings —the daughter of a mere paid lackey—I never had any doubt. For all that, the thing had been done—and I would be forever in his debt on account of it.

Strangely, he never once referred to the events of that night, nor to the time when he had come to tongue-lash my father. Indeed, as I have said, during the journey from Jamaica, he seldom addressed me at all, and only about commonplace matters.

So it was that, on that October afternoon, we ill-assorted four came to Castle Mallion.

* * *

The last turn in the lane brought us to a pair of great gates of wrought iron, hung from two high columns of granite. On top of each column stood a carved granite lion—I knew that the family crest was a black lion.

"Mallion," murmured Benedict Trevallion.

I glanced sidelong at him. He was staring ahead, through the gates and up the drive beyond. There was a strange, visionary light in his deep-blue eyes; a light of something like awe.

It was then that I realised, for the first time, that his elder brother's death had brought him to the succession of the Trevallion estates, and all that entailed. This was the master of Castle Mallion coming to claim his birthright.

Beyond the gates, the drive swung away in a curve that was flanked on each side with high rhododendron bushes that reminded me of Roswithiel. Through gaps in the bushes, I saw a sweep of rocky headland, and beyond that the deep azure blueness of the sea. The sharp tang of ozone prickled at my nostrils, and I experienced the strange excitement of the spirit that always comes with tantalizing glimpses of the unaccustomed and beautiful.

The view ahead of us was obscured by a screen of high trees, and it was while I was craning my neck for a first glance at the upper parts of the castle over the top of them, that the curve of the drive took a sudden and unexpected flourish—and all of Castle Mallion stood in its glory before us.

I have loved and hated Mallion, and I shall do so till the day I die—but, on that never-to-be-forgotten October afternoon, my feeling was all love, and awe.

Seven tall towers of granite rose above the battlemented, ivy-girt walls, each tower capped with a pointed bonnet of warm red tiles. From the peak of each of the towers that flanked the entrance archway there fluttered white banners bearing the black lion of the Trevallions. The huge sprawling bulk of it lay close to the sea. The tide was high, and the unruly waters surged in the deep moat that encircled the high walls. Our way into the castle lay across an arched stone bridge that spanned the moat. It was like the gateway to fairyland: through the entrance arch, I could see a hint of green lawns and splashing fountains.

"It's beautiful," I cried impulsively. "So beautiful!"

"Mallion is all things to all men," said Benedict Trevallion unexpectedly. "But you are quite right, young lady. When everything else has been said, no one can deny Mallion its exquisite and very special beauty."

I looked at him, and, to my surprise, I found that he was

smiling at me. Instantly, I felt the hot blood rush to my cheeks, and in a sudden confusion, I dropped my gaze. Nor did I look up again till we clattered over the bridge, causing a row of gulls to rise from their perch on the balustrade and flap skywards, screaming hoarsely.

Our carriage swept under the cool, shady archway and into the sunlight of a flagged courtyard, where it came to a halt.

"Welcome home, Mr Benedict. Welcome back to Mallion, sir."

A man and woman stepped forward from the wide entrance porch: they both wore dark clothing and I took them to be servants.

Benedict Trevallion leapt down from the carriage and held out his hand to the man.

"Hello, Prendergast," he cried. "Is all well?"

"Yes, sir," replied the other.

"Good. And Mrs Prendergast, how are you? I must say, neither of you has changed in the last few years."

"We both continue to enjoy good health, sir, thank you," said the man, and his wife gave a stiff little curtsey. They looked to be in their late fifties, a solemn-faced pair with pinched mouths and close-set eyes. They looked to me more like brother and sister than man and wife.

"Me and the wife were sorry to hear about Mr Saul," said Prendergast. "It was very sudden and shocking."

"You received the note I sent ahead, then," said Benedict Trevallion. "And you took special care that my mother didn't get the news from one of the servants? It's important that I break it to her gently, in my own way."

"We have naturally obeyed your instructions," replied the other primly.

"And how is my mother?"

"Mrs Trevallion keeps well," interposed the woman. "When the weather isn't too cold for her, I wheel her every day to the old garden and read a while to her. She likes to be read to."

Benedict Trevallion turned to me. "There, I've found a task for you already, Joanna," he said. "I appoint you official reader to my mother. Here, by the way, as you will have gathered, are Mr and Mrs Prendergast, who are respectively the general factotum and housekeeper of Castle Mallion. And this is Miss Joanna Goodacre, daughter of our late bailiff at Roswithiel, who has come to live at the castle."

"How do you do," I said.

They both nodded to me. The woman looked me up and down from hat to hem, and seemed to set a price on all my clothes. Her eyes, when they met mine, were sullen and hostile. It occurred to me that she would be the sort of person who would resent anyone taking over any part of her duties—particularly any other woman, and a young woman at that. And I was right.

"I'm sure Mrs Trevallion will like to be read to by an educated young lady," she said. And there was no mistaking the malevolence in her tone.

If Benedict Trevallion heard, he ignored it. He was helping little Jackie down from the carriage, and the child's mother followed after. I saw the Prendergasts' eyebrows go up at the sight of the beautiful mulatress in her dark purple gown and startling yellow shawl. They exchanged glances, and I smiled privately. Sort that one out, my dears, I said to myself.

"Well, now, and what do you think of your new home?" Benedict was crouching beside the boy with his arms round him. "See those fine battlements, where you'll be able to play soldiers?"

But Jackie was too overawed to respond. Squirming free of the other's embrace, he ran to his mother and buried his face against her skirts.

Benedict laughed. "He'll lose his shyness, soon enough," he said. "We'll have him the thoroughgoing little Cornishman in no time at all."

With that, he turned and strode towards the entrance porch, motioning us to follow him. Neither then nor at any other time did I see him introduce Mayana and her child to the Prendergasts, nor indicate their relationship, or their status in Castle Mallion.

It was with a strange feeling of awe that I stepped out of

the October sunlight and into the shadowy interior of the ancient castle. Great, iron-studded double doors led straight into a vast hall, all of stonework, and hung with tattered banners high up against the echoing roof. There was an open fireplace in the centre of one wall, in which a whole tree trunk lay crackling cheerfully. The tangy scent of burnt wood was clean and sweet to the nostrils, and a pleasant contrast to the smoky railway train that had brought us to Cornwall. There must be a score of scents and smells that I associate with Mallion, and all of them pleasant: smouldering oak in the great fireplaces; the heady perfume of night-scented honeysuckle coming in through my window; the rose garden in all its summer glory; well-waxed furniture; the burning of leaves in autumn; the strange, astringent fragrance of ivy.

At one end of the hall was a wide stone staircase embellished with carvings of heraldic beasts, among which the lion of the Trevallions was prominent. The other end was dominated by a medieval screen and minstrels' gallery. Four narrow windows, reaching from waist-high to the ceiling, admitted the sunlight through many-coloured glass, so that the vast chamber had the soft and muted light of the interior of a cathedral.

"You find it impressive?" I gave a start. So absorbed in my surroundings had I been, that I had quite forgotten my companions. Benedict Trevallion was standing at my elbow. To my embarrassment and confusion, he was smiling at me again —an inscrutable smile that seemed to probe inside my skin.

"Yes. It must be—very old," I faltered.

"It's the oldest part of the castle," he said. "It was built before the Normans came, by my ancestor, Roc Trevallion, to house his family, his men-at-arms, his animals—they all lived together under this one roof. They ate, slept, quarrelled and made merry on an earth floor strewn with rushes. There were no windows then, and a hole in the roof served to let out some of the smoke that came from a fire in the middle of the floor. The smell must have been stupefying."

"He was a great lord—this ancestor?" I asked.

"He was a very great scoundrel," he replied flatly. "The local robber baron, and uncrowned king of this part of Cornwall.

I admire him tremendously. To me, he exemplifies all that is best—and worst—in the Trevallions. What he wanted, he took. And devil take anyone who tried to stop him!"

Again that inscrutable smile. All at once, I had the feeling of being a mere puppet, with Benedict Trevallion holding the strings and jerking me to his will.

"Well, we'll speak more of that later," he said. Then, turning to the Prendergasts, who had followed us into the hall: "Perhaps one of you will show Miss Goodacre to her room."

"Aye. That's the green room in the south central tower," said Mrs Prendergast. She reached out and took the carpetbag from my hand. "Come this way, will you . . . miss?"

I followed her towards the stairs. Looking back, I saw Mayana and her little boy standing together in the middle of the great sweep of stone-flagged floor. They were both staring about them, and some trick of the diffused light made them both look darker and more alien than usual: two exotic creatures of the sun, rudely transplanted—like tropical flowers—to a climate and a way of life in which they could scarcely be expected to flourish and be happy. Not for the first time since we left Jamaica, I wondered at Benedict Trevallion's motive for bringing them. If, indeed, Mayana was his mistress, it was a strange sort of relationship, for neither by word nor gesture did either of them show any affection or regard for the other. But, then, I remembered the way she had looked when he had carried the girl into the fountain on the night of the ball.

I ascended the stairs after the housekeeper, and followed her down a long, echoing corridor that lay beyond. The corridor was panelled with dark oak and hung with painted portraits in heavy gilt frames. Some of them were very old: I recognised some of the styles of dress to be Elizabethan or earlier. All, I guessed, were likenesses of past Trevallions. In fact, one could recognise the Trevallion look: the dark features, the raven hair, and deep-blue eyes. The womenfolk were the same: dark, blue-eyed and splendidly made. Even in advanced old age— white-haired and emaciated—they did not lose their arrogant poise of the head, nor the way those sea-coloured eyes out-stared the beholder.

At the far end of the long corridor, my guide led me up another flight of steps that brought us to another level of the vast building. This part was a maze of connecting rooms, all of a much later date than the great hall. There were huge crystal chandeliers hanging from painted ceilings of the last century. The walls were hung with tapestries that showed ladies and gentlemen in wigs and court dress, disporting themselves in gentle dalliance. Everything in these rooms spoke of riches almost beyond counting. Any one piece of the carved and gilded furniture that graced them must have been worth enough to keep a Jamaican cane-cutter and his family for twenty years.

We came at length to a double door that led out into a wide spiral staircase.

"The south central tower," said Mrs Prendergast. "The green room's at the top of the tower. Follow me."

More to break through the barrier of her surly manner than to glean information, I said: "It's all very confusing. I'm sure I shall get lost at first. Do I have to go all the way back to the hall to get outside?"

"You do not," said the woman. "You go straight down these steps to the bottom of the tower, where there's a door leading out into the courtyard."

The green room was semicircular; panelled and painted in a deep sage green that gave it its name. The bed was a four-poster and looked deliciously comfortable. A deeply recessed window looked out towards the illimitable blueness of the sea.

Mrs Prendergast did not stand on ceremony, but laid down my bag and stalked out, with the parting information that supper would be served at six-thirty o'clock. I was alone in my tower room.

On closer inspection, the view from the window was an enchantment. From it, I could see the sweep of the coast in both directions, to distant, shadowy headlands. The tide was receding, and already a wide sweep of smooth sand was showing beneath the castle walls, where gulls were swooping and screeching as they picked up fragments of marine life left abandoned by the retreating sea.

The low-cast October sun was casting long shadows over

the foreshore: from my window, I could see the imprint of all seven tall towers of the castle—including my own—and each tower joined to the next by a battlemented wall.

As I watched, a flickering movement in the corner of my eye resolved itself into the figures of a horse and rider coming from afar off, along the virgin beach; coming towards the castle, round the gentle curve of a bay, so that my first view of them was of the plunging head and mane of the horse and the rider's head bent low above. It was a white mount, and the rider was a woman: a woman with unbound hair that streamed wildly in the wind: blonde hair, that seemed as one with the animal's mane. They came with a great flurry of kicked-up sand, and were soon abreast of the castle and passing directly below and in front of me. The woman was young, scarcely more than a girl, and she wore a black habit. As a cavalryman's daughter, I had the eye to see that she was a superb horse-woman. Perched sidesaddle on the galloping white, she forever urged him on to greater efforts. I heard her cries of encouragement above the drumming of the hooves.

Though utterly absorbed in what she was at, her attention wavered for a brief moment. It was when she was immediately abreast of the castle. I saw her glance sidelong and upwards at the walls, and it seemed to me that she raised one gloved hand as if in a wave or salute. Then she was past—and I could see only her back view, above the mount's flowing tail.

I watched till the strange Diana was no more than a dot near the far headland. And I wondered who she was.

I was soon to find out—to my cost.

* * *

My first afternoon and night at Castle Mallion passed without any further notable event. Shortly before six-thirty, a young maidservant tapped on my door and told me that supper was laid. She led me down to a tidy-sized refectory overlooking the courtyard which we had first entered, and opposite the great hall. Places were laid for four, but I ate alone off cold mutton and pickles, with delicious homemade bread, and a

47

very potent cider—of which I was careful to drink only half a mugful.

Weary, then, of the long day's travelling, and having no one to talk with, I decided to save any exploring for the following morning, and went back to my room, where I reread a chapter of Mr Dickens till sleep overcame me.

In my dream, that night, I seemed to be translated back to Jamaica and Roswithiel. It was dark, and I was afraid. Someone was chasing me through the dark undergrowth bordering the cane fields—a man dressed all in black and carrying a hunting whip. I knew it was Saul Trevallion, though he was masked. When he overtook me and seized me, I screamed and ripped away the mask from his face—to disclose the features of his brother Benedict. Then I awoke, panting and overheated, so that it was a blessed relief to go over to the window and, opening it, to look out across the moonlit beach, where the incoming tide was already beginning to creep and cover the tracks that the white horse had made the previous afternoon.

How strange, I thought, that I should dream of being pursued by Benedict Trevallion—he who, most of the time, seemed scarcely aware of my existence.

* * *

I woke early—before six o'clock—and refreshed, dressed myself in a sprigged muslin that had survived the journey pretty well, put my hair back in a broad band—and set out to explore my new home.

The seven towers of Mallion formed a rough square that enclosed the main buildings, courtyards and a pretty formal garden set with lawns, flower beds, and ornamental fountains. Outside the walls, however, and reached by an archway and a steep flight of steps, was another garden that was quite different from the prim orderliness of the one within. It was overgrown and unkempt, save in those parts where the long grass had been scythed down, and the flowering bushes had grown rank and tall as trees. Despite that, there was an informal friendliness about the place; and in time to come, it became my favourite retreat. Looking back on that first morning, as I strolled in the lush wilderness, it seems strange that I never had the slightest inkling of what lay before me—the terror and the misery—and how my sole consolation would be to hide myself away in the old garden.

An hour of my exploring gave me a rough idea of the layout of the castle and its surroundings, so far as could be seen from outside. What lay within—apart from the great hall and the other rooms in which I had been—remained an unknown labyrinth. I easily identified the kitchen quarters—a group of buildings behind the refectory where I had eaten supper—from the early sounds of servants singing about their work, the sound of pots and pans, and the aroma of roasting coffee. The rest of the castle—the barrack-like blocks that lay under the ramparts, the remaining six towers, and the main buildings that surrounded the entrance courtyard—was a brooding mystery of empty rooms and eyeless windows. At least, I presumed nearly all the rooms were empty, for, apart from the servants and the four of us who had arrived the previous afternoon, there was no one else in residence save Benedict's mother.

The thought of Mrs Trevallion brought to mind her son's remark about my reading to her—and I remembered the housekeeper's jealous reaction.

My meeting with the old lady of Castle Mallion was not long delayed. The same maidservant of the night before searched me out and informed me that breakfast was ready in the refectory (this was the place, I learned, where the family had been in the habit of taking most of their meals together; on more formal occasions they sat down to eat in the great hall); and I arrived there to find Benedict Trevallion already at table. He dabbed his lips with a napkin, and nodded when I entered.

"Good morning. I trust you slept well," he said.

"Yes, thank you, Mr Trevallion," I replied. Then I remembered my dream, and how he had figured in it—and I had a wayward impulse to giggle.

"I'm sorry you were left to your own devices last evening,

and had to take your supper alone," he said. "Mayana was occupied with the boy, who became rather feverish—excitement of travelling, I suppose. And I was heavily involved with my mother."

"You . . . you've broken it to her?" I asked.

"About my brother. Yes."

"Poor lady."

He coughed, and gestured towards the dish that stood in front of him.

"Let me carve you some ham," he said. "It's very good. Raised and cured on our own home farm."

"Thank you." I watched him wielding the carving knife and fork. His eyes were quite inscrutable—as always.

"There's some hot pease pudding."

"No, thank you, Mr Trevallion."

"The bread's at your elbow, and the coffeepot. Help yourself."

"Thank you."

We ate in silence for a while. And then:

"Are you easily shocked, Miss Goodacre?" he said. And, when I stared at him in surprise: "No, I seem to remember you as a young person of some considerable moral resilience. Would you be interested to hear how my mother took the news of the demise of her second son?"

"If—if you wish to tell me, Mr Trevallion," I faltered.

"She took it very well. In fact, you might say she was quite pleased about it."

"Pleased, Mr Trevallion?" I nearly choked on a swallow of coffee.

He laughed mirthlessly. "After all, you are quite easily shocked," he said. "I should explain to you, Miss Goodacre, that we Trevallions are not a very loving lot, and Mother is herself a Trevallion, born and bred. In further mitigation of her lamentable lack of grief at the news, I should add that my late brother's character was not of a sort to inspire anything but detestation, as you are yourself aware, from personal experience. He was, in short, the sort of creature that even a mother could not love. My mother's reaction to the news was, firstly, surprise. Secondly, relief. Relief that the Trevallion estate had passed from the hands of her odious second son, to those of her slightly—but only slightly—more civilised third son. More ham, Miss Goodacre?"

I shook my head.

He took another mouthful of food and washed it down with a long draught of coffee. "By the way, I told her about you, and she's very much looking forward to meeting you. I'm to present you this morning at the dower house. There's just one thing I must warn you about."

"Yes, Mr Trevallion?"

"It concerns my elder brother Piers, who was killed in the war. You will see—you can hardly avoid noticing—that Mother reveres his memory to an almost unbelievable degree. It's no use asking you to steer the conversation away from the subject of Piers, because she simply won't be steered." He looked gravely down into his coffee cup. "All I ask is that you humour her, and don't appear bored or impatient. Not that I think you would, I hasten to add." He looked up at me, and there was a great sadness in his deep-blue eyes. "You see, Miss Goodacre, a Trevallion or not, Mother had one great love in her life, and that was my brother Piers. When he was killed, part of her died too. And nothing that anyone could ever do— nothing that I could ever do—will ever fill the gap of her great loss."

The expression in his eyes was gone almost as soon as it came, and he looked down again.

And I thought, on reflection, was it sadness that I had seen written there, after all? Or was it—jealousy?

* * *

"*Darling Benedict! Benedict!*"

We were crossing the courtyard in the direction of the building at the far side of the garden, called the dower house, when the excited cry brought us to a halt.

There was the harsh clatter of hooves on cobble, and a horse and rider came from under the gateway arch. A white horse—*the* white horse—and his black-habited rider: the girl who rode on the pristine beach.

"Feyella!" cried my companion. "How splendid to see you again!" He stepped forward and took the horse's rein. The girl kicked herself free of the stirrup and slid lithesomely to the ground. Next instant, her slender arms were wrapped around his neck, and she was pulling his face down to meet hers. Benedict Trevallion responded readily enough. I stood and fidgeted with embarrassment till they were done—and they took their time about it.

It was he who broke the embrace. He reached up and gently disentangled her hands from behind his neck.

"Enough, Feyella," he laughed. "Enough for now. By God, you are spoiling me for all other women, you jade."

"There will be no other women for you," retorted the girl. And for good measure, she dragged his head down again and implanted another kiss on his mouth. "Remember that you are promised to me."

"That was a childhood caprice," he said. "Less than that, it was a threat. I promised I'd marry you when you grew up—unless you behaved yourself."

"It was real for me," she declared. "I've saved myself for you, Benedict Trevallion. I chose you before Piers, whom everyone swooned over, and before that awful Saul—naturally . . ." She drew away from him, and searched his face closely . . . "Is it so that Saul's dead, and you're the master of Mallion?"

Benedict nodded gravely. The girl's response was to throw back her head and give a laugh of pure delight. This was my first real chance to study her face. It was delicately boned and beautiful, with a finely structured nose and an upper lip that might have been thought to be a trifle too short for perfection. In the middle of her peal of laughter, she opened her eyes and met my glance, seeming to see me for the first time. Instantly, her jawline hardened, and her violet-coloured eyes grew cold.

Benedict Trevallion followed her glance. "This is Joanna Goodacre, who came with us from Jamaica," he said. "Joanna,

I should like you to meet a very dear friend and neighbour, Feyella Mapollion."

"How do you do," I said primly.

She did not offer her hand; nor did I offer mine. We simply stared at each other: she in some kind of hostility, and I in a watchful and guarded manner.

Presently, she said in a high, clear voice: "Goodacre?—one of the Falmouth Goodacres?"

Benedict Trevallion saw my confusion, and answered for me. "I don't think Miss Goodacre lays claim to any Cornish blood," he said easily. "In fact, she's a foreigner and I believe her people hail from London."

"From Jamaica, also," persisted Feyella Mapollion, and I felt her eyes on my sprigged muslin: suddenly it felt like a bit of crumpled old rag on me. "Do your people own a plantation there?"

"No," I replied.

"Then you travelled there for a vacation? How lucky of you. I've never been farther abroad than Bath. Do you know Bath, Miss—er—Goodall?"

"Goodacre," interposed Benedict Trevallion flatly.

"No, I've never been to Bath," I said.

"Then you must swiftly rectify that omission," said Feyella Mapollion. "Bath is terribly smart. It has enormous style." And with that, she dismissed me out of her mind and turned her attention back to Benedict Trevallion. "Now that you're home, we must see a lot of each other. Ride over and see me very soon. Tomorrow. This afternoon. Father is in London, and I'm nearly going mad with boredom."

"Give me a few days to sort out my affairs, Feyella," he replied.

"No, tomorrow," she insisted.

"Three days," he said.

"Two," she said, with the air of someone who knows she has won an argument. "I shall expect you for tea on Thursday." Before he had time to make any protest, she kissed him lightly on the lips, and turned to her mount. He helped her into the saddle. She turned the horse to go. And as she was moving off, she flashed me a tight-lipped smile.

"Good day, Miss Goodacre," she said, with just enough accent on the "Miss" to make it sound like mockery.

I watched her ride out through the gateway arch, with an imp of envy nagging at a corner of my mind.

One thing was clear from the encounter: though Benedict Trevallion had had the grace to introduce the two of us as social equals (and, come to think of it, why had he thought it necessary to do that?), Feyella Mapollion had immediately discerned that we were worlds apart. Educated I might be, with some of the superficial trappings of gentility, but the aristocratic Feyella had seen through the false golden sheen to the common pinchbeck underneath. She knew me for a servant—a nobody. I hated her for it, and envied the breeding and assurance—and the unself-conscious beauty—that allowed her to carry it off.

And, as I walked with Benedict Trevallion across the lawn to the dower house, I gave him a covert, sidelong glance—and admitted to myself that I envied her also for the way in which she was seemingly able to twist this somewhat awesome man round her elegant and capable little finger.

* * *

"Mother, this is Joanna Goodacre."

"Come here, child. Come closer to me and let me have a look at you." At first sight, the dowager of Castle Mallion seemed older than I had imagined she would have been. She sat in a Bath chair in the cool, ground-floor parlour of the dower house. The windows were shaded with heavy crepe, which gave a twilight appearance to the room, and it was not till I stood close to her chair that I could see that her face was quite unlined by age. Suffering alone had placed its imprint about her eyes and at the turned-down corners of her mouth.

I took her proffered hand, which felt like the dried claw of a bird beneath the black mittens she wore. She was dressed completely in funereal black, with widow's weeds on her cap.

"Very pretty. Charming." She touched my cheek, and commented in a voice that was like an expiring breath. Her hand fell wearily back on to her lap. "So this is the child of that brave fellow who brought my darling Piers from that dreadful Valley of Death?"

"Yes, Mother," said Benedict Trevallion. "This is Corporal Goodacre's daughter. He was killed with Saul in Jamaica, as I told you. All in all, this family owes a very great deal to Joanna."

Mrs Trevallion closed her eyes wearily and nodded.

"I'll leave you two together, then." He gave me a brief glance, crossed over to the door, and was gone.

"Sit down, my dear," said Mrs Trevallion, "and tell me all about yourself. I never met your father, though I wrote him a letter of thanks after I had heard the dreadful details from Lord Cardigan. He came to Mallion to see me, you know, Cardigan. They made him a national hero on his return from the Crimea, and, of course, Mr Tennyson wrote that glorious poem immortalising the Charge. To tell the truth, I did not like Lord Cardigan—very shifty about the eyes, and a terrible reputation with women—but he spoke very warmly of my poor darling Piers. My poor wounded boy was carried straight from the battlefield, from which your father had brought him, to Lord Cardigan's yacht—a great honour. His lordship's own surgeon tended my boy, and it was thought that he would recover from his wounds. When Lord Cardigan set sail for England very soon after the battle, he brought my darling Piers with him" . . . Mrs Trevallion's voice, which had taken on an unaccustomed animation during her story, began to break, and I saw a tear course down her smooth cheek . . . "You must forgive me, my dear, for a mother's grief, but seven years have passed and the wound is still fresh in my heart." She touched her eyes with a cambric handkerchief and went on: "During the voyage through the Mediterranean, his lordship told me, darling Piers rallied and was able to be brought up on deck to enjoy the winter sunshine . . ." Her voice faded away to nothing.

"Please don't upset yourself, Mrs Trevallion," I said. "Please."

"The end came very quickly," she continued. "There was a

sudden relapse. Darling Piers was very weak. They managed to feed him a few morsels of biscuit soaked in wine, but he just drifted away from them. There was nothing to be done. Lord Cardigan was holding his hand when he fell asleep and passed away soon after. He was buried at sea—a soldier's funeral, with a salute of guns and his blue hussar's coat wrapped round him."

"It was tragic," I said feelingly.

"It was a glorious end! *Glorious!*" Her head jerked round to face me, and I saw the flash of those unmistakable Trevallion eyes, deep blue as the sea. "If he had lived forever, my darling boy could not have brought more honour upon himself and upon the family. To have ridden at Balaklava and to have died in the arms of his general—though, as I have told you, there was much that I did not admire in Lord Cardigan, even on a brief acquaintance."

"But—to die so young," I said. "When he had so much to live for. And in that dreadful, bungled charge . . ."

"Miss! You are insulting my son's memory!"

Too late, I saw that I had blundered. Too late, I remembered Benedict Trevallion's warning to humour his mother. And it was quite clear that I had put Mrs Trevallion badly out of humour: a bright spot of colour had appeared on each cheekbone, her mouth hung slackly, and the eyes—those marvellous Trevallion eyes—had taken on a wild and frenzied light.

"I'm sorry, ma'am," I said hastily. "Sorry if I said anything to offend you. I only meant . . ."

"I would not have had it other!" she cried. "Though I have mourned my darling boy, day and night, these seven years, I have mourned with pride. Five hundred years of breeding went into his making. I am a Trevallion, you know; my husband and I were second cousins. My Piers was a Trevallion of the heroic mould. The modern world was not a big enough place to contain his spirit; he was destined for glorious death."

I stared at her in silence, listening to her babblings, scarcely believing that such sentiments could come from the lips of a woman who had borne the son of whom she was speaking. But the astonishing Mrs Trevallion had scarcely even begun to unburden her feelings . . .

"We no longer live in days of greatness," she said. "My Piers should have been alive in the Middle Ages, when Castle Mallion was one of the principal bastions of the West. He carried the quality of greatness about with him like an aura. In a former age, he could have been another Roc Trevallion. He could have been—he could have been the King of Cornwall!" She sank back in her chair, panting with the intensity of her feelings.

When she spoke again, her voice was weary and flat—the way it had been before. "What could my Piers have done here now?" she asked. "All that is called for here now is a keeper of accounts. A bailiff. A curator of antiquities. Counting stooks of corn and heads of swine. My son Benedict can do all those things uncommonly well. Better than that creature Saul, who made Benedict go with him to Jamaica to put things in order when Roswithiel was in such a dreadful state of neglect after the war—while he, Saul, amused himself with hunting, drinking, and wenching."

She closed her eyes and was silent for a while. And then, she said: "Waste no tears on Piers Trevallion, child. He needs only mine. That great spirit was called away, and the beautiful body it inhabited lies at rest in the deep, wrapped in its military coat of honour."

There was a long silence between us, marked by the ticking of an ormulu clock above the parlour fireplace. I regarded the woman before me, who sat in her invalid's chair with her delicately boned and grief-ravaged face bowed over her hands; and I remembered that it was only a few brief hours since she had been told of the death of her second son—yet how briefly and contemptuously she had dismissed the memory of Saul. It was clear that—as Benedict had hinted—Mrs Trevallion's whole life was taken up in the adoration of the memory of her beloved Piers. Half of her mourned; the other half exulted in the manner of his death. She was like one of those pagan women of bygone days who urged their menfolk to return from battle carrying their shields with honour—or to be carried back, dead, on those same shields.

Presently, she looked up, and when she spoke, her voice was

tired and toneless. "I must put my mind to other things," she said. "I should like you to read to me, to distract me."

"I shall be happy to, ma'am," I replied. "What would you like?"

"Prendergast is doing *David Copperfield*," she said. "She reads very badly."

"Oh, but that's my favourite novel," I cried. "I must have read it six times at least, and it will be a great pleasure to devour it again."

"The volume is over there, on the sewing table," said Mrs Trevallion disinterestedly.

There was a bookmark at the beginning of Chapter Eleven, and I started to read. I had just reached the part where David is first introduced to Mr Micawber, when my companion broke in:

"He said—Lord Cardigan said—that my darling boy's last words were of me."

I could think of no comment to make; but simply waited a respectful half minute and re-commenced my reading. I scarcely got to the bottom of the next page before she interrupted me again.

"My Piers bore his wounds with great fortitude," she said. "His lordship told me that he never complained of the terrible pain."

It struck me that she was not listening to a word of what I was reading; that I was no more than a background to her thoughts, and merely someone to be a sounding board for the memories that welled up in her tortured mind. And so it proved to be. She called for no replies from me, and after a while I went on reading again, till the next interruption.

In this manner, we got through most of Chapter Eleven before midday.

* * *

My first week at Mallion took on a pattern of living that lacked nothing in the way of comfort. I rose early, made my own bed and tidied out the green room. It was wasted effort: the bed was always remade and the room dusted out and cleaned again while I was out—presumably by Mrs Prendergast's orders.

Meals were always served at regular hours in the refectory. Table was always laid for four, but Mayana and the little boy seldom put in an appearance. They had a suite of rooms, so I understood, in one of the other towers, and I suppose the mulatress prepared food there that was more to her taste and the child's.

Benedict Trevallion was always at table when I went in to breakfast, which was the only meal that he never missed. His early-morning manner was self-absorbed and uncommunicative: a brusque nod of greeting, and he returned to whatever he had propped up before him—either a book, a newspaper, a letter, some accounts, or other. More often or not, he was away from the castle on some estate business and did not turn up for the midday meal. Again, he was often too late back for supper. I was quite happy to eat alone, for his presence was always a trial to me: I became all fingers and thumbs, and incapable of handling knife and fork properly, on the few occasions when he addressed me.

I took to reading at meals when I was alone (Mrs Trevallion also subscribed to *All the Year Round*, and to my joy she had the copies up to date, including the ending of *A Tale of Two Cities*). The food, served by one or another of the many parlourmaids, was simple and wholesome: fresh meat and vegetables from the home farm; newly baked bread and creamy butter; home-brewed cider. I never saw, at Castle Mallion, any of the pies, pasties, potato cakes, and suchlike concoctions that the poor peasantry of Cornwall eat.

At around ten in the morning, I went across to the dower house, where Mrs Trevallion had by this time been attended to by her ladies' maid, and was ready for her morning's diversion. I continued the reading of *David*, sometimes in the parlour, sometimes in the old garden—which was a great favourite of Mrs Trevallion. This called for the assistance of Prendergast, because I did not feel capable of negotiating my charge and her Bath chair up the steep steps into the garden. He always carried out this task with his customary sullenness, and pointedly addressed his remarks only to Mrs Trevallion—even when it was I who had spoken to him in the first place.

The readings continued in the same pattern as the first. I doubt if she ever took the slightest notice of, or interest in, Mr Dickens's story. Instead, it formed a background of sound to her thoughts and recollections. I became used to her interruptions: was able, eventually, to predict the moment, when her face began to soften, that she would come out with one of her remarks. And, of course, the subject was always the same—the tragic and glorious death of her firstborn.

This apart, she treated me not as an equal but as a paid servant. This was to be expected, and I did not resent it. I was, after all, living in some considerable comfort by the grace and favour of the Trevallion family. I knew enough of the outside world to realise that girls of my station were hard put-to to make an honest and virtuous living. I only had to scan the crowded advertisement pages in *The Times*, where such inducements as "unexceptionable references" and "wages immaterial" indicated the desperate competition amongst the servant classes to get themselves sheltered and fed. And I was luckier than most. Though not "genteel," like the daughter, say, of an impoverished clergyman, I was at least educated. Because of this, I had come to occupy a place in Castle Mallion of a ladies' companion, which is one better than a childrens' governess, entitling me to a place at the family table.

And yet, and yet . . .

I could not forget the shadow of resentment that had always lain across my feelings for the Trevallions: the rich and powerful Trevallions, who, with their dark good looks and their haughty sea-blue eyes, had had such complete control over my comings and goings for so long. And, if anything more than another tended to soften this shadow it was not the gruff courtesy of Benedict Trevallion, nor his mother's increasing dependance upon my companionship. It was—Mallion.

In that first week, I began the unspoilt period of my lifelong love affair with the Cornish seat of the Trevallions. My first glimpse of its fairy-tale towers had not been followed by the slightest sense of disillusionment. My fairy castle continued to be a constant delight. Every new corner, every fresh viewpoint, each new trick of the ever-changing Western skies showed me Mallion in another of its enchanting guises.

That first October week, in that Indian summer of 1862, I took Mallion to my heart. In the afternoons, when Mrs Trevallion rested, I wandered in the old garden, or on the foreshore, but never very far away from its ivy-covered walls.

Once, I walked as far as the nearest headland, and looked back across the sweep of smooth, hard sand left by the tide, to see its distant, silhouetted bulk—like some tall ship with castellated bulwarks and seven pointed towers. And then I remembered how Feyella Mapollion had galloped her white horse across the same foreshore towards Mallion, when I had watched her from my tower window.

What, I wondered, did Mallion mean to her?

For that matter, what was she to Benedict Trevallion?

Curiosity had driven me to discover if he kept his promise to visit her two days after his return, on the Thursday. That Thursday afternoon, I had found my way to the long corridor above the refectory, which had windows out on to the courtyard. And it was from there, in the midafternoon, that I had seen him ride out through the gateway arch, to keep his tryst with the aristocratic Feyella. I had watched him go, tall and lean in the saddle, dressed in a coat of dark green broadcloth and wearing the same broad-brimmed Panama hat he had brought from Jamaica—and his going had filled me with a strange and unaccountable sense of deprivation. And this was ridiculous, I told myself, because Benedict Trevallion and I were as far apart, in every way possible, as the North Pole and the Equator.

In that first week, when we met briefly at breakfast and occasionally at other times, I had the opportunity to study this strange man who had come to play such an influential part in my life.

The cast of melancholy on his face, and the touch of bitterness in his mouth were, if anything, more pronounced since our arrival at Castle Mallion—and I thought I knew the reason.

61

It seemed obvious to me that his inner sadness was connected with his mother. He loved her, but she was entirely indifferent to him—even contemptuous. To her, he was no more than the caretaker of the castle and the estates: a keeper of accounts, counting stooks of corn and heads of swine, as she had slightingly put it. He was not hated and despised, the way that dead Saul had been; but he could scarcely derive any consolation from that.

No, the way I saw it, Benedict Trevallion—for all his awesome poise and strong will—was a man who had always lacked a mother's love; someone who had lived in the shadow of an elder brother more attractive and more loved. I remembered the portrait of the smiling hussar in the picture over the great fireplace back in Roswithiel. Poor, sombre Benedict. What chance could he have had against a firstborn who had looked like that?

Looks, of course, are not everything. In my childish way, I had fallen in love with the portrait of Piers Trevallion. But—allowing for Mrs Trevallion's overblown mother love—had the dead hussar's virtues really lived up to his appearance? My father had always spoken of him as "a fine fellow, a brave officer, a real gentleman through and through"; but that was only the judgement of a rough soldier—a man's judgement; a better opinion than that was needed, to set against that of his mother. And Feyella Mapollion's might be the opinion well worth remembering: she had known the three brothers since her childhood, and had chosen Benedict before the other two, before even the marvellous Piers. This answered the question, also, of what Benedict meant to her.

I had no doubt at all—it had been obvious when she first greeted him—that Feyella's well-tended and capable hands were clutching for the new master of Castle Mallion. When I examined the idea in my mind, I found it curiously displeasing to me.

And so, in this way—with intriguing speculation and in agreeable surroundings—I passed my first week at Mallion, in a period of deceptive calm.

It was a calm that was suddenly to erupt into a destructive

storm. Had I but known it, the storm was giving plenty of warning of its arrival; the danger signs had been there, if I had had the eyes to see them, as far away as Jamaica in time and place.

* * *

It was just after breakfast, and Benedict had just ridden out to do a day's business at one of the outlying farms, when a carriage came into the courtyard. I heard Prendergast call out as I was leaving the refectory. He was holding the horses when I got outside.

Feyella Mapollion was just getting down from the driving seat. She was wearing a white muslin dress and a pretty bonnet trimmed with pink rosebuds, with her smooth blonde hair piled up beneath it. She had driven herself to Mallion. But—why?

She smiled in a most friendly manner when she saw me. It was as if our first meeting—with her searching questions and cold glances—might never have been.

"Hello and good morning," she said. "Is Benedict around?"

"He—Mr Benedict—is doing some estate business today," I said. I felt nervous and gauche before her, and despised myself for it.

"No matter," she said. "I've come to do some painting, not to see him. Prendergast, when you've put the horses away, would you be so kind as to lift down my paintbox and easel and take it down on to the beach below the walls?"

"Certainly, Miss Feyella." Prendergast's grim face broke into an unaccustomed smile and he ogled her with the special look that higher servants reserve for only the very best people.

"I've always wanted to make a colour sketch of Mallion from the beach," she said to me. "It's the aspect of the place that I see so often when I'm riding out. Do you paint—er—Joanna?" There was no doubt about it, she was really making a determined effort to be friendly and agreeable to me.

"No," I admitted. "I can't draw a straight line, and wish I could." Then, remembering my manners, "Have you had breakfast?"

"I never touch it," she said, wrinkling her nose prettily, "but I wouldn't say no to some coffee."

We drank coffee together, facing each other across the refectory table, till the time came for me to go to the dower house and give Mrs Trevallion her morning read.

I remained shy and nervous of Feyella most of that time. Everything about her underscored my own inadequacies. She carried her fine-boned, aristocratic beauty in such a way that I felt like some raw country wench up from the country selling eggs. At closer quarters, her simple muslin dress was of the finest linen and cunningly cut to make the most of her elegant slenderness, while the bonnet could only have come from Paris. Every detail of her appearance suggested leisure and wealth lightly borne. I particularly noticed a blue brooch that she wore at her bosom: it was of a simple oval shape. On anyone else it would have been quite remarkable; on Feyella Mapollion, you just knew that the blueness came from a real semiprecious stone and not from coloured glass, and that the encircling frame was of solid gold.

Gradually, because of her friendliness and her lively and pleasing manner, my self-consciousness thawed out. She asked me about myself: of my life in Jamaica and before then. I found myself warming to her, and even gave her—with a bit of prodding—a version of what happened when I spied on the revels on the night of the Roswithiel ball (I omitted to mention the horrifying encounter with Saul and his hunting companions). Feyella found this very amusing. In return, she told me more about herself. This she did without any affectation. What she told were simply a few disconnected fragments from the life of a young girl living in the country, her hopes, her fears, her simple amusements. She made light of the cosseted surroundings in which this life had been lived: the servants obedient to every beck, the lack of nothing, the assurance of plenty. I found her very sweet and charming. When ten o'clock came, and time for me to go to Mrs Trevallion, it was quite a wrench to leave my new friend.

We parted in the courtyard: she to her painting, I to my reading.

"We must have another gossip very soon," she said. "I want to do lots of paintings of Mallion. We shall see plenty of each other, Joanna."

My troubles began from that very day.

* * *

I never saw Feyella's departure. Mrs Trevallion was particularly garrulous that morning. Very little reading was done, and it was past one before I returned to the courtyard, by which time the carriage was no longer standing there.

Later, it rained, and I spent a lazy afternoon in a pleasant, high-ceilinged room overlooking the sea. I sat there, nodding over some sewing, till evening light took over, and I decided to go up to my room and change for supper—in case Benedict put in an appearance.

I had a premonition of horror before I even opened the door of the green bedroom at the top of the tower. Even with my hand on the latch, I sensed a presence of evil within.

Inside the room, it was nearly as dark as pitch: only the faint loom of light seeping in below the drawn window curtains—and that struck me as strange, for why should anyone have taken the trouble to come up and close the curtains when it was barely dusk?

There were two choices open to me: either to light a candle in the gloom, or to cross the room and pull aside the curtains. I decided upon the latter almost without thinking.

Two paces across the room, and the door creaked—then snicked shut behind me. It had a habit of doing this. No cause for alarm. I paused to get my bearings again. Without the light from the open door, all was blackness. The faint glow from the direction of the curtained window seemed to have disappeared completely.

I took a couple of hesitating steps forward, hands extended in front of me—and stumbled against a chair that surely should not have been standing in the middle of the room.

Then something fluttered past my ear. I distinctly heard the beat of leathery wings!

My own scream—coming shockingly loud and quite beyond

my control—further added to my sudden terror. I clasped one
hand across my mouth to shut off the sound. My other hand
went instinctively to my hair: whatever happened, I had to
keep the thing of horror from becoming entangled in my hair.
Sobbing with desperation, I made another step forward—and
fell headlong over the chair that I had upturned.

*The thing came low over my head, and I thought I heard its
tiny shriek!*

Now I was crawling, with one hand and forearm scrabbling
to cover my hair, and the other hand questing the darkness
ahead. Somewhere from afar off, I could hear a woman screaming like a soul in torment—and I knew it was me.

If the horror had touched me, I think my heart would have
stopped beating. I knew it had to happen sooner or later. No
hope, now, of ever reaching the window. The room no longer
had shape or direction: it was an endless black pit from which
I should never escape. I was alone with the thing of horror.

My cheek against the cold floorboards, I lay and listened,
stifling my shuddering breath.

Nothing . . .

I swivelled my eyes to their full extent, both sides, without
daring to move my head. There was a sunburst of hope in my
heart. It seemed to me that there was a faint patch of lightness
away to my left.

I listened again, stretching out my nerve ends, as if to probe
every corner of the green room. No sound. The thing had settled somewhere.

Gathering myself together, I prepared to leap to my feet and
run to where I believed the window to be. Only, it had to be
done in one swift movement; my first sound would disturb the
thing, and it might take flight towards me.

I brought my right knee up; stretched out my left hand,
scrabbling lightly with my fingertips, to gain a purchase—however slight—in the cracks of the floorboards.

*And then—something small and cold flapped, lurchingly,
across the back of my hand!*

How long I cowered there, I shall never know. Huddled, like
an unborn child, with my hands clasped over my head. They

66

must have heard my screams across the courtyard and in the kitchen quarters.

I did not hear them come in. There was no warning. Suddenly, the dying daylight flooded over me, and I looked through the chinks in my fingers, to see the shocked face of one of the kitchenmaids standing by the window, still holding the edge of the curtain that she had just drawn.

"Lawks a-mussy, miss. What's happened to you?"

There was a sound behind me. I looked round. There was another girl. She was stooping to pick something up from the floor. Something dark. Something that flapped, protestingly, in her hands.

I hid my face with a moan.

"It's only a little fruit bat, miss. Don't know how it could have got in here, not with the door and window closed and all. Does it scare you, miss? Frightened of bats, are you?"

It was useless to try to explain. I simply nodded and struggled to my feet. Tried not to see the amused contempt on their young, unformed faces as they went towards the door. The girl who had picked up the thing still had it in her hands.

"You'll be all right now, miss?"

I nodded, keeping my eyes averted from the thing she was carrying.

"Don't you worry. We'll get rid of your little old bat. Won't we, Rosie?"

They both sniggered.

I looked out of the window; out across the tumbled breakers that were advancing across the sands in the evening light.

Useless to explain, given the situation. I had always had a horror of bats; an unreasoning instinct that had the power to lay me prostrate and helpless.

Tomorrow, I would be able to talk about it, but not now. In the daylight, I was perfectly able to talk—even to laugh—about it.

Why, I had even spoken of it to Feyella that very morning.

* * *

Benedict Trevallion did not come in to supper that evening, which was a blessed relief. My nerves were still in a jangled state, and I think I would have burst into tears if he had mentioned the episode of the bat. And mention it he would, for the story was all over the castle. The servants had obviously passed it among them as a great jest. The young girl who served me at table could scarcely smother her grin. I was glad to retire early to my room. And I was careful to take a three-branch candlestick—already lit—up with me.

Benedict Trevallion had almost finished breakfast when I came into the refectory the following morning. He nodded a greeting to me and got to his feet.

"I'm off," he said. "And I shall be back for supper with three gentlemen. Would you be so good, Joanna, as to tell Mrs Prendergast? Tell her to prepare plenty. We shall have been in the saddle all day, and hound-hungry."

"Is there anything particularly you'd fancy?" I asked.

"A leg of pork would suit," he said. "Yes, a leg of pork. And a game pie. And a couple of side dishes. Tell her that, if you please. Mrs Prendergast will see to it."

"Very well, Mr Benedict."

"Good day to you, Joanna."

"Good day, Mr Benedict," I said.

A few minutes later, I heard him mounting-up in the courtyard. I went to the window, and watched him ride out under the archway. Just before he went out of the sunlight and into the shade, he turned in the saddle, and looked back towards the refectory window. I stepped swiftly to one side, out of sight, and hoped that he had not seen me watching after him.

Mrs Prendergast was standing at the door of the kitchen quarters when I crossed over towards the dower house at ten o'clock. The housekeeper kept her close-set eyes on the level of my shoulder, never meeting my gaze, as I gave her Benedict's message. She nodded briefly in acknowledgement of the instructions, but made no comment. I had the impression that there was the ghost of a smile lurking at the corners of her pinched, pursed lips. She was probably reflecting with amusement on the incident of the bat, I thought.

Mrs Trevallion still had her lady's maid with her when I went into the parlour of the dower house. The maid—a thin-faced, dark-eyed Cornish girl—was fussing with her mistress' shawl and causing her some irritation.

I tactfully intervened, and sent the maid to fetch Prendergast to carry the chair up the steps into the old garden. And then—an unaccountable thing—when I went over to the sewing table to pick up *David Copperfield*, it was not there. Nor was it anywhere in the parlour. I searched everywhere, and Mrs Trevallion was quite adamant that no one had borrowed it.

In the event, we spent the morning in the old garden without a book. I had to forego the delights of Mr Dickens, and try to divert Mrs Trevallion from her morbid obsession with her dead son by telling her gossipy anecdotes about life back on the plantation in Jamaica. I failed miserably: within a very short time, she was in full spate. She rambled on about Piers till weariness overcame her. Then she fell asleep. I never spent a longer morning.

That afternoon, mindful of the fact that Benedict was bringing guests back to supper, I took out my only evening dress—a white velvet that had been made for me the previous year by a seamstress at Roswithiel—and subjected it to a critical scrutiny. It was quite clean, and still fitted me well, but it smelt musty from the long journey in the trunk. It occurred to me that a few hours in the afternoon sunlight might help to sweeten it, so I hung up the dress from the branch of a tree in a quiet corner of the old garden, where no one would comment on the unsuitability of hanging old clothes about in the grounds of a stately home of England.

Just before six o'clock, I went up into the garden to recover my dress. It was no longer there—the branch was empty.

I found my dress lying in the long grass some distance away from the tree where I had hung it. The material was badly crumpled, and I thought that it must have been blown there by a fitful gust of wind—though the air had seemed to be still all day.

When I picked up the dress, I saw the destroying stain on the back of the skirt: a blackberry stain the size of a hand, or larger; the sort of stain that could be made by deliberately rubbing a handful of ripe fruit into the material. The fragments of seed and skin were still sticking to the discoloured velvet.

Of course, I told myself that it was unthinkable that anyone in or around Castle Mallion would have dreamed of playing such an evil and malicious trick on me. There had to be some mistake. I estimated the distance from the tree branch, where the dress had hung, to the clump of grass where it had landed—and persuaded myself that a sudden eddy of strong wind had blown through the old garden and carried the dress, hanger and all, to the spot where I stood. The explanation, though unlikely, was the only one that I could bear to accept. Any other explanation opened up possibilities that I just did not want to consider. I could not begin to explain the blackberry stain.

I met no one on my way back to my room carrying the dress. If I had—if, for instance, I had come across Mrs Prendergast— I might have shown the damage and demanded information. As it was, I reached the green room none the wiser, hung up the dress, and had a good cry.

I had scarcely washed my face and composed myself when I heard the clatter of horses' hooves coming into the courtyard. Benedict had come back with his guests. I gave myself a swift look in the mirror, hoped that my old sprigged muslin would pass muster, and went downstairs.

As soon as I turned into the courtyard, I knew that something was badly wrong. The Prendergasts were with the group in the middle of the yard. There was Benedict Trevallion with three cloaked and hatted men.

He was angrily addressing the man and wife:

"Not expected? What the blazes do you mean, not expected —didn't you get the confounded message?" I had never heard him so angry. In such a tone of voice as that he must, surely, have spoken to my father on the memorable occasion after the Roswithiel ball.

Mrs Prendergast mumbled something, and all eyes were turned to me as I approached.

"Good God, girl! Can't you pass on a simple message?"

I stared at him, trying to come to terms with what he was

saying to me. His deep-blue eyes were clouded with fury, and the lines of ill temper were drawn deeply between his brows.

"I—I'm sorry," I faltered. "I don't understand . . ."

"Don't understand?" he repeated, turning to his three companions and making a gesture of disbelief. "Do you hear that, gentlemen? We've ridden over half the duchy this day, and all I can offer you for supper is stale bread and cold cuts. And all this child can say is that she doesn't understand."

"But I told her!" I cried out indignantly, glancing towards Mrs Prendergast. The housekeeper was white-faced and cowed. She continued to look at Benedict Trevallion.

"Well, I didn't hear her," she said sullenly. "If I had, I would have done it, wouldn't I, sir?"

"But I told you quite clearly," I cried. "You were standing at the door, and . . ."

"What the blazes does it matter now?" shouted Benedict Trevallion. "Between the two of you, you've condemned my guests to a kick at the pantry door. But remember this in future . . ." He pointed his finger straight at me. His face was a mask of mingled fury and arrogance. Not for the first time in my life, I was suddenly and frighteningly aware of the might and power of privilege . . . "When I give an order here, I expect it to be obeyed. I demand obedience, and I will get it. Do you understand?"

I faced him, willing myself to protest, to begin to explain all over again. Suddenly I knew it was useless. I was beaten.

"Yes, Mr Benedict," I said flatly.

Then I turned and walked back towards the tower, hating the tears that scalded my cheeks.

Behind me, I heard him say: "Well, then, gentlemen. Come and let's have a drink while something's being got together. I can only apologise for this mess."

I slammed the tower door behind me. That much, at least, I permitted myself.

* * *

I did not go down to breakfast next morning. Shortly after nine o'clock I heard Benedict Trevallion calling good-bye to his guests as they rode out of the courtyard. Then all was silent about the castle, till just before it was time for me to go across to the dower house. Then a carriage arrived. It was Feyella. I went down to her.

"Hello, Joanna," she greeted me brightly. "How are you?"

"Very out of sorts," I replied ruefully. And I flashed an angry glance towards Prendergast, who kept his face averted as he unharnessed the carriage horses. "People seem to have been going out of their ways to make things unpleasant for me!"

"I'm sorry to hear that," she said, tucking her hand in my arm. "You poor dear. What's happened?"

We strolled towards the formal garden and sat down beside one of the fountains. I told her the business of the message that I had been accused of not having delivered. In the morning sunlight, it all sounded very trivial. Feyella was gracefully sympathetic.

"You ran full-tilt into one of Benedict's fits of bad temper," she said. "He's famous for them. He was the same as a child. They were never able to keep a nursemaid for him. Such a cross old bear."

"But it was so unfair," I said. "Mrs Prendergast obviously forgot and was too scared to admit it. I was put into the position of either persisting in calling her a liar to her face, or keeping my peace."

"You relapsed into a dignified silence," said Feyella. "And I applaud you for it."

"But it made me look such a goose," I said. "Now he thinks I'm a scatterbrain."

She laughed. "Not he," she said. "Now, put the whole thing out of your mind and come and tell me how you think my painting's getting along."

I helped her carry her paintbox and easel down to the smooth sands below the castle walls. She set up her canvas, on which there was already a very good representation of Mallion as seen from the low viewpoint of the beach. I am no judge of art, but it was quite obvious that she was a very competent sketcher in oils. She had caught the feel of the great, brooding bulk with its ivy-hung walls. I praised her work, and we said good-bye because it was ten o'clock and time for my reading.

I fervently hoped that *David Copperfield* had turned up. It had not.

Mrs Trevallion's maid was full of protestations. "I've searched the dower house from top to bottom, miss," she said. "Are you sure you brought it in from the old garden the day before yesterday?" I assured her that I had. We both agreed that it was a mystery.

Remembering how inadequate had been my attempts at conversation the previous day, I decided to take another book with us to the garden. Not wanting to become involved in the delights of another Dickens while still in the middle of *David*, I picked an undistinguished-looking novel by an author who was unknown to me, and we set off for our morning constitutional in the fresh air.

The wind, coming in from the sea, was driving flurries of leaves from the treetops that overhung the castle walls. The year was dying, and we would soon see the end of our Indian summer. Perhaps, I remember thinking, this will be our last morning in the old garden.

I had no wish to confront Prendergast again that day, so I made some pretext for asking the lady's maid to help me up the garden steps with the Bath chair. The two of us managed it pretty well, despite some protests from Mrs Trevallion that we were jolting her uncomfortably.

The maid left us at the top of the steps. I wheeled my charge to our usual spot—a sheltered place under an old wall, above a grassy slope—and started to read.

By the end of the second page, it was clear that the novel was a piece of trivial rubbish. I found myself yawning with boredom, and Mrs Trevallion—after interrupting me, in her usual manner, a couple of times—soon began to do likewise, for yawning is as infectious as measles. Very shortly, she was nodding over her folded hands, and, after a while, her gentle snoring told me that she was fast asleep.

I laid aside the book, and studied her bowed head, with its bone-white hair set with a cap of black widow's weeds.

73

Save for the slight movements of her breathing, she could have been a dead person; the almost transparent pallor of her face was like the pallor of death. I had but the vaguest notion of the source of Mrs Trevallion's infirmities. Her maid had told me, in an awed whisper, that her mistress had collapsed, and never walked again, on hearing the news of her firstborn's death. That had been eight years ago, and Mrs Trevallion's sorrows had set their imprint deeply on her since then. I found it impossible to form any affection, or even liking for the poor woman; but, on that October morning in the dying year, I experienced a great wave of compassion when I looked at her sitting there, huddled and terribly vulnerable, in her invalid chair, with the golden leaves falling all about her. Surely, with all that weight of grief, she was not much longer for this world.

I shuddered, as if someone had walked over my own grave. Come, girl, I said to myself, this sort of morbid thinking won't do, and I stirred myself and got up on my feet. To shake off the cobwebs of boredom and depression, I busied myself in gathering a posy of fallen leaves and the overblown roses that abounded everywhere in the old garden. Then I took some long strands of ivy and plaited them into a wreath, in which to tuck the flowers and leaves. It made a fine chaplet, of the kind worn by pagan gods and goddesses; and I found a marble bust of a laughing boy—all green with lichen and hung about with delicate spiders' webs—on top of a crumbling stone wall, and crowned him with my chaplet.

I was taking a few steps back, to admire the effect of the flower-crowned boy, when my eye was taken by a flash of something white under the bushes, nearby the path leading down to the steps. Thinking it might, perhaps, be a handkerchief that someone had dropped, I went to have a closer look.

It was not a handkerchief, but a book. And, even as I stooped to pick it up, I guessed what book it was.

I was right. In my hands, I held the copy—our copy—of *David Copperfield*. Its handsome leather binding lay close by—ripped from the body of the book by a vandal hand and

74

dropped there. And whoever had done it had been to no great pains to conceal his or her crime: the remains were in such a place that they could scarcely have remained undetected for long; in fact, I was almost certain that they could not have been there on the previous day. It was more likely that the pieces had been put under the bush early that very morning. And this meant that the culprit had wanted me to find them; had wanted me to come across the evidence—*so that I should know that there was someone who hated me!*

Yes, it had to be me against whom the act of senseless vandalism was directed; it could hardly likely have been aimed at Mrs Trevallion.

I was standing there, holding the ruined book and trying to come to terms with the sudden sense of unease, when I clearly heard my name being called:

"Joanna! Joanna—come quickly!"

It floated up from the direction of the castle courtyard: an urgent cry for help—and it was the voice of Feyella Mapollion.

My first instinct was to run to her. Then I thought of my charge. Mrs Trevallion was still asleep, her head bowed. She would be quite safe, and I would only be gone for a minute or so: her chair was at the top of the grassy bank, but not facing the slope, and the brake was on. I had no idea, of course, what was ailing Feyella, but it sounded like a crisis.

One last glance back towards the sleeping woman, and I gathered up my skirts and ran down the path, down the steps into the castle courtyard.

"Feyella! Miss Mapollion! Are you there?" There was no one to be seen in the courtyard, so I called her—and received no answer.

I crossed the yard, and went into the coolness of the great hall, just as Mayana came down the wide staircase with her little boy.

"Have you seen the lady?" I mouthed at her. And when she stared at me uncomprehendingly, I pointed through the long window and tried again. "The young lady—have you seen her out there?" This time, I threw the question at Jackie, but the child only hid his face in his mother's skirts, and Mayana was glaring angrily after me when I went out into the yard again.

My alarm for Feyella was rapidly increasing. There was still no sign of her outside. I scanned the lines of battlements above, thinking that I might see her there, in some situation of peril. There was no one about. But, just as the mulatress and her child came out of the porch behind me, I saw Mrs Prendergast approaching round the corner of the kitchen block. She looked like some forbidding black crow in her funereal dress and shawl. I called out to her:

"Where's Miss Mapollion?"

The woman came close to me before she replied:

"What did you say, miss?" Her pinched lips barely parted to mouth the words.

"Miss Mapollion," I cried. "Surely you heard her call out for me. Her voice came from the courtyard. Have you seen her about?"

She looked from me to Mayana and back, puzzled.

"I'm sorry, miss," she said coldly. "I scarce know what you're asking me. I heard no call. As for Miss Mapollion . . ."

"Yes?" I asked.

"Why, she was down on the beach, when last I saw her from a window, and has been all morning since she came, miss."

The woman was looking me straight in the eyes. There was malice in her glance—and I knew, with startling clarity, that she was lying to me.

But—*why?*

I had scarcely asked myself that question when there came an unearthly sound from the direction of the old garden: a long drawn-out wail, as of someone in mortal terror; it ended abruptly with a scream of pain. Then—silence.

"It's madame!" Mrs Prendergast's voice lashed at me accusingly. "Madame's come to some mischief, up there on her own!"

My heart gave a lurch. Gathering up my hem, I raced to see what awful thing was amiss with my charge. To tell the truth, all thoughts of Mrs Trevallion had been erased from my mind by the unaccountable incident of Feyella calling for me and then disappearing. I prayed to Heaven that nothing serious had happened up in the old garden. As I toiled, panting, up the steep steps, my mind assembled hideous visions of Mrs Trevallion lying beneath her overturned chair, broken-necked and glassy-eyed.

The reality was scarcely less awful.

"Look at poor madame! See what you've done with your neglect!" came Mrs Prendergast's accusing voice at my elbow. She had followed close behind me, and I could hear others following up the steps.

My charge lay, as I had imagined her, close to her upturned Bath chair, at the foot of the grassy slope down which the chair must have rolled. She was sprawled on her side, and her mittened hands were scrabbling at the tangled grass, while she whimpered piteously.

I ran to her; flung myself on my knees beside her and took her hands.

"Oh, Mrs Trevallion," I cried. "It was all my fault for leaving you. Are you badly hurt?"

There was an already-darkening bruise on her right cheek-bone that was smeared with earth and the green stain of grass. She continued to whimper—half frightened, half puzzled—like some child who has wakened from a nightmare and does not yet know where it is. I took my handkerchief, and was making a dab, to clean some of the soil from her pale cheek, when a powerful hand closed about my arm and wrenched me roughly to my feet.

I looked round, and into the face of Benedict Trevallion. To say that he was angry is simply to make a general statement about the condition of his mind. The expression on his face far eclipsed—in sheer savagery—anything I had seen there before during any of his other explosions of fury. It was more the face of a wild animal than that of a human being. And yet, strangely enough, I had the impression that he was perfectly in control of his overheated passions—and this made it all the more horrifying to me.

"I saved you from the gutter," he snarled close to my face. "Is this how you repay me—by trying to kill my mother?"

"I—I never dreamed it would happen," I faltered.

"You left her all alone and untended! An invalid in a wheel chair!" he cried accusingly.

"I—thought she'd be safe for a little while," I pleaded.

He lifted his foot and kicked at one of the rear wheels of the Bath chair. To my horror and amazement, it spun round quite readily.

"But I left the brake on!" I cried.

"That you did not!" he said savagely.

My mind was all confusion. By this time, most of the castle servants had appeared on the scene. Prendergast and one of the gardeners had lifted up Mrs Trevallion—who was still only in a half-conscious state, and wailing brokenly—and were slowly carrying her towards the steps. The kitchen staff and the housemaids were grouped together at a respectful distance from where I was standing with Benedict Trevallion and the overturned chair; they were muttering together, and I could not but be aware that the gazes they threw at me were hostile.

I tried to cast my memory back to the events of the morning. Had I really applied the brake to the Bath chair as soon as we arrived at our usual place by the old wall? Had I checked that the brake was securely on before I left Mrs Trevallion? Both these things I was sure I had done; but the conviction melted away before Benedict Trevallion's savage glance. He truly believed that I had been callously neglectful of the helpless woman placed in my charge.

At that moment, Feyella Mapollion came up into the garden, accompanied by a maid who had probably been dispatched to fetch her. Feyella cried out with alarm to see the two men carrying Mrs Trevallion towards her. She ran to them, and had some words with Prendergast, who, in answer to a question, pointed towards where I was standing. I saw Feyella's eyes open wide with sudden shock.

She came up to us. "What a dreadful thing, Benedict," she said.

"What happened to you—are you all right?" I asked her.

The gaze that she turned on me was blankly hostile; I felt a cold finger of unease trail the whole length of my spine.

"What are you talking about?" she demanded. And, without

78

waiting for me to gather my wits and summon a reply, she readdressed herself to Benedict. "Have you sent for the doctor?" she asked.

"The groom rode off to the village straightaway," he replied.

"I hope she'll be all right. But a fall can be terribly serious to one so frail," she said.

"It never should have happened," he cried. "It was unforgivable. Unforgivable!" Then both of them were looking at me again. I felt trapped in a web of anger and misunderstanding.

"Please believe me," I appealed. "I realise now that I shouldn't have left Mrs Trevallion, but when I heard Feyella . . . Miss Mapollion call out . . ."

"What are you talking about?" snapped Feyella irritably.

"But—you called me," I said.

"You would need a good pair of ears," she said coolly. "I never left the beach all morning, till the girl fetched me just now with news of the accident." She turned to Benedict. "I'll go and see if there's anything I can do to help make your mother comfortable."

Benedict nodded absently, still glowering furiously at me. It was as if he could scarcely bring himself to unleash the fury in his mind. In that instant of time, I knew that I would have given anything to have convinced him that I had not been callous and neglectful; but it was hopeless; every circumstance was against me.

I gazed helplessly about me, trying to read something from their faces, and finding only hostility. Yet, surely, there was more than that in the glance that Feyella Mapollion threw me as she turned to go; it was only momentary, but quite unmistakable.

She had her back to Benedict, and her short upper lip was curled in a smile of malicious triumph that was echoed in her violet-blue eyes.

Then my world broke and fell apart in confusion. I was scarcely aware of Benedict Trevallion as he turned on his heel and followed her. I could only stare at Mrs Prendergast, who was standing a short distance away and regarding me out of the corners of her narrowed eyes.

The black shawl that the housekeeper wore had slipped—or had been purposely moved, perhaps—from her shoulders, revealing the bodice of her black bombasine dress, revealing, also, an oval-shaped blue brooch that was pinned in the centre of her narrow bosom.

I knew, with a startling certainty, that it was the selfsame brooch of semiprecious stone encircled with a frame of gold that I had seen Feyella Mapollion wearing on the first day that she had come to call in the carriage, on the day that she had gone out of her way to make herself agreeable to me.

Feyella Mapollion had given Mrs Prendergast the quite valuable brooch—and now the housekeeper was flaunting it before me.

She had given the brooch to Mrs Prendergast—*in return for what?*

* * *

October 28, 1862.

Dear Mr Benedict,

I am very glad to hear that Mrs Trevallion is not seriously hurt and is expected to make a quick recovery.

In view of what has happened, you will not wish to be burdened with me any longer, so I am going to leave and make my own way in the world.

I should like to take this opportunity of thanking you for all you have done for me and mine. Also, that you should consider that the service which my father was able to perform for your brother at Balaklava has been more than repaid by your family over the years.

That my thoughtlessness in leaving Mrs Trevallion alone contributed to her accident will always be on my conscience. I hope you will, in time, come to forgive me.

Again, many thanks for all your kindnesses.

Believe me I remain,

Yours sincerely,
Joanna Goodacre

I folded the letter, wrote his name on the front and laid it on the chest of drawers in the green room. Even if it fell into the Prendergasts' hands, I had no doubt that they would deliver it to him, since the contents made no attempt to lay blame on anyone but myself. In fact, it absolved the Prendergasts, Feyella Mapollion, and anyone else who might have been involved in persecuting me.

For now I knew the reason for Feyella's sudden blossoming of friendship for me; I could see how my artless confidences about my horror of bats had led to the thing being insinuated into my curtained room: the defacing of *David Copperfield*; the "misunderstanding" over the ordering of supper for Benedict's gentlemen guests; and, finally, the contrived means by which I had been trapped into leaving Mrs Trevallion on her own (and who had quietly slipped the brake and sent the sleeping woman hurtling down the slope?—almost certainly Prendergast himself)—all these incidents had been fiendishly devised for one reason, and one reason alone: to drive me out of Castle Mallion.

They were in it together. The Prendergasts, because they saw in me a member of the upper servant-class who might challenge their authority at the castle; Feyella Mapollion—I could hazard a female's guess as to why she resented me and wanted me out. And it was ridiculous, of course, the jealous fantasy of a spoilt she-cat. What was I to Benedict Trevallion?—a man who treated me like a piece of furniture, or a purchased slave.

Well, I told myself, they've had their way with me, they've driven me out.

What use of making any trouble? Benedict Trevallion would never believe me. I had no proof of any of the things they had done to me.

I touched my farewell letter again. Better to part this way.

I took one last look round the green room that I would never see again. It was growing dark, and there was a slight mist closing down over the sea. A gull gave its melancholy call, and I saw its white shape dip low over the waves on the foreshore.

There was someone down on the beach. A man. I ran

towards the window for a closer look, and saw that it was Benedict Trevallion.

He was standing close to the shoreline, his back turned to the castle, looking out to sea; bareheaded, with the wind of the new night ruffling his dark hair. He was wearing a dark coat, and he looked for all the world like some phantom that stalks lonely places; silent, melancholy, and abandoned. There was nothing of the angry man who had so terrified me earlier in the day. He looked so forlorn and solitary that I had the impulse to fling wide my window and call out to him, though he never would have heard me across the distance that lay between us. The impulse soon passed; as I turned away, I saw him stoop and pick up a stone from the shallows and send it skimming across the wavetops.

I took up my carpetbag and went out of the tower room and out of the castle. No one saw me go. It was a short walk to the village, where I managed to hire a trap to take me to the railway station.

It was not till the train was carrying me away from the wild and beautiful Western land that the awful sense of loss descended upon me.

CHAPTER 3

I arrived in London on the fine, chill morning of the following day, by the first train up from the West country, after an uncomfortable and wearisome night in an unheated station waiting room.

Stepping out of the carriage and looking about me, at the great iron-and-glass train hall of Paddington, I was overwhelmed with my remoteness from it all. Everyone seemed to be in a hurry, and everyone had a place to go, somewhere in that sprawling city beyond the station walls. They eddied round me, like a tide receding past a pebble in the sand, till I was all alone. Then, picking up my heavy bag, I went out into the noisy street.

My sprigged muslin did little to keep out the cold. I had no coat, and the shawl that had served me well enough on the voyage from the West Indies gave only scant protection from the morning wind. I shivered, and looked about me for a place where I could get a hot drink and a bite to eat. All I could see was a seedy chophouse close by the station, where rough labourers with munching jaws eyed me through the steamed-up windows. Pulling the shawl more tightly about my shoulders, I went on my way.

There was a lot of traffic in the broad street that ran past the station. Cabs and carriages of all sorts, tradesmen's carts and drays, and brightly painted omnibuses. I hailed the conductor of one of these and asked him how I could get to Kennington. He gave me directions to catch a certain omnibus at the corner of Edgware Road—and very soon I was in it, and being carried southwards through the great metropolis—past the wide sward of Hyde Park with its leafless trees of approaching winter; past the crowded pavements and all the bobbing, tall hats; over the grey river to Kennington.

St Martin's vicarage looked smaller than I remembered it, and the houses all about had been pulled down to make way for blocks of new terraces that seemed to be going up all over the borough. When I knocked on the door, I noticed that it was sadly in need of a coat of paint, and that the windows of the ground floor were grimed with London soot—whereas in the Reverend Smithers's day everything about the vicarage, inside and out, had been as clean and neat as a doll's house.

My feeling of depression was greatly increased by the appearance of a middle-aged little man in a dark suit and twice-about white neckcloth, who answered my knock. He was pale and pinched of face, and he eyed me as if I might have been someone who had called to dun him for a grocer's bill. When I introduced myself and told him my former connection with St Martin's, his attitude softened slightly and he asked me inside.

"I am the Reverend Julius Cope," he said. "You will find the place in something of a mess, but my dear wife is unhappily unable" . . . he made a vague gesture that embraced the peeling walls of the hallway and the debris piled in the corners ". . . she is, I am afraid, incapacitated on account of her present condition."

"Who is it, Julius?" came a cry from above the stairwell. "Is that the doctor?"

"No, my love," replied Mr Cope. "It is a young person who once lived here in the Smitherses' day."

"What does he want?"

Mr Cope was rescued from further explanations by the sudden cry of an infant baby, which was followed by sounds of the mother trying to comfort it. The vicar spread his hands in a gesture of helplessness and motioned me go precede him into the living room.

"The child is sickening for something," he said, "and my wife is far from well. Now, is there any way I can be of service to you, Miss—er—Goodacre?"

It had been my hope to take lodgings with the new incumbent of St Martin's and perhaps contribute towards my upkeep by assisting in the work of the parish. One minute in the company of the Reverend Julius Cope was enough to tell me that this was out of the question: the man—and his home—looked and smelt of failure and despair. There was nothing I could do here, and no home for me.

"You say you have just arrived from Cornwall?" he went on. "How very remiss of me. Perhaps you are famished. Can I offer you some refreshment?"

Though I was nearly faint with hunger and my throat craved the comfort of a hot drink, I implied that I had already breakfasted. He looked very relieved, and waved me to a seat and took one himself—the only other one in the barely furnished room. He cracked the knuckles of his bony white hands and eyed me uneasily—anxious, I imagined, in case I should make any great demands upon his slender resources.

"I've come to London to make my living," I said. "I have a little money with me—enough to see me through till I can find myself a suitable position of employment—so I can pay my way from the start. I wondered if you might be able to recommend somewhere for me to lodge; someone in your parish, perhaps, who's looking for a business lady to accommodate?"

"You speak of employment," he said. "What kind of employment did you have in mind, Miss—er—Goodacre?"

"I haven't given it a lot of thought yet," I admitted. "But I read and write, speak a little French, and sew and cook quite well. Something on the lines of a companion to an elderly lady, or an invalid. Or perhaps a governess to a child. Either visiting or living-in."

"You have some experience?" he asked.

"Very little," I said. "I—I did something of the sort in Cornwall for a short time."

"Do you have references?" he asked.

I shook my head.

"Not from your previous employer, in Cornwall?"

(From Benedict Trevallion? The very thought made me shudder. I imagined myself asking him for a reference before I ran away from Castle Mallion—and pictured the expression on his face.)

"I—I wasn't there for very long, Mr Cope," I said.

He looked stern and said: "You can hardly know what a task you have set yourself, Miss Goodacre. There are hundreds—nay, thousands—of young persons like yourself in London—and many more less well endowed, by reason of youth, good health and education, to command a living wage. Add to that, there is a massive criminal and near-criminal population in the metropolis. All these unfortunates are clamouring for food and shelter—and there is not enough food and shelter to go round. In consequence, as far as employment is concerned, the places go to the best of those who are willing to work for the least profit. And, because of the massive criminal and near-criminal element I have mentioned, employers are concerned more than almost anything else with the characters of their employees."

I could see what was coming. "So I won't get a place without a reference," I said miserably.

The Reverend Cope spread his bony hands in the familiar gesture of helplessness. "That, I am afraid, is the way of the world," he said. "You have only to run your eye down the columns of advertisements in the newspaper to see what an importance is attached to references."

"Then you don't think I shall be able to find employment?"

"Your choice will be strictly limited," he said. "And insofar as any position of trust is concerned—such as the sort of position you have in mind, which would call for entering another person's home—I am afraid" . . . and he pursed his thin lips and shook his head . . . "However," he went on, "in view of your connection with the late Reverend Smithers, I would be willing to act as referee as to your character and background, Miss Goodacre."

I stared in awe at the shabby little man before me. My heart overflowing with gratitude, I reflected on the strangeness —the wonderful and unpredictable strangeness—of people. Who would have thought that such an unpromising person as this poor man would turn out to be an angel in disguise? I could have kissed him.

"Thank you," I said. "One day, I'll repay your kindness."

He made a fussy gesture with his hands. "That will not be at all necessary, my dear young lady. And now, I'll give you the address of one of my parishioners who has some accommodation to offer, which may suit your taste and—what is probably more to the point—your pocket." He took out a notebook and scribbled a few lines. "Mrs Purvis is a widow who carries on a small business on the premises. She is a worthy body, but, like so many worthy bodies in this parish, does not often feel called upon to seek the consolations of religion. Pray give her my regards and say I hope she is keeping well." He smiled a tired smile and gave me the paper with her name and address.

I thanked him again and got up. As he showed me out to the hall, the woman's voice came from upstairs again, harsh and peevish:

"Julius, you must go to the doctor and bring him here, do you hear me?"

"Yes, my love," he replied wearily.

"Tell him we shall pay—in good time."

"Very well, my love."

He opened the door for me, and took my hand.

"Refer any prospective employer to me at this address," he said. "And I will write as good a testimonial as I can."

"Thank you, Mr Cope," I said. And then impulsively: "Mr Cope . . ."

"Yes?"

"I have five sovereigns with me," I said. "The baby—if your doctor isn't willing to come without payment, I should be only too happy to help."

He squeezed my hand, and my heart turned over, to see his tired eyes begin to moisten.

"Thank you, my dear, but we shall manage," he said. "You are young and healthy and full of hope, but you will find that you will need all of your resources to survive in this city. Good-bye and God bless you. You must call and see us again when—things—are better."

"Good-bye, Mr Cope. Yes, I will."

"I have been most inhospitable," he said. "Are you quite sure I can't offer you some refreshment?"

I tactfully refused again—and again he looked relieved.

* * *

I found Mrs Purvis's address to be a narrow cul-de-sac off Kennington Lane, in a part of the borough that still remained as I remembered it from my days there in the war: a place of narrow streets where the sunlight seldom reached, and where the overhanging eaves of the upper floors nearly touched overhead, so that it was like walking through caverns of brick and mortar. The house I was seeking was near the end of the turning, and a small queue of women and children were grouped by the door. Their eyes turned to regard me—they turned slowly and expressionlessly like the eyes of patient sheep—as I approached.

I never saw such pathetic-looking creatures. The women, both young and old, were stamped with the marks of toil and poverty, with sunken cheeks and lacklustre eyes and hair. The children (and every woman had several of them about her, some in arms) were all undernourished, raggedly dressed, and barefoot. It was impossible to meet their gaze without quailing; I lowered my eyes when I spoke.

"This is Mrs Purvis's house?"

None of them replied, so I tried again:

"Is she in?"

At this, one of the women spoke up angrily. "Aye, she's in, right enough," she said. "But you'll take your place with the rest, fine lady!"

"Leave her be, Martha," interposed another. "If you 'ad

eyes in yer 'ead you'd see that she ain't 'ere after work . . ." This more helpful woman smiled at me, showing toothless gums ". . . go you straight on in, young lady. You'll find Mrs Purvis takin' and givin' out the work."

It was then that I noticed most of them carried large wrapped bundles, or had them piled in rickety perambulators or roughly made barrows. I wondered what work it was that Mrs Purvis dispensed to these poor wretches.

The street door of the house led straight into a large parlour, where a stout woman in a mobcap sat behind a trestle table that was piled high with what appeared to be Chinese lanterns, but which proved on closer acquaintance to be silk lampshades. She had one of these in her hands and was loudly berating a little woman cowering servilely before her.

"What do I pay you for this work, hey?"

"Twopence three-farthin' a dozen, Mrs Purvis," faltered the other.

"Twopence three-farthin' a dozen," repeated Mrs Purvis. "And all you're called to do is sew on the eight panels and trim 'em with the fringe. It ain't what you'd call heavy work, is it? I mean, it ain't like fetchin' coals, or loadin' wagons, is it? Nice clean work, and handsomely paid. Why—I know women in this borough who can do as many as six shades in a day, and do 'em beautifully."

"Mebbe after a while I'll get the 'ang of it better," said the little woman brokenly. "If you'll give me another chance, Mrs Purvis."

"Another chance?" Mrs Purvis's many chins sagged with an expression of affront. "Did I clearly hear you askin' for another chance? Work like yours would quickly put me out o' business. Then what's to happen to the good workin' women o' this borough who look to me for their gainful livelihood, eh?" She turned and addressed the small line of anxious-faced creatures who stood waiting their turn at the trestle table. "Would you have me give this woman more work, to put me out o' business and deprive you of your daily bread?"

The question was greeted by a chorus of "no," and the women gave the cringing victim to understand, in no mean

89

terms, that rather than allow her to deprive them of their livelihood, they would gladly watch her starve in the gutter.

"You heard what they said," commented Mrs Purvis smugly. "I'm not the one to deprive you of a second chance, but I has to think of them who depends on me. Right, who's next with the work?"

But the little woman lingered.

"Mrs Purvis . . ." she murmured hesitantly.

"Well, what is it now?"

"The dozen what I've done already. You—you wuz going to pay me for them, wasn't you?"

"Pay you?" Again, the heavy jowels sagged. "Pay you for spoilin' good silk an' best fringe? Get away with you! Get you gone afore I set the law on you."

The woman fled. It was then that Mrs Purvis saw me standing there. Her shrewd, berry-black eyes took in my appearance, and lingered on my heavy carpetbag that I had laid on the floor beside me.

"What was it you were wantin', my dear?" she asked me, in honey-like tones.

"The Reverend Cope," I said, "gave me to understand that you have accommodation to offer."

"Indeed I have, my dear," cried Mrs Purvis. She turned to the waiting women and pointed to the door. "Come back later, all of you. Wait outside till you're called." She rose to her feet and waddled across the room towards me. "It's a lovely room, and I know you'll be happy here, Miss . . ."

I told her my name, gave her Mr Cope's good wishes, but contrived to create the impression that I had far from decided to accept the offered accommodation—even if it turned out to suit me. But there was no checking the formidable Mrs Purvis; she took hold of my carpetbag and motioned me to precede her out of the room and towards a staircase beyond.

" 'Tis a lovely quiet neighbourhood, and respectable, as Mr Cope well knows, or he wouldn't have sent you here, my dear," she said. "O' course, there's the Bermondsey women who work for me—scarcely better than animals, them an' their broods—

but I keep 'em well under control. No trouble I have with them—and I don't allow their menfolk near the place, either."

"They all seemed very wretched," I suggested.

"Like animals!" she retorted. "Only to be ruled by fear an' starvation. An' how is the dear Reverend Cope? I must be puttin' on my bonnet one o' these bright Sundays an' goin' to Mattins. Lovely preacher is Mr Cope. Spiritual. Speaks very well of the Life Hereafter, he does, though I'm not myself partial to the thought o' dyin'. Here's the room. Lovely, like I said, ain't it?"

The room was on a small landing at the top of the stairs. It was neat enough, though barely furnished with an iron bedstead, chest of drawers, and a single chair. The windows were curtained with dark-coloured crash, and they looked out over the rooftops to distant fields. The bed was covered with a patchwork quilt and looked deliciously comfortable. I suddenly became aware that I felt terribly weary, and longed to lay myself out across its inviting surface and shut my eyes.

"That'll be six shillin's a week for the room and use o' sittin' room," said Mrs Purvis. "Or ten shillin's with the entire use o' the sittin' room. Attendance is included o' course, and I can do you full board if you choose."

The lure of the bed drove any doubts from my mind. "I'll take it, please," I said.

"Month in advance," said Mrs Purvis firmly. "Seein' as how Mr Cope the vicar recommended you to come, I'll not insist on references. You'll be up from the country, I take it?"

I nodded.

"Lookin' for employment, I suppose, miss?"

"Yes."

"Well, then, you'll pay me a month in advance, please. With or without the entire use o' the sittin' room, was it?"

I counted out twenty-four shillings from my reticule, and considered that I had done well to get a clean and comfortable room with the use of a sitting room and service. Service meant that Mrs Purvis employed a maid-of-all work and that I should not have to do my own cleaning-out and laundry. I dismissed the notion of full board; this would cut too deeply into my slender hoard of money—all I had to live on till I found employment. I should have to exist on short commons, I decided. A far cry from the well-covered tables of Castle Mallion.

Mrs Purvis checked the money carefully and slipped it into a purse at the end of her chatelaine.

"Well, I'll leave you to unpack," she said. She paused with her hand on the door, looking back at me. "You look wore out with tiredness," she said, "an' that's a real nasty cough you've got. Why don't you lie down an' have a nice rest, while I get Alice to bring you up a cup o' warm milk an' a bit o' bread an' butter?"

I thanked her, and did as she suggested. It was true that I had had the beginnings of a cold before I left Cornwall. I was now coughing, and felt slightly feverish. I lay back on the bed—which was not quite so soft and comfortable as it had promised to be—and closed my eyes. Almost at once, the silhouette of Castle Mallion sprang to my mind, and with it a vision of a dark figure on the shore; the figure of Benedict Trevallion looking out to sea.

I was asleep before the maid-of-all-work arrived with the tray of refreshments. She had to wake me up.

* * *

Next morning, I felt much worse. After a restless night, punctuated by bouts of coughing, my chest felt painful and my head ached. Nevertheless, I resisted the temptation to stay in bed; instead, I was up and ready to go out by seven o'clock. With just under four sovereigns between me and destitution, it was vital to get some employment immediately. Throwing on my shawl, I went downstairs and into the street. There was a greyness in the sky and a touch of frost. The queue of wretched women, with their children and their covered bundles, were waiting patiently by the door for Mrs Purvis to open up and give them work. They probed at me with their lacklustre eyes; and I gave silent thanks that my slender accomplishments might win me better employment than slaving all hours for Mrs Purvis's pittance—or so I hoped.

There was a respectable eating house on the edge of Kennington Common, close by the Horn Tavern, where I ordered a pot of coffee and a hot meat pie. This, the first substantial meal that had come my way since I left Cornwall thirty-six hours before, I was determined to make last all day; so I forced myself to eat every morsel, though the very thought of food nauseated me, and I was finding it agony to swallow.

There was a copy of *The Times* newspaper on the counter, and I asked to see it. The coffee was good, and a blessed relief to my sore throat. I sat sipping it while I scanned the long columns of advertisements for employment.

All London, it seemed, was looking for domestics—and an army of cooks, housekeepers, nurses, kitchenmaids, and the like were offering themselves. The only enquirers for governesses and companions very firmly demanded the best of references; but there was one item that caught my eye:

Mr Albert, Surgeon-Dentist of 45, Ludgate-hill seeks a refined Young Lady willing to act in the capacity of assistant in his practice of *Supplying Teeth* without extracting stumps or causing pain. Also to receive patients, assist with accounts, etc. Apply in person between 9 a.m. and 6 p.m.

I had never heard of such a thing as a female assistant to a dentist, and it seemed to me that the very unlikelihood of any young lady of refinement wanting any part of such employment must account for the most unusual course of the advertiser giving his name and address and inviting callers, and also for the fact that Mr Albert asked for no references. It was my guess that he would have very few applicants for the post, but one thing was very sure, I told myself firmly: he would have to consider Joanna Goodacre.

Supplying teeth, with or without extracting stumps or causing pain, may not be to everyone's taste; but I was a cavalryman's daughter, the offspring of a corporal of horse who had charged at Balaklava—and not a girl who was easily put down.

If only, though, I did not feel so ill . . .

Paying my fare, I left the warmth of the eating house for the cold greyness of Kennington Common, where sheep were unconcernedly nibbling at the wintry grass.

From a man who clattered past me on a black horse, I asked the best way to reach Ludgate Hill; he doffed his tall hat and directed me to take an omnibus to the north side of the river, then to walk to Trafalgar Square where I would find another omnibus going east up Fleet Street and Ludgate Hill. When I thanked him, he asked me if I was well, for I looked pale, he said—which was strange, for a few steps in the chill air had left me feeling hot and flushed.

The journey was a nightmare. Somewhere towards midday, walking along the river embankment towards Trafalgar Square, I stumbled and would have fallen but for the support of a tree against which I lurched. I leaned there for I don't know how long, with my cheek resting against the cold bark, eyes closed. The exertion of walking had set my heart pounding in a most unaccustomed way and I was having difficulty in breathing. I'm ill, I told myself. Really ill, and I shouldn't have come out today. A sudden paroxysm of coughing left me gasping for breath; and it was while I was recovering from the worst of this that my gaze happened to fall the way I had come— and I saw—*him*.

He was a nondescript individual in a long grey overcoat and battered tall hat, who was lolling by a tree some fifty paces behind me. He had something in his hands—perhaps a penknife—with which he was unconcernedly cleaning his fingernails. And I knew, with an awful certainty, that his whole attention was upon me—even though his eyes were lowered to his task. I could not see his expression; just a long, pallid face bent over his task. He looked like some bedraggled grey bird of prey.

Suddenly alarmed, I summoned up my strength and set off again. The road ahead was empty of people, though an occasional carriage went past. It was very still; only my own footfalls on the dusty road and the pounding of my heart in my ears.

And—something else . . .

Footsteps behind me.

There was no doubt about it. Above my own footsteps, another pair of feet were drumming out another—and faster— rhythm.

The man in grey was following me; was hurrying to over- take me!

Not daring to look round, for fear of what I should see in his face, I quickened my step. The exertion set my heart pound- ing anew, and a knot of harsh pain began to throb in my chest. What lay ahead: the grey buildings, the towers, steeples and domes of the city, became a wavering blur before my eyes; but somewhere there had to be busy, cheerful crowds and kindly voices. I hurried my pace even more, till I was nearly running.

And I knew in my heart that he was running too!

All of a sudden, I seemed to come out of shade into sun- light, and out into a wide space full of people. There was the merry jingle of harness and the clip-clop of high-stepping car- riage horses. I crossed a crowded, dusty square and entered a wide street, where I saw the unmistakable shape of Nelson's Column against the skyline ahead.

I dared to look round: there was no sign of the man in grey. Of course, it had all been my feverish imagining. I laughed to myself, and this set up another paroxysm of coughing. A kindly woman—poorly dressed and carrying an enormous basket of dried lavender—took me by the elbow and asked me if I needed any help. I thanked her for her kindness and said that I was quite near where I had to go; and, indeed, this was so.

When I reached Trafalgar Square, someone directed me to wait by the church for the arrival of the next eastbound omnibus; and a quarter of an hour later, it rattled into view, all red paint and bright lettering. Thankfully, I climbed aboard, and found a seat on the lower deck, near to the door.

Bowing my head, I closed my eyes and realised how com- pletely weary I really was. The panic-stricken flight down by the river had drained the last of my strength. The day's project should never have been entertained; for what condition was I in, to inspire anyone to employ me? The best thing I could do, I decided, was to throw myself on Mr Albert's mercy,

95

tell him I was ill (as if he would need to be told!), ask to be allowed to rest for a short while, then break into another of my precious sovereigns to pay for a cab to take me back to Kennington. Yes, that was what I would do. For the moment, it was strangely pleasant, just to sit and be jolted gently up Fleet Street in the crowded little omnibus. A small haven in a morning of weariness and pain.

I was roused from my reverie by a tap on the shoulder: it was the conductor, demanding his twopenny fare. I took the money from my reticule and received my ticket. In the act of so doing, I looked down the carriage, and felt every hair of my head suddenly prickle with horror.

Sitting three places away from me was the man in grey!

There was no doubt about it at all. The battered tall hat was stuck at the jaunty angle I remembered; and he was so close to me that I could see the dandruff on the back of the collar of his shabby overcoat. His back was inclined towards me, so I still could not see his face—and that was my only consolation.

What to do? He had clearly followed me to Trafalgar Square and boarded the omnibus behind me. My skin crawled at the thought that he must have brushed right past me, touching me—and I had not noticed him—when he entered the lower deck and went to the seat farther down.

Escape—that was the answer. But—to where?

If I leapt to my feet and demanded to be put down before my destination, he would only follow me, and I would be as badly off as before. No—the thing to do was to get out, as planned, at the bottom of Ludgate Hill and take refuge with the dentist-surgeon. I tried to quiet my pounding heart, averted my gaze from the figure ahead of me, and let time slip past . . .

"Farringdon Street fer the Fleet prison! Bridge Street fer Blackfriars! Bottom o' Ludgate 'ill!" cried the conductor.

The omnibus rattled to a halt by the kerb, and I clawed my way to my feet, to be out and away before the creature in grey could come after and get near to me. Before I reached the step, I was overcome with a cloying weakness, and it was only by holding onto the handrails that I prevented myself from falling into the muddy gutter. With a sudden, sickening horror, I realised that my follower might seize upon any excessive sign of my weakness as a pretext to, perhaps, take me by the arm and lead me off—anywhere. I did not have the strength to resist a determined effort. This last thought steeled me to take the step onto the kerb and direct my wavering footsteps away from the omnibus.

I was on a corner, and the shop on the corner was an outfitter's: the windows were full of bolts of cloth, neckties and tall collars, silk handkerchiefs displayed like fans. Next was a woollen draper's, and I put out my hand for support and rested there for the space of three laboured breaths. After that, I passed the open door of a shop that gave off the tangy, male smell of tobacco. I searched the door for a number: BARRACLOUGH—TOBACCONIST it said; and, after that: INFANT ORPHAN ASYLUM.

Then—blessedly:

Mr Albert
Surgeon-Dentist

Supplies teeth without extracting stumps or causing pain. A tooth, 5s; an upper or lower set, mounted on gold, from £5. Decayed teeth restored, 2s.6d. Mr Albert has no other establishment than this at 45, Ludgate-hill. Advice gratis.

I knocked on the door, and leaned against it, shrinking there with the dread that I might feel a hand—*his* hand—upon my shoulder.

Only then did I see the piece of card tucked into the corner of the notice on the door. I read it with despair:

Called away on fmly. business.
Back soon—pl. wait.

Then I felt the hand on my shoulder . . . *his* hand . . .

I screamed—and was immediately choked by a fit of coughing. But terror came to the aid of my weakness, and I wrenched myself away from the grasp of the man in grey, and turning, stumbled off the kerb and into the street. I had a vision of a quartette of horses passing before me, that and a pair of spinning carriage wheels. Someone blessed me with a round curse. I paused for an instant, to let a jouncing wagon go past the other way, then I gained the far kerb. There was a man and a woman, arm-in-arm, and they stared at me with something like affront, as I brushed past them and set off again at a lurching run up the hill. There were others walking the pavement, and groups of people looking into the elegant shopfronts of Ludgate Hill—but not one of those respectable folk so much as put out a hand, or uttered a word to question what was amiss with me. No help in the crowds.

I came to a turning off; a narrow lane that promised other turnings and eventual concealment. Casting a glance behind me, and not seeing the creature in grey, I began to run down the lane. Surely, there, I would find some dark corner to hide till he had tired of searching for me. My brain, I should add, was now numb with fever and fear.

Somewhere down the lane, between the high canyon walls and the dark windows that looked down on me, I was aware of *his* presence again. Looking back, I saw the tall figure striding straight down the middle of the narrow road. He appeared to be in no hurry: he walked with the air of a man who knew where he was going and what he was about.

I panicked then. There as an alleyway, scarcely wide enough to pass along without gathering my skirts closely about me. It smelt foully of rottenness, and the daylight hardly reached halfway down its blackened walls; but it promised the beginning of the concealing labyrinth for which my shocked mind craved.

The alleyway took a sharp bend. I leaned against the rough brickwork for a few moments and took a few pain-racked, deep breaths. A backward glance revealed my pursuer not twenty paces away: only the gloom of the alleyway and the shade of his hatbrim prevented me from seeing his face and the expression in his eyes. Choking, I went on.

Time and space were now without meaning; I was wandering in a state that was dictated only by the need to keep moving at any cost. Somewhere, and at some time, I came to the end of the dark alleyway and out into an enclosed space that was crowded with people and clamorous with noise. Nightmare small figures capered on the filthy cobbles; a woman sat on an upturned basket, puffing on a pipe; she looked up at me and grinned to show blackened teeth; there was a baby rolling and cooing in the dirt by her bare feet; someone shrieked with laughter from an open window above me.

"Wotcher, lovey. Lookin' for somethin', was yer?" An evil-smelling creature with a black eyepatch barred my way and began to knead my arm. I cried out—and a row of watching faces split into a hellish chorus of laughter. A small boy, monkey-like and half naked, plucked at my skirts.

They were all laughing at me now: the faces that surrounded me and the faces high up at the windows. And, above it all, there seemed to tower the tall, sombre figure of Benedict Trevallion. He was pointing to my surroundings and crying out to me in an angry, condemning voice:

"*You have found your way to the stews at last!*" he thundered. "*I warned you that it would happen if you ever left the protection of the Trevallions. You are here, my girl. And here you will stay till you rot . . . till you rot! . . .*"

His face closed in on me; his and the others; their mouths gaping. My heart thudded in my chest, threatening to burst with anguish, and my head ached till it was agony to keep my eyes open. Everything was going away from me. I reached out my hand for a support, but met only the empty air. Next, I was lying and looking up at the patch of blue sky that was framed far above me by the square of blackened brickwork.

A ring of faces were looking down at me. A new face swam into view, and I saw the man in grey for the first time. The face under the jaunty tall hat was not terrifying; it was only the leering, weak face of a sneak thief.

"Best not touch her," said a woman. "There's a bad sickness on her, or I ain't never seen it afore. Cholera, like as not."

The man in grey sniggered. "Cholera or no cholera, I'm having what I came for," he said. "It's cost me a long walk, and I'll bash in the face of any who deny my right!"

And, before the clouds of unconsciousness closed in upon

me, I saw him stoop down; felt his hand take my wrist and detach the handle of my reticule—containing the mite of money that stood between me and the utter destitution that Benedict Trevallion had predicted for me.

* * *

I opened my eyes and saw the stars and scudding grey clouds like gunsmoke across a field of battle. A great weight lay upon the upper part of my body, and the act of drawing breath set my heart pounding with the effort. I told myself that I was dying.

I peered to left and right, but saw no one in the shadowy square. They had all departed, leaving me where I had fallen. No lights, save the flickering loom of a candle in an upper window of one of the high-walled tenements. A dog barked. There was a bellow of drunken laughter, followed by a woman's scream. Silence.

Somehow, by rolling myself over on one elbow and raising myself by degrees, I managed to get to my feet and support myself against the nearest wall. Despite the October night, I was ablaze with fever. I could feel hard cobblestones against my bare feet, which meant that my shoes had been stolen from me while I had lain there—it scarcely made any difference.

I knew instinctively that I had been given a brief respite from the agony of the fever, but that it could not last long. In a very short time—minutes, perhaps—my strength would give out for the last time, and I would be stretched out dead on the cold stones when they found me in the morning's frost.

The wall was to be my salvation, and I pressed my hands to it, feeling the hard roughness of its texture. For so long as the wall continued—and for no farther—so would the span of my life be measured out; where the wall ended, would end also Joanna Goodacre.

One hand advancing; then the other to meet it; one dragging step following the other! I set off to find my way out of the hideous stew where my reckless flight had taken me.

I think I would have given up many times; let everything go, and succumbed to the pain and the weakness—but for the image of Benedict Trevallion's sardonic face that remained before me all the time. He seemed to be taunting me to failure, condemning me to remain in the darkness and the filth. I was determined to defy him and all the Trevallions. This night—I croaked aloud from out of the depths of my burning lungs—I shall stay alive to prove you wrong!

The good wall saved me, as I had hoped it might. I never let it go for an instant; hand over hand, by tortuous and devious ways, it led me out of the darkness and into the light.

The fever was closing in on me again, and my legs barely had the strength to support me, when I came out into the wide bright street again, and saw the carriage lamps come bobbing up Ludgate Hill.

One last gulf to cross: I let go with both hands and willed myself across the street. My legs were numb when I gained the other side, and there was a wild roaring in my ears.

The shape of the building before me was blessedly recognisable and so was the doorway, with the painted sign upon it.

Mr Albert
Surgeon-Dentist . . .

My nerveless fingers trailed down the sign, down the door, and I sank to my knees upon the step.

* * *

The cosseting warmth of soft sheets and the smell of dried lavender were the first things to break in upon my consciousness. Before that, there were shadowy figures that always dissolved into darkness, and alien voices that sounded so loud that I wanted to cry out, because of the pain they caused in my ears.

After a long while, the voices became easier to bear, and took on a friendliness that seemed to be directed towards me personally. When the faces drew close to me, to look at me, the voices became soft and compassionate.

I knew that I was ill, but that I was mending. This was

confirmed when two of the faces resolved into those of middle-aged men.

"The crisis is over, Mr Rowley," said one.

"Thank the Lord, so it is, Mr Albert," replied his companion. "It has been a long struggle. Fortunately she has a basically strong constitution, or the lobar pneumonia would have carried her away."

"It is a blessing we owe to your good physicianship, Mr Rowley," said Mr Albert.

"I did little enough," said the other. "It is a disease that will forever remain obdurate to medicines. I would put the credit to the excellent nursing of your wife and daughters."

"I think she is about to speak to us," said Mr Albert, and he took both of my hands in his. "How are you feeling now, my dear?" he asked.

"Much better, thank you," I replied, in a voice that did not sound one bit like my own.

The surgeon-dentist of Ludgate Hill had a plump, rosy face and curly grey hair. It was a face that radiated kindliness and good will.

"You have been very poorly for over a week," he said. "Ever since last Tuesday night, when you knocked on the door and we found you on the step."

"You've looked after me," I said. "You've been very kind."

Mr Albert spread his hands and indicated his companion, a tall, spare man in a black frock coat. "Despite his modesty, all the credit goes to my friend," he said. "Miss Goodacre, may I introduce Mr Robert Rowley, physician-accoucheur."

"How d'you do, Miss Goodacre," said the physician.

"You know my name!" I exclaimed.

Mr Albert twinkled. "Ah, we know a very great deal about you, my dear," he said.

"But—how?"

"Well, there is no very great mystery about it," he said. "We immediately informed the Fleet Street Police Station that an unknown young lady had delivered herself into our hands. Such is the efficiency of the Metropolitan Constabulary that, by Thursday, you had been identified as the Miss Joanna

Goodacre who had been missing from her lodging in Kennington since Tuesday morning."

"Mrs Purvis must have informed the police," I said.

"I understand that the lady took the problem to her vicar, who escorted her to the constabulary," supplied Mr Albert. "And now, my dear, I'm sure that Mr Rowley would advise sleep, so we will leave you now, and my wife or one of the girls will bring you some nourishment at midday."

I thanked them both and closed my eyes. Hardly had the door closed behind them when the terrible thought occurred to me that I was now financially destitute—for had not the thief in grey snatched my money?—and unable to pay the physician for his services, let alone offer the kindly dentist and his family anything in return for their attention and hospitality. Looking farther ahead, I was now without any resources for my life in London—except for the balance of the month's advance rent I had paid to Mrs Purvis.

The prospect seemed black, and my weakened body was unable to direct my mind to come to grips with the problems of my immediate future. Still worrying, I drifted into sleep.

* * *

The dentist's family comprised his wife and five daughters ranging from fourteen to twenty. Mrs Albert, with her plumpness, pinkness, and curly locks, could have been her husband's twin sister, and the girls were of the same likeness.

It was the youngest daughter, Nellie, who attached herself to me on the first day of my return to consciousness; demanding to know of my adventures in Jamaica, on the high seas, in Cornwall, and in London. Her china-blue eyes grew big and round with delighted horror when I told her about my flight from the man in grey.

"You wandered down Creed Lane!" she cried. "Oh, Miss Goodacre, it's a wonder you're still alive to tell the tale. You went into the 'rookeries'—where no respectable folk dare set foot."

When I expressed surprise, Nellie explained to me about the "rookeries": teeming tenements where the wretchedest poor of the great city lived like animals, and in close contact with the special crimes of the hopelessly rejected. Such colonies of degradation existed just behind the prim shopfronts of Ludgate Hill, and within the very shadow of St Paul's Cathedral itself. Looking back, I told myself that I was lucky to have come out of that nest of horror with the loss of only my money and my shoes.

On the second day, I was strong enough to be propped up by pillows and take some solid food. It was then that I put to Mr Albert my reason for coming to Ludgate Hill in the first place.

"Ah, the position I advertised," said the dentist. "That caused some raised eyebrows among my professional colleagues, I can tell you, Miss Goodacre. The notion of a lady—and a lady of refinement at that—acting as assistant to a surgeon-dentist is thought to be close to revolutionary."

"I don't see the slightest reason why," I replied tartly.

"Nor do I, my dear lady," said Mr Albert. "Indeed, I can see the day coming when we shall have dentists of the fair sex, aye, and physicians too." He laughed. "I shouldn't wonder if we don't have you all seated in Parliament, one day. Ha! How do you fancy succeeding Lord Palmerston as Prime Minister, Miss Goodacre?'"

"I shouldn't like that at all," I replied. "But, Mr Albert— tell me, please—is the position filled?"

"It is not, Miss Goodacre," replied the dentist. "Nor, on the showing so far, is it likely to be."

"You've had some applicants?"

He nodded. "Three—all of them excellent ladies of refinement."

"And?"

"All three fainted at the sight of my tray of instruments!"

We both laughed.

"You're mending well, my dear," said Mr Albert. "Already you've quite a good colour. We'll have you up and about in no time."

I said: "Mr Albert, you've all been very kind to me, you and Mrs Albert and the girls—and I'd like to ask you one more favour. As you say, I'm very much better and I'm sure I shall be on my feet in a few days' time. Will you then, please, give me a trial as your assistant? I promise you that I'm not the sort to faint at the sight of the tools of your profession—nor the sight of blood, either."

"There is little shedding of blood connected with my own branch of dental science," said Mr Albert, with a slight note of reproof, "my discipline lies largely in restoration."

"But you will consider me, please?"

Mr Albert glanced at his watch and seemed rather embarrassed by my persistence. "Dear me," he said. "It's nine-thirty already and I've a patient in the waiting room. It's been very pleasant talking to you, and I'm delighted to see you looking so well."

"Mr Albert," I said. "You haven't answered my question."

He was already on the way to the door, and he paused there with his back still turned to me, hand on the latch.

"We shall have to think about it, Miss Goodacre," he said. "Later, when you're quite recovered." He paused for a moment, and then: "But I'm of the opinion that you'll have other plans in mind, when the time comes."

And with that cryptic observation, he left me.

*　*　*

That afternoon, the five girls brought their needlework to my bedroom and bombarded me for more information about myself. They seemed to be sharing a private, particular interest in me—and it seemed to concern my short stay in Castle Mallion.

"It must have been a very grand feeling," said Prudence, "to live in an ancient castle and to be waited on by servants, hand and foot."

"Hardly hand and foot," I said, "but it was certainly a very strange and enchanting experience to live in such a place as Mallion."

As I said this, the recollection of Mallion—its sights, its colours, and its myriad scents—came swinging back to me, as if out of a cherished dream. I felt my throat tighten with emotion, and my eyes prickle with treacherous tears.

"Then why did you leave it?" came young Nellie's flat question. "Why did you come to London, and take lodgings in Kennington, if you loved it so much in your Cornish castle?"

"I—there were certain misunderstandings," I replied.

"Nellie, you've no right to quiz Miss Goodacre," admonished Harriet primly. "It's very rude to ask personal questions."

"Oh, no, I don't mind," I said. "There's nothing secret about it. I had—certain differences of opinion—with the man and woman who kept house for Mr Trevallion. They resented my being there. In the end, it seemed simpler to go away and let them carry on their existence as they had done before I came."

"Did Mr Trevallion approve of your going?" asked Nellie.

"Nellie!" chorused the others.

"I hardly think so," I smiled. "In any event, I didn't wait to ask for his opinion."

"You mean . . . you ran away without saying good-bye?" asked Nellie.

I felt the colour mount in my cheeks. "I left him a farewell note," I said defensively. "He and his family had always been very kind and generous to me and mine, and I told him as much. But I didn't feel . . . equal to the task . . . of saying good-bye to him personally."

"Are you in love with Mr Trevallion, then?"

"Nellie!"

"Nellie, take your sewing and leave this room at once!"

"Miss Goodacre, please forgive that awful child. She doesn't know what she's saying when her tongue runs away with her like that."

They chorused their apologies, and little Nellie was allowing herself to be thrust towards the door. I was aware—yet strangely uncaring—that their five identical pairs of round blue eyes were upon me, watching for my reaction. All that—the five girls and the bright little room, the bed in which I lay, and the sound of the traffic rumbling up and down the cobbled hill outside the window—were suddenly apart and insubstantial.

My whole attention was fixed upon the vision of a tall, bareheaded man standing on a seashore in the dying light of an October day of an Indian summer. After a breathless moment of silence, it seemed as if the whole world moved and sighed.

"*I don't know . . . the thought never occurred to me before now.*"

Five pairs of china-blue eyes grew even rounder. I realised that I had spoken the words aloud.

* * *

That night, in my dream, my footsteps carried me back to Castle Mallion; and a man awaited me on the sea-swept shoreline, under the arched crescent of the moon. The night wind plucked at the dark cloak he wore, and he looked like a knight standing vigil, his face hidden in the shadow of his hood.

I walked towards the tall figure, my bare feet sinking deeply in the warm, yielding sand, and he turned at the sound of my coming, and held out his hands to receive me; but, try as I might, I could get no nearer to him; the faster I directed my tread, the slower became my advance—till I could see that, instead of coming nearer, he was drawing farther and farther away from me.

I cried out, then, in my fear of losing him: pleaded with him to help me, and not to allow us to be parted forever. He called back to me in a voice of unutterable sadness and melancholy; telling me that it was for the best that we should never be together. He cried:

"*I am Death. If you come with me, I shall only destroy you as I have destroyed others—and myself!*"

And, when I pleaded with him that this could not be so— and, even if it were, it made no difference—the tall man turned his back to me and wrapped his cloak more tightly about him. With despair, I saw that he was deliberately walking away from me; away from the shoreline and towards the dark bulk of the castle, which I should never be able to enter.

Despair lent me a strength that was far beyond my own. A will that was not mine directed me to greater efforts, so that

my bare feet were lifted out of the cloying grip of the sands—
and I flew towards the retreating figure in the billowing black
cloak.

I cried out:

*"Turn and hold out your arms for me—I am coming to
you!"*

He turned as I came upon him, and my hands met his cold
hands. Because I still could not see his face, and eyes, I then
reached up and drew back the concealing hood. But there was
no face there, no eyes that looked down into mine; only
smooth, polished bone and the eyeless sockets of a skull.

I knew, then, that he had spoken the truth to me: he was
Death.

* * *

Mr Rowley the physician came to see me every morning at
eleven, and by the end of the first week of my convalescence,
I was strong enough to receive him sitting up in a cosy little
button-back armchair by the window. Maria, who was much
my size, had lent me nightdresses and a pretty, pink *peignoir*.

It was Friday. Nellie had cleared away my breakfast tray,
and the girls descended upon me in force. They had curling
tongs and hair ribbons galore, and a very splendid housecoat
of sprigged muslin that, they explained, had been worn by
their mother when she was young. They set-to to dress my
hair; piling it up at the back and allowing it to fall to the
nape of my neck in a wild confusion of curls. I laughed at
the folly of trying to add to the disorder of my own unruly
mane; but they all declared that it looked very *soignée* in the
French style. I humoured them, let them have their own way
with me, because they were so sweet and well meaning.

"But," I said, "all this is a most unnecessary fuss to make
for Mr Rowley. I'm sure he'd never notice if one were *soignée*
in the French style or otherwise."

This sent them into peals of laughter, and there was a certain
amount of whispering behind raised aprons.

"What are you little minxes up to?" I demanded. "What

have you been saying to poor Mr Rowley? I'll not be a party to your teasing that nice old gentleman."

"We wouldn't *dream* of it!" cried Harriet, all round-eyed with innocence; and the others all added their reassurances.

"I think a touch of kohl at the corners of the upper eyelids would give a hint of mystery," said Prudence.

"And the merest hint of rouge on the cheekbones—it would simulate a slight feverishness, and that's always associated with passion," said Maria. And that sent them into more peals of laughter.

"You *are* teasing!" I cried. "Away with you, and take your kohl and your rouge with you. The very idea!"

They ran to the door and grouped there, looking across at me with their lovely pansy faces and dancing blue eyes.

"You *do* look beautiful, Joanna," said Prudence. "We were determined to make you so—though it wasn't a difficult task."

"Thank you," I said, softened. "You are sweet girls, all of you. And now—be off with you, and let me compose myself, in peace, till Mr Rowley comes at eleven."

The sonorous tones of St Paul's chimes echoed down the hill and over the rooftops of the great city. Eleven chimes . . .

I let my book slip on to the floor, as there came the sound of a hansom cab drawing up outside. There was the time it takes to pay off a cab driver, and then the thud of the door knocker below. The door was answered smartly (presumably by one of the girls waiting in the hall with an eye on the clock); a discreet murmur of voices—and then the tread of footsteps ascending the stairs. A man's footsteps; but not those of poor Mr Rowley, who walked slowly from the gout; these were the light and springing footsteps of a younger man.

Again, that great stillness was closing down upon my world, and I was poised on the brink of a splendour that was just beyond the reaches of my questing fingers. Time moved with a solemn deliberateness, marked out like the organ notes of a fugue that swelled to fill the vastness of some mighty cathedral. Somewhere in the high, blue skies there were angels shouting for joy.

The door opened—and we were looking at each other across

a vast distance of space. He had not changed; only my heart had changed. Still the same dark, lean face that set off the deep-blue eyes. He looked thinner, and there were lines of tiredness about the eyes; but I searched in vain for the deep clefts of ill humour between his brows.

"I've come to take you home, Joanna," said Benedict Trevallion.

CHAPTER 4

Our private railway compartment was upholstered, seats, walls, and all, in red plush—and deep red was the colour, also, of my velvet dress. I watched and wondered at my reflection in the mirror opposite: my eyes were strangely large and bright, the illness had left my complexion good, and surely it was not my own untidy chestnut mane that was coiled and cosseted so suavely under the delicious confection of Parisian millinery perched saucily forward on my brow.

I told myself it was all a dream: a figment of my sleeping state, and I was still delirious with the pneumonia.

But the rattle of the carriage wheels was a true sound; we flashed through a station, and it was Reading—biscuit factory, gaol, and all. The train was carrying us westwards with the sun; a miracle of modern science come to the aid of the wanderer's return. I was going back to Mallion. Back home— as Benedict had said.

Without moving my head (lest he should see the movement and meet my glance), I slid my gaze towards him. He was sitting by the window opposite, reading a newspaper; still wearing the broad-brimmed, flat-crowned straw hat that he had brought back from the West Indies; the smoke from his long cigar curling in a wraith about his cheek; totally absorbed in his reading, and completely oblivious of my regard.

I marvelled at the lean strength of the hand that held the paper; it was so close to mine that I could have reached out and touched the smooth, sun-bronzed skin with its faint pelt of jet black hair. His dark blue broadcloth coat was tailored snugly about the upper arms and shoulders, and gave some hint of the lithe, catlike power beneath.

Catlike . . .

Yes. That was it. Benedict Trevallion's real power lay in his repose, more than in his fierce, all-consuming anger. Sitting before me as he was—one leg crossed with careless elegance, head slightly on one side—he looked for all the world like a big cat, a jungle killer, in easeful rest. A black panther relaxed after the hunt and the kill.

I shuddered, and the small, wayward movement made him lift the gaze of his searching blue eyes to meet mine.

"You look tired," he said. "Why don't you rest? I'll wake you long before it's time to alight."

I nodded, and closed my eyes obediently—to hide myself from his disconcerting regard.

Safe in the pink gloom of my lowered eyelids, my mind was able to wander far and wide. He would not know, he could not know, where my thoughts were taking me, along what delicious and forbidden paths my fancy might lead. He might be watching me, still—but what matter? My shielded eyes and my expressionless face would tell him nothing.

The wheels rattled a rhythm that suggested the cadences of a child's jingle; a skipping song that came back to me across the years with a very special newness, on this day, in this railway carriage speeding westwards. I remembered it well:

> Rosy apple, lemon tart
> Tell me the name of my sweetheart.
> Black currant, red currant, gooseberry jam,
> Tell me the name of my young man.
> When will he marry me? . . .

January, February, March; Monday, Tuesday, Wednesday; Silk, Satin, Cotton, Rags; Tinker, Tailor, Soldier, Sailor . . .

The probing questions, so long sought after in a childhood game, were all answered for me now. 🙋

This very morning, this bright October morning, in St Martin's Church, Kennington, the Reverend Julius Cope had joined Benedict Trevallion and me in holy wedlock; and, even though I shrank from opening my eyes, I could touch the proof of the astounding truth of it—in the plain gold band that encircled my ring finger.

* * *

Benedict had followed me to London as soon as he had read my note, which had been on the morning after my flight: had caught the first Paddington-bound express, and arrived at the Reverend Cope's vicarage only a few hours after my departure from there. He was astute enough to have realised that, as the only London address with which I had ever had any connection, St Martin's Vicarage would most likely be my first port of call.

From then on, his footsteps had fallen only a few paces behind mine, all the way . . .

From the vicarage, he traced me, of course, to Mrs Purvis's house in the narrow Kennington street; and a brief enquiry of the slatternly work-women grouped outside the house told him that a young woman was newly arrived there as a lodger.

He could have come to me then, but he decided to wait till the following morning (guessing that I would be tired and not amenable to his persuasions).

The following morning, after a late, gentleman's breakfast at the Horn Tavern, on Kennington Common, where he had stayed overnight, he went back to Mrs Purvis's and found me already gone.

I can only imagine the intensity with which he addressed himself to tracing my whereabouts during that fateful Tuesday, Wednesday, and Thursday—before the Metropolitan Constabulary established that the pneumonia victim who had turned up on the doorstep of a dentist in Ludgate Hill might be the same missing lodger from Kennington. From kindly Mr Albert, I had the story that a tall and terrifying young man ("looking,

113

for all the world, my dear Miss Goodacre, with his pride and arrogance, like Lucifer on the point of his fall") descended, with the police, on 45 Ludgate Hill within an hour of the receipt of the information about me; immediately took over charge of my welfare, instructing that the best physician available (who also happened to be the dentist's friend and neighbour, Mr Rowley) be retained for the purpose of attending me; and gave the Alberts complete *carte blanche* in the matter of the costs of my nursing and welfare (not that the dear dentist of Ludgate Hill and his family would not, I know, have cared for me out of their own charity and loving-kindness).

From the girls—wide-eyed Nellie, Susannah, Harriet, Maria, and Prudence—I heard how that terrifying man had stalked the hallway of their house during the dark hours of the night when my fever had mounted to its dangerous crisis; how he had been there in the dawn, haggard of eye yet curiously gentle of countenance, when the physician brought down the news that I was going to live. He had told the family that no mention was to be made, to me, of his name and presence, till I was strong enough to come to grips with the hard realities (for so he put it) of life.

This was why dear Mr Albert had been so embarrassed when I pressed him for a promise about the appointment as his assistant: he had rightly guessed that another plan would appeal to me better when the time came. In the same way, the girls, sworn to secrecy, regarded me, from the first, as a highly romantic creature—a sort of pantomime Cinderella who would shortly be carried away by her Prince Charming in a golden coach.

The five of them were my bridesmaids at the wedding. Benedict was not for waiting a day longer than necessary to return to Cornwall, and there had scarcely been time to make preparations. The girls wore assorted white dresses, and I was grateful to Mrs Albert for lending me a bridal gown of wild white silk and Brussels lace that both she and her mother before her had worn to the altar.

The Indian summer of 1862 granted us one last, memorable day of high blue skies and warm sun for our wedding morning;

and the dusty walls of St Martin's echoed and re-echoed to the loud peal of bells from the high tower, as I walked back down the aisle with my hand on the arm of the man who had, so miraculously, hunted me down and taken me for his own.

The bells of St Martin's tolled the knell of that long summer: even as they—the Alberts, Mrs Purvis, Mr and Mrs Rowley, the Reverend Cope—waved our carriage on its way to Paddington Station and home, the grey clouds were closing in from the east, and the first, chilly winds of the overdue winter were rustling the dry leaves of Kennington Common.

* * *

"Exeter! This is Exeter!"

The train came to a stop with a flurry of steam and a great squealing from the wheels. I opened my eyes; Benedict was looking at his watch; with an uneasy pang of regret, I saw the two indentations between his brows—their first appearance since our reuniting.

"On time," he said. "We'll be at the castle before ten o'clock tonight. You'll be glad to get there. It's been a tiring day for you, the more so because you've only just recovered from a serious illness, Joanna."

"I'm really not tired," I protested gently. "Mr Rowley commented many times on my robust constitution, and how it helped me overcome the pneumonia."

I had the impression that my remark only irritated him: he turned his head from me and stared out of the window; the frown lines deepened, and he repeatedly snapped the cover of his watch open and shut. I determined to try another approach, to humour him.

"Will they be expecting us at Mallion?" I asked. "Did you send them the news?"

"I wrote a letter to the Prendergasts," he said shortly. "They'll have made all the arrangements."

The Prendergasts. This was the first mention of the couple that had passed between us, and I felt a sudden wave of despair. Somehow, I had assumed that, in bringing me back to Mallion as his wife, Benedict would first have got rid of two servants with whom he must have known I had had serious differences. That, at least, he must have noticed; the deeper and more serious wrongs the Prendergasts had done me—or had attempted—had been concealed from him, and it was no intention of mine to dredge them up.

He must have gauged my feelings from my expression. "Is there anything the matter?" he asked.

I took a deep breath, summoned up my courage, and said: "The Prendergasts—do they have to stay at Mallion?"

"Of course," he said, surprised. "Why should they not, Joanna?"

"I—I don't think they like me," I replied, and my slender resolve broke in a thousand pieces, and I looked down at my hands and the unfamiliar wedding ring. Miserably conscious of the weakness of my reply, I added: "They resent my presence at Mallion. They're jealous of me, and have been from the first."

"This is nonsense, my dear," he said; and, when I began to protest again, he held up an imperious hand. He was not angry; merely trying to be patient to a rather silly and uninstructed girl. "No—listen to me if you will . . .

"Joanna, you're returning to Mallion a very different person from the one who went away. No longer a privileged servant but the mistress of Mallion and my wife. It isn't important, Joanna, that the Prendergasts like you or don't like you. All that's important is that they respect and obey you—which, as good and well-trained servants, they assurely will. That, my dear, is all there is to it. That's the beginning, the middle and the ending of it."

I could have told him, then, about the campaign of deliberate hurt and provocation that the couple had directed against me; carried out, almost certainly, at the instigation of Feyella Mapollion. I could have done all this—but, to my everlasting regret, I did not. Too many hopes were soon to be dashed, and too much bitterness quickly to grow between Benedict and me—and I tell myself that most of it could have been avoided if I had spoken then. But perhaps I am wrong; perhaps it would have made no difference to what followed.

Whistles blew. There was a wild hissing of steam, and we were hauled grandly out of the station; past water meadows with fat cows; along the bank of the broad river, with the towered cathedral rising above the rooftops of a hill. There was the estuary, and a distant line like beaten silver that was the horizon of the sea. We were being carried deeper and deeper into the wild and beautiful Western land.

Benedict returned to his newspaper, and from the inclination of his bowed head, I could not see if the lines were still there between his brows.

I closed my eyes, and let my thoughts wander along the easiest and most agreeable path they knew: to the savouring of that noon, a few days ago, when Benedict had come for me, to take me home . . .

* * *

My daydream faded off imperceptibly into a dreamless sleep, and when I woke it was already dusk. Benedict sat with a wicker basket open on the seat by his side, a glass in his hand.

"I've supped," he said. "You looked so peaceful that I didn't have the heart to waken you. Something to eat—a piece of game pie?"

I shook my head.

"A glass of wine?"

"No thank you."

"Oh, come—you haven't touched a thing since we got out and stretched our legs at Taunton."

"A small glass, then."

He poured red wine from a dark bottle and passed the glass across to me. Then he raised his own; his face lay in the shadow of the dying sun, and I could not tell if the signs of strain had gone from about his eyes.

"A toast to the bride," he murmured.

"To us," I said.

"To us, then."

The unfamiliar claret tasted bitter and dry to my palate, but curiously warming. I felt strangely relaxed, and put it down to the beneficial effects of my nap.

"One of the first things facing you back at Mallion," I said, "will be the unenviable task of breaking it to your mother that you've married a little nobody."

He grunted. "Mother will accept it with the same aplomb with which she received the news of Saul's death," he said. "You've seen and heard enough of Mother to know that the enclosing wall of her grief isn't to be breached by any other considerations whatever." His voice grew bitter. "I could marry whom I chose."

I felt the blood rise, hotly, in my cheeks—and I turned my head to look out of the window at the passing landscape of shadowy hills.

"To be fair to Mother," he went on, "she had the grace to speak quite kindly of you, when we found you'd gone: said that you were a steadfast and reliable girl, and didn't hold you one bit responsible for that ridiculous business of the runaway chair. Too much was made of that runaway chair—by me, more than by anyone."

I did not reply; but I had a disquietening image of the savage look he had given me on that awful, unforgettable morning.

"Joanna," he continued, "what I'm trying to say is that I'm fully aware that I behaved badly to you on that occasion, as on many others. Please look at me . . ."

Obediently, I turned to face him again. No longer did he wear the image of the big, predatory cat that he did in repose; now, he was all earnest appeal—like some large and lovable dog that pleads with you to forgive him some naughtiness. I smiled at the thought; and realised that this strange and complex man, whom I had married only that morning, was indeed begging—in his own fashion—for my understanding; and I could appreciate the effort it was costing a man of his proud mettle.

"What I'm trying to say, Joanna," he went on, "is that, from time to time, I may behave badly to you again. There's a dark and violent streak in my nature that I find very hard to live with, but live with it I must for there's no changing it, you see." He smiled in the shadows; it was a smile that would have sent cowards out to die, or charmed away the hearts of stronger women than I. "However, I accept that there is room for improvement, and I will do what I can. But you must bear with me and try to accept my shortcomings as well as you are able. Now, will you agree to try and do this?"

"Of course," I replied readily.

"Then give me your hand on it."

I held out my hand and he took it in his; leaning forward, he brought it to his lips and briefly kissed my ring finger.

"Between us, in good times and ill, there must always be understanding," he said. "Agreed?"

"Agreed."

With this simple act of faith, then, I put all my doubts and reservations behind me—and these included the reasons that had sent me away from Castle Mallion.

I accepted that, though the Prendergasts had first resented my coming to the castle, things would be very different now that I was returning as its mistress.

Also because the banishment of doubt and fear cleans away many dark corners from the mind, I was willing to accept that it was unlikely that the Prendergasts—or, indeed, Feyella Mapollion—had been responsible for all the hurts that had been done to me; some of them, surely, had been blown up out of all proportion by my own heated imagining.

In short, because of my love for Benedict, I was happy to make the best possible construction on everything that had gone before.

The thought of the aristocratic Mapollion girl made me smile quietly to myself. Encouraged by Benedict's good humour, I said, with a touch of mischief:

"Another person you have to break the news to is Feyella. I think she'll be quite furious."

He only grunted noncommittally in reply.

I turned away and looked out of the window, well content with what had just passed between us.

There were many girls, I knew, who might think that Benedict's wooing of me had been less than romantic; a long way from the sighing and impassioned protestations you read in novels. For me, the unexpected realisation of my love for him,

119

and his pursuit of me, seemed to be of the finest and most splendid fabric from which romance is woven.

Even the brief, shocking manner of his proposal had the power to make my nerve ends tingle every time I thought of it —as I did at that moment, with the secret hills of Cornwall sliding past my gaze in the gathering darkness . . .

"I've come to take you home, Joanna."

"Home?"

"Immediately. As soon as possible. I can't abide the stench of London a day longer than necessary."

"To Mallion?"

"No need to wait for banns to be read, or any of that tomfoolery. Cope says he can get us a dispensation from his bishop. For reasons I won't go into now, it's better that we be married in London."

"Married? You're asking me to marry you?"

"Yes, Joanna. *And you are accepting me.*"

Considering how, even from the days of my young girlhood in Jamaica, I had fretted under the yoke of Trevallion arrogance; considering the way they had always managed to make me feel like a creature without a will, dancing to the tune of their power and their riches—it is surprising how deliciously easy it was to succumb to Benedict's curt blandishments.

The truth is that the manner of his proposal was part of the whole man; nothing else would have been right, coming from Benedict. I was in love with the whole man; I was, therefore, enthralled and delighted by the form of his proposal.

One thing, only, marred the delight: if he had kissed me, it would have been perfection.

We had been engaged for a week and married all day—and still we had never kissed. It was an omission I intended to rectify, I told myself, at the first convenient moment.

Now he was reflected in the dark window pane before my eyes, and I could regard him unseen.

Strange how, with what detachment, I could look the truth in the eye and not flinch from it . . .

To be able to say to myself: You don't love me, Benedict

Trevallion. You wanted me enough to follow me to London; enough, even, to marry me, in order to entice me back to Cornwall, to your fine castle, where I shall be another one of your Trevallion possessions.

You don't love me. Not yet. But you'll learn to love me.

I shall make that my everything, the beginning and the ending of all I do—to make you love me.

* * *

A groom and a boy from the castle were waiting for us at the station: the two of them touching their forelocks, while the chill night air traced the shape of their breaths. They loaded our luggage, and Benedict handed me into the old-fashioned, closed coach and tucked me about with warm rugs, afterwards taking his seat opposite me. Then we were away, out of the loom of the station lights and into the dark mysteries of the high-walled lanes.

It was too dark to see Benedict's face, save when he drew on his thin cigar and it made a ruddy halo about his mouth, but hid his eyes.

We travelled in silence. Nothing but the clip-clop of the horses' hooves, the rattle of the wheels in the rutted lane, and the sound of the wind roaring overhead, over the top of the stone walls. When we came out on to open moorland, and into the full force of wind, the coach was buffeted by the sudden onslaught of sound and fury.

In this manner—and on a moonless night of storm and darkness—I came home to Castle Mallion, and it was as unlike my first arrival there as anything that could be imagined: I saw nothing of the building, or of its approaches; only the hollow sound of the wheels as we rolled under the gateway arch, then the door was opened, and Prendergast was standing there with a blazing flambeau.

"Welcome home, sir. Welcome home, madam." As smoothly as you please.

"Thanks, Prendergast," said Benedict. "Tell me—is all well?"

"Indeed it is, sir."

"That's a relief, at any rate."

Benedict helped me to alight from the coach, and the man-servant followed behind us towards the open doors of the great hall, where the curling flames of an open fire quenched the light of many candles.

"We informed Mrs Trevallion that you would be returning this evening—but mentioned nothing of the circumstances."

"Good, good," replied Benedict. "And Mayana and the child —they're both well?"

"Yes, sir. The little boy was a bit poorly yesterday and we sent for Dr Mayo. Its nothing, I think."

The dark figure of Mrs Prendergast stood between us and the fire. The wide sweep of the flames framed her, surrounding her with a bright halo that obscured the expression on her face. Yet I knew, quite well, that she had eyes only for me, and I could guess at her expression.

"Welcome, sir," she said. "I hope that you and madam had a good journey."

Benedict acknowledged that we had.

"I've prepared some hot soup," said the woman, indicating the table, "and Prendergast can mull a jug of cider or claret."

"I may take a drink later," said Benedict. "What about you, my dear? You've scarcely had a bite to eat since breakfast."

I was now positioned so that I could see the light falling directly upon Mrs Prendergast's face, and the expression in her eyes—which were turned to me, but away from Benedict—struck me with a near-physical shock. I had prepared myself for all sorts of attitudes from the woman: everything from sullen resentment to a fawning adulation, for there was no telling how she might react to the news that I had become her mistress. The reality was beyond all belief; I had to look twice before I could take it in.

Mrs Prendergast was giving me a look of gloating triumph.

There was no doubt about it; she was making no effort to hide her expression.

"Are you having some refreshment, Joanna?" Benedict's voice broke in on my stunned bewilderment, and I dragged my gaze from the woman's.

"No thank you, Benedict. I'm not at all hungry."

I looked back at her again, but Benedict had moved forward, and could see her face. She lowered her head—but the turned-up corners of her thin lips showed that she was still wearing the tight-mouthed malevolent smile, and the close-set eyes were surely still smouldering with hateful mirth.

Why? I asked myself. Here was I, returned to the castle with the power and splendour of the Trevallion name so recently settled on my shoulders—what reason was that for the ill-disposed housekeeper to be so cock-a-hoop, and in such a gloating manner, almost as if she was exulting in some misfortune that had come upon me? It was most puzzling. Puzzling and disturbing.

Benedict was asking them about the arrangements:

"You've made the alterations in my bedroom as I instructed?"

"Yes, sir," said Prendergast. "And Cox is taking luggage up there at this moment. A fire had been laid and fresh flowers set out in vases. I think madam will find everything to her satisfaction there, and we've . . ."

"Yes, I'm sure she will," broke in Benedict. He took me by the arm. "You really do look tired, my dear. Why not a reasonably early night? Come, I'll show you the way."

He led me across the hall, towards the staircase. As we passed the Prendergasts, the woman bobbed a little curtsey, but I did not look towards her. I dared not—for fear of what I might have seen in her eyes.

Benedict led me down the portrait gallery at the head of the stairs; and once more I ran the gauntlet of the rows of staring Trevallions.

"You're one of them now," said Benedict. "They don't appear to have accepted you yet, but I've no doubt they'll get around to it in time."

I answered absently, for my thoughts were suddenly elsewhere. Somewhere ahead of me, down this echoing corridor lined with the likenesses of countless generations of Trevallions, lay the bedchamber that I would shortly share—and share, as our vows told us, for the rest of our lives together—with Benedict Trevallion.

So far, in our strange courtship, we had spent very little time alone together, and the journey down to Cornwall had been the longest period that we had been in each other's company. At this eleventh hour, I became discomfitingly aware of how little I knew—*really* knew—about the man who had become my husband. Fragments of memory crowded my mind: the Benedict Trevallion who had used to terrify me so much at Roswithiel, who had so wildly kissed the blonde girl in the fountain; the look on his face when his mother's Bath chair had run away; Benedict being greeted and kissed by Feyella Mapollion, she with her arms wrapped about his neck; Benedict with Mayana, with the light-skinned child clinging to the skirts of the beautiful deaf-mute.

A score of unanswered questions crowded in on me, questions I should have asked in London, before we were joined in marriage—questions that, left too late, had now better be laid away in a bottom drawer among the dried lavender and the dead memories.

Too late, now, to probe. We had made a special pact of trust and understanding, and this was the ground on which our lives together would be built. For better or worse.

Meanwhile, we were drawing closer to our bedchamber . . .

"This is the wing of the castle," said Benedict, "that was largely rebuilt at the beginning of the last century by my great-grandfather, Mark Trevallion, who went out to Jamaica and founded the family's sugar empire at Roswithiel. He did the Grand Tour in his youth: visited Italy and Greece and got himself bitten by the bug of Classical antiquity. The tapestries are Gobelins that he brought back from France, and that marble statue is a copy of the Aphrodite from Cyrene—with head and arms added, as you see . . ."

I had first come through these lofty rooms with Mrs Prendergast, and it seemed so long ago. The richness and the elegance made me feel that I should be wearing my Sunday best clothes. I had never been used to anything like such surroundings, and whispered a silent prayer that our bedroom would be well away from this particular part of the castle.

"And here we are," said Benedict, opening a great double

door at the end of the most sumptuous of the tapestry-hung apartments. "Yes, they've got a good fire going in here. I hope you approve."

"Oh, it's beautiful," I said impulsively. "Beautiful!"

The bedroom was quite large, but so cunningly proportioned that it gave an immediate impression of cosiness. The walls were covered in chocolate-coloured silk that was offset by doors, window frames, and other mouldings of white. The soft furnishings were coloured in all variety of reds, from the palest of magentas to rich plum. The huge, canopied double bed was of carved and unpainted pine, like the graceful pine overmantel of the fireplace. And my feet trod upon a scattering of Persian rugs that yielded silkily beneath them.

"Most comfortable bedroom in the castle," said Benedict. "I took it for myself, very smartly, when we first arrived here from Jamaica. It is also the warmest—and, considering Cornish winters, that is no mean advantage."

The fire glowed and crackled amiably, and muted candlelight threw diamond points of reflected glass lustres on the mouldings of the ceiling. Despite the splendour of it all, I was completely won over, and suddenly felt at ease and at home.

"Why, it's beautifully warm and comfortable," I cried. I crossed over and patted the silk counterpane that sank so suavely beneath my touch. I sat down on the edge of the bed and bounced myself up and down for a few moments.

He was watching me from over by the window, and a trick of the firelight seemed to cause a shadow to pass across his face, and created the impression that his eyes were unnaturally bright. Unaccountably, I felt very silly and gauche, and got hastily to my feet, embarrassedly smoothing down the wrinkled counterpane.

When I looked towards him again, he had opened the shutters and was gazing out of the window.

"The moon's up," he said, without turning round. "And there's a halo round it, which means frost." Was it my imagination, or was his voice hoarse and strained?

"Thank Heaven for this lovely fire, then," was all I could think of by way of a reply.

Silence. No sound but the gentle crackle of the logs on the open fire. A strange tension had entered the lovely room, all unbidden. I looked about me, seeking for inspiration. There was a partly open door leading into a dressing room, and I could see my luggage piled up just inside the door: the brand-new leather trunks and hat boxes from Bond Street, that contained my trousseau. I thought of a certain night dress and matching *peignoir* of lilac silk—and wondered how on earth I would find the courage to change into it and climb into that splendid bed.

"Well," said Benedict, "I promised myself a tankard of mulled claret, and, since it's still only ten-thirty, I think I'll go down and indulge myself before turning in."

"Yes," I said hastily. "That would be a wonderful idea. I mean—it will help you to sleep more soundly."

I blessed him for his thoughtfulness. While he was having his nightcap, I would have the bedroom suite to myself, to make my toilette and to be grandly established in that marvellous bed by the time he returned. Only a man of breeding would think of such a course. I thought how different it must have been for my poor, gently reared mother, wedded to a common soldier.

"Oh, well," said Benedict, turning from the window, "I'll be off."

I took a very deep breath. "Don't be too long," I said, greatly daring.

"I'll not be late out of my bed," he said. "It's been a long day, and there's plenty to do tomorrow. Good night, Joanna."

He took my hand and stooped over it, to kiss my ring finger. I stared down at the crown of his head, at its mane of thick, blue-black hair, and absently noticed how it was clustered in tight curls about his ears and in the nape. My heart began a treacherous pounding, as an awful possibility sprang to my mind.

"Good night," I said—and it was half a question.

He nodded towards the window. "I've had my things moved over to a room in the northeast tower, which you can see directly across the courtyard. I hope you'll be quite comfortable here. If not, merely say the word, and we'll have any alterations made to improve the room. Or, on the other hand, you could always try another room. There are plenty to choose from."

"Thank you," I heard myself say in a very small voice.

"Don't rise early," he said. "I'll give instructions that you're not to be called. Have all the sleep you need. I have to go to Bodmin and won't be back till nightfall, but I'll be joining you at supper."

I nodded. All that mattered now was that he should leave without noticing that I was fighting back the tears. Fortunately, he did not seem to be looking into my face.

"I shall call in at the dower house after breakfast and break the news to Mother," he said.

"Yes," I said.

"I'll see you tomorrow, at supper, then."

"Yes."

I felt a hot tear course down my cheek, and touched it away with a fingertip.

"As to meals, you can leave everything to Mrs Prendergast, who'll provide an adequate choice of dishes at every meal. On the other hand, if there's anything you particularly fancy, you only have to tell her, and she'll provide it specially."

"Of course," I said.

The tears were now coming too fast to check. He still was not looking directly at me, but I turned my face away.

"I'll be off then, Joanna."

He crossed to the door and opened it. In another instant he would be gone, and I would be alone.

"Benedict!" I called to him.

"Yes?"

There was some distance separating us now, and I hoped he could not see that I was crying, for I did not want to use a woman's tears against a man.

"What is it, Joanna?" he repeated, and there was a note of harshness in his voice. Clearly, in the candlelight, I could see the telltale clefts of anger between his brows. He was exasperated with me and anxious to get away to his mulled claret.

"Nothing," I said. "Good night, Benedict."

He shut the door without replying. I heard his footsteps die away down the long room; another door opened and closed; and I was alone in my bridal chamber and in that whole, echoing, empty wing of Castle Mallion. On this, my wedding night.

I sat down on the edge of the bed, numb with misery and despair. I had known that Benedict did not love me as I loved him, as I would have wished to be loved in return.

But—to leave me on my wedding night . . .

It was a release to let the tears flow unchecked. I lay back against the silk coverlet and gave myself up to the bitterness in my heart. I had not moved when the candles guttered low and burned out; and when the last ruddy glow of the fire died away into ash, I fell asleep where I lay, all uncaring of the gathering cold in my beautiful bridal chamber.

* * *

The dream was like the one that had gone before: another Figure in the strange Quadrille of Death. Two more were to follow.

In this, the second dream, I was once more on the shoreline below Castle Mallion in the moonlight. I was alone, but away at the distant headland, a lone horseman was approaching along the wide sweep of the sea-washed sand: a white-clad rider on a white horse. He was coming to me.

There was no fear. I could have moved and run away; the castle was no longer forbidden; the great gates were open and the drawbridge lowered for me to go inside whenever I pleased.

Instead, I was waiting by the shoreline, with my gaze fixed upon the distant, approaching horse and rider; watching the night wind plucking at his flowing white cloak; listening to the growing thrum of the hoofbeats, coming to me above the hiss of the surf among the rocks.

This time, I told myself, I would gaze upon his face without flinching. With an act of faith, I would clothe those bare bones with living flesh; make him quicken with the flow of warm blood in his veins. With my will, I would make him whole.

Now, he was near enough for me to see the plumes of sand

sent up by the flying hooves, and the rise and fall of his hand as he urged on his mount to even greater efforts. He was directing the white horse straight at me; taking it through the shallow pools, so that the kicked-up water rose breast-high and fell in jewels of moonlight.

He was hooded, as before. But as he thundered close, his hand came up, to draw back the covering from his head. And instead of checking his mount's wild onrush, he gave a jerk of the rein, directing it to pass close by me at the gallop.

It was then I saw that I had been mistaken. The rider of the white horse was not a man, but a woman; the torso was too slender to be a man's, and the hand that was raised to the hood was fine-boned and delicately blue-veined.

Who was the horsewoman who was hurtling past me on the wings of the night wind?

I asked the question aloud; next moment I reeled back, sobbing with horror, hands pressed to my face to shut out the sight, fighting with my will to obliterate the memory of what I had seen.

In the instant of her passing, the rider had pulled back her hood and had shown me her features.

It was the face of a dead woman, with waxen pallor of skin, and half-closed eyes that saw nothing.

And it was my own face: I was the white rider on the white horse.

* * *

My windows were rimy with a lacework of frost, and a band of thin sunlight stretched halfway from there to my bed. I shivered and sat up. By the gold fob watch that Benedict had given me (it seemed an age ago) for a wedding present, I saw that it was nine-thirty.

There was a thin plume of smoke still rising from the grey ash and the partly consumed log in the fireplace, and I soon had a small blaze going among the remains. It kept me warm while I washed—in a handbasin by the fire—and dressed myself in a warm tweed skirt and coat from my trousseau. When I was ready, I threw a fur cape about my shoulders and went swiftly down to the refectory.

Benedict had already left. A young servant girl whom I had never seen before was clearing away his place at table. She bobbed me a curtsey and in answer to my question, she told me that the master had ridden out not a quarter of an hour ago. I thanked her, and asked her to bring me some fresh coffee.

I sat alone in the large and cheerless room, warming my fingers on my steaming coffee cup—for the fire had scarcely taken the chill off the air—and gazing out of the mullioned windows on to the courtyard. The day's activities of the castle were well advanced: a maid ran across the yard with a bundle of laundry, her nose and cheeks pink with the cold; two more came past, gossiping brightly, great trays of new-baked bread on their heads; and I thought I saw Mrs Prendergast opening a window opposite.

It all seemed very remote from me. It was scarcely believable that the busy comings-and-goings of this vast establishment would be, from that day forth, very largely ordered for my benefit: I—an outsider.

I marvelled at my apparent composure. The truth was, I felt much better than I would have believed possible. After having been scorned and thrown aside, as it were, on my wedding night; after having awakened from a most hideous and affecting nightmare—despite these vicissitudes, I found myself in remarkably good order. My mind was clear and calm, and I felt ready to face whatever the day might bring. The indestructible quality of the human spirit is really quite remarkable.

Mrs Prendergast came in. She was dressed all in black, as ever, and a heavy bunch of keys jangled at a long chain from her waist.

"Good morning," she said. "I hope you slept well, madam."

"Very well, thank you," I replied.

She had the same tight-mouthed, mean smile of the night before, and the cause of her amusement was now obvious to me. She had seen to the arrangement of our rooms, at Benedict's orders. She knew that I had spent my wedding night alone. Suddenly, the thought that Benedict had so little regard for my feelings that he had not taken the trouble to hide his neglect from the servants hurt more than the neglect itself.

"Will madame continue to sleep in the same bedchamber?" she asked.

"Certainly," I replied.

She raised an eyebrow, and the mean smile broadened.

"Why should I not?" I asked calmly.

"The master is more concerned that you might have found it uncomfortable," she said. "He asked me most particularly, over his breakfast, to make sure that you found your bedchamber comfortable, and if not, to suggest other rooms that you could try."

I looked down at my hands, and was surprised that they were not trembling.

"That's very kind of Mr Trevallion," I said. "But the room is quite suitable. Rather grand for my taste, perhaps. But I don't think I would change, Mrs Prendergast—unless it was to go back to my old room—the green room in the South Central tower."

"Not the South Central tower, madam," she said. "The South Central tower's for servants. The higher servants, of course—but servants for all that. And you're not one of us any longer. Are you, madam?"

I met her gaze. The contempt and the mockery were written there quite unashamedly and without concealment. It struck me that I was being deliberately goaded into either losing my temper or my composure. And I was not going to let that happen.

"Thank you, Mrs Prendergast," I said quietly. "That will be all."

The close-set eyes narrowed angrily. Mrs Prendergast had not expected the former servant to show such spirit.

"Well, if you change your mind—about the bedchamber, I mean . . ."

"Thank you, Mrs Prendergast. You may go," I said.

But the woman had one last gibe that she had been waiting to deliver. She left it till she reached the door.

"You have only to say the word, madam," she said. She gave

me a very deliberate stare, and treated me to that hateful smile again. "You have every bedchamber in the castle to choose from. At least . . ."

The unspoken words came across the distance that separated us as clearly as if they had been shouted:

". . . *at least, every bedchamber, save your bridegroom's!*"

* * *

The Prendergasts would have to go. I would tackle Benedict this very evening when he returned; tell him that I would not have them under my roof for another day. My roof. I liked the sound of that. My roof.

I stood in the old garden, with the last of the dead leaves whirling about me in the keen wind from the sea—and, for the first time, I felt the heady sense of proprietorship.

Let them do their worst—the Prendergasts and anyone else who resented my intrusion into Castle Mallion. My bridegroom did not love me as I wished, and that would be common knowledge around the countryside in no time, I didn't doubt; but I was the undoubted bride of the Trevallions, and no one would shake me.

I felt strong. My handling of the malevolent housekeeper had greatly heartened me. It was as if I was drawing my strength and inspiration from the very granite stones of the castle itself. It was not too far-fetched to suppose that the great, sentient bulk—stronghold of the Trevallions through five centuries—would give aid to the new bride of the family. Perhaps even the long rows of proud faces in the portrait gallery would soften towards me.

I repeated to myself my earlier resolve: I would make Benedict love me, no matter what.

Last night had been a bad beginning; but a night is not a lifetime.

And the Prendergasts would go.

I stood for a long while, in my favourite garden, watching the gulls swooping over the offshore islet; drinking in the keen air of the wild Western land; filled with pride and confidence.

How little I knew. How empty my pride, and how fragile the hopes upon which my confidence was built.

* * *

When I went back through the courtyard, I saw that there was a carriage waiting outside the dower house, and I instantly recognised it as Feyella Mapollion's. She had come to call, and was with Mrs Trevallion. Well, then, I would kill two birds with one stone and greet them both together—my new mother-in-law and the woman whose girlish dream had been to stand in my place as wife of Benedict Trevallion. The spirit of Castle Mallion had certainly given me courage.

The diamond panes of Mrs Trevallion's parlour reflected back to me the unfamiliar—and greatly reassuring—image of Jo-anna Trevallion (née Goodacre), warmly and expensively dressed, and with her unruly chestnut mane tamed and or-dered by the best *coiffeur* in Mayfair. Armed thus, I would not stone these two formidable birds, but charm them down from their boughs, I told myself.

Mrs Trevallion's maid opened the door before my hand had reached the knocker. They had seen me crossing the courtyard, and Feyella Mapollion was on her feet and half across the parlour to greet me, hands extended in welcome; all smiles, for all the world as if we were the nearest and dearest friends.

"Dear Joanna," she cried. "How very nice."

One glance at her, and my fine tweeds became suddenly baggy and ill fitting, and my fabulous fur cape an old sack that market women wear about their shoulders against the rain. I caught a glance of myself in a wall mirror—and, surely, my *coiffure* was a disaster, and my nose and mouth even larger than usual.

She wore a simple grey velvet dress trimmed with grey lace at throat and cuffs, and her blonde hair was drawn up in a stylish chignon. The deceptive simplicity of her turn-out, added to her ease of manner, drained away my confidence. It wasn't fair. How could anyone who had behaved so badly to a person greet that same person with such artless grace?

She took both my hands and squeezed them affectionately. The violet-blue eyes were completely without guile or malice.

"Welcome home," she said. "We're all so happy for you."

It was then I noticed, with a shock, that she was wearing the blue brooch—the one that I thought I had last seen on Mrs Prendergast. So I had been mistaken, after all, in supposing that Feyella had given it to the housekeeper in return for conspiring with her against me. I felt suddenly confused. Was I incapable of getting *anything* right?

I stammered my awkward thanks and turned to Mrs Trevallion, remembering that we now bore the same name, and wondering how to address her.

She gave me a cue by offering her waxen cheek for me to kiss.

"You look tired, my dear," she murmured expressionlessly. "Benedict has told me that you have been ill. I hope you're on the way to recovery. It will be a hard winter in Cornwall, and many of the weakest will be taken to swell the graveyards —perhaps myself included."

I caught Feyella's eye, and she winked at me.

"Tell us about the wedding," said Feyella. "And I may as well inform you that we are all furious at you for choosing to get married in London and cheating us out of a memorable rout."

"I was married from the castle," said Mrs Trevallion. "There were eight hundred guests, and my gown came from Spain. My bridegroom and I were cousins and had both lived at Mallion all our lives. If my darling Piers had been spared, I would have used what influence I had to urge him to marry out of the family . . ."

Feyella broke in: "Did you wear white, Joanna?"

"Why yes," I said, "but it was a very simple affair. The gown was borrowed, and the only guests were the people who had been so kind to me in London when I was ill."

"Some came from as far away as Yorkshire," said Mrs Trevallion. "And, of course, everyone of note in the West Country was here. My husband had no connections with the Army, so there was no guard-of-honour at the church. It would have been a different tale at the wedding of my Piers, of course . . ."

"What are your plans for the black woman and her child?" asked Feyella.

I stared at her. There was nothing to read in her face.

"I—I'm afraid I don't understand you," I faltered.

"The little boy is ill," said Mrs Trevallion. "They had to send for the doctor again early this morning. He arrived before Benedict left. I saw him ride in, and he was here for quite a while."

I made a mental note that I must call and see little Jackie at the earliest opportunity. Meanwhile, there was Feyella's surprise question. She had dropped her eyes, and was tracing the side seam of her dress with a questing finger.

"I don't understand you," I said bluntly. "What plans should I have regarding Mayana and her child?"

She shrugged, without looking up.

"Oh, I don't know," she said. "It's just that the woman seems a bit—*de trop*—at Mallion. And the more so now."

While I was digesting that, Mrs Trevallion's wavering voice broke in again.

"I went to the West Indies only once," she said. "It was during the time of our honeymoon. My husband and I stayed at Roswithiel. I found the climate uncomfortably hot—it was during the summer—and we quickly returned. By the time we were back at Mallion, I was carrying my darling Piers . . ."

"I would have thought she'd be happier with her own people," said Feyella. "She must find Cornwall dreadfully cold, and the food not to her taste." She was smiling at me now, quite ingenuously; but I had the distinct impression that the question of Mayana's comfort had not been what she had had in mind in the first place.

I was determined not to let slip the opportunity of letting Feyella—and the rest of the district—know my own position in regard to the beautiful deaf-mute and her child.

"Mayana was very glad to come to England," I said. "She is part-white herself, and with a part-white child. There is a lot of unrest in Jamaica at the moment, and I suppose she is content to put up with the climate here, in return for the security it offers for the child. She's very grateful to Benedict for offering them both a home in reward for the faithful service she gave to the family as housekeeper at Roswithiel. And he's very happy—we're both very happy—to have her here," I concluded.

So you can spread that round the duchy, my dear, I said to myself. That should go a long way towards scotching any rumour that my bridegroom is keeping his black fancy woman and her love child under the same roof as me.

Feyella made no comment. She got up and put on her cape.

"Good-bye, dear Mrs Trevallion," she said, leaning down to peck my mother-in-law's cheek. "I can't say how much I enjoyed our little threesome chat. Now I'll leave you and Joanna to talk private family matters."

Mrs Trevallion shifted uneasily in her Bath chair and muttered something. I had the impression that she was not very pleased with Feyella.

I walked Feyella to her carriage. There was a sharp wind blowing in from the sea, and the mummified heads of the summer's hydrangea bushes were being tossed wildly to and fro, and rustling against each other like bunches of dry parchment.

"Are you and Benedict planning to go away during the honeymoon time?" she asked.

"I don't think so," I said. "He's terribly busy with the business of the estates."

She smiled.

"Besides, we've both done quite enough travelling this year," I said defensively.

"I'm sure you have, Joanna," she said. "And that's nice, because it means I shall be able to see plenty of you. And this I intend to do." She slipped her hands in mine and gave me the benefit of her lovely eyes. "We'll be good friends, Joanna. How can we do other—we've so much in common."

With a light laugh, she sprang into her carriage and snatched up the reins. I watched her drive out under the archway, and wondered what it was that we had in common.

Mrs Trevallion had called her maid to build up the fire, which was already halfway up the chimney breast, and the parlour was pulsating with heat like an orangery.

My mother-in-law was still fidgeting angrily.

"That wretched girl," she said. "I've never trusted her. She set her cap on my Piers, you know, when she was barely out of the nursery. Unnatural child. Never have trusted her."

I resisted the impulse to tell her that, from my knowledge, it was my husband Benedict, and not her precious Piers, whom Feyella had coveted—and, for all I knew, still coveted.

"There's bad blood there," she went on. "Not only bad, but mad. Her mother killed herself, threw herself from a cliff into the sea, and they never did find her body. The father—that Mapollion fellow—is even madder. With him, it's drink. No, I don't like her. She never listens to a word I say. Always interrupts me."

And that, I thought, is the measure of this old woman's opinion of anybody, whether of Feyella, or me, or anyone else.

"It would have been such a wedding," she went on, after a while, dreamily, "if my darling Piers had been taking a bride, to be mistress of Mallion. Half of London would have come down here, including my Lord Cardigan . . ."

She was well away with her daydreams about her beloved dead son. I let her ramble on without interrupting her.

Now I knew—and I should have guessed from the first—what my mother-in-law thought of her surviving son's marriage to a woman of the upper-servant class: the matter was scarcely allowed to ruffle the surface of her mind.

Mrs Trevallion simply did not care, one way or another, who her son married. Piers did not survive to be master of Castle Mallion; all other considerations were unimportant.

She found me more agreeable than the aristocratic Feyella because I listened to her ramblings without interrupting her. Ramble on, you poor creature, I thought. Your life is empty enough, and I'd be the last to deny you the thin comfort of your memories and your fantasies about what might have been. The reality is me: I am the mistress of Mallion, and I have plenty of problems of my own.

And I had the thought that, despite her new reassurances of friendship, Feyella loomed very large as one of my problems.

* * *

I had never visited Mayana's quarters; indeed I had to enquire of their whereabouts from one of the serving girls. It turned out that she and little Jackie were lodged in a suite of rooms on the second floor of the northwest tower. This was the twin of the northeast tower and the two of them flanked the massive gatehouse block. It was to the northeast tower, of course, that Benedict had removed himself.

The smell of pine and balsam prickled at my nostrils when I reached the second floor of the tower staircase. In an alcove at the head of the stair, Mayana was warming a saucepan of milk over a spirit stove. Though deaf, she quickly sensed my presence and turned to regard me with her unbelievably large and lustrous eyes.

"How is little Jackie?" I mouthed, pointing to the open door of her apartment, and accompanying the word and gesture with a look of grave concern.

Her splendid bosom rose and fell in a sigh, and she made a brusque shake of her black-maned head. The milk sizzled in the saucepan. She poured the contents into a mug and walked past me into the apartment. I followed her.

The child lay on a couch in the semicircular living room of the tower apartment. At first, I could scarcely make out his pale face among the sheets that swathed him. The curtains were drawn, the narrow windows closed, and the apartment was filled with aromatic steam that issued from a vapouriser near the sick bed.

Mayana dropped smoothly to her knees beside the couch and, raising up the child's head, she placed the mug to his lips.

I was shocked by the change in Jackie's appearance. He had never been a particularly robust child; but the passing of a few, short weeks in these northern climes had taken the native bloom from his magnolia-like fragility and left him a poor, sickly little thing indeed. The small bones of his face, neck, and shoulders stood out in pathetic clarity, with the dead-looking skin stretched tautly across them. The eyes were closed with a heavy weariness, and the first sip of the warm milk sent him into a paroxysm of hollow coughing that racked and contorted his frail body.

Mayana gave a great sigh, dabbed his lips, and laid him back against the pillows. She swept me with a tragic glance, as if to say: well, you asked how he was, and now you see him.

I scarcely knew what to say. The mulatress's affliction was no bar to her communicating with her child and with Benedict, but she had never presented anything to me but a blank wall of incomprehension. I wanted to offer my help, to assist her in nursing the child, but I sensed that it would not be received. So I contented myself by symbolically stroking the child's damp curls and drawing my finger across his hot cheek.

"Is there anything you need, Mayana?" I asked, gesturing to the surroundings. "Would you like to move to another, perhaps more convenient, room?"

No reply. She looked away from me, towards the child.

In fact, as far as I could see, the living room of the apartment was well suited for a sick room; being dry, warm, and free of draughts. Jackie's couch was well upholstered, and handy for the chores of washing and tending for the needs of the little invalid. I was sure that Benedict would have seen to it that all the resources of Mallion were available, and the doctor was in attendance. I made up my mind to hear the doctor's opinion when next he came.

Mayana was still kneeling by her son when I left the room. She gave no sign of being aware of my going when I gave her shoulder a comforting pat and went out, closing the door behind me.

When I came out of the tower doorway into the courtyard, the clock over the stable block chimed the hour of midday. The sky was high and clear, but the wintry sun was doing nothing to dispel the rime of frost on every grass blade and ivy leaf, and the very stones of Mallion glistened as if they

139

had been glazed with sugar icing. The wind still blew from the sea.

I shivered, and recalled my mother-in-law's doleful prediction about the weakest being taken, in the coming winter, to swell the graveyards—and I prayed that the poor little love child from far-off Jamaica would not be numbered among them.

With the prayer still on my lips, I gathered up my skirts and ran across the courtyard.

There was a small and cosy sitting room, at the far end of the great hall, that was reached by a door in the screen of finely carved woodwork supporting the old minstrel gallery. There were two maids dusting in there, and they bobbed me embarrassed curtsies when I went in. Still sufficiently unaccustomed to such marks of servility, I was as embarrassed as they, and would have left them to their work, but they assured me that they could come back and finish the room—they called it the solar—later in the day. They threw more logs on the cheerful open fire, and curtsied their way out, leaving me alone.

It was from the diamond-paned windows of the solar that I was witness to a strange incident that was to be the first in a chain of disquieting facts and fancies which were to lead me towards the greatest tragedy of my life.

* * *

I had not been there long—seated by the fireplace, with a view across the yard to the gatehouse—before I noticed that a man and woman were lurking under the archway by the moat bridge. They were too far away to recognise, but they were clearly not members of the castle staff; more like the poorest kind of Cornish peasantry. The man was dressed in a ragged countryman's smock, and the woman was all but enveloped in a rusty black shawl. She was barefoot, despite the biting cold. I had not noticed them when I came out of the northwest tower, so I supposed that they had only just arrived. This was borne out when, after some hesitation and discussion, the man reached up and pulled the gatehouse bell.

The thin tinkle of the bell reached me across the courtyard.

A few moments later, a door under the arch opened, and I saw the black-clad figure of Prendergast.

Again, I was too far away to read the mime that took place between Prendergast and the couple—and, in any event, I was only idly interested. It soon became pretty clear, however, that Prendergast was telling them to be off: he pointed away across the bridge, and made to go back into the gatehouse.

The couple showed reluctance to move, and made some protest to the manservant. Prendergast retorted by again pointing across the bridge, delivering a final remark, and slamming the door in their faces.

A thin flurry of light snow slanted across the courtyard from the direction of the sea. The man and woman shrank closer together against the stonework of the arch, turning their backs on the courtyard and the wind. They huddled there, looking out of the far end of the arch and across the bridge, to where the drive snaked back through a belt of trees and out of sight. It was as if they were waiting and watching for someone to arrive at the castle.

The clock struck half hour past midday, and I looked round from making pictures in the shifting red ash of the fire, to see a mounted figure riding up the path towards the bridge. Even at that distance, I could recognise Benedict and the black hunter that he usually rode.

I leapt to my feet, heart pounding. Benedict was home again. But he had told me that he would not be back from Bodmin till nightfall. What had, then, caused him to change his plans? Surely . . .

His heart had softened towards me, that was it, and he had realised the hurt that he had done to his new bride by his neglect. He had taken pity on me. It was not his pity I wanted, but his love; but I was ready to snatch at anything, with both hands, till the day that he learned to love me . . .

I ran across to the window and watched as he drew nearer; over the moat bridge and under the archway. The sound of his arrival brought Prendergast and a groom. The latter took the reins when Benedict dismounted and fired some question at Prendergast, who replied with a shake of his head. It was at this moment that the waiting peasant couple—whom I had completely forgotten—stepped out from the shadows of the archway and went up to Benedict, the man touching his forelock and the woman making a clumsy attempt at a curtsey.

Benedict stared at the man, and even from that distance I could see the mounting anger in his face and attitude as he listened to what the other had to say. I was reminded of the time when I had looked from the kitchen window of our house at Roswithiel and had seen him with my father: there was the same silent, brooding regard while the other man did the talking; the same impression of a tempest about to be unleashed.

The tempest was not long in coming. The peasant came to the end of what he had to say, and made a gesture towards the woman, as if calling to her to support his argument: she merely nodded vigorously—and Benedict ignored her completely. Without a word, he shook out the coils of the long hunting whip that he carried, and cracked it at waist-level: I clearly heard the cruel snap.

The man backed away, and the woman with him. Again, Benedict flourished the whip, and this time the lash cut through the air and struck the man. He cried out with pain and his hand went to his cheek. Next moment, the pair of them turned tail and raced away, through the arch and over the bridge, down the long drive and out of sight. Benedict watched them go.

The tableau of which I was the unseen observer was not yet finished. There was a splash of colour at the door of the northwest tower: a mauve skirt slashed with the end of a yellow shawl. It was Mayana.

Benedict turned to her and asked a question: he asked her how was the child Jackie—I knew it as surely as if I had been standing there facing him. She made an expressive gesture with her hands—a gesture of despair. Then she turned and went back into the tower. And he followed after her.

I had to accept it then: the flat truth that it was Jackie's condition—and not any feeling for me—that had caused Benedict to alter his arrangements for the day and return to the castle so early.

He had been so concerned for the child that he had cut short his business and come back to see how he had progressed during the morning.

Common humanity and kindness apart, what was Jackie to him, I asked myself—or, for that matter, what was Mayana, still?

* * *

The winter afternoon was already closing in and shadows were gathering in the solar when a maid came in to tell me that luncheon was ready.

"What about Mr Trevallion?" I asked her. "Has he been told?"

"Yes, ma'am," said the girl. "And master asks particularly that you don't wait for him, but start your meal while it's warm. He'll join you in the refectory later, master says."

I ate in the silence of the refectory, and knew not or cared not what I was eating. It was a silence broken only by the clop-clop of the serving girl's clogs as she went back and forth, serving me with dishes that remained unfinished. My ears were strained for the sound of Benedict's heavy tread. It was not till I had finally given up toying with my dessert that he came into the room and crossed over to the sideboard and poured himself a rummer of spirits.

"What did you think of Jackie's condition?" I asked, marvelling at my composure.

He half drained the glass before replying.

"No worse than he was first thing this morning, thank God."

"I had no idea he was ill till I had it from your mother," I said. "How long has he been like this?"

Benedict went over and refilled his glass. His back was towards me when he replied.

"The poor whelp has ailed ever since he came here. Early this morning he had a slight haemorrhage. Mayana came to see me in a great tizzy, as well she might. I sent a groom to fetch Dr Vyner."

"It's the consumption?"

"I'm afraid so."

"Benedict," I said. "It's quite clear that poor child's constitution won't stand up to the cold and damp of a Cornish winter. He never should have left the West Indies, and you must, you really must, see that he goes back without any delay. Now. Tomorrow—or as soon as he's fit to be moved."

He shook his head. "Out of the question," he said flatly. "They can't leave here."

"Can't?" I asked incredulously.

"Can't!" he repeated. And he drained the rummer again and poured another brimming measure. The deep indentations of anger had appeared between his brows, and his deep-blue eyes were smouldering.

"Why can't they leave here and go back to Jamaica?" I demanded.

Benedict walked the whole length of the refectory towards the fireplace, where he laid his rummer on the mantelpiece and engaged himself for some moments by rearranging the half-burnt logs with the toe of his riding-out boot. I waited, watching my husband: broad shouldered and tall, with his mane of unruly black curls.

When he spoke again, his voice carried a false note of heavy good humour.

"Christmas will soon be upon us," he said. "We must throw open the great hall for the celebrations. It hasn't been done since my father's day. You'll enjoy it, Joanna" . . . he turned to face me, and the deep-blue eyes held mine defiantly . . . "first we have to give a ball for the castle servants and the estate tenants. Then there's a party for the children. Finally, on Christmas Eve, there's a grand ball for the local landed gentry, with the Lord Lieutenant and so forth. You'll enjoy it, you really will. Perhaps you'll want to go up to London and buy yourself a ball gown or two."

I took a very deep breath.

"Benedict. Why can't Mayana take her child back to Jamaica?" I asked quietly.

I think he had been watching me very closely and was

prepared for my return to the attack. In any event, he did not explode with fury as I had half expected him to do. Instead, he raised his head very high, and, looking down at me along the edge of his straight and very well-shaped nose, he said:

"Mayana and the child will stay here because I choose that they stay here. That, my dear, is the end of the matter."

"Even if your decision puts Jackie's life in hazard?" I countered.

His glance did not waver. "I am not to be convinced," he said, "that the care and attention which can be lavished on him at Mallion will be less beneficial to his condition than the rigours of a long sea voyage in the season of winter gales. That, I'm almost certain, will finish him off."

I had to admit it was a reasonable point. But I intended to probe a little further.

"And, if he survives the winter, with all the care and attention we are able to lavish on him," I said, "would you agree that he should go back to Jamaica in the spring or early summer?"

He stared at me for a few moments, then picked up his glass from the mantelpiece.

"Possibly," he said. "But I wouldn't be prepared to discuss the possibility at this time."

And that, I could see quite clearly, was as far as I was going to get my husband to unburden himself on the topic of Mayana and her child. So I decided to abandon the subject. The next thing I wanted to bring up was the dismissal of the Prendergasts, and I did not look forward to it. To delay the moment, I sidetracked to something else.

"Who were that couple who accosted you at the gatehouse when you came in?" I asked.

He looked at me over the rim of his glass.

"You saw that?" he said.

"Yes. From the window of the solar."

To my surprise, the fact that I knew of the encounter was obviously causing him some concern and embarrassment. Once again, he turned to the decanter and recharged himself with

145

a stiff measure. His face, when he turned round again, had grown suddenly haggard and drawn.

"They're a pair of worthless creatures," he said. "The man used to work for the estate in my father's day, but had to be dismissed for thieving. From time to time, they descend on me and badger me for a hand-out."

"They looked very poor and wretched," I said.

"The poor are always with us," said Benedict.

"But, if they have no work, they may be starving," I protested.

"Work?" he cried. "They wouldn't take it if offered. People like that, Joanna. People like that" . . . he slurred the words, and I realised that the spirits were taking effect . . . "people like the Pollitts enjoy money the more if they've begged it, or stolen it. Money earned by the sweat of their brows, they regard as the fruits of damned exploitation. Gallows-meat they are, and the sooner they hang the better."

He slumped into a chair and passed a hand across his brow. As never before, he reminded me of my father, with his wild and brutal judgements on people for whom he had no sympathy. Yes, my father had been just like that—particularly when he was in his cups.

There did not seem any point in pressing the subject any further. It was hardly likely that I should ever see the unfortunate couple again, after the harsh way that Benedict had driven them from the gate.

Something else needed to be aired; and I was determined to have it out with my husband—no matter if he was drunk or sober.

"Are you having some luncheon, Benedict?" I asked coolly.

"I'll have a bite later," he said. "When I've finished my drink."

"Please sit up at the table with me," I said. "There's something I really have to talk to you about, Benedict. Something that's worrying me."

"Worrying you?" He gave a mirthless laugh that made my whole skin prickle with an unpleasant thrill. "What in Heaven's name should be worrying you, my dear? You—the mistress of one of Cornwall's finest great houses, and a bride of only two days."

There was no mistaking the mockery in his tone. And there was something else: something that half sounded like—bitterness.

"It's a matter we've discussed before," I began.

Benedict smiled and made a wide gesture with both his hands, spilling some of the spirit from his glass as he did so.

"It won't hurt for being aired again," he said, still in the mocking tone. "There are no secrets between us, my dear Joanna. We are of one accord in everything. The marriage of true minds, as the Bard has it. Any topic can be taken out, dusted down, and discussed freely. At any time. Any time at all" . . . he took another long pull at the glass . . . "Please proceed, my dear."

"It concerns—the Prendergasts," I faltered.

His eyes flashed up to meet mine; and the two indentations appeared; warnings of a coming storm.

"What of the Prendergasts now?" he demanded dangerously.

"Mrs Prendergast's attitude to me . . ."

He cut in: "I was of the opinion that we had settled the question of the Prendergasts, quite adequately, in the train coming down from Paddington. I believed I had managed to persuade you that the absurd private attitudes which servants have the effrontery to adopt should not be allowed to impinge on the mind of the master, or mistress; and that, providing the Prendergasts obey you in every particular, their attitudes are no more to be probed than if they were mechanical figures of clockwork."

"That's all very well for you, Benedict," I said. "You who've been used to an army of servants all your life. With me, it's different. I'm not so far removed from Mrs Prendergast—as a fellow human being—that I don't notice that she hates and resents me."

"Nonsense!"

"I am not talking nonsense!" I retorted with heat.

"I'm sorry," he conceded. "I should have said that you exaggerate. The feeling will pass."

147

"Benedict, I can't stand to have that woman in the place any longer," I cried. "You must tell them to go. Now. Please."

He shook his head, closing his eyes as he did so, with an expression of boredom.

"You won't do as I ask?"

"The Prendergasts stay," he said flatly.

With that, he uncoiled his long legs, rose, and walked unsteadily to the sideboard and refilled his rummer from the decanter. I stared at him, undecided on what to say next—if, indeed, there was anything to be said in the face of his callous obstinacy.

He turned to face me; leaning back against the edge of the sideboard and twirling the glass in his fingers, close to his nostrils, savouring the smell of the spirit.

"This attitude of Mrs Prendergast's that you complain of," he said. "It's of no importance, but let's pursue it for a while; drag it out into the light of day and see what manner of attitude it is, and if it isn't indeed a figment of your own imagination that disappears under inspection. Tell me the quality of this . . . attitude."

Faced by his demand, my assurance subsided again. I felt the colour mount in my cheeks.

"Well, she's—insolent!" I said.

"I find it hard to believe," he said. "Sullen, perhaps. Occasionally taciturn, certainly. A mite overbearing with the lower servants, but that's the way she gets things done. You might find her a bit short in manner if it came to your criticising her in matters concerning the housekeeping which you, as mistress of the castle, would do best to leave alone. But, insolent—I think you may be putting it too high, my dear."

He was mocking me now. The drink had taken hold of him, and he was enjoying the situation: enjoying the privilege of his five hundred years of ancestry; delighting in being able to talk down to the little nobody whom he had picked up—on a whim, surely?—from out of the gutter.

Suddenly, I felt my fury rise, as I looked into his flushed

face and saw the telltale puffiness around those sea-blue eyes
that had so enchanted me. And, all at once, he reminded me
not only of my father, but also of his detestable brother Saul.

"I don't think I'm putting it too high," I retorted.

"Do you not?" he smiled.

"No," I said. And, taking a deep breath—for I was now going to leap headlong into the fray: "I don't think it's a servant's
place to make veiled allusions about her employers' sleeping
arrangements—do you?"

"To . . . *what?*"

I had hit the mark, all right.

"Mrs Prendergast took great delight in dwelling on the fact
that I spent my wedding night alone," I said. "By word and
by implication, she had me know that she thought the situation
very amusing."

It had been said. It was out in the open. Benedict was
rising to his feet, and I did not dare to look into his face.
Instead, I gazed steadfastly ahead.

"By all the devils in hell!" he cried. "She dared to do that?"

"She did," I said.

I saw him draw back his arm and hurl the rummer across
the refectory. It landed in a far corner and fell in bright
shards and a widening pool of amber liquid. The sound made
me give a violent start.

When I looked at him, he was staring towards the window.
The indentations were scored into his brow as if cleft there
by an axe; and his eyes were awful with anger.

But anger towards—whom?

"Fool!" he gritted between clenched teeth. "What a fool!"

"Benedict . . ." I began.

His head flicked round at the sound of my voice, and his
eyes flared, as if in surprise to see me there. His expression
was coldly hostile. The placatory comment that I had assembled
was driven from my mind like leaves before the wind of the
dying year.

He stared at me for a full minute, and it seemed an eternity.
In that time, I came to know, with sullen hopelessness, that I
should never, never be able to fulfil my resolution. Benedict

149

Trevallion would never grow to love me, no matter how hard I tried.

To him, I was just a piece of chattel he had picked up on a whim. And, to make it worse, I had just revealed myself as a piece of chattel who had the effrontery to stir up trouble; to disturb the unruffled, unquestioned superiority that was the birthright of his class.

The wronged bride had actually had the effrontery to feel hurt. More, she had had the bad taste to notice the servants' reactions to her misery. To cap it all, she had come whining to her lord and master.

Not the actions of a lady—no Trevallion bride of the past would have committed such a shower of solecisms.

His eyes were still upon me: blank and uncaring. I seemed to hear a great oaken door slamming across the corridor of my life.

I turned on my heel and walked out of the refectory, and all the time, I told myself how important it was to keep my head held high. At least, the Trevallion ghosts up in the portrait gallery should not fault me for that.

He did not call after me, nor follow me, to bring me back. Not then, nor after—though I stayed all day in my room, hoping against dying hope that he would.

* * *

Darkness brought a gale that raged over Castle Mallion and sent tiles crashing down into the courtyard from the high-pitched roof of the great hall. My chimney moaned like an organ pipe, filling me with unease; I would have given the earth for companionship and the sound of a friendly voice.

It was past ten o'clock when I threw aside my book and went over to the window, first dimming the lamp, so that no one should see me from the courtyard.

The moon was up, and racing between lines of scudding clouds. The air was filled with flying debris of leaves and branches, and the ornamental trees surrounding the fountains were bent over like bows. The whole air was filled with sound and fury.

I thought of the mighty waves pounding the rock-girt shore below the castle, and of the hell on earth for the sailors out at sea on such a night, when the whole, perilous shoreline of rugged Cornwall was besieged by the tempest. I shivered—and would have closed the shutters and shut out the awful night; but something stayed my hand.

Something moved at the base of the tower that flanked the gatehouse on the left-hand side—the northwest tower. Mayana's tower, as I had come to think of it.

A splash of colour in the moonlight—instantly quenched, as a dark shawl was shaken out and draped tightly about a tall, willowy figure.

It was Mayana. The night made her olive skin seem darker and her eyes brighter by contrast. They shone like the eyes of a cat, as she craned her head and cast a darting glance round the courtyard. I instinctively stepped back into the shadows as her gaze took in the window of my room. When I looked down again, she seemed to have gone.

But no . . .

A door opened—the door at the base of the northeast tower at the other side of the gatehouse—and two figures were momentarily silhouetted against a faint gleam of lamplight beyond them. They were posed there, immobile, for a brief instant in time—then the door closed on them and they were gone.

In that short moment out of all eternity, I saw enough to destroy the last, cold embers of all my burnt hopes.

The man who had opened his door in the night to Mayana was my bridegroom of two days.

I knew, then, what I had always half guessed and had latterly come to thrust into a dark corner of my mind: I knew what he was to Mayana and what the beautiful octoroon was to him.

CHAPTER 5

The gale had blown itself out by morning. I heard the going of it, because I lay sleepless till cockcrow, turning over and over in my mind the bitterness of my misery: when the wind stopped moaning in my chimney, I slipped into a fitful half sleep that lasted till the first, thin shafts of daylight straggled through my bedroom window.

Through the window, from where I lay, I could see the battlemented top of the northwest tower—Mayana's tower—and I wondered if my bridegroom's mistress had by now left her lover's side and returned to her sick child. In my heart, I could find no means to hate the beautiful deaf-mute for the wrong she was doing to me; but it seemed strangely out of character for Mayana neglectfully to leave her child untended while she visited her lover, and this I found unforgivable.

I lay awake from dawn till nearly half-past nine, in the languorous warmth of my lonely bed, trying to decide how best to handle the situation in which I now found myself.

Clearly, yesterday's scene with Benedict could not be allowed to be the end of it; the topic would have to be resumed—though I cringed at the thought of raising it again with him. The question of my position as his wife was something that simply could not be swept away under the carpet, not by me at any rate; I had not had the aristocratic upbringing that schools a person to put on a bold face and accept an impossible situation with dignified calm. Benedict was different, and anyhow he was a man. Men can turn their backs on a situation—or forget their troubles in drink.

Which reminded me that I must never again stay around and argue with Benedict when he was in his cups. I had not realised it before, but he was obviously capable of heavy and compulsive drinking. Coupled with his violent temper, it could make him difficult—even dangerous.

I had half decided to go to Benedict and—as calmly and quietly as I could—reopen our discussion where we had left off, when there came a tap on my bedroom door. It was a maid with a tray of tea. She also had a letter for me.

"Master rode out early and didn't say when he'd be back, ma'am, but he told me to give you this."

"Thank you, Emmy," I said, my fingers already ripping open the envelope with trembling eagerness. "That will be all, thank you."

The girl bobbed and departed. Not till I heard her footsteps fade away down the passage did I trust myself to open the sheet of writing paper with the black lion of the Trevallions engraved at its head.

I read the words written there in his thick, slashing script. There were many alterations, all done with brutal strokes of the pen that betrayed the high emotional state in which he had composed the letter.

It was a letter that went as near to breaking my heart as any I have ever received, or hope to receive . . .

My dear Joanna (it began),
Firstly, it is necessary for me to offer my most sincere apologies for my behaviour. There were certain matters which, weighing heavily on my mind, tended to impair my judgement and my conduct.

Touching on the matter which you raised—the matter of our married state—there is, again, little I can offer but regretful apology. I am sorry that you may have detected anything hurtful in the manner of one of the servants. Believe me, I had not the slightest suspicion of this. The woman concerned has been severely reprimanded by me, and I have every confidence that the incidents will not be repeated.

I am not so blind as not to be aware that you are unhappy in your present state. The blame is entirely mine, but I regret that it is quite beyond my power to do anything to change matters. The sorry truth is that I have committed a ghastly mistake in so hastily condemning you to the state of wedlock with me.

I call to your mind the pact we made on the train down from London (was it only two days ago?—it seems an age), in which I extracted from you the promise that you would bear my intolerable shortcomings as well as you are able.

My dear Joanna, that was a most unfair demand I made of you. And I now release you from the obligation of making any allowances for my conduct.

Mistakes, though they cannot be put right, can be made as tolerable as possible. I cannot be the husband to you that one might have wished, but in matters of material comfort, of position, and (though this may be of little consequence to you, as I quite understand and appreciate) in my own personal esteem of your qualities, you will find nothing of which to complain.

Finally, be assured that I shall do all in my power to avoid any friction between us; neither making demands upon your time or your patience. In company, we can meet as friends. In our private lives—I'm sure you will agree—we had best maintain a polite distance. To this end I shall, in future, take all informal meals in my own quarters.

> With every respect,
> I remain, my dear Joanna,
> your devoted servant,
> Benedict Trevallion.

The storm that had lashed the ivy-girt walls of Mallion all the long night had left behind a legacy of driven leaves and torn branches. But the courtyard below my window now lay in a warm hush of unseasonal sunshine that was like a promise of the summertime that lies at the end of the long winter's burden.

I stood by my window, the fateful letter in my hands, looking out upon the sunshine, and finding no echo of it in my heart.

Though I knew I should never completely give up the pathetic hope of making Benedict love me as I wanted to be loved, I could see nothing ahead of me at the end of the long winter of my despair. No summertime would ever lay its warm touch upon the withered blossoms of my dreams.

I gazed over the battlements and turrets of Castle Mallion, the proudest stronghold of the wild Western land, of which I was undoubted mistress. What had Benedict written?—that I should have nothing of which to complain in matters of material comfort and position, not to mention his own personal esteem. His . . . esteem . . .

No. Not that. Hold back the tears. There'll be a lifetime for tears for the mistress of Mallion.

The wife in name only.

* * *

My remembrance of the days that followed Benedict's letter of rejection—the period of agonised adjustment to the grim realities of my true situation—have blessedly faded into a grey blur of images.

It is strange, but I do not remember even being particularly unhappy. I suppose that kindly Nature spins a cocoon of forgetfulness around the hurtful memories of our lives. In any event, there are only two things that stand out in my memory of that time. The first was the arrival, in my life, of Robert Vyner; and the second was the occasion of the first painting lesson from Feyella Mapollion.

One day, I was walking across the courtyard on my way

back from my beloved old garden, when a man came out of the northwest tower, closing the door behind him.

"Mrs Trevallion, is it, ma'am?" he called to me.

I had an impression of a kindly, open face framed in russet-coloured hair and whiskers, and a pair of grey and rather shy eyes. He came towards me, holding a hat and bag in his hands.

"Why, yes," I replied. "Mr? . . ."

"Robert Vyner, ma'am," he said. "Dr Robert Vyner, at your service."

"Oh, yes, Doctor. You're attending little Jackie, aren't you? How is the patient today?"

I offered him my hand, which caused him some confusion, because both his hands were occupied and he was of two minds whether to put the hat on his head and change the bag to his left hand, or to lower both hat and bag to the ground. In the event, he compromised by putting down the bag. I could not help smiling at his disarming clumsiness of manner. He seemed so young and gauche, though he must have been some years older than me, and only a couple less than Benedict.

"Pleased to meet you, Mrs Trevallion," he said. "As to the little lad, I'm afraid I'm not very happy. Not happy at all."

"I'm very sorry to hear that," I said. And I spoke the truth. I had no quarrel with Mayana's poor little love child. "It is the consumption, isn't it?"

"Oh, yes, ma'am," he confirmed. "Not greatly advanced, mind you, but he's a poor, weakly mite by constitution, and the disease is taking a heavy toll on his slender strength. The mother's nursing is doing wonders for him, but I've grave doubts that he'll survive the winter."

I thought of Mayana, in all her splendour of beauty—my husband's lover—deprived of her child; and I could feel nothing but compassion for her; nothing but unutterable sorrow at the grief and desolation that was coming to her, for I knew the depth and intensity of feelings she had for her child—the she-cat and her cub.

"Can nothing be done for him, Doctor?" I cried.

156

Robert Vyner pursed his lips and shook his head.

"In my experience, medicaments scarcely have any effect on the progress of the disease," he said. "We can only hope for a light winter and an early spring, so that the little lad can be shipped off back to his own warm clime just as soon as the weather permits a storm-free passage."

Remembering my conversation with Benedict, I said: "My husband is reluctant to send the mother and her child back to Jamaica—even in the spring."

He looked surprised.

"Well, now, you astonish me, ma'am, you really do," he said. "I was speaking to Mr Trevallion only last evening, and he was most insistent that Jackie should be moved at the first opportunity. I remember him saying that we'd have him on the first boat out of Plymouth or Southampton after the first daffodil shows in Mallion."

"Did he now?" I said wonderingly.

So something had happened to change Benedict's mind. Was it the force of my argument? I wondered. There seemed no accounting for the strange man I had married.

There was a clip-clop of hooves, and a groom brought a big grey horse across the yard towards us.

"I must away and continue my rounds, ma'am," said Dr Vyner, and he strapped his bag to the saddle, then vaulted lightly up. He bowed and doffed his hat to me. "It has been a pleasure to make your acquaintance, Mrs Trevallion," he said.

"Good day, Doctor," I said, and watched him ride out under the archway, thinking to myself what a very kind and reliable-looking man he seemed to be—the sort of person who would make a good friend in time of need. I made up my mind, there and then, to make a point of cultivating Robert Vyner; for if anyone ever needed a friend, it was I.

And so the days dragged on. I had little to do with the management of the household, Mrs Prendergast coped with all that. Every morning, she brought the day's menus for me to approve. Her manner was polite and icily withdrawn, but I had no cause for complaint. As to the menus, I never criticised, nor made any alterations or suggestions; and when it was done, she gave me a stiff curtsey and withdrew without a word. It was obvious that Benedict had frightened her; but she still hated and resented me.

I saw very little of my husband. Our first meeting after the letter came as an absurd anticlimax: we merely passed on the stairs above the great hall; Benedict stepped to one side and said good morning to me, to which I replied. It was a calm exchange of courtesies that was to set the pattern for our new relationship.

My days became set in a routine that varied very little. I felt no longer obliged to dance attendance upon my mother-in-law, but I generally called on her for an hour or so every other day. One of the young parlour maids had taken over the duty of reading to her—and as the girl was also a patient listener to the interminable tales of the long-dead Piers, she prospered in her task.

Then there were my painting lessons. These were Feyella's idea. She arrived at the castle one afternoon with her folding easel and paintbox.

"My dear," she cried. "You must be dying of boredom in this place, so I've decided to teach you how to sketch in oils."

In vain, I protested. "I can't even draw a straight line," I told her.

"A good sense of colour is much more important," she said, "and we women have it as a natural birthright. You see—I'll have you sketching like a dream in no time at all."

She was wearing a very pretty dress and jacket of deep green velvet with a lace jabot at the throat. As always, she made me feel like a poor relation; but in certain of her moods—and it was one of these that she was presenting to me at the time—Feyella could be a truly enchanting and vivacious companion. She could also be very persuasive.

"There's a long window in the gallery above the great hall that gives a marvellous view of the sea and the beach," she said. "It's a scene I've painted many times, and it shall be your first lesson. Come, my dear. Your art awaits."

Ten minutes later, I was nervously dabbing spots of blue paint on to white canvas, in the forlorn hope of catching an impression of the tumbled mass of water that lashed about in the rocks at the head of the beach below me. My tutor stood at my elbow, directing my hand.

"Don't get the paint too liquid, or you'll have it dripping long streaks down your work. See, it's already happening. Dab it with your rag."

"It's hopeless," I wailed. "I'm much too clumsy with my hands to cope with all the things that have to be done at once. Why—the sea's not only greeny-blue, but it's grey at the same time. How can I get an effect like that with only one pair of hands—particularly when it's moving all the while?"

"Patience, my dear. Patience. It'll come, never fear," promised my mentor.

Later, when I had become resigned to my daubing, and was quite enjoying myself, Feyella left me to it and wandered about in the gallery. Absorbed in the novelty of my task, I became barely conscious of her presence; only the occasional click-click of her heels on the parquet, as she moved about, looking at the pictures and glancing out of the windows. I did notice, after a time, that she seemed to be concentrating most of her attentions on the window behind me—it looked down on to the courtyard and the gatehouse.

Presently she asked: "What time are you expecting Benedict home?"

It was the sort of question I had grown to dread, though, fortunately, there were all too few people around me to ask such a thing.

"I don't know," I said bluntly, and concentrated my attention on painting a large wave lapping against a rock.

"He never seems to be home," said Feyella. "And neither of you go visiting. Do you know you both have gained a reputation for being recluses?"

"He works hard with the management of the estate," I said. "This keeps him away most days, visiting the outlying farms."

"He was always depressingly conscientious," she said. "He took Mallion and everything concerning Mallion terribly seriously, even as a boy. My earliest recollection of him is of an unsmiling big boy on a pony, riding behind his father, traipsing all over the countryside, counting heads of sheep and all that rubbish. Not like his brothers—they didn't give a fig for anything but their own amusements."

"Not even Piers?" I asked, interested. "Surely, as the heir to the estates, he must have had a very real interest?"

"He certainly never showed it," said Feyella. "No sooner had his father died and left him his own master than he bought himself a commission in the Army and went off. Mallion could have gone to rack for all he cared—so long as it provided him with enough money for his horses, his drink, and his doxies."

I remembered the portrait of the beautiful hussar with which I had fallen in love all those years ago. What a pity that one's illusions have to be shattered. Feyella had obviously not liked Piers; had justifiably detested Saul. But she had been infatuated with Benedict. Did she still feel the same way about him? I wondered. It seemed likely.

"Nothing would have got Benedict away from Mallion," said Feyella. "He bitterly resented having to go out to Jamaica, but Saul insisted, and by then Saul was holding the purse strings. He had to go, or be cut off without a penny. That odious Saul would have been quite capable of doing such a thing, even to his brother. Saul had no family pride; Benedict's stiff with it—the pride of the Trevallions. They loathed each other, of course. Do you know, Joanna, I sometimes think . . ."

"Think what?" I said, absently mixing up another dab of greeny-blue paint.

"I sometimes think," she said, "that Benedict would have done anything . . . *anything* . . . to get Mallion for himself, and away from Saul's clutches."

I glanced round at her. She was standing by the window opposite, her back to me, looking down into the courtyard. I could only guess at the expression in those violet-blue eyes.

"Feyella, what do you mean?" I demanded.

She turned to face me, and those lovely eyes were wide and candid; perhaps a little too wide and candid.

"Why, Joanna, I mean just what I said," she replied. "There was no hidden message in my remark. Why should you think there was?"

I made no answer, and there the subject died. We went on with the painting lesson, and my tutor took the brushes herself and made some corrections to my work, commenting all the time on what she was doing.

I gave her profile an occasional, covert glance—and something in Feyella's face left me with the impression that she was feeling very satisfied with herself about something.

It was very puzzling.

*   *   *

As the weeks went on, in the dying end of the year, I took to exploring the countryside that lay beyond the winding drive of Castle Mallion. Well wrapped in a fur-lined cloak and hood, I ventured for the first time beyond the confines of my grand home, and walked the high-walled lanes and the broad uplands where the earth seemed to meet the sky. There was a jaunty little terrier named Pinkie, who lived in the kitchen quarters and who took to accompanying me.

The village stood half a mile from Mallion gates, in a narrow valley through which a stream torrented between the tiny, white-painted cottages and the ancient church. I only walked through the village once, and it seemed to me that I was watched from every curtained window. Not a soul to be seen; only desolation and the sense of watching eyes. After that first experience, I never ventured there again; but took a fork in the lane that carried me high above the valley and on to the moorland, where the sheep cropped the frost-darkened grass, and the horizon on three sides was bounded by the greyness of the sea.

One afternoon, I went farther than usual, led on by the unfolding of a new horizon of wooded hills and by the fineness of the weather. Pinkie had chased a hare and several rabbits and was feeling very full of himself; running on far ahead, so that I had to call and call him for a long while when I decided we must turn back and go home.

By the time the rascal had reluctantly come back to me, the wintry daylight was more than half gone, the westerly wind had taken on a keen, damp edge—and we had every prospect of arriving home in rainy darkness.

Calling encouragingly to my little companion, I set off back at a brisk pace; over the wind-swept moorland, with Pinkie bounding keenly ahead, nose to the ground.

We came at length to the entrance of a rutted lane that I had not noticed before, but which promised a quicker return to the coast in the direction of Mallion. I decided that we should take it. We had not gone more than a quarter of a mile before I regretted my decision.

In the first place, the lane, which had started off being unwaveringly straight, very quickly became a maze of turns, so that I had no idea if we were still heading for the coast, or if we had turned upon ourselves and were going back inland. Pinkie was no help in the matter: he found plenty of scents in the hedgerow, and for all he cared we could go anywhere.

Even more disturbing, the stunted trees of yew and hawthorn that lined both sides became thicker and taller, till they met overhead and formed a gloomy tunnel that shaded off into almost pitch darkness ahead. And it had begun to rain.

Useless to retrace our steps; by the time we reached the entrance to the lane it would be quite dark. Better, I decided, to go on and hope that we should soon come out in familiar ground.

It was just after I had come to this conclusion that Pinkie stopped and stiffened all over.

"What is it, boy?" I whispered, alarmed. "What have you heard?"

For answer, the little terrier drew back his lips in a soundless snarl. I craned my eyes to pierce the tangled darkness ahead—but could see nothing. A nameless dread struck at my heart, which began pounding heavily. I sensed the presence of evil—as indeed the dog must have done.

I steeled myself to go on, but, try as I might, I could not persuade Pinkie to follow me.

"Pinkie, it's all right," I pleaded. "Don't be afraid. No one's going to hurt you, I promise."

The hairs at the base of the terrier's neck stood up like the quills of a porcupine, and he uttered a low growl.

At the same instant—someone laughed, close to my ear!

I screamed. Pinkie tucked his tail between his legs and fled; I saw his little white form bounding off back the way we had come. Something moved at my elbow. Turning, I saw a man standing in the deep shadow of a hawthorn tree, leaning against the drystone wall and regarding me from under the shadowed brim of his hat; a man in a ragged countryman's smock.

"No call to worry, ma'am," he said. "'Tis foolish o' the dog to run off like that. Gave him a fright I did, just standing so still, like."

It was then—with a small shock of disquiet—that I recognised him as the peasant who, with his wife, had been driven so brutally from the gates of Mallion by my husband. At close quarters, he looked to be a big and powerfully built man in his late forties. Of the cringing attitude that he had displayed to Benedict on the last occasion, there was no sign; he seemed to be all swaggering confidence, now. And there was a hint of something else—was it, perhaps, menace?

I put a bold face on my nervousness. "Is it much farther to the end of this lane, please?" I asked him in what I hoped was a loud and fearless tone of voice.

"You be out late, ma'am," he replied. His eyes were hidden from me, shaded by the brim of his hat, but the lips were bent in a grin. "Ain't usual to see a lady o' quality in the lanes these nights."

"I am out for a walk," I replied coldly. "Would you please tell me if I have much farther to go to the castle?"

"You be the new lady o' the castle," he said wheedlingly. "Long life to you, ma'am. 'Twould give me pleasure to drink your health and long life. Which I'll be happy to do, ma'am —if you was to give me a few coppers to buy the wherewithal."

"I carry no money with me," I said, turning to go on. "Good night to you."

To my alarm, I heard him moving after me.

"That's a bad man you're wed to, ma'am. Black-hearted as hell he is, begging your pardon for the strong words, like."

I stopped; turned to face him.

"How dare you say a thing like that to me?" I demanded, with more assurance than I felt.

Again that sneering grin.

"For all that, I'll drink your health, lady. Aye, and the master's as well, if you be so minded. But I'll need the money for it, you see."

To my horror, he had circled round me and was now blocking my onward path. Behind me lay my only way of escape—assuming that I could outrun my tormentor—and that led only to the dark and trackless moor. I fought to keep my nerves steady and my voice under control; the last thing I must do, I knew instinctively, was to show fear.

"I've already told you—I have nothing with me," I said. "I've no call to carry money." And this was perfectly true: I had never touched money since arriving back at Mallion.

"You'll have a little something about you, now," he said, moving closer to me. "Some little geegaw that you'll not miss?"

I backed away, tugging at a bracelet that I wore on my right wrist: only a tawdry thing of pinchbeck, set with paste diamonds, but it had belonged to my mother. I was reluctant to lose it—but my situation looked desperate and could be even worse than I believed.

"Thanks, lady," he replied, taking my bracelet and slipping it into the pocket of his smock. "'Tis kind o' you to take pity on a poor feller. There's some who'd strike a poor feller for doing no more than begging for a little to wet his whistle. That black-hearted devil you're wed to, he whipped me like a dog. Like a dog!" The voice was raised in fury, now.

"I'm sorry," I said. "I saw it happen, and I'm ashamed that you should have been treated so. Believe me. And now—will you please let me pass?"

He made no move to release me; instead, his hand came out and closed about my wrist. His face came close to mine, and I smelt a foulness on his breath.

164

"This will be just between you and me, my lady," he hissed. "What's passed between us shouldn't reach his ears."

I struggled to free my arm, but he only held me tighter.

"You'll promise this?" he cried.

"Yes," I said. "I promise. Now will you let me go?"

He drew me even closer to him, so that our faces were nearly touching. I closed my eyes, nauseated.

"For, if that devil ever got wind o' what's passed between us this night," he said, "he might seek me out with the whip —or worse. And that would bring no good to the castle folk. That man you're wed to strikes before he considers the cost, and 'tis a folly . . ."

He let go my arm, and I stumbled away from him, the way I had to go. He called after me, and what he said will be forever imprinted on my mind; it became, at the time, yet another link in the chain of horror that was—insidiously and almost unnoticed—beginning to encircle my life.

What he said was:

"Let that devil lay a whip across me again, and I'll lay evidence against him as shall bring him to the gallows! Mark that, lady!"

The terrible words puzzled and shocked me; stung me to near-panic. I started to run. I was still running, with the low-slung tendrils of hawthorn and yew clawing at my hair, when the lane suddenly debouched into a wide road and open countryside. Below me lay the lights of the village, and I knew that I was not far from home.

Before I had gone a few yards down the road, I heard the sound of hoofbeats coming up behind me, and, turning, I saw a horse and rider. My first thought was that it might be Benedict on his way home—but the newcomer was wearing a tall hat, and not the broad-brimmed one that my husband favoured.

When he saw me in the road, the rider checked his mount's pace to a walk, and I saw who it was.

"Good evening to you, Mrs Trevallion," cried Dr Robert Vyner. "You're out late, and alone."

"Hello, Doctor," I said. "I'm afraid I went much farther than I should, and I also lost my way."

"Then it'll give me the greatest pleasure to escort you as far as the castle," he said. And, slipping from the saddle, he gathered up the horse's reins and took up step by my side.

"Thank you," I said. "To tell the truth, I've just had rather a bad fright, and I'm blessedly glad of your company."

"Have you indeed?" he said. "What happened to frighten you, in our peaceful Cornish lanes?"

After a moment's consideration, I told him a certain version of what had just happened. Two things I omitted: any mention of the man having demanded money from me and any reference to what he had said about Benedict.

Robert Vyner was appalled, and wanted to turn round and go after the blackguard, as he called him.

"His name's Pollitt," he cried. "I know him well. A worthless wretch of a worthless family. Mind you, Mrs Trevallion, I'm sure you were in no real danger, but things have come to a pretty pass when a lady can't walk unmolested in these parts."

I restrained him, saying: "Please don't make a fuss about it, Dr Vyner. And, most of all, I beg you not to tell any of this to my husband. It will only worry and anger him—and then he'll take steps against the man for speaking to me."

He looked doubtful.

"Well, if you're quite sure, ma'am . . ."

"I'm quite sure I want it to end here, Doctor," I said. And then, on an impulse, I added: "Let this incident remain a secret between us—a kind of bond of friendship."

He looked very pleased at that, and, though it was dark, I would swear that he blushed. I felt mean on account of my coquettishness, as if, somehow, I was cheating him.

"Still, I'm surprised that Pollitt didn't try to wheedle a florin out of you," he said.

"He would have been unlucky," I murmured, "for I'm not carrying any money."

"Then as you say, there's no harm done," he said. "And

166

you'll be able to put it out of your mind. But it was impertinent of the wretch to address you."

Put it out of my mind? Not so easily, I thought . . .

It had been some comfort, though, to talk to Robert Vyner about the incident—even if I had not admitted my new friend and confidant into the raw and appalling details of my transaction with the man Pollitt.

That, I decided—casting a sidelong glance at the tall and capable-looking figure loping along beside me—might come later, if the need should ever arise.

We walked together in silence, till we came to the gatehouse of Mallion and there Robert Vyner took my proffered hand and held it longer than was strictly necessary—but only by a mere hairsbreadth of time.

* * *

I bore the sleeplessness that night, for as long as I was able; then I flung out of bed and crossed over to the window.

The courtyard was a well of darkness, with only one light burning in an upstairs window of Benedict's tower. I closed my eyes against it, pressing my forehead to the cold panes, letting the scalding tears run unchecked.

"Benedict! Benedict!" I cried aloud. "What is it? What have you done, that torments you so?"

And the hateful voice of the man in the dark lane came back to me again, clear on the wings of the night wind . . .

". . . I'll lay evidence against him as shall bring him to the gallows!"

Another voice broke in: the drawling, aristocratic voice of my self-appointed friend, the charming and accomplished Feyella Mapollion . . .

"I sometimes think that Benedict would have done anything . . . anything . . . to get Mallion for himself!"

The darkest speculations teemed into my mind, till I thought that my brow would burst with the pressure of the horrors that were mounting up within my head.

I prayed for the strength of will that would take me out into the night and across the courtyard, to my husband's tower

—there to throw myself upon his mercy and beg to be allowed to share in his life, all of his life, the sunshine and the shadows; but I knew that the strength was not in me; I also knew that it was to another that he turned for whatever he needed.

And, as I began to become aware of the dark shadows that were gathered about the strange life of the man I had married, so did I begin dimly to realise how desperate must be his need for comfort and consolation.

* * *

Christmas came and went without the celebrations of which Benedict had spoken on that never-to-be forgotten night when the division between us was dragged out into the open. There were no balls and parties in the great hall. The blazing yule logs lit up the ancient walls and filled the air with their merry crackling—just as on any other day. No laughter of happy children. No tread of dancing feet and the sound of gay music.

Two souvenirs of Christmas: the village church choir sang carols under the gateway arch; a circle of pale faces under a flickering lantern. The tunes carried me back to the happiest part of my childhood, when my mother was alive and we sang them together. I went out into the night with a handful of coins and pressed one into each chill palm. They were too overawed to thank me, but just stared at me with their great, hungry eyes. Most of them were barefoot, and I was ashamed of my fur-lined cloak.

The second souvenir was brought to me on my breakfast tray on Christmas morning. It came in a wrapping of coloured paper, and inside it was a ring of garnets and diamonds lying in a bed of black velvet. There was no message, but I did not need to be told who it was from. The ring fitted me perfectly; and when I had tried it on, I put it away in a drawer with all the rest of my beautiful and expensive toys.

The new year of 1863 brought a hand of ice that lay over all the wild Western land, so that even the sea was frozen below the walls of Mallion, and a cruel wind scoured the humped hills. Almost every day, the wind carried the sound of the chuch bells from the village, ringing the dirge for the dead; but though the barefoot poor fell victims to the bitter winter, Mallion's invalids continued to survive, cosseted and protected against the fury of the elements by Mallion's wealth and warmth.

I never saw little Jackie, but Robert Vyner called to attend him regularly, and we sometimes met in the courtyard and exchanged the time of day. From him, I learned that the boy was holding his own against the dreadful disease.

As for my mother-in-law (I still found it difficult to think of her as such, and frequently found myself addressing her as ma'am), the excessive warmth—almost like that of a tropical plant conservatory—at which she kept her parlour made her positively glow with health, and I had never seen her better. As ever, her talk was of nothing but her dead son; and I listened to it with dutiful patience.

Feyella came often. I made so little progress with the oil sketching that we abandoned the project by mutual consent. She painted a portrait of me: a flattering thing that was far from being a likeness, with its tactful playing-down of my overlarge nose and mouth and its concentration upon the lustre of my hair.

It became obvious to me that Feyella was still quite hopelessly infatuated with Benedict, and that she had only engineered her friendship with me in order to have an excuse to be a regular visitor at Mallion. Of course, since she was always with me, and the paths of my husband and me seldom crossed, the poor girl hardly ever saw the object of her passions.

I continued to speculate about her disquietening remark concerning Benedict, but could make nothing of it—nothing that added up to any sense. And whenever I tried to bring the conversation round to Benedict and his inheritance of Mallion, Feyella pointedly changed the subject. It was as if—having once dropped a cryptic comment in my lap—she was content to leave it so.

There was a dreadful evening a week or so after New Year, when she and I dined with Benedict. It happened this way: Feyella arrived after luncheon and met Benedict in the courtyard. I witnessed their encounter from the window of the solar. He greeted her pleasantly, and, by his manner and gestures, seemed to enquire after her health and that of her father, perhaps. Feyella replied with heavy coquettishness, head on one side, eyes sparkling—so that I had to smile, despite my feelings. Then she laid an entreating hand on his arm, seeming to be trying to extract a promise from him. He seemed hesitant, but, after a moment's pause, he nodded and smiled with indulgent good humour.

She ran into the solar a few moments later, eyes dancing, to tell me that she had invited herself to dine with me—and had, furthermore, coaxed Benedict into joining us.

The poor girl was in such a tizzy that I could not bring myself to be angry with her. The situation promised to be embarrassing for both Benedict and me. According to the terms of his note, we should only take our meals together on formal occasions, in company—but, as things had turned out, this would be the first time we had entertained since our marriage. When I thought about it, the idea was both disturbing and exciting.

Feyella did not stay for tea, but went straight home to begin her toilette. She arrived back at seven o'clock in a dinner gown of orange taffeta with the most breathtaking *décolletage* I have ever set eyes on. I had, by some instinct of modest withdrawal, chosen a gown, from my trousseau, of grey silk; very demure at the neckline and long in the sleeve.

The dinner was a disaster. Benedict was late at table, and already drunk. He greeted me with scarcely a glance, and devoted the whole of the meal to humiliating Feyella.

His manner of doing it was typical of him: subtle, tortuous, and catlike. He began by enquiring after various of her girl-cousins of her own age who were already married; after this, he wrung from her the grudging admission that she would prefer to marry than to stay single; then he pounced, and demanded to know why—since there was no shortage of eligible young men in the duchy—she was still a spinster?

Poor Feyella's answer was written all over her; in her white face and in the treacherous quivering of her nether lip; in the shameless gown that must suddenly have felt like a sackcloth shroud draped about her bare shoulders.

I wished I could have taken the words from her silent lips and screamed them into his flushed, sneering face:

"*She's never married because she's loved you all her life, you heartless brute! And, when she realised that I'm your wife in name only, she had hopes of becoming your lover . . . but now you're spitting in her face!*"

Only, of course, I kept my own counsel. Satisfied with his work, Benedict poured himself a bumper glass of brandy, rose to his feet, bid us both a mocking good night—and left the refectory.

The episode had penetrated Feyella's aristocratic calm; broken through the assurance that came from a lifetime of knowing her highly valued place in the world. In my case, rejection by the man I loved was all of a piece with the common fabric of life; my harder schooling had made it easier for me than for the poor little rich girl who, in all her born days, had only needed to ask for something and it was immediately hers.

I felt a sisterly compassion for her as I walked her to the door where her coach waited to take her home through the night. She had not said a word after Benedict's departure, and her eyes were swollen with the unshed tears. As she got into the coach, she cast a yearning glance across the courtyard, towards the northeast tower.

Remembering her words on my return to Mallion, I thought of the truth of them: how it was that, by a cruel twist of fate, she and I could indeed be good friends because we had so much in common.

We were both unwanted—rejected.

* * *

It was a morning of bitter frost, and I was gathering some branches of holly in the formal garden when I heard a hoarse, animal-like cry from the direction of the gatehouse.

Out of the door of the northwest tower came Mayana, her

171

blue-black hair streaming in the chill wind, her slender arms flailing the air.

Again that unearthly cry: it burst from her open mouth as from a stricken she-wolf of the forest; the call of a wild thing in mortal agony.

Then I was running across the courtyard towards her, and doors were flying open and others were coming from all sides.

"Mayana! What is it, Mayana?" I cried.

Her eyes were crazed with horror and she could only mouth this same horror with incomprehensible sounds. But her intention was plain: she was pointing towards the open door at the base of the tower.

"Jackie!" I blurted out. "Something's wrong with Jackie—yes?"

The beautiful deaf-mute nodded violently.

By now, we were surrounded by a small crowd of castle servants. I saw Prendergast and one of the grooms.

"Ride for Dr Vyner at once," I told the latter. "Ask him to come immediately. Tell him I said so, and that the child's taken a bad turn."

The man raced away to do my bidding. I took Mayana by the arm. "Let's go and see if there's anything we can both do till the doctor comes," I said.

Mayana followed me up the spiral stair of the tower to the door of her apartments, and when I went in she stayed at the door, tragic-faced and keening quietly to herself.

Jackie lay, half on, half off the couch. My first thought mirrored what must have been in Mayana's mind—that he was already dead. The pathetic little body seemed no bigger than a doll. I stooped and lifted him up. The head lolled forward and I saw a trickle of bright blood coming from the corner of the pale, pinched mouth. Then his unbelievably big, dark eyes flickered open and met mine in a look that spoke for all the agonies of sick childhood. I choked on a tear.

"He's all right, Mayana!" I cried. "He's alive, and we'll save him yet, you'll see!"

Uttering an incomprehensible cry, the mulatress ran across the room and gathered her child in her arms, pressing the blood-dabbled face to her breast and rocking him backwards and forwards, keening all the time. She stayed like this, holding him to her, while I changed the bed linen and found a clean nightgown to put on the little invalid. Then, together, we laid him down and made him as comfortable as possible.

Then followed the agony of waiting for the arrival of the doctor. In that seemingly interminable time, a strange bond was forged between Mayana and me; a bond that, so far as I was concerned, was in no way weakened by the thought that I was in the presence of the beautiful, alien woman who was almost certainly my husband's lover. In the span of time while we waited together by that frail little life huddled on the couch, we were just—two women.

Two women united in the primitive state of supporting life: watching over a small, sick young of the tribe . . .

I thought we had lost him soon after. His little body was suddenly hunched and torn by a flood of uncontrollable coughing, and this was followed by a choking as the poor mite threatened to drown in his own blood. Somehow, by dint of moving him this way and that, we managed to drag him back from the threshold of the tomb; air was gasped into the afflicted lungs, and the dreadful tinge of purple faded from his face.

Mayana's glance met mine. There was no need for words to pass between us at that moment. We had both heard the beat of the wings of the angel of death.

It must have been quite soon after that—though it seemed an added age—that I heard the pounding of running, booted feet on the tower stairs—and Robert Vyner burst into the room.

He took one look at the small figure on the couch.

"Hot water, please," he said crisply, without glancing at me. "As hot as possible, and plenty of it."

"Yes, Doctor," I replied meekly, and went to obey.

All that day, till long after the wintry sun had cast its last rays through the narrow windows of that tower chamber, Robert Vyner fought for the little life on the couch. While Mayana and I took turns to lay cold compresses on the pa-

173

tient's fevered brow and to chafe his thin limbs, the doctor applied a heated cupping glass to various portions of the emaciated chest with a view to—as he put it to me—drawing the blood to the surface and away from the inflamed parts around the lungs. The process must have been painful to the poor mite, for he cried out in anguish; and soon the olive skin of his chest was blotched with ruddy circles where the cup had sucked at him like a leech.

Presently, there was no more bleeding from the mouth, the racking cough ceased, and Jackie closed his eyes in sleep.

I glanced across at Mayana, but her dark eyes were fixed on her child. Neither then nor later did she acknowledge my presence in the room: the hours of crisis—when we had stood together, united in our womanhood—were over; our relationship was back where it started, and the barriers between us had been set up again.

With a sigh, I set-to to help clear up the mess. It was past seven o'clock, and I realised with a sudden sense of unreality that we had been labouring for over nine hours without rest or refreshment. My forehead was damp with my own sweat, and I fumbled in my pocket for my handkerchief, but it was gone, nor could I find it lying about anywhere.

Robert Vyner was gathering up his instruments. He smiled across at me.

"You are a natural nurse, Mrs Trevallion," he said. "You'd be a credit to Miss Nightingale's new school at St Thomas's, if you had the mind."

"I don't think so," I said. "I'm much too selfish to care very much for others over long periods of time."

"You underestimate yourself," he smiled.

I picked up the last of the cold compresses and dropped it in a pail.

"You must be worn out, Doctor," I said. "Come across to the solar and have a glass of something and a bite to eat."

To my surprise, he looked embarrassed.

"That's very kind of you, ma'am," he said. "But—I must pay some further calls this evening before I return home."

"You must have a swallow of brandy to revive you and keep out the cold," I persisted.

"Well—all right." He still looked doubtful, avoiding my eye as he rolled up a canvas instrument case with slow care, preparing to put it in his bag.

His bag was lying open beside the sofa. The hem of my skirt brushed against it in passing, and I idly looked down. What I saw there almost—but not quite—made me give an exclamation of surprise.

Lying among the other things in the open physician's bag was—*my missing handkerchief!*

There was no doubt about it; no possibility that I—or anyone else—could have mistaken it for anything other than what it was: a scrap of pink cambric edged with white lace and monogrammed with my initials *J.T.* at one corner. It was part of a set that had been hastily embroidered for my trousseau.

Before I had properly taken it in, I was several paces across the room. Turning, with a remark already forming on my lips, I saw Robert Vyner very deliberately place his roll of instruments into the bag and close it.

The remark died on my lips. What point would there have been, after all, in calling his attention to the fact that a piece of my property was lying in his bag—when he must have seen it? What point in speculating how it could have got there— when it was quite obvious that he himself had put it there?

A last look at the little invalid, and we went down the steps together and across the dark and wind-swept courtyard towards the great hall, where the glow of firelight danced behind the diamond-paned windows.

"Your brandy, Doctor."

Having poured him a generous glassful in the solar, I crossed over and very deliberately placed it in his hand, watching him as I did so, my gaze deliberately challenging. I let my hand linger longer than was necessary for him to take hold of the stem of the glass, and my little finger brushed against his thumb. He met my glance with his sober grey eyes. I saw honesty there, coupled with shyness: the shyness of a basically strong man whose very honesty might make him doubtful of the propriety of his emotions, and who might perhaps resist those emotions to the very death.

"Your health, Doctor."

"And your very good health also, ma'am."

He tipped the glass and drained the spirit in one swallow. This done, he bowed to me and picked up his bag.

"Good night to you, ma'am."

"Good night, Doctor."

I stood by the window, watching him as he emerged from the hall door and crossed the yard to where a groom was waiting with his big grey. I heard him exchange some pleasantry with the man, then swing himself into the saddle and clatter off through the yawning archway without as much as a backward glance in my direction.

Taking with him the talisman of my handkerchief . . .

They were waiting for Benedict when he arrived back at the castle soon after nine: I saw Prendergast run forward and take his horse's head, mouthing the news about the child. With a treacherous lurch of my heart, I saw Benedict leap from the saddle and race across towards the entrance of the northwest tower; and I turned away, trying to shut out the thought of his reception by Mayana at the head of the tower stair, and how they would creep into the sick room together and look down at the peaceful face of the sleeping child.

It was another long and sleepless night for me: a fact that left me ill-prepared to face the heavy demands of the hideous day that followed.

The next morning, a groom rode over from Mapollion Grange with the news that Feyella was missing!

* * *

I received the fellow: Benedict had left early and it was not known when he would be back.

"Missing?" I cried. "But—since when?"

"Since the night afore last, ma'am. The night that Miss Feyella did come here, to Mallion."

The groom was a tall, stringy man well past his middle

years, with a shrewd, peasant's face that was cracked and crazed all over like a piece of old leather.

"And you left it all this time before making any enquiries about her?" I demanded in amazement.

A cunning, knowing look came into his eyes. Behind the superficial politeness, I sensed a contemptuous amusement.

"There weren't any call for alarm, ma'am. Arrived back home from here, she did, and went to bed—or so 'twas thought. Next morn—yesterday morn—nothing was seen of her, and 'twas thought she'd ridden out at dawn, maybe to come here. Her white horse were gone from the stables, you see, ma'am, and her maid says as how her riding habit be gone too. 'Twas thought she'd spent the day here."

"And no one gave a thought when she didn't arrive home last night?" I asked.

Again the contemptuous smile of the overfamiliar servant.

"Ain't nobody at the Grange who'd question Miss Feyella's comings-and-goings. More than your place be worth to do that, ma'am."

"But what about her father? Didn't he raise any query when she didn't come home last night?"

The groom sneered. "The master weren't in no condition to know if Miss Feyella had come or gone, if you do get my meaning, ma'am. I carried him to bed myself. 'Twas not till he came down this morning that the master were in any condition to be told what had happened."

"And so he sent you here?"

"That's right, ma'am. And all the men be out searching the moors and the cliffs for her."

I felt suddenly alarmed: the man's voice had taken a grim tone.

"Of course, there may be some perfectly simple and straightforward explanation," I said. "Miss Mapollion could have ridden out to visit other friends and stayed overnight."

The groom grunted noncommittally.

"Still, it's very sensible of Mr Mapollion to order an immediate search," I said. "The countryside's very wild, and in this weather . . ."

"Master's seen it all before," interjected the man cryptically.

I stared at him in puzzlement. "Seen all what before?" I asked.

He looked very knowing. "Like mother, like daughter," he said meaningfully. "The master knows well enough what might have happened to Miss Feyella—same as happened to the mistress, seventeen years ago this very winter's month!"

I remembered what my mother-in-law had told me about the tragic end of Feyella's mother.

"But—surely not . . ." I began.

"Just such weather as this, it was," said the groom, who was obviously enjoying the situation. "Mistress rode out into the winter's night and told nobody of her going. We found her mare wandering on the moor next day, and her cloak at the top of Beacon Cliff two days later. Nobody ever did find the body of her. The sea creatures had that."

I shuddered and turned away from him in distaste. "Well, there's nothing for you here," I said. "And I suggest you join the others in the search."

"I'll be doing that, ma'am," he said wryly.

In the event, there was a clatter of hooves in the archway before the man had left the room. Three men arrived on horseback, all of them from Mapollion Grange. And one of them led a riderless white horse that I immediately recognised as Feyella's.

I went out to them.

"He was cropping grass on the moor, about three miles yonder, ma'am," said the man leading the white horse. "It do look as if he's been tethered, an' broke away like."

The reins were snapped into two parts. I felt suddenly as if I was standing at the brink of a newly dug grave. Feyella Mapollion had been a question mark in my life—indeed, it was quite possible that she had done me a very great deal of harm—but, for all that, she had exercised a curious attraction of which I had been deeply aware. If anything had happened to her, I knew that I would feel diminished, almost as if I had indeed lost a true friend.

The men were all watching me. I particularly sensed the

gaze of the groom who had first brought me the news. It was he who spoke next.

"Best take the news back to master, lads," he said heavily. "Then get on with the search."

"I think the police should be informed," I interjected.

"Don't you worry about that, ma'am," said one of the men. " 'Twas the first thing the master ordered us to do."

"This is the second time for the master, you see, ma'am," said another. "He's been through it all before, like."

* * *

"Why did Feyella's mother kill herself seventeen years ago?" I fired the question at Benedict, and saw it strike home.

I had left a message at the gatehouse that he was to come at once to me in the solar when he returned—and I had framed the request to sound like an order. He came straight to me, and it was from my lips that he heard of Feyella's disappearance. My question about her mother followed swiftly after, before he had time to collect his thoughts.

My husband looked confused and embarrassed—or so it seemed to me. This served to confirm the belief that I had assembled, in my mind, during the time that I had been waiting his return.

"I—I really have no idea," he replied. "Why do you ask that?"

Brushing aside his counterquestion, I persisted. "But, surely, you were a grown boy when it happened, and you and your family have known the Mapollions all your lives. This is a closed community—the gentry and the lower orders are tightly knit with each other. There can surely be nothing like a true secret in all this part of Cornwall. You are not trying to tell me that there was no speculation—that you have not the faintest idea of why Feyella's mother might have done herself to death?"

Excepting the night when we had had our terrible verbal encounter, I had never dared to address my husband in such a fearless manner—and he had been drunk on the previous occasion; now he was stone cold sober; and set-faced and shocked

179

with it. My words were striking home, and it was as if the overwhelming majesty and power of the Trevallions had never been.

"Well," he said hesitantly. "There were—rumours."

"I'm not surprised to hear it," I replied tartly. "What were these rumours, Benedict? Why did people say that Mrs Mapollion threw herself from—where was it they said?—Beacon Cliff?"

"There was some disagreement with the husband, I believe," replied Benedict. "There was some talk of—a lover."

"Was there now?" I said. "Who was the lover, according to rumour?"

He crossed over to the sideboard, where the tray of decanters and glasses stood like a row of sentries. His hand hovered over one of the cut-glass stoppers, paused for a while, then fell. He turned back to me—and there was a look of defeat in his lean face.

"A naval officer, so I heard. Stationed at Plymouth. The captain of a frigate there. It's possible that he abandoned Mrs Mapollion and that she killed herself in consequence."

"I see," I said. "From something Feyella once mentioned to me, I had a notion that it might have happened like that. Well, now, Benedict . . ."

There was a long silence. He did not meet my gaze.

"Do you think Feyella has killed herself, also?" I demanded.

His eyes flared widely as his head snapped up. To my surprise, there was genuine shock and astonishment in his expression.

"Kill herself?" he breathed. "Feyella? That's quite impossible."

"Why should it be so?" I demanded.

"You don't understand," he said. "Anyone who had known Feyella for any length of time would know that she would be quite incapable of such a thing."

"They may well have said the same for her poor mother," I responded wryly.

"But Mrs Mapollion had reason."

I took a deep breath. "It might be thought that Feyella had reason, also," I said quietly.

He looked at me narrowly. Like the mare's tails in the sky that predict a storm, the merest suspicion of folds appeared between his brows.

"What do you mean?" he asked.

"I mean you," I said. And when his eyes flared with shock, I went on: "No. Don't interrupt me, Benedict. This has to be said. You know as well as anyone that Feyella has been infatuated with you ever since she was a girl, and she has remained so. Your marriage to me has, if anything, only intensified her passion."

"I have never offered her the slightest encouragement," he said coldly.

"I believe you," I replied. "Indeed, you treated her on at least one occasion with the most incredible cruelty."

He turned from me and walked the length of the room. Once again, his passing gaze lingered upon the spirit decanters on the sideboard; but again he resisted the impulse to indulge. He stood with his back to me, looking out of the window; nor did he turn when he next addressed me.

"What are you trying to imply?" he asked.

"I think you have got to prepare yourself for the possibility that history has repeated itself and that Feyella has destroyed herself as her mother did before her," I said. "What's more, whether she killed herself for love of you, or not, the world is going to say that she did. You're going to have to learn to live with that, Benedict; whether here or in Jamaica; no matter where you go, you'll never be able to escape the whispers, the gibes, and the pointing fingers. It's already happening, Benedict. The very servants from Mapollion Grange already believe it, and showed it in their manner to me."

He did not flinch under the lash of my tongue, but remained with his back towards me, his hands loosely held by his sides, his fingers limp. When he turned, his face was drained of all emotion.

"Thank you, my dear," he said mildly. "If what you say is true, then I must indeed prepare myself for it, mustn't I?"

With that, he gave me a brief bow, and walked out of the room, leaving me staring after him. With every fibre of my being, I longed for the strength to call after him: to tell him that nothing had changed for me, but that I loved and supported him, no matter what; to beg him to lay his head on my breast and pour out his inner agonies for me to share.

I did none of those things. I merely watched him go.

When I think of the heartbreak I could have spared myself if I had declared my feelings then! But we who love are incredibly stupid: we see the light quite clearly, then seek to obscure it with evasions and fantasies of our own imagining.

The truth is that I dared not declare myself to Benedict, for fear of the rebuff that would surely have followed. I knew with a searing clarity that Feyella was no longer among the living, and I told myself that I knew the reason for her death. I did not for one minute suppose that I could bear to see my last faint hopes of happiness extinguished with any more fortitude than she had shown.

* * *

A day and a night passed, and Feyella Mapollion was not found—either living or dead. I was told that notices were posted throughout the duchy, announcing a reward of a hundred guineas for anyone giving information that would lead to the discovery of her whereabouts. Such a large sum, offered in a poverty-stricken area like Cornwall, at a time of the year when there was so little work, had the effect of turning almost the entire peasant population to the task of searching for the missing girl. From the walls of the castle, one could see them scouring the beaches and prodding the rock pools: dark, shuffling figures of men, women, and children, poorly clad against the biting winter wind.

On the afternoon of the second day, a sergeant of police came to Mallion and spent some time with Benedict. Afterwards, he requested to speak to me.

"Sergeant Menhenitt of the Truro Constabulary, ma'am." He was a shortish, lightly built man in his middle forties, dressed in a loud check caped coat. He had a most alarming squint, and I was immediately put at the disadvantage of not knowing which of his eyes was regarding me and which was looking over my shoulder.

The interview took place in the great hall. I took a seat by the fireplace and motioned the sergeant to make himself comfortable in a chair opposite, but he nervously declined. His nervousness was further revealed when he produced a notebook and pencil in trembling hands. I decided that he was overawed by his surroundings.

"Concerning Miss Mapollion," he began.

"She hasn't been found?" I asked. Everything about Sergeant Menhenitt—his squint, his nervousness, his ridiculous coat and general unattractiveness—conspired to give me confidence for the interview. I was able to pitch my voice in tones of unhurried calm, with the right note of gravity.

"Not as at midday, when I received a message from my headquarters, ma'am," he said.

"There is no chance that she may have left the district?" I said. "Taken a train to London, perhaps?"

"The young lady was wearing a black riding habit, ma'am," said the policeman. "It is not a costume that would pass unobserved in a railway train."

The promptness of this shrewd reply jolted me out of my complacency. There might be more to Sergeant Menhenitt, I thought, than first impressions promised.

"Then what do you think has happened to her?" I asked.

"What do you think has happened to her, ma'am?" he countered, with a suddenness that made me start. I searched his gaze, to see if he was staring into my face, or merely glancing idly in my direction. The eyes told me nothing.

"I—I've no idea," I stammered weakly.

"Mr Trevallion has formed certain opinions," said Sergeant Menhenitt, "that you no doubt share, ma'am."

My mind raced. What was he getting at? What had Benedict told him?

"I—I don't really know," I faltered. "I—I haven't given it very much thought."

"But you've discussed it with Mr Trevallion, ma'am?"

"Yes, I have. Yes." I felt a thin edge of panic entering my voice.

"At some length, or so I understand?"

"Yes." I was fencing in the dark, not having any idea of what Benedict had told this man—this suddenly alarming man.

"And you arrived at a conclusion, the both of you—or so I understand."

"Well, of course, we—speculated," I heard myself say in a whisper.

Sergeant Menhenitt nodded and wrote something in his notebook. I had been quite mistaken about him: his hands were not trembling.

"How would you describe your relations with Miss Mapollion?" he asked without looking up from his writing. "Would you describe them as cordial, perhaps, ma'am?"

"We—we were the best of friends," I said.

"*Were*, ma'am?" One eye was looking right at me now.

"I mean—we are very good friends," I corrected myself hastily.

"Ah, but you said *were*, ma'am. And that's very interesting, in view of the—what was the term you used?—*speculations*—you and Mr Trevallion had about the young lady's whereabouts, isn't it?"

"You're twisting my words," I cried. "You're trying to trap me!"

The eye that I was looking at suddenly slewed away and addressed itself to something over my shoulder.

"Trap you, ma'am? Now, why should you be thinking that?" asked Sergeant Menhenitt mildly.

Realising that I had made a fool of myself (how could I have thought, only a few brief minutes ago, that I should have command of the interview with this insignificant little man?), I took a deep breath before I spoke again.

"I'm sorry, Sergeant," I said. "That was a very silly remark. But, you see, this business of Feyella—Miss Mapollion's—disappearance has upset me very much."

"I don't wonder at it, ma'am," he replied. "And it's upset

Mr Trevallion too, as I could see. This would be on account of your—mutual speculations, wouldn't it?"

I avoided his gaze and looked down at my hands. "Yes," I said.

"And these speculations concerned certain possibilities regarding the explanation for Miss Mapollion's disappearance?"

I nodded. To my sudden horror, I found that my nether lip was trembling uncontrollably.

"And this didn't concern the possibility of her taking a train to London?"

I shook my head.

"Or anything like that at all?"

There was no need for me to make any reply. The truth was staring him in the face: the mouse was cornered. The cat's steely claws were out of the velvety pads. All he had to do was strike.

He struck.

"These speculations, then—what were they, ma'am?"

I was defeated, and I knew it. "We thought . . . we think . . . that she has made an end to herself," I whispered.

"Like her mother before her?" supplied Sergeant Menhenitt.

"Yes," I nodded.

The sergeant let out a sigh and moved nearer the fire. From the corner of my eye, I saw his lean fingers reach out and spread themselves in front of the warmth. I waited for his next question, fearful of what it might be.

"So then, ma'am," he said, at length. "We come to the truth at last. And yet, you were at first reluctant to give me your opinion. Said you had no idea of what might have happened to Miss Mapollion. Now—why did you say that? I wonder."

I had a good reply for that—or so I thought. "Miss Mapollion was my friend," I replied with some heat. "My private opinions are one thing, but to bandy scandal about a friend is quite another thing!"

Too late, I saw that I had blundered. Menhenitt turned to face me, and it almost seemed that both his eyes were straight upon me now, and looking into my brain.

"Scandal?" he exclaimed. "Now, who spoke of scandal, ma'am? Concerning friendship, wouldn't it be the best duty of a friend to give every aid to those who're concerned with finding the missing lady? But, as to scandal—well, that's another matter entirely, isn't it? What kind of scandal had you in mind?"

Again, I had this helpless sense of being jockeyed into a corner.

"Just—scandal," I faltered weakly.

"Such as might be connected with the reason for Miss Mapollion making an end to herself—in your opinion?"

I nodded. My nether lip had begun its trembling again.

"Like as in the case of the lady's mother?" he prompted.

"Perhaps," I whispered.

"Concerning a man, perhaps?"

Both the eyes were upon me again. I glanced around, wildly, as if some way of escape might suddenly open up for me, but there was none: just the two of us—the lady of Mallion and the inquisitor from Truro—in that empty, echoing hall.

"There are other reasons for a woman to kill herself," I said, with even less conviction that I felt.

"But not in the case of Miss Mapollion, perhaps?" It was a question, and I could not bring myself to answer it either way, but stared into the fire and said nothing. Sergeant Menhenitt could not possibly be in any doubt about my opinion.

"Well, ma'am," he said. "I'm greatly obliged for your time. What you've told me has cleared my mind somewhat over several points. I'll take my leave now."

I walked across the hall with him, towards the great doors. At the sound of our footsteps, the dark-clad figure of Prendergast appeared from the corridor leading to the servants' quarters. He glided ahead of us and opened the doors. The outside air struck chill, and I shivered despite my fur wrap.

Sergeant Menhenitt paused. "Thank you for your help, ma'am."

One eye wavered over my shoulder; the other may have been watching me very closely.

"If anything else occurs to you, ma'am," he went on, "anything concerning your past acquaintance with the lady that you might think useful to our search, I'd be grateful if you'd communicate it to my headquarters in Truro."

"Certainly, Sergeant," I said. And I offered him my hand. "I—I hope you find her."

"I think I can promise we shall do that, ma'am," he said. Then he was gone.

Prendergast shut the doors. As I was walking back down the hall, he called after me.

"A bad business, Mrs Trevallion. They're no further to finding her then?"

"No," I said. Then I had a thought. "Prendergast, have you any idea where my husband is at this moment?"

The man's close-set eyes looked shifty, and he ventured the opinion that Benedict might be in the library, which lay beyond the solar. It was a room I seldom entered, being filled from floor to ceiling with shelves of books that smelt of ancient mildew and seemed mostly to be printed in Latin, a language in which I have no competence. Benedict was there. He was sitting at a table in the chill, fireless room with a thick sheaf of papers before him. He looked up as I entered.

"The police sergeant from Truro has just left," I said.

Benedict nodded. "I doubt whether that fellow will make any progress in finding her," he said. "We are certainly very badly served in our local constabulary."

I had a sudden pang of new unease. "You didn't find Sergeant Menhenitt very impressive?" I asked. "He didn't strike you as being very astute?"

Benedict stared at me blankly. "He did not," he said. "The fellow was a bundle of nerves and incompetence. Scarcely asked me anything at all. Why—he hadn't even got my name right: insisted on calling me Tregannon. He spoke to you, did he? Did he ask you any questions?"

"A few," I said.

He gave a brief, mirthless laugh. "Harking back to your remarks after the news of Feyella's disappearance," he said. "Whether or not the locals think she killed herself for hopeless love of me, they'll not pass on their opinions to a policeman from Truro—a foreigner. That much embarrassment I shall be spared. And it isn't likely to occur to a cretin like Menhenitt."

Fool, I said to myself. Fool . . .

Don't you see that he *has* found out? He tricked you, as he tricked me. And it was me he goaded and cajoled into confirming the impressions that his uncanny, inquisitor's mind must have picked up around the countryside.

* * *

I was filled with a sense of being oppressed by my surroundings: even the vast bulk of Mallion, with its spacious interiors, seemed to be closing in on me and pressing me down. With barely an hour before the winter's night fell, and yearning for the outdoors, I called across the yard for the terrier Pinkie, and took the winding stone stair at the corner of the courtyard that led down to the beach. Pinkie's eager, rushing footfalls came down the steps behind me as I emerged from the arched doorway on to the yielding sand, and saw the breathless sweep of the ever-shifting grey sea before me.

The roar of the breakers was like a constant drum-roll; it dinned in my overwrought brain and seemed to soothe my jangling nerves. I walked closer to the hissing surf, where the black sea kelp lay in long streaks down the shingle. Now, the boisterous wavecrests were higher than me as they came rolling in, and I could only see the rocky tip of Wreckers' Isle above the curling breakers; the fine spray soon covered my face and cloak with its shimmering droplets.

I called to Pinkie, but he had already found himself some other sport at the top of the beach, where the dry bracken, clinging to the foundations of the castle wall, must still have been carrying the ancient scents of summer's excitement for the little dog.

The sun was already dying behind the far headland, and I did not plan to go far. It was bitterly cold, but I was well wrapped-up in my furs and my cosseting tweeds, and the closeness of wild nature was blessedly exhilarating—and at the same time soothing.

It was then that I saw—him.

He appeared as a dark shape looming out of the sandhills. His ragged coattails fluttered about him like the wings of a bat. A bat!—the very word made me almost turn and run. He came towards me, the sinking sun behind him, turning him into a featureless creature out of a nightmare. I had made up my mind to retreat from the apparition, but, to my horror, I realised that, by going so close to the water's edge, I had placed myself farther from the castle wall than he was. My way of escape was blocked. The only retreat lay in the wide waste of the darkening beach—and to venture there was out of the question.

I waited as he approached me: nor did I have to wait long.

"You be out on another o' your lonely walks again, ma'am."

I recognised the face and figure even as the wheedling voice came to me in all its hateful familiarity. It was the man Pollitt.

"Be searching for your friend, I shouldn't wonder," he said. "There be many poor folks a-searching for Miss Mapollion this day. A hundred fine guineas, it ain't to be sneezed at, nor it ain't . . ." He was close to me now, and the mouth was bent in the familiar sneering grin. He made to tap my forearm, to reinforce his remark, but I withdrew it hastily, ". . . with a hundred fine guineas, the likes o' me and my missus could live out the rest of our lives in a manner which we've never dreamed of."

"Then I would advise you to carry on with your search," I replied coldly, making to brush past him. "I wish you a good evening."

He let me go readily enough, and, as I passed him, he uttered a remark that struck upon my ear but did not register properly till I had walked several paces. I stopped, turned and faced him again.

"What did you say?" I demanded.

"I said, 'twould be a waste of time, ma'am—to look along the seashore for your friend Miss Mapollion," he replied. "That was what I said, ma'am, and that I'll stand by afore any court in the realm."

"What do you mean?" I cried.

He laughed. "There be many who'd like the answer to that, ma'am. And I can't think of any person—be they genteel, or common folk such as me—who it wouldn't be a pleasure to give the answer to but you, ma'am." He took a step closer and laid a hand on my arm. This time I was too bemused to resist him. "Are you carrying any money with you this day, ma'am?" he hissed close by my ear.

I shook my head. "No," I whispered. "Nor anything of value."

" 'Tis a pity," he said, releasing my arm. "I tell you, ma'am, you'll have to get into the habit of carrying a few guineas with you when you walk abroad, in case you should happen across me."

"I will not be threatened by you, nor will I be blackmailed by you any more," I cried. "If you have something to tell me, out with it. If not, let's have an end to your insinuations!"

"Hoity-toity!" he laughed. "That be a fine spirit, a right and proper spirit it be for a fine lady of a fine castle . . ." his voice took a turn, and a grating note of menace entered it . . . "But the gentlefolk will have to learn to pay for their pleasures, ma'am. You be wanting news of your friend from Pollitt— then you have to be ready to slip a few guineas into Pollitt's pocket."

"I told you I have no money with me," I said.

"Next time we meet, you'll bring money," he said blandly.

"Perhaps," I said hesitantly.

"Oh, you will, my fine lady," he said. "You will, 'cos you be confused in your mind concerning this and that, and you have a notion that Pollitt be the feller to straighten out your mind on a few things. Things concerning—*him you're married to, for a start!*"

"What do you know?" I cried. "For God's sake stop playing cat-and-mouse with me. You'll be paid. I'll see that you have money."

Again his manner changed. Like a trader who has struck a bargain in the market place, he became all businesslike and incisive.

"Concerning the night o' Miss Mapollion's disappearance . . ." he began, with a quick look over his shoulder, as if spying for eavesdroppers.

"Yes?" I said.

"Concerning that night," he went on, "the lady in question rode out of her home right soon after returning there from the castle."

"I know that," I said. "Everyone knows that. She had dinner, that night, with my husband and me."

"And came back!"

"*What?*"

"Back to Mallion," he said. "She rode out and back to the castle, and tethered her horse in the drive there, out of earshot o' the servants and such as she didn't want to hear her. It were two o'clock of a starlit morning, you see, ma'am, and not such an hour as ladies go a-visiting as a rule. She wasn't going a-visiting of you yourself, ma'am, I take it?"

"No," I replied dully.

"Well, there you are," he said. "There it be. The lady came back to the castle in dead o' night to see somebody, and she tethered her horse in the drive. Come the morning and the horse tugged and broke his rein and made off on his own devices."

"How do you know this?" I demanded.

"I saw it all," he replied simply. "I made it my business."

"How do I know you're not lying?"

He did not answer for a while: then he said: "You know I'm not lying."

"And you've told no one else?"

"I know," said Pollitt. "The missus knows. That be all. No one else shall know but you. But it'll cost you, lady. Like I said, the gentry will have to learn, come sooner or later, to pay for their pleasures. That feller you be married to—*he'll* have to learn to pay."

I shuddered at his taunt, and said: "But you haven't told me all. You implied that you knew where Feyella Mapollion has gone. Where, then, is she?"

Again his manner changed, and he reverted to the sneering,

evasive creature of before. He tapped the side of his nose and grinned.

"Next time," he said. "Mark that you be carrying money with you next time you be walking abroad, my lady. As much as you be able to lay your pretty hands on. Money or valuables. You'll have plenty o' them, I shouldn't wonder."

"But . . ." I began.

He turned and walked away; back towards the sandhills from where he had come; the low-cast sun turned him, once more, into an insubstantial creature of menace and shadow.

"What of the rest?" I called after him in anguish. "You must tell me the rest of it now!"

The dark shape reached the top of the sandhills, and the chill wind of the new night stirred the ragged coattails. He raised his arms, and the likeness to a bat was hideously increased.

"We'll speak o' that next time," he called out to me across the space between. "You'll bring money or valuables, for by then you'll know well enough, my lady, what I mean when I say that the gentry must pay for their pleasures!"

And then, he added: *"Look in the old garden—but don't you let any of 'em see you looking!"*

* * *

The moon had come out from behind the scudding clouds when I came to the old garden. It was past midnight and the last light had died in the windows of the castle—all save the dim glow in the narrow window in the northwest tower, where, I knew, Mayana kept solitary vigil over her sick child: I knew this because I had watched from my window till I was sure that Mallion and all within its walls were still for the night.

I had not dared to bring a lamp, but the full moon made it all as bright as day. Every evergreen leaf, each blade of grass and dead flowerhead, was jewelled with frost.

Somewhere beyond the swaying cypresses, an owl hooted. I gave a start and stood still, till my heart had ceased its pounding.

With only an instinct to guide me, and a nameless dread to

prod me on, I made a circuit of the garden; past the still statuary and the looped strands of the naked rose bushes; under the dark caverns of yew hedge.

I found what I was seeking in a hidden spot near the path leading down to the steps—a place not far from where (how long ago it seemed) I had found the ruined copy of *David Copperfield.*

There, by an old wall, and beneath a bust of a grinning satyr, I was looking down at a piece of ground, six feet long and two feet wide; with freshly dug sods that had been relaid and roughly scattered with earth.

More than enough space for a girl whose violet-blue eyes would mock no more.

CHAPTER 6

From my window—the window of the lovely, lonely bed-chamber—I could see the tips of the dark cypresses swaying above the ivy-covered wall of the old garden; and it struck me then, as it often has, how fitting that cypresses are so often planted in cemeteries. And now the old garden, my beloved garden, had indeed become an unconsecrated resting place for the unquiet spirit of Feyella Mapollion. I shuddered at the thought, and dragged my sleepless eyes away from the scene.

It was morning, and I still had not come to terms with the hideous thoughts and events that crowded in my mind. It had to be done: I had to make some decisions before I took any action—for to rush blindly into an unconsidered move might spell disaster. Think. Reflect and consider . . .

I calmed myself as best I could: stooped and rearranged the half-burnt logs in the fireplace till they blossomed again into warming flame. Then, wrapping my dressing gown snugly about my shoulders, I settled down in an armchair by the fire and began to put my thoughts in some sort of sensible order.

I instinctively shied away from the first and most dreadful fact: that Feyella was not only dead, but that someone had seen fit secretly to bury her within the walls of Castle Mallion;

but, despite the horror of it, I clung on to the thought, biting the knuckle of my forefinger till it pained intolerably.

Someone had buried her. Then, who?

Benedict . . .

Benedict certainly, with or without assistance from some other person or persons.

Mayana? The Prendergasts?

Feyella had come here, secretly, that night. The man Pollitt had seen her arrive (there was not the slightest reason to disbelieve him—not now), and had probably witnessed her secret internment.

Why had she come?

To see Benedict.

And why?

There was a whole world of reasons, some of them beyond my imagining. As a woman, I could easily grasp the most likely: she had come, in desperation, for the last time, to throw herself at his feet and beg him to make good his youthful promise to her.

(How had it gone? I took my mind back to the October day when I had first seen them together in the courtyard of Mallion.) *"You are promised to me . . . I've saved myself for you, Benedict Trevallion . . . I chose you before Piers and Saul . . ."*

That was it: driven to despair by his heartless treatment of her at the dinner table that awful night, when he had played cat-and-mouse with her in his drunken ill humor, she had come back: the hurts that she had suffered—as a woman in love, with the burden of an unfulfilled childish infatuation bearing down upon her and driving her crazed—had made her so that she no longer cared for her pride, for her self-respect, for anything. She had come to prostrate herself before the only man in her world—perhaps with no hope that her shamelessness would touch at his heart, but merely to prove to him, once and for all, that there was no limit, no plumbing the depths of her adoration.

That done—the debasement over—what then?

How did she kill herself? Was it done before the mocking eyes of the man she knew that she could never have?

Had she wiped the tipsy mirth from his lips by drinking poison in front of him—or had his brandy-inflamed eyes been shocked to sanity by the sight of her taking a knife to herself? Had her lifeblood flowed thickly in his room in the northeast tower? Or had she hurled herself from the tower window, to perish on the granite flags of the courtyard far below?

By whatever means, she had done for herself—for hopeless love of a man—just as her poor, star-crossed mother had done seventeen years before. Only, in Feyella's case, there had been no kindly sea to bear away her corpse and hide it decently within its wide fastness.

Benedict had seen to the hiding place . . .

Why had he done that? Why the dark and unholy internment in the silent garden under the cypresses?

To avoid the scandal that would surely follow the news that the newly married master of Castle Mallion had been the cause of a young girl taking her own life? Perhaps, even—and the thought of it made my eyes prickle with new tears—he had the wish to save me from hurt and anguish. I dwelt on that for some time, and found a grain of comfort there.

The logs in the fireplace were collapsing into grey ash when I came to the end of my reflections. I decided that I had found the answer—and that my best course was to do nothing, say nothing, for the time being.

So—by dwelling on the thoughts that are the most comforting to us, and by shutting out those that are unbearable to the mind and the heart—do we utterly deceive ourselves.

* * *

I had no premonition of the next horror that was to descend upon me; though if I had not been sitting with my back to the solar window, with its view across the courtyard to the gateway arch, I might have seen its bearer come into the castle.

The first I knew of it was when the maid tapped on the

solar door, curtsied and said: "There's a young lass says her must see you, ma'am."

"Who is it?" I asked.

The maid partly closed the door and whispered across to me: "Don't know her name, ma'am, but I mind her do come from Mapollion Grange, though she weren't raised in these parts. Yes, I mind her do work at the Grange."

"Show her in, please," I said, puzzled.

The newcomer was a child of about fifteen, wide-eyed and nervous, looking about her in frightened awe. She was dressed in a worn cloak over a dark dress such as indoor servants wear, and she was decently shod.

"Come over by the fire and warm yourself," I said. "You look half frozen to death." And when she hesitated, "Don't be frightened, girl, I won't bite you. What's your name?"

"Janey, ma'am. Janey Maddern."

"And you work at the Grange?"

"Used to work at the Grange, ma'am." The girl's eyes filled with tears and her lip trembled. "The housekeeper did dismiss me this morning. Said there be no work for me any longer at the Grange, seeing as how the young mistress, Miss Feyella . . ."

I stared at her. "Miss Feyella—yes? What of Miss Feyella?"

The girl was crying uncontrollably now, her thin shoulders shaking with the helplessness of her emotion. I took her arm and led her to a stool by the fire.

"Come now, Janey," I said. "Have a good cry, then tell me all about it. You've been dismissed, you say? What were your tasks at the Grange?"

"I—I acted as lady's maid for Miss Feyella, ma'am," she sobbed. "Miss Feyella did once have a real lady's maid, but she went back to France. Then—then Miss Feyella said she'd give me a try, and I did try very hard and was getting along nicely, ma'am . . ." Her words were lost in another flood of tears. I understood, now, what had happened.

"And now Miss Feyella's . . . disappeared . . . the housekeeper has decided to dismiss you," I said.

"Yes, ma'am," she sniffed. "And I've nowhere to go."

There was all the tragedy of the working poor in that child: without a place, she was now completely destitute, with only the puny strength of her frail body against the whole, frightening world. I had seen enough of utter destitution during my brief adventure in London to know something of what might lie ahead for little Janey Maddern.

"So you came to me," I said. "Now, why did you do that, Janey?"

"Why, ma'am, because of the letter," she said.

"The letter?" Without any further prompting, I gave a shudder. "What letter?"

She was fumbling in a small black reticule that hung from her wrist. A moment later, her trembling hand held out a sealed letter to me.

"What's this, Janey?" I asked.

"Miss Feyella did tell me to give this to you, ma'am. She did give it to me on that night—that night she rode out. Woke me up, she did, and her all in her riding habit. 'Take this to the young Mrs Trevallion, Janey,' she did tell me. 'And mind you give it to no one else, nor mention about it to a soul. No hurry to deliver it, Janey,' said she, 'the important thing is for you to give it into the hand of Mrs Benedict Trevallion yourself.' So I came as soon as I could, ma'am."

I broke the seal of the letter and opened it up. There was a full page, written in a tight, backward-sloping script. There was no address and no superscription. The first line leapt out of the page at me in an assault that was a physical shock. I reached out and placed a hand on the fireplace wall for support.

"Ma'am—are you all right?" asked the girl, frightened.

"Yes, I'm all right. It's nothing" . . . I had to get rid of the girl for a while . . . "Janey, would you like to go along to the kitchen and tell them from me to give you a warm drink and something to eat? Later, I'll send for you again."

"Yes, ma'am. Thank you, ma'am."

"And Janey—you'll remember Miss Feyella's instructions," I added. "Not a word of this to anyone, and that includes anyone here at Mallion."

"Never fear, ma'am. Miss Feyella were always very kind to me, and I wouldn't disobey her word for all the world."

She bobbed a curtsey and went out. I waited till the clatter of her footsteps died away at the end of the corridor, then I reopened the piece of paper in my hand—and began to read past the first, dreadful line, and onwards, with ever-mounting horror.

I shall be dead when you get this. I despise and detest you, but I'm content that misery enough will have come your way by the time you read this letter. The letter is just to turn the knife in the wound, my dear!

As to the man you married, I guessed from the first that he must have killed that swinish brother of his—or had it arranged, for murder is cheap in Jamaica. Your father was with him, so he had to be killed too.

As I told you before, Benedict would have done anything to repay Saul's treatment of him, and to get Mallion for his own. He loves Mallion beyond all belief. I think he's incapable of any other kind of love.

You wonder why he married you? I'll tell you. He married you for the same reason he bundled you out of Jamaica so smartly—to prevent you from prying too deeply into the circumstances of your father's death. He intended that you should never go back to Jamaica —and as his wife, he could enforce his wish. Did you once *really* think he married you for love? You fool! I could have told you he's incapable of it!

As soon as I heard that your marriage was an empty charade and he was sleeping in the northeast tower, I knew that I had guessed right. You poor little dupe. One could almost find it in one's heart to feel sorry for you.

Do you think I blame Benedict for what he did? I do not. I applaud him for snatching what he wanted with both hands. That is my way—to take and never count the cost.

The pity is that all I want is Benedict. And the

more I call to him, the more he reviles me. I can bear it no longer.

It is past midnight. I have drunk a very great deal of my father's brandy and I have purloined one of his double-barrelled pistols. I shall give this letter to my maid—and then I shall ride to Mallion and put a bullet in the heart of the man who has rejected and destroyed me. Then I shall use the second bullet on myself.

Now you know the answer to the questions that must have puzzled you. I hope you will have a long and thoroughly wretched widowhood in which to turn them over in your mind.

Farewell, my dear,
Feyella.

P.S. If there was ever the slightest doubt in your mind, the black strumpet has been his mistress for years, and the brat is his son by her. When you send them packing, you will have repaid the slight to us both. F-

I reread the dreadful letter time and again, till the words became a meaningless blur on the page and my mind swam.

Gradually, the full import of Feyella's last message came through to me, and I panicked. Alone in that silent room, I fought against my mounting terror—and quenched it.

It must have been an hour later—and the winter shadows were gathering in the courtyard outside—that I got to my feet and examined my face in a mirror on the wall.

In that dreadful hour, I had grown older inside, and, to my eyes, it showed in my face. Any shred of youthful innocence that I might have brought with me to Mallion had been stripped away from me. Joanna Trevallion, née Goodacre, was now a woman. A woman forged in fire and anguish.

I rang the bell for attention, and marvelled at the calm and crisp tones in which I instructed the maid to have the girl Janey Maddern brought to me again.

"Yes, ma'am?" Janey stared at me, wide-eyed. Did she see, I wondered, that I was quite a different person from the one to whom she had given the letter all those ages ago?

"Do you have your things with you, child?" I asked.

"I—I left my box at the lodge at the Grange," she said. "They said they'd keep it till I send for it when—if I get another place ma'am . . ." here she burst into tears, as the hopelessness of her situation came back to her again.

"I'll have a coachman drive over there and pick it up, Janey," I said. "For you're going to come and work for me. If you'd like to, that is."

I silenced the child's tearful thanks, with an admonition: a warning delivered by the new Joanna Trevallion; the cool calculating woman of the world who knew how to protect her own . . .

"You shall be my lady's maid, Janey, and you must serve me as faithfully as you served Miss Feyella. And one thing you must do is to forget that letter you brought to me. Put it right out of your mind. Pretend to yourself that it never happened, do you understand?"

* * *

The next dream in the awful Quadrille of Death came upon me that night, during the brief, fitful sleep that I snatched in the unearthly hours between midnight and cockcrow.

As before, I was on a shoreline, but it was a white-sanded and tropic strand—and not the wintry beach below the walls of Mallion. A gentle night wind sighed in the great curved palms behind me, and the shifting water was bright with the phosphorescence of a million tiny sea creatures. A full moon rode the cloudless sky, and the very stars of the Milky Way were matched by the winking lights of houses that studded the mountain slope behind the palms. I was, I knew, back in Jamaica—and not far from my old home at Roswithiel.

With no premonition of horror, with no fear in my heart, I kicked off my shoes and set off to walk along the beach, whose smooth sand was still warm from the previous day's sun.

Then I heard—*them* . . .

They came out of the palms ahead of me and turned on to

the beach, skirting close to the spent wavelets: two horses and riders.

The horses were blacks, and the riders were indistinct against the sky. They came on at a plunging canter. And they were coming straight at me.

I stood my ground for a few instants that spanned the compass of an eternity; and in that time, the riders' faces were turned towards the moonlight so that I recognised their features quite clearly. I could see that they were shouting—mouths agape and faces grotesquely twisted with the effort—though no sound of it reached my ears.

There was not the strength in me to run. I simply fell on the spot and buried my head in my arms so that I should not see them when they rode over me.

When the first hoof was planted in my shrinking back, I woke up screaming, with the vision of their faces still clearly set in front of my waking eyes: the faces of the two riders—my dead father and Saul Trevallion.

* * *

Next morning, I ransacked my drawer and laid out the expensive presents that Benedict had bought for me in London at the time of our short courtship: they amounted to an amethyst brooch and earrings to match, a jade signet ring engraved with my new initials, a double string of pearls, a bracelet of enamel set with sapphires and diamonds, and a very regal-looking tiara in silver filigree and pearls. There was also the garnet and diamond ring he had given me for Christmas. I had no money save a handful of loose change lying at the bottom of the drawer.

I weighed the Christmas present ring in my hand and decided that it would suit my purpose best; wrapping it in tissue, I hid it away in the inside pocket of my warm tweed cape.

My next move would be to find Pollitt and—bribing him with the ring—get him to tell me what else he knew about the strange and frightening man I had married. That the wretch had more information to sell—and at a high price—was obvious from the fact that he scorned to claim the reward of a hundred guineas. I only hoped that I had the nerve to bear the sort of revelations I might be buying with Benedict's Christmas present; and I had the sense to realise that, being already in the hands of a blackmailer, I should only be able to buy his confidence and his continued silence while my jewels lasted. Beyond that, I did not dare to look.

I passed the days that followed in a state of limbo: half alive and divorced from the reality of my surroundings. I suppose I ate some meals, alone and in my room, but I have no recollection of them. I went about my usual, slight activities in and around the castle—even visiting my mother-in-law on one occasion—as if nothing had happened; I even said good morning to Benedict when we passed in the courtyard.

Every evening, I walked down to the beach below the castle walls, down by the sea edge, and waited there for as long as I dared, till the wintry night closed in about me; hand clutching the screw of paper inside the pocket of my cloak—waiting, waiting for my informant to come.

And so the days went by.

I visited my mother-in-law because one of the maids told me she was poorly and in bed. I found her much changed: a grey-faced ghost lying in damask sheets, with only the deep-blue Trevallion eyes alive and vital still. In a voice that sounded like the distant rustle of dry leaves, she told me to sit down beside her and give her all the latest news. There being no topic of interest except Feyella's disappearance, I informed her that, despite continued searchings, no one seemed to have come up with any news of her whereabouts. Gloomily, the old woman gave it as her opinion that Feyella was dead and gone, never to be seen again—like her mother. With unconscious irony she added that she was confounded if she could think of a man in the district with enough about him to drive even a silly flibbertigibbet like Feyella to suicide. But there was a man behind it somewhere, she assured me. There had to be a man behind it. She had been crazy for men—why, she had even set her cap, once, on Piers.

Which brought us back to Piers, as ever. I sat and let my thoughts wander, while she rambled on about her dead son.

The windows of Mrs Trevallion's bedroom were curtained against the thin winter sunlight. I had never entered the room before, and, looking about me, I was intrigued to see that there was a picture over the fireplace that appeared to be a smaller version of Piers Trevallion's portrait that I had first seen all those years ago at Roswithiel. I broke in on my mother-in-law's monologue, and she was only too delighted to inform me that this was so, commanding me to throw wide the curtains and feast my gaze upon her beautiful dead son.

With a stab of emotion, I saw that my memory had not been at fault. Piers Trevallion was everything I had remembered of him: he was the gay and handsome hussar, with eyes that were full of some private merriment; he was a livelier and less complicated Benedict; Benedict without the shadows. I sighed—and redrew the curtains.

That night, the wretch Pollitt came to find me on the shore.

* * *

"Looking for me, fine lady?" He was openly sneering now.

"I've brought you—this," I said, holding out the unwrapped screw of tissue, to reveal the ring. The diamonds glinted in the light of the low-cast sun.

"Very pretty. I'll have it."

He reached out to take the ring, but I withdrew my hand and put it behind my back.

"You'll earn it, Pollitt," I said, with more firmness of resolve than I felt. After all, he was a big and powerful man, who could quite easily wrest the ring from me; and, if I called out, what explanation would I give to the servants from the castle who came running to my rescue?

"Reckon I've already earned it," he grinned at me, head on one side. "Did you look where I did tell you? Now, I'll bet that you did, ma'am."

"Yes, I did," I whispered.

"So," he said. "And now you know, just like me, what happened to Miss Feyella. Just the two of us know it—and no one else. No one, that is, save them as laid her there.

And they'll keep their mouths shut about it, never you fear. Heh!"

I took a deep breath, and: "Who were they—the ones who buried her?" I asked.

"'Twas him you married . . ."

"Yes—who else?"

"Prendergast and his missus. Prendergast it was as dug the hole."

I exhaled a shuddering breath: now I knew the answers to many more tortuous questions that had haunted my nights.

"Anyone else?" I demanded.

"There was another party, but it was too dark to make out for sure who it might have been. Maybe it was the nigger woman. Yes, I be pretty sure it was her."

"I want you to tell me something else," I said. "And then I'll give you the ring."

"What's its value?" demanded Pollitt. "You'll not forget that I've only to open my mouth and there's a hundred pounds for the asking that'll keep me and my missus in style for the rest of our born days?"

"The ring must be worth at least that amount," I assured him. "And there'll be more for you, if you continue to do as I say."

He grinned, showing blackened teeth. "What do you want to know, ma'am?"

An incoming wave slapped against one of the black rocks in the shallows and sent droplets of icy spray over our heads and upon us. I shuddered and backed away up the beach. The walls of Mallion looked down, and there was no one in the eyeless windows that loomed above. It was doubtful if anyone up there could have picked out our two small figures on the dark shore.

"You'll remember the first time we met . . ." I began.

"Aye! I remember it well, ma'am."

"You told me—you called after me," I said, "words to the effect that you had evidence that could send my husband . . ."

"Ah!" There was a note of savage triumph in his voice.

205

"I thought to myself 'twould not be long afore we were discussing that, ma'am. Dang me if I didn't!"

"Tell me about that," I demanded. "For that, I will give you the ring here and now. And more to follow."

Silence. Had he been bluffing? I asked myself. Was he still bluffing?

And then, he said: " 'Twas a girl. My girl."

"Your girl?"

"We had a daughter," he said. "I say 'had,' though the good Lord knows she never was much of a thing—a poor, simple-minded creature as didn't know God's ways from the devil's ways. She went to work at the castle."

"Yes?" I said, with a premonition of horror mounting in my mind.

"She wasn't there for long," he said. "No more than a month. I mind it well, the day that Prendergast brought her home in a carriage. That black-hearted devil you're wed to, he'd been at our Lucy: been trying to work his evil will on the poor mindless little creature of God."

I heard someone cry out, and realised it was me. The night wind plucked the sound from my lips and away from the direction of the castle. I clasped my hands against my mouth and kept them there, staring hard at the man before me; willing him to pour out the rest of the horror so that I should hear the worst and get it over with; silently entreating him to say no more.

"We never did right know what had happened to her," he went on. "But that child was now nothing more than a poor husk of a human creature. She was never the same again: just lay huddled in a dark corner like a plant that's been cut off at the roots and must surely die. She did survive the next hard winter, but a cough came upon her, and a damp spring did carry her off. She lies buried in a sack in the churchyard for we couldn't afford the price of a box."

"And you're telling me that *my husband* did—that?" I breathed.

"Ask Prendergast," he replied. "Prendergast it was who brought her home and told me that your man had come upon

206

her while she was alone, and that only her screams had saved her from God knows what; brought Prendergast and his missus running, and they had to drag him from her the way you'd drag a fox off a chicken."

"And when—when was this?" I asked numbly.

"I mind 'twas the year that the war ended," he said. "That fine Mr Piers—the only good apple out of a rotten bushel if you do ask my opinion—was dead after the Great Charge. On the summer that our wronged child was laid to rest, your man and Mr Saul—another black dog if there ever was one— went off to Jamaicy."

My mind was in a whirl, utterly confused. "But, this is monstrous and appalling!" I cried. "Didn't you report this outrage to the magistrates or someone? Your child was ill used —don't tell me you did nothing about it?"

On that wind-swept seashore, by the dying light of the winter's sun, I learned a hard lesson about human degradation; about how people can be coarsened and brutalised by oppression and grinding poverty, till they are capable of selling everything—even their children's very flesh—to provide the means to struggle on through the wretched, crooked path down to paupers' graves.

"Who'd have believed us, me and my missus?" he demanded. "Oh, I know full well as how I told you that I could send that man o' yours to the gallows—but 'twere but an idle boast. What notice would any magistrate take o' the likes of us against the Trevallions? For poaching a rabbit, my two brothers was transported to Australia for life. My missus was but six when she saw her own mother hanged at Bodmin for taking a pair of shoes—and her with a babbie at her breast."

"So you did nothing?"

"We took the money and kept our peace."

"Money?" I cried. "Do you mean to say that my husband offered you money, to buy your silence?"

He nodded. "I mind that Prendergast brought half a guinea when he came home with the girl," he said. "There's been a florin or two for the asking up at the castle ever since. Only— the last time we went to ask, your man laid about him with a whip. I reckon he thinks that he's paid off all he need for the life of a half-wit child."

I gave him the ring: pressed it into his hand with thankfulness; glad to rid myself of the taint of the loathesome gift.

"Thanks, ma'am," he chuckled. "Never you fear, Pollitt ain't the one to spoil everything by blabbing his mouth around the countryside. You be a friend to Pollitt, ma'am, and Pollitt be a friend to you and yours. Not a one to bear a grudge ain't Pollitt. Heh!"

But I had already left him; running away towards the dark bulk of Mallion, to seek out the privacy and silence of my own room; away from the degradation and the horror. His final words faded and were lost to me in the wild singing of the wind, the bass crash of the waves on the shore, and the frenzied beating of my own anguished heart.

* * *

There was the sound of horses in the courtyard before dawn, much coming-and-going and the murmur of voices. I guessed —rightly as it turned out—that little Jackie had had another relapse and that Dr Vyner had been sent for in a hurry.

I was dressed, and thoroughly composed in my mind when the doctor came out of the door of the northwest tower followed by Mayana. I waited, looking away from them and tapping my foot with feigned impatience, while he mimed to the deaf-mute some last-minute instructions about the care of her child. Inside, I was ice-calm. The new and calculating Joanna Trevallion had a plan to ensnare the susceptible medical practitioner and bind him to her aid in her time of dreadful need.

I only hoped that my nerve—and my scruples—would not fail me at that last moment.

"Good morning to you, ma'am." Robert Vyner came towards me, bag in hand and raising his hat. He had returned to the awkwardness of manner that I had noticed in him at our first meeting, and when I turned to meet his gaze, he dropped his eyes in embarrassment.

"How are you, Doctor?" I said coolly.

"Well enough, ma'am. And I hope I see you in good health. We—we have suffered a little anxiety for the little boy. Nothing much—a slight haemorrhage, nowhere near so grave as the last time—but dangerous in his weak state. He's now resting comfortably."

"I'm glad to hear it," I said. "And very glad to see you, Doctor. Come into the solar and have a cup of coffee."

The healthy skin of his face took on an even ruddier hue. "Er—I'm sorry to have to refuse your kind hospitality, ma'am . . ."

The new Mrs Trevallion told herself she was having none of that . . .

"I have need of you, Doctor!" I snapped, and turned on my heel. It was with a small feeling of triumph that I heard him walking after me.

A maid was laying coffee for two on a side table in the solar. I waited till she had gone before I stooped to pour out. Robert Vyner stood before the fire, shifting uneasily from one foot to the other.

"Do you take sugar?"

"A little, ma'am."

As I handed him the cup and saucer, he cleared his throat and said awkwardly: "Er—how can I be of service to you, Mrs Trevallion?"

"I should like you to return my handkerchief, Doctor!" I said abruptly.

The cup and saucer fell to the parquet and smashed to smithereens. My skirts were splashed by the hot fluid, and Robert Vyner was falling to his knees as the last skittering fragment came to a halt against the far skirting board.

"Leave the pieces," I commanded him. "A servant can pick them up later. Get to your feet, Doctor."

He obeyed me—slowly. His honest grey eyes were like those of a whipped dog, and my heart turned over with compassion, as he took from his breast pocket the handkerchief—my pink cambric handkerchief, edged with white lace and monogrammed with my married initials—and shamefacedly held it out to me.

"My—my apologies, ma'am," he said hoarsely. "It—it was an unforgivable impertinence."

I turned my back on him and walked to the window. "It was more than that," I replied. "It was an indiscretion that, if it had come out, could have led to scandalous talk."

"Ma'am, I assure you that I would never have dreamed of showing the handkerchief to anyone," he protested. "The very thought . . ."

I turned round to face him. Forcing a severe note into my voice, I said: "I accept your assurance, Doctor. But wouldn't you say that the very act of purloining my handkerchief violated your code as a physician? Did you not take some kind of oath when you qualified?"

"You're referring to the so-called Oath of Hippocrates, ma'am," he said. "I never took the oath, but I try to abide by its principles, as do most of my profession."

"Can you recite the oath, Doctor?" I murmured.

His brow furrowed with an effort of recollection. "Not in chapter and verse," he said. "But I remember the main points, and some of the rather splendid phraseology."

"Quote from it," I demanded.

"Er—which part, ma'am? It covers many aspects of medical practise."

"The part that relates to a doctor's relationship with his patients," I said coolly. "Particularly with regard to his relationship with his women patients."

"Women patients, ma'am? Ah—yes!" Robert Vyner licked his dry lips and turned crimson again. I hated myself for tormenting him, but it had to be done. I had to know exactly where I stood with the susceptible young physician.

"Have you forgotten that part, Doctor?" I asked dryly.

"It goes somehow like this," he said. " *'Whatsoever house I enter, I will go there for the good of the sick, refraining from all wrongdoing. And especially from any act of . . . er . . . seduction, of male or female, bond or free.'* I think that's the part of the oath to which you were referring, ma'am."

I let a moment of time go past, and then I asked, in a very small voice:

"And you don't think, Doctor, that you have transgressed that oath—the spirit, if not the letter, of that oath?"

His chin went up, and I saw the mature man behind the gentle, shy manners of the boy. "I do not, ma'am," he replied firmly. "I have no right to make this declaration—to you, a married woman, and nominally my patient—but, since you question me closely, I have to tell you that I admire and esteem you greatly. I would say that I admire you more than any woman I have ever met, or ever hope to meet."

Treacherous tears of gratitude and relief were prickling at my eyes. I bowed my head and heard myself whisper, "Thank you, Doctor."

"If it hadn't been for this incident, I can promise you that you would never have been embarrassed by my declaration," he said. "I was—I am content to go through life as your faithful friend, if you would accept me as such. As to the Hippocratic Oath—if to steal a token possession of yours and treasure it to my breast is a violation of that oath, then I have certainly been at fault. But I have to tell you that— apart from any embarrassment it may have caused you—the act lies very lightly on my conscience!"

The handkerchief was suddenly a blessed godsend: I hastily wiped my eyes with it, and hoped that he would not notice. Then with a feeling of heartfelt relief, I gave him my hand.

"I'm sorry I probed you," I said. "It was very unkind, but, you see, there was something I had to know about you, and now I know. And now I should like for us to be friends."

"Gladly!" cried Robert Vyner. "Nothing would give me greater pleasure than to be your true friend and to serve you."

"You may come to change your mind—Robert," I warned.

I pulled the bell cord for a maid and had her bring fresh coffee and another cup. When we were alone again, I motioned Robert to sit opposite me.

"Tell me how I can help you," he said encouragingly.

"First, we have to go back to that Oath," I said. "Is it also true that you're bound to secrecy—like a priest?"

He sipped at his coffee for a few moments, and then he

211

said: "Not quite, Joanna. A physician isn't in the favoured position of a priest in a confessional. The Oath goes something like this: '*Whatsoever things I see or hear concerning the life of men, in my attendance on the sick, which ought not to be noised abroad, I will keep as sacred secrets.*' The key phrase, you see, is '*which ought not to be noised abroad*'—and that moderates the oath very considerably. It puts the physician in a very different position from the priest who hears a confession of a crime; for, whereas the priest's lips are forever sealed, it is the physician's common duty to 'noise abroad' any evidence of crime—as it's the duty of any law-abiding citizen. Does that make it clear, Joanna?"

"Yes," I said, my spirits suddenly flattened.

"And that makes a difference to what you were going to say—to what you were going to tell me?"

I nodded. "Yes."

"You're worried," he said. "You're in trouble—real trouble. I sense it. Am I right in supposing that it concerns someone near to you?"

"Yes," I replied.

A long silence, broken only by the ticking of a French clock on the table under the long window looking out on to the courtyard; that, and the moaning of the wind in the stone chimney of the open fireplace.

Presently he said: "And there is crime involved in this?"

"Perhaps," I whispered. "But I really don't know—I'm not sure. Yes—I think that crime has been committed," I had to add.

"I see," said Robert. "Then, if you confide in me, you'll have to disregard the Hippocratic Oath—and accept my simple promise as one friend to another that I will remain forever silent about what you tell me, or until you give me leave to break your confidences. Will that suit, Joanna?"

Hope—hope and relief—were rekindled in my heart. "That will suit perfectly, Robert," I told him.

I had tested my admirer and found him to be true. As I had suspected, there was a real worth beneath Robert Vyner's shy exterior. He was forthright and strong, and I could trust him.

"Tell me all, Joanna," he said.

I told him—all. Beginning with my days at Roswithiel until the tragic deaths of my father and Saul Trevallion; continuing with the story of my arrival at Mallion, the misunderstandings that sent me running to London and to my unexpected marriage with Benedict. When it came to telling him of the early breakdown of that disastrous marriage I found the going difficult; but he listened with an expression of such compassionate understanding that I spared him nothing of the details. It was only when I began to skirt around the horrors that had later closed in about me that he found the need to step in and question me.

"This letter that you had from Feyella Mapollion," he said. "It was undoubtedly from her, I take it? Did you keep the letter?"

"No—I burned it almost immediately," I said. "I didn't dare to keep it, but it was definitely from Feyella. I know her handwriting, and there were things in it that could only have come from Feyella."

"You mean things like the assertion that Mayana's child sprang from a union between her and your husband?"

I nodded miserably.

"Leaving that aside for the moment," he said, "do you believe—do you really believe—that Mr Trevallion murdered your father and his own brother, or caused them to be murdered—is that what you think in your own heart, Joanna?—had the thought ever occurred to you for one moment before you had that letter?"

"No," I was able to reply with perfect honesty.

Robert spread his hands as a small gesture of triumph. "Well now," he said. "We've gone some way to demolishing that idea, haven't we? We now see it for what it is; a vile accusation from a scorned woman—a highly emotional woman who was always used to having her every wish granted and who, when she was scorned, was ready to strike out like a tigress, wounding everyone in sight—including herself."

"But the letter changes things," I pointed out. "Before the letter, it seemed certain that she had killed herself for the sake of Benedict. Now we know that she came here, before anything else, to kill him. And she failed."

He drew down the corners of his lips and nodded gravely. "Not only failed but—if that wretch Pollitt's to be believed—he buried her. Yes, that takes some explaining away. What do you make of it?"

I had thought long and hard about that question: in the sleepless hours of the nights between, I had gone over it again and again.

"Either he killed her in the defense of his own life," I said, "or she failed in the attempt and then destroyed herself in his presence."

He nodded. "Yes—and which alternative do you prefer, Joanna?"

"Can you ask?" I cried.

"You believe he's innocent?" he asked. "You *want* to believe he's innocent?"

I also had the answer to that question—forged in the long and tortuous hours of sleeplessness.

"If I were to believe that Benedict killed his brother for the sake of gaining Mallion, and my father because he was with Saul at the time," I said, "I would have to believe that he brutally attacked Pollitt's daughter. And if he did those dreadful things, he would have been quite capable of killing Feyella the instant he found out that she had come here with the intention of turning her father's pistol on him. It's all of a piece, don't you see? If I believe one thing about him, I have to believe all. I have to accept that the man I married is—*a monster!*"

"And you can't bring yourself to do that?"

Again in my mind's eye, I saw—like the shifting patterns in a child's toy kaleidoscope—the many faces of Benedict Trevallion: the man who had saved me from the loathesome embrace of his hateful brother; the stern figure who had reduced my father to slack-mouthed impotence; Benedict on the never-to-be-forgotten morning at eleven precisely when he won

214

my heart and my hand with his brusque proposal; the strange pact—so soon fated to be broken—that we had made on the westbound train . . .

"I know him as a man with a violent and terrible temper," I said. "In such a temper, he's probably capable of doing almost anything. What's more, he's well aware of his failing, and I believe he sincerely would wish to change his nature if he could. I can imagine him killing his brother Saul in a fit of uncontrollable rage, but not in cold blood, for greed. Anything like that, I can't imagine. But, you see, I have to face up to the possibility."

"You were right when you said it's all of a piece," said Robert. "If he's guilty of one, he's guilty of all. If Feyella's letter was nothing but an hysterical outburst and Pollitt's story a tissue of lies to extract money from you, we're left with only the fact of Feyella's death and secret burial—and there's nothing in that to brand your husband as a monster; he could simply have been concealing her suicide to shield your feelings."

"That's what I thought," I cried. "If only we could prove it was so."

"Pollitt's the key," he said. "We can get no further evidence about what happened in Jamaica, but we can possibly find out what really did happen to that daughter of Pollitt's. When did he claim it happened?"

I thought back to my meeting on the seashore. "He said the child came to work here the year that the war ended," I said. "That would be six years ago."

"Six years ago, eh?" said Robert. "That was before I came to this practice; took over from my predecessor, old Trelawney, who died in harness. The likes of Pollitt wouldn't have the money for doctor's fees, but, from what I gather, old Trelawney wasn't the type who'd have let a child die unattended if news of it reached his ears."

"You mean . . . ?" I began.

"I've a tin trunk full of Trelawney's case-notes in my attic," he said. "Notebooks, diaries, and the like. He was a methodical old bird, was Trelawney. I think it highly likely that, if he attended Pollitt's child in the hours of her death, he would have left some record of it."

I shuddered—and not because of the winter's chill that even the blazing logs in the wide fireplace were not able to quench.

"When I heard that story," I said, "from Pollitt's lips, I was horrified and revolted by the idea that a human being—any human being—could have been responsible for the death of a helpless, mindless creature; and the thought that Benedict could have done it was too much to bear, so I crammed it out of my mind; told myself that there must have been some mistake, that Pollitt was lying—anything."

He nodded. "I can quite understand that, Joanna," he said quietly.

I laid my hand on his arm. "Robert," I said. "Robert, my good friend, if you come back and tell me that the man I married did that awful thing, after all, I think . . . I think I shall go out of my mind."

* * *

Janey Maddern, my new lady's maid, served me luncheon in my own room: lamb cutlets and an apple pie, for which I had no taste. Little Janey needed hardly any pressing from me to eat it up herself with the gusto that comes from a healthy young appetite sharpened by childhood deprivation. The girl had settled down quickly to the routine of the castle, and I was careful to keep her in my personal charge—away from the influence of the Prendergasts. She also provided me with an extra set of eyes and ears on to the comings-and-goings about Mallion. From her I learned—while she was gobbling up my cutlets— that, thanks to Robert Vyner's attentions, young Jackie was sitting up and taking nourishment from his mother. A further item of news sent me rushing into my dressing room, to snatch up my tweed cape and bonnet.

While collecting my luncheon from the kitchen, she had heard someone say that the master had ordered his horse to be saddled and ready to go out by two o'clock.

It was one thirty-six . . .

I saw no one on my way across the wind-swept courtyard

and under the shadowy archway that led to the bridge. The tide was in and I could hear the roaring of the dark waters in the deep sea moat beneath the bridge. At the far side of the bridge, I cast a backward glance at Castle Mallion, silhouetted against the wintry sky: the ivy-covered walls, the five pointed towers, and the black leopard banner of the Trevallions snapping and streaming high above the gatehouse. Neither before or since has Mallion seemed so alien—so strangely *hostile*—as it did that freezing afternoon. Shivering, I went on my way.

I went only a short distance down the drive, to the first bend, then I took shelter from the biting wind against the smooth trunk of one of the tall elms that bordered the gravel carriageway, to wait for my husband. I had not long to wait.

Like the spectres in my nightmares, he came round the turn of the drive on his cantering black, with his caped coat fluttering behind him. He drew rein, as I stepped forward and raised my hand to him.

"Good lord, Joanna!" he cried. "Are you out walking on a day like this? You'll catch your death."

There were signs of strain on his face, and the familiar lines of anger were visible between his brows. I all but panicked and forgot what I had come to say—my reason for waylaying him. But not quite.

"I—I'm glad you came by, Benedict," I said. "For I've been wanting to have a few words with you, and it's so difficult to arrange a meeting when we live . . . so far apart."

He bowed his head and replied stiffly: "I'm sorry for the way we live, Joanna. But, if you'll pardon my saying so, it's neither the time nor the place to enter into a long discussion about that. Was there something else you wanted to talk to me about?"

My lip was beginning to tremble. "I'm worried for you, Benedict," I faltered. "It seems to me that you may have a lot of troubles on your mind."

His horse tossed his head and snorted. Benedict patted the beast's neck, soothing it with a calming voice. A few moments passed before he replied to my remark.

"I'm really at a loss to know why you should think so," he

said, looking down at me from his great height with those cold and disdainful Trevallion eyes—deep blue, like the merciless sea beneath the walls of Mallion.

"It seems to me," I persisted, "that you must still be worried about what's happened to Feyella."

He spread his hands and shrugged his broad shoulders. "I am desolate about the poor girl," he said, "but I shall recover from it, as we all shall. You are making too much fuss, my dear, you really are."

"Then you're not worried?" I asked.

"About what?" he demanded.

"About what people might be saying about—you and Feyella," I said. "And about what that policeman—Menhenitt—may have found out."

He gave me a pitying glance. "Joanna, did you really take the trouble to waylay me for this?" he asked. "Do you really think that I'm walking round in terror of what local gossip might make of my relationship with Feyella Mapollion? As for that incompetent nincompoop of an inspector—last time we had this discussion, I gave you my opinion of *him*."

And how wrong you were, I thought. And how wrong you still are!

I said: "Then there's nothing I can do to help you?"

"Help me?" he asked, in what seemed genuine surprise. "Help me in what, Joanna?"

"I would help you, if it lay within my power, in anything," I said. "If you were in any trouble, I would gladly share it with you."

As I looked up at him, trying to communicate the depth of my anguish for him, Benedict deliberately looked away from me, chin high, towards the dark towers of Mallion and the sea beyond.

"You are very kind, my dear," he said distantly.

"I mean it, Benedict!" I cried. "You have only to tell me what's the matter, and I would gladly share your burdens. Offer you what comfort's in me. Help you against the whole world."

The stallion snickered impatiently and tossed his head again.

"Thank you," said Benedict flatly.

My heart sank. I was getting nowhere with him, and his attitude to the morass of danger that surrounded him on all sides only confirmed my worst suspicions. But what hurt me most was his cold, blank-faced rejection of my offer of help.

"That's all I have to say," I murmured. "I'm sorry to have taken up so much of your time, Benedict."

He sighed. "My dear," he said, "I'm very grateful for your concern, I really am. But I promise you that it's quite misplaced. I have my problems—don't we all? However, I'm happy to be able to assure you that—at this moment—my problems are no greater than usual: indeed, I'd go so far as to say that, considering all things, I have cause to congratulate myself that I'm coping with my problems very well. Now—does that reassure you?"

"Yes, Benedict," I whispered, lying.

He smiled, and suddenly I saw a vision of the man who had come bounding up the stairs and into my sickroom at Ludgate Hill—and my heart turned over.

"Let a little time go by," he said, "and things—my affairs, the affairs of Mallion—will get very much better still. Hold on to that idea, Joanna. One must only be patient, and all will be well."

With that, he took off his wide-brimmed hat, nodded to me gravely, and set his horse into a canter. The wind took the skirts of his coat as he rounded the corner of the drive and was borne away out of my sight.

"Oh, merciful Heaven!" I breathed, burying my face in my hands.

After a time, I retraced my footsteps to the castle. The walls were as high and seemingly impregnable as ever, and the black leopard banner of the Trevallions fluttered just as boldly as before; but now it all seemed to me to be a hollow mockery, a fruitless posturing of strength to hide the rottenness within.

The dreadful fact that had emerged from my encounter with Benedict was that he was living in a fool's paradise of his own self-deception. Because some days had gone past since Feyella's disappearance, and nothing had happened to suggest that he

219

was in any way implicated, he believed that the danger was all but over.

"I'm coping with my problems very well," he had said; and: "let a little time go by and things will get better still."

* * *

A sense of impending tragedy guided my choice of what to wear that evening: I decided upon a black silk gown that had lain, all unworn, among my trousseau. Janey Maddern hung it up to air before the roaring fire in my bedroom, while I lay in the bath that she had prepared for me. The young girl ran her fingers over the smooth material and over the jet embroidery at the bodice, lingering and marvelling at the stiff white lace ruffling that fringed the *décolletage* and provided the sole touch of relief from the severity of the gown.

"'Tis loverly, ma'am," she breathed. "Really loverly, 'tis. But it ain't you, ma'am, if you don't mind my sayin' so. You're the sort o' lady as should be wearing gay and pretty things, all flowers and such-like. That's your style."

"All flushed in the cheeks, and hung about with bows and beads," I said, "like a woman up from the country selling eggs."

"Ma'am?" the girl looked puzzled.

"It's nothing, Janey," I smiled. "You're quite right, I don't have the style and breeding to carry off simple clothes. Not like Miss Feyella had." And I thought of the way my self-confidence used to collapse before Feyella's cool stylishness.

"Don't you go believing any such thing, ma'am," declared the girl. "Miss Feyella were good to me, and I'd be the first to admit it. But there's more of what you call style and breeding in your little finger than that poor lady had in the whole of her— and I tell you no lie, ma'am."

"Get away with you, Janey," I said. "Now I know you're a poor judge of people. Miss Mapollion was a lady, born and bred, and it showed in her every move, in everything she did. Me—well—I'm someone who has to try very hard to be an imitation of a lady. That's the difference, don't you see?"

Janey did not see, and said as much. She continued to praise me, and I felt flattered by her impression of me, while knowing

220

that it was mistaken. I shut my ears to her talk, and it was while I was soaping my arms and thinking back to Feyella and the first times we had met, that I heard—or thought I heard—something that shook me out of my daydream.

"Would you mind repeating that?" I cried. "Something you said about Mr Trevallion . . ."

"Why, the way he do look at you, ma'am," the girl faltered, with the air of someone who has uttered an indiscretion and is now being called to account for it.

"In what way does my husband look at me?" I asked.

Janey's nether lip trembled. "Why, in *that* sort of way, ma'am," she said.

"And what is *that* sort of way?" I demanded.

"Well, ma'am. He do look at you, and . . ."

"Yes?" I cried, angry, now. "Go on, child!"

At this point, Janey burst into tears, and there came a knock on the bedroom door. It was one of the housemaids. She called out that I had a visitor.

"Who is it?" I cried.

" 'Tis the doctor, ma'am," came the reply.

Then the voice of Robert Vyner, very cool and loud, with a meaningful undertone that was intended only for my ears. "Mrs Trevallion, I'm sorry to bother you, but I have brought the medicine I prescribed for you, and it's rather important that I show you exactly how it's to be taken!"

I knew why he had come, and I felt the hairs of my scalp crawl with dreadful apprehension.

"Just a moment, Doctor!" I called out. And to Janey: "Stop that snivelling, child, and pass me my *peignoir*. Then help me to carry this bath into the dressing room."

She threw me an anguished glance. "Yes, ma'am," she sobbed. "You'll forgive me, won't you, ma'am. I swear as I didn't mean any harm."

"Of course," I said. "We'll speak of it later."

The question dinned in my mind: Had Robert found anything in his predecessor's files—and, if so, what . . . ?

We had the room cleared and reasonably tidy within a few minutes. I put my hair up inside a silk scarf and cast a glance at myself in the mirror. I looked dreadful: thin in the cheeks, and my nose and mouth unnaturally large. Oh, dear God, I thought. Don't let it be true. Not Benedict. I couldn't bear that . . .

"Come in!" I said in a voice that was not my own.

I avoided looking towards the door when Robert Vyner entered, for fear of what I might see written on his face. I waited till Janey had gone out, till her footfalls and the housemaid's had died away down the corridor beyond. And then I turned.

I saw it in his clouded grey eyes.

"*No!*" I breathed. "Oh, no!"

He crossed over to the window and peered down through a crack in the curtain into the courtyard. My legs were suddenly deprived of their strength, and I lowered myself into the chair by the fire.

"Is your husband in the castle?" he asked.

"He—he went out this afternoon," I said. "And I haven't heard a horse come back into the courtyard." I bit my forefinger till it hurt, and then: "Robert. Tell me the worst . . . please!"

He turned to face me, and his face was quite calm and matter-of-fact. "Do you have anyone you can go to?" he asked. "Here, in the West Country, or London—or anywhere?"

I found myself trembling.

"Only in London," I whispered. "The Alberts—the dentist and his family who took me in when I fell ill. They're the only friends I could turn to in that sort of way." When he nodded brusquely, my nerves seemed to snap. "Robert! You don't mean . . . you're not suggesting I should leave?"

He stood over me, the lamplight forming a halo of brightness around his russet-coloured hair. He looked like some big, fatherly, amiable bear.

"It has to be faced, Joanna," he said quietly. "You are almost certainly in immediate and dreadful peril every moment you stay within these walls!"

My senses swam, and his head wavered in my vision. I must have swayed and nearly slipped to the floor, for his hands came down, took me by the shoulders and steadied me.

"You don't mean . . . *from Benedict?*" I breathed.

He nodded gravely.

"No! It can't be true!"

"It's true enough, Joanna."

"Then tell me about it," I cried. "Tell me everything. I have to know."

"There isn't time, my dear," he said. "What I want you to do is to pack a few things in a valise—enough to see you through the journey to London—then I'm going to drive you to the station—I brought the trap with me—and put you on the night train. If you like, I'll gladly go with you to London and deliver you to your friends."

"No!" I cried, shaking my head till the scarf fell loose and my hair cascaded about my shoulders. Blinded by tears, I appealed to him. "You must tell me everything!"

"Later," he said. "On the way to the station. Now, get ready, Joanna. There may not be much time."

"Now," I grated. "You'll tell me now!"

"Joanna . . ."

"I'm not moving till you've told me what you've found out!"

"Very well, Joanna," he said quietly. "If that's how it must be, so be it." He took a silver flask from his coat pocket and poured a measure into the cap of the flask, offering it to me. I shook my head. "You won't?" he said. "Then I will." He drained the cap in one swallow. I watched him all the time, through my tears.

"You found what you were looking for in Dr Trelawney's papers?" I said, dully.

He nodded, watching me carefully (did he think, I wondered, that I was going to throw a fit of hysterics and bring the whole castle full of servants down about our ears?).

"Yes," he said. "I went straight home and to the attic, where Trelawney's stuff is kept; turned out the old tin trunk and went through it. It should have taken me a week, I promise you, Joanna—but I had the most extraordinary luck, if luck you can call it . . ." At this, he walked over to the window again. I clenched my hands till my knuckles showed white.

"I found a daybook for the year of eighteen fifty-five," he

223

said. "The volume had its date written on the cover, so there was no need to look any farther. Trelawney, I learned, had indeed attended the Pollitt child during her last illness. The Pollitts had not sent for him, that was scarcely to be expected; but neighbours, hearing the child's cries, had spread the news that Lucy was suffering, and so it came to Trelawney's ears. He went to see her."

"Yes," I whispered. "And what did he find?"

Robert coughed, and dabbed his lips with his handkerchief. "There were multiple abrasions and some superficial lesions," he said, in a cold and clinical-sounding voice, "consistent with a physical assault by a person or persons possessing considerable strength. Some of the child's teeth were newly missing and one eye was so contused as to give some anxiety about its sight. The right arm was broken, though someone—presumably the Pollitts—had made a fruitless attempt to reset the limb . . . do you really want to hear any more, Joanna?"

I nodded. I was past all hurt. My mind and my spirit was numb and cauterised by the horror of it all.

Robert continued briskly. "Trelawney examined the girl and found her to be *virgo intacta*. He was of the opinion that by far the worst part of her injury lay in the effect upon her mind—and, indeed, this proved to be the case. A lifetime of undernourishment, coupled with the shock of her injuries, contributed to the child's end. She died of a massive debility in the summer of that year. It's a phenomenon that is frequently observed in persons of a low mental calibre and in the lower animals—this inability to survive an experience of gross injury." He was silent for a few moments; then the cold clinical voice gave way to the one I knew better: "I really am very sorry, Joanna. I would have given anything to be the bearer of better news."

My mind was still fighting with all that I had heard. Somewhere beyond the mists of horror, there had to be some hope that I could reach out and seize.

"But did it *have* to be Benedict?" I cried. "Are you sure— was Dr Trelawney himself sure—that it was Benedict who ill-used that poor child? Couldn't it have been done by Pollitt himself? I'm positive he's capable of such a thing!"

Robert Vyner shook his head. "I'm afraid you haven't yet heard all, my dear," he said. "There's more—much more, and worse—to come."

A convulsive tremor ran through my frame. Looking down at my hands, I saw that they seemed to have taken on some separate existence of their own and were fluttering like a pair of dying doves on my lap. His hand touched my shoulder.

"Drink this," he said. "You need it, after all."

He lifted the silver cap to my lips and the fiery, unfamiliar spirit scored my mouth and throat till I choked on it. I gagged and retched. He took me in his arms, pressing my head against his chest and soothing me with gentle words.

And then, he said: "You've heard enough, Joanna. Will you now get ready so that I can take you away from here?"

"Please!" I sobbed. "Please, tell me why it has to be Benedict!"

"All right, my dear," he said softly. And he released me. "If you feel equal to hearing it, it's right that you should. In that same daybook, I learned that Trelawney had been attending your husband for what he described—in somewhat unmedical terms—as 'brainstorms.'"

"Brainstorms?" I stared at him, aghast.

"Trelawney wasn't very specific, but it seems that Benedict Trevallion had some kind of mental breakdown about that time," he said. "It took the form of an uncontrollable violence where he was a danger to himself and all about him. The elder brother, Saul, sent for Trelawney, swore him to secrecy in the matter, and ordered him to do anything short of killing Benedict to quieten him. In the event, Trelawney prescribed massive doses of alcoholic tincture of opium, which reduced the patient to a condition of stupor in which it was possible to keep him under physical restraint."

In the long silence between us that followed, I was conscious of the wind howling in the chimney, and somewhere in the distance, a door was banging with a rhythmic insistency. I shuddered.

225

"Brainstorms!" I repeated.

"Fits of violent behaviour," said Robert Vyner, "in which, according to Trelawney, he acted like a maddened beast and was a danger to himself and all about him."

I closed my eyes, but the image of Benedict's face persisted: the face that had looked at me across our plush-upholstered railway carriage on that dreamlike journey together to the wild Western land of his forefathers . . .

"There's a dark and violent streak in my nature that I find very hard to live with, but live with it I must, for there's no changing it, you see . . ."

"He was honest with me," I whispered. "Right from the first, he told me of his affliction. But I never realised . . . never dreamed in my wildest dreams . . . that it was . . . was . . ."

"Madness!" supplied Robert Vyner. "There's no point in my trying to persuade you any other, Joanna. Your safety—your very life—is at stake, and I'll not have you running any risk. The man's mad, and you must get away from here—for good— before it's too late."

"But, why should he hurt me?" I cried. "He thought enough of me, once, to marry me. And nothing's passed between us —nothing of which I'm aware—that could have changed his feelings about me. And no matter what Feyella Mapollion may have thought, I'll never believe he married me to secure my silence."

"The child Lucy Pollitt had done nothing to cause him to hurt her either!" he said savagely. "But that didn't save her from his bestial attack! Old Dr Trelawney, who was loved by all who met him—he didn't merit any ill-treatment, either. But that man for whom you're still trying to find excuses, Joanna— that man, would you believe it?—he threw himself at the old fellow and tore at his throat with his teeth, like a rabid wolf!"

A distant door was still banging, but the wind had died down to a barely audible whisper in the chimneytop.

"I won't be long getting ready, Robert," I said quietly. "Give me time to dress and collect a few things."

He squeezed my hands. "My dear, I shall be so relieved to see you gone from this accursed place," he said.

But I was not fated to leave Mallion—not that evening.

When we reached the courtyard, where Robert's horse and trap were waiting, my husband was there—and he was not alone. With him was the Nemesis—the figure of retribution—from whom, in my heart, I had known he could never escape.

CHAPTER 7

There were two covered vans parked in the shadow of the gate-house, with dark-caped figures grouped by them. Benedict had obviously just returned: he stood by his horse, speaking to Sergeant Menhenitt. They all turned to regard Robert Vyner and me as we walked towards them. I noticed Benedict's eyes widen with surprise to see me in travelling clothes, but if he connected this with the valise of mine that Robert was carrying, he made no comment.

"The sergeant has something important to tell us, so I understand, my dear," he said with a drawl that contained more than a suggestion of contempt. "I suggest we repair to the great hall and hear what this momentous piece of news is all about."

Menhenitt's uncomely face was quite impassive and his disconcerting squint was turned towards me.

"Yes, I should like Mrs Trevallion to be present when I deliver my remarks," he said calmly.

Benedict tossed his reins to a groom and led the way towards the door of the hall. I followed after him with Robert Vyner at my elbow.

"Do you want me with you?" Robert murmured in my ear. I nodded, and, seeing Menhenitt's gaze upon us, I had a sudden pang of nameless guilt.

The double doors closed behind us, echoing hollowly in the banner-hung recesses of the high ceiling. The fire crackled in the fireplace, and there was a sudden flurry of sleet against the high windows.

"Come over by the fire and warm yourselves," said Benedict. "Then let us hear what the excellent sergeant has to say." He was in a brash and sardonic mood: if he had not just returned from his ride I would have thought that he had been drinking heavily. His gaze, when it fell upon Menhenitt was blatantly contemptuous; but the officer of the law seemed all unaware of it. I could not bring myself to look upon the man to whom I was married—but some part of my mind was trying to reach out to him and warn him that his brash confidence was unfounded, that he was in mortal danger, that he must be careful.

"One needs some inner fortification in this confounded weather, don't you agree?" cried Benedict, and he crossed over to a side table where stood a decanter and glasses. "I expect you will all join me in a brandy. How about you, Menhenitt?"

"Thank you, sir," said the sergeant. "But I never partake while on duty."

"You, then, Doctor? No? How about you, Joanna my dear? Really? Then, unless you bring in your fellows from outside, Menhenitt, I shall have to drink alone. And drink alone I will."

He poured himself a bumper and tossed it back, while we all watched him, not moving—the three of us standing before the crackling fire, with the sleet and the wind beating against the ancient outside walls.

Benedict laid the glass on the table and poured out another measure.

"So, Menhenitt," he said. "What is the nature of your business here this afternoon?"

Menhenitt took from his pocket a piece of paper which he unfolded and held out to my husband. Benedict made no attempt to take it, but merely fixed the police officer with an arrogant stare.

"What might that be?" he demanded.

"It is a warrant, sir," replied Menhenitt. "Duly signed by a magistrate."

"What kind of warrant, pray?"

"A warrant empowering me to search these premises, sir," replied the other quietly.

I have no recollection of fainting: no pain as I struck the flagged floor with my head in falling; there was suddenly a sick emptiness through which my body fell into a yielding softness. When I came to—how much later, I shall never know—I was sitting in an armchair in the solar with Robert Vyner kneeling beside me. His face, and that of Janey Maddern, filled all my vision. My head ached intolerably; and, reaching up my hand, I found that I had raised a lump the size of a bantam's egg at the side of my temple.

"You fainted clean away," said Robert. "How are you feeling now?"

"Benedict?" My first thought was of him.

"He's in the hall with Menhenitt. The men have begun searching. They're starting with the grounds, so as to get as much as possible done before nightfall."

We were both acutely aware of Janey's presence, as our eyes met and I drank in the significance of Robert's information. I was about to make some comment, when Menhenitt came into the solar.

"Ah, just the young lady I was looking for," he said, nodding towards the terrified Janey. "I understand you formerly worked for Miss Mapollion, is that so?"

Janey nodded, wide-eyed.

"Then I should like to put a few questions to you, young lady—in private, if that's convenient, Mrs Trevallion. No—please don't move. The young lady and I can go elsewhere. Come, my dear."

Janey threw me an anguished glance as she went out on the heels of the police officer. The door closed behind them.

"Robert, what's going to happen?" I cried. "He's sure to worm the business of Feyella's letter out of the poor girl, and they're bound to find that freshly dug grave up in the old garden."

"There's nothing you can do, Joanna," he said. "And nothing I can do, either. Benedict Trevallion is beyond all help. We can only hope that they get the thing over quickly."

"Oh, Benedict," I found myself saying, over and over again. "Oh, Benedict, have I been at fault? Was there something I could have done, or said, to prevent it happening?"

And then I found that Robert Vyner's shoulder was good to cry on, and that the wholesome man's smell of his broadcloth coat was curiously comforting, like the touch and scent of a beloved childhood plaything.

* * *

Time was without meaning. It simply passed in an empty limbo as I sat there in the growing darkness with Robert. When we heard men's returning footsteps in the yard, he went over to the window.

"Steel yourself, Joanna," he said. "I think they've found what they were looking for."

There was a resounding knock on the double doors of the hall, that echoed hollowly through the corridor down to the solar. I was halfway across the room before the sound died away.

Benedict was slumped in a chair by the side table, an empty glass by his elbow, chin in hand, gazing expressionlessly into the fire. Menhenitt had just come in from the door leading to the servants' quarters, and Janey was behind him. It only needed one flashing glance in my direction for her to tell me, as surely as if she had spoken the words, that she had revealed all about the letter from Feyella.

It scarcely mattered now . . .

Men were filing in: three of the caped policemen. One of them touched his hat to Menhenitt and whispered something in his ear. The sergeant nodded.

"There'll be no need to look any further," he said. "Dr Vyner, would you be so good as to accompany my men, to make an identification?"

Robert cleared his throat. "Certainly," he murmured hoarsely.

They went out together. Menhenitt took out a spotted handkerchief and blew his nose noisily. I noticed that one of the policemen had stayed behind. He backed away against the wall, and remained a dark and menacing observer to what followed.

"Well?"

The grating monosyllable from Benedict had the power to shock me. I looked across at him and saw that his face was still quite expressionless. Whatever thoughts were racing through his mind, they were not connected with fear—of that I was certain.

"The body of Miss Mapollion has been found," said Menhenitt. "Buried in the garden above the courtyard. The doctor will confirm the identity and perhaps make some indication as to the cause of death. You knew of this internment, sir?"

"Yes," said Benedict.

There was a chorus of muffled gasps and exclamations of horror from the group of servants who had gathered, all unnoticed, by the door leading to the kitchen quarters. I saw Mr and Mrs Prendergast standing like a pair of carrion crows in the front: their eyes never left Benedict.

"Would you have any knowledge of who buried the body of this young woman, Mr Trevallion?"

"I buried her," said my husband without hesitation.

There was another concerted murmur of comment, and Menhenitt turned his head to look at the servants with a small frown of irritation. "Would you people be so kind as to keep silence, please," he said primly. Then, back to Benedict: "What assistance, if any, did you have in this task, Mr Trevallion?"

"I carried it out myself," said Benedict.

"You dug the grave?"

"Yes."

I stood, not daring to move, lest I bring Benedict's glance towards me. For some reason I never questioned, I did not wish him to look at me—and, indeed, he had given no indication that he was aware of my presence since I had reentered the great hall.

Something had changed in his manner. Gone was the taut-ness and tension; instead, his attitude was almost that of a man from whose shoulders a vast and unbearable weight has just fallen. I took this to be the relief from carrying the secret guilt. His manner to Menhenitt was now gentle—almost friendly.

"Mr Trevallion," said the sergeant. "It will now be my unpleasant duty to arrest you and take you to Truro."

"Of course," replied Benedict.

"For the present, I am charging you with the unlawful concealment of Miss Mapollion's death."

"Yes," replied my husband.

"It is only fair to warn you that various other charges may be levelled at you at a later date."

Benedict nodded. "I understand," he said.

"Then will you please accompany my officer outside to the van?"

"Am I permitted to say a few words to my wife?" asked Benedict.

I felt a sudden compulsion to run—anywhere, to be away from him, from that hateful hall and all its associations. Menhenitt looked across at me with a lugubrious expression on his homely features. For the first time, I was aware that there might be a real man behind the façades and poses of the official.

"I can't allow a private meeting at this stage," he said. "But it will be quite in order to say your good-byes . . . if that's Mrs Trevallion's wish." And, when I made no reply, but only bowed my head, he turned and walked across the hall to where his uniformed man was standing sentry.

Benedict came up to me. He was smiling: a smile so gentle and candid that my fear and revulsion vanished like smoke in the wind—and all I could think of were those few and far-off days in London when we were planning our hurried wedding.

"Good-bye Joanna," he said. "You were quite right to warn me this afternoon. I had thought myself into a state of false security, but I was living in a fool's paradise."

There was a treacherous tightness in my throat and I could not trust myself to reply to him.

"So much to say," he went on, "so inadequate the means to express it all. I can only beg your indulgence, and ask you to forgive me for the many hurts you've suffered at my hands."

Was this the monster of Castle Mallion? No—shut out the thought! Cling to the memory of the morning he won your heart. Coming into your room. Bearing you off to be his forever.

Oh, Benedict . . .

"Good-bye, then, Joanna."

"Good-bye," I whispered.

He turned—and my whole heart went out to him in one tremendous wave of compassion. He was the prisoner of his passions and his infirmities and no more to be blamed, I told myself, than a beast of the wilds. And now the beast was going to be chained up. Or destroyed.

I watched his tall figure cross the hall, saw him pick up his hat and gloves from the table by the door; then he went out, followed by the uniformed officer. Menhenitt remained. A minute later, there was the rattle and clatter of a horse-drawn van leaving the courtyard by way of the gatehouse.

The master of Mallion had gone from the ancient stronghold of his ancestors. Would he ever return?

Menhenitt broke the silence that followed. "I'm sorry for this, ma'am. I really am. But it had to happen. It was inevitable. I wish you'd communicated with me when you had that letter from Miss Mapollion—the letter the girl told me about—but I appreciate your reasons for keeping it to yourself. Do you still have the letter?"

I shook my head. My thoughts were only partly with what Menhenitt was saying; nearly all of me was with the man who was being borne through the wintry night to some dark cell, to await the slow and soul-destroying processes of the law.

"No matter," said Menhenitt. "I'll not ask you to tell me the contents, for you're privileged not to say anything that might further incriminate your husband. But I'm sorry you didn't confide in me."

The wild beast has been hunted down; dragged from the lair where he thought himself to be safe; carried off to whatever end they dictate for him . . .

I followed Menhenitt out into the courtyard. Driving sleet struck sharply at my cheek. A small procession came out of the gloom from the direction of the kitchen garden. With a sudden shock of horror, I saw that two of the policemen were carrying a stretcher and that its burden was covered by a grey blanket. They loaded the stretcher on to the remaining van, assisted by Robert Vyner, who was with them.

"You've made the identification, Doctor?" asked Menhenitt.

"Yes," said Robert. "It's the body of Feyella Mapollion."

I closed my eyes and shuddered.

"And have you formed any opinion as to the cause of death, sir? Please don't feel committed to giving me a hasty opinion, but some indication would be helpful."

Robert glanced in my direction, then answered quietly: "The cause of death is in no doubt at all, Sergeant. She died by . . . manual strangulation."

Now it was dark, and the whirling sleet was turning to snow. It spiralled down from above the tall ramparts of the castle, and took on a bright new life in the loom of the lantern that hung over the gatehouse arch. I was barely aware of Robert taking off his coat and draping it round my shoulders.

* * *

The new and capable Joanna Trevallion was in command of the situation, and I was quite firm with Robert. He had insisted on my eating some supper, and I had compromised with an egg beaten up with warm milk—which had nearly made me retch.

"No, Robert," I said firmly. "You've done enough—more than I should have asked of any friend, but now you must leave me to fend for myself. I have all my life in front of me, and I might as well get used to it from the start."

"Let me stay at the castle," he pleaded. "Just for this first night, to be at hand in case you need me."

"No," I said. "Don't you see?—if I give way on this first night I shall never be able to stand on my own two feet again. Poor Robert, you've already paid a high enough price to become my friend; would you take me on as a lifetime burden?"

Too late, I saw the unwisdom of my remark.

"Yes," he said, with the directness and simplicity of a good and honest man. "There is nothing more in the whole world that I would rather do than care for you your whole life through, Joanna."

This was too much for me; even the new and capable Joanna Trevallion was out of her depth in such uncharted waters. Already, Robert was rising to his feet from the armchair opposite me; next, he would be kneeling by my sofa . . .

"I don't need to be cared for," I exclaimed brutally. "Neither by you, nor by anyone else, Robert . . ." his face took on the look of a chastised dog, and I could have swallowed back my words . . . "I'm sorry, my dear, but you mustn't probe me too deeply. I can't see very far ahead, and most of what I see terrifies me greatly. Some time soon—and I suppose it had better be tomorrow, before she hears of it from some other source—I shall have to break the news to my mother-in-law. Then there's the question of what's to happen to Mayana and the child. With Benedict gone, these things have all become my responsibilities."

He stood irresolutely before me, hands hanging limply by his side. "I'm sorry, Joanna," he said. "It wasn't fair of me to take advantage of your situation by forcing my attentions on you. Forgive me. But remember that I will do anything for you. Anything. You've only to ask."

I painfully assembled the question that had never been out of my mind since the moment that Benedict had walked out of the great hall and into the darkness and sleet . . .

"Will they . . . hang him?" I asked.

Robert shook his head. "I've already taken opinion on this," he said. "A barrister friend of mine in Bodmin—I rode over to see him yesterday and put the question to him, purely hypothetically—confirmed what I believed: that Trevallion will almost certainly escape the scaffold."

"Even after . . . the things he's done?"

"He's not responsible for his actions," said Robert. "This principle is already accepted in British law. You won't remember the case, but a fellow named McNaughton shot and killed Sir Robert Peel's secretary about twenty years ago. He was quite mad, and under the delusion that Sir Robert was persecuting him. McNaughton fired on the secretary, thinking that he was his tormentor. He was found not guilty, and this verdict gave rise to a set of rules which, I'm convinced, will save your husband's life. In short terms, he'll be found to have been unaware of the awfulness of what he was doing, at the times he committed the acts. I shall be there to testify to this, backed up by old Trelawney's case notes."

So the wild beast of Mallion—who had once won my heart to the eleven o'clock chimes of St Paul's Cathedral—would evade the slaughterers. But, what then?

"They'll shut him up for life, of course," said Robert, as if in answer to my question. "There could be no hope of his release."

I saw an image of the Last of the Trevallions then: crouched in a bare cell in some insane asylum, festering in a lifetime of emptiness. I thought of Benedict Trevallion galloping the native moors of his wild Western land—and I could not but wish that he had ridden away forever, to be swallowed up in a bog; or hurled, broken-necked, in a dead heap at the other side of some far, high wall. Any fate would have been better than for that highly tempered spirit to eke out his days in captivity. No matter what he had done to deserve it.

The ormulu clock on the solar chimneypiece sounded eight o'clock. Eight o'clock—and there was much that I had to do before morning.

"Come and see me tomorrow, Robert," I said. "Tomorrow, I shall have arranged things more clearly in my mind."

"And you're sure you don't need me to stay?" he asked.

"Quite sure. I feel quite strong; strong enough to survive

till morning. And, if I last till morning, I can bear everything that comes."

He took my hands.

"I really think you'll rise above this tragedy, Joanna," he said admiringly. "In one sense, I'm glad and happy for you. But, in another, since your inner strength puts you beyond the need for my poor help, I can only regret." And he smiled ruefully.

"I shall always need your help, my dear," I said. And I kissed his cheek.

Not till I heard his horse's hoofbeats fade beyond the moat bridge did I ring for my maid. When Janey came, I brushed aside her tearful pleas for forgiveness for having allowed Menhenitt to wheedle the story of the letter out of her.

"It scarcely matters now, Janey," I said. "And I wouldn't have expected you to lie to the police. Put it out of your mind. You're a good girl. Don't worry—your place is safe here."

"Oh, Mrs Trevallion . . ." The child was falling to her knees beside me. I raised her up and told her to blow her nose and calm herself.

"What I want to know is, where are Mr and Mrs Prendergast to be found?" I asked.

"Why, ma'am, they be having their supper in the big kitchen," said Janey. "They always do eat alone, and none o' the servants be allowed in the big kitchen while they be at table."

"I want to see them," I said.

"Oh, 'twould be quite in order for me to go in and take a message from you, ma'am," she said. "I'll go right away, ma'am."

But another plan had suddenly come to my mind. "No, Janey," I said with a certain feeling of pleasurable anticipation. "What I have to say to that pair can just as well be delivered in the big kitchen. I'll go to them myself."

With that, I left the solar and found my way, through the great hall and the long, echoing corridors beyond, towards the kitchen quarters, where I had never dared to tread before, so great had been my nervousness of the Prendergasts and their opinions. With every step, my courage and resolve was strengthened. My footsteps sounded loud and brave in the flagged corridors, and flickering tallow dips made giant shadows of my figure on the dank stone walls. The mistress of Mallion was coming to settle her score!

The big kitchen was an immense, stone-vaulted chamber rivalling the great hall itself. The walls were hung with gleaming copper saucepans, trays, dishes, skillets, pot lids; and a macabre display of animal skulls decorated the tall chimneypiece. In contrast to the corridor outside, the room—for all its size—was cosy and warm. The Prendergasts sat facing each other across a refectory table in the middle of the chamber.

As I closed the door behind me, I heard Prendergast hiss to his wife (whose back was towards me): "By God, it's *her!*"

"Yes, it is I!" I commented in a loud voice.

Mrs Prendergast turned to face me, her jaw frozen in the act of chewing a mouthful of food. I noticed, with some interest, that the table was laid with a handsome choice of dishes, including game pies and joints of meat, some of them uncut. The Prendergasts were obviously accustomed to doing themselves very well. But the sands were running out . . .

I gave them my ultimatum without any preamble. There seemed no point in beating about the bush: these people were my enemies; had been my enemies ever since I first set foot in Castle Mallion.

"It is now eight-fifteen," I said. "I give you an hour. Within an hour, you are to be out of this place. Pack what you will need for tonight and tell one of the grooms to drive you to Bodmin, or wherever you can conveniently find lodgings. Your belongings will be sent after you in the morning. Is that quite clear?"

It was the man who replied. He had already risen to his feet, and was staring at me, his close-set eyes suddenly vulnerable and puzzled.

"You can't mean this, Mrs Trevallion," he cried hoarsely. "What have we done to deserve such treatment?"

"Fifteen years," said his wife, who had emptied her mouth.

"Fifteen years come Easter we've been here, and always given satisfaction to *the Family*." She accented the final words.

The duplicity of these people! They were adopting the pose of the faithful retainers who were being cast out by an upstart. The Family, indeed!

"I've nothing further to add," I said icily. "I've no wish to abuse you. You will simply leave my house and not come back again!"

But Mrs Prendergast had no intention of departing quietly. "And what if we demand compensation for all we've done?" she cried. "And there's plenty we're entitled to. There's things we've done for this family that wouldn't bear examining by folks outside these walls."

"I'm aware of that," I said. "I know that you helped my husband to bury Feyella Mapollion—there's no need for you to deny it, for I have a witness. I don't doubt that you were well paid for that—and you have escaped the consequences of your act, as you very well know. My husband took the entire blame upon himself."

"Martha!" cried the man. "She knows—she *knows!*"

Mrs Prendergast's boot-button eyes flashed towards me. "Aye, she knows," she said. "But what does she know, and how much does she know—that's the question? Does she know the real reason why the master made sure we weren't taken away with him this eve?"

"I'm aware," I said, "that you must have been well paid to help conceal my husband's . . . activities. I know now why he refused to dismiss you both, even at my request, when you had grossly insulted me. Because he dared not. You knew too much."

"Grossly insulted you, eh?" Mrs Prendergast's pinched, humourless lips were twisted in a travesty of a grin. "That's a good one. And who are you, that you should be spared from insult, my fine lady?"

"Martha!" urged her husband. "Let it be. Don't vex Mrs Trevallion. I'm sure she'll see reason and reconsider . . ."

"Not she!" grated the woman. "Not that scullery slut trying to be a lady. I know her sort. There's none so haughty and quick to strike back as your skivvy-turned-mistress. She'll have us out of here, like she says"—the woman's malevolent face was thrust close to mine, and I shrank back from the spittle that showered from her tormented lips—"she'll have us out of here, but let her take the consequences! *Let her take the consequences!*"

I was dumbfounded by the unexpected vehemence of her attack, so that I could only murmur weakly: "You've done all the evil you're going to do to me, Mrs Prendergast. It isn't in your power to do any more."

She laughed shortly. "Aye! We've had our sport with you, my grand lady, me and Miss Mapollion." She pulled aside her shawl and revealed the oval-shaped blue brooch that I had seen her wearing on the fateful day that I ran away from Mallion. "Remember this, eh? Gave it to me, she did, for helping her to get you away from here because she was jealous of you and the master. Took it away from me again, she did, when she found I'd flaunted it in front of you, and you coming back as his wife. But I got it back from milady, as you see. Oh, yes! I'm one as takes what's rightly mine."

A dreadful possibility came to me. "How?" I breathed in horror. "How and when did you get the brooch back from her?"

Mrs Prendergast showed her blackened teeth in a grin of pure, exultant evil. "Took it from her pretty neck," she said. "Wearing it as a stickpin she was, as part of her riding habit. Took it from her before my man started a-shovelling the cold earth down upon her dead face."

I drew back from her, from them both, in revulsion. They stood together, pale-faced, ill-smelling and shifty, dressed in their identical seedy black. Not for the first time, it occurred to me that they could easily have been brother and sister.

"You're evil—evil!" I cried. "And you'll leave my house within the hour. Now, get out of here and collect your belongings. The Trevallions owe you nothing—you've been well paid for all you did."

Turning my back on the ghoulish pair, I strode to the door.

When I reached it, I was arrested—shocked—by a hissed exchange that took place between them.

"She's sending us away, Martha. What's to be come of us? We're done for—finished!"

"And so is she," came the reply. "She's sown the wind, let her reap the whirlwind—like the Mapollion wench before her!"

Like the Mapollion wench before her?

What could that possibly mean?

I turned, and they were both staring after me. Prendergast's mean eyes were widened with something that looked like shock; and the woman was smiling her awful smile.

It was an hour before I heard the coach taking them away from Mallion, and not till then did my limbs cease their unaccountable trembling.

* * *

So many questions, still, to ask—and who was going to answer me?

The northeast tower was beckoning me from across the blizzard-swept courtyard, as it had done so often when Benedict was there. Surely, there I should find some of the answers; perhaps, to me, the most important of them all.

I lit a lamp and carried it out into the night. The snow was ankle-deep in the courtyard and it swiftly soaked through the slippers I was wearing as I ran, head down against the force of the blizzard. My hands reached out and, scrabbling for the heavy iron latch of the tower door, turned it and let myself in. My lamp revealed a circular stone vestibule and an archway with the beginnings of a spiral staircase had curved away upwards into gloom.

Benedict's apartments, I knew, were on the second floor. Gathering up the hem of my skirts, I began to climb. There were arrow slits cut into the massive stone walls of the stair, and the wind sent flurries of snow on to the worn steps. The silence was eerie; nothing but the moaning of wind in the high battlements above. And only my feeble lamp to lighten the blackness that surrounded me. Suddenly, halfway up the steps, I felt very alone and frightened.

The door to his apartment was carved with linenfold panels and bore a knocker in the shape of a grinning imp. The latch yielded to my touch—and then I was standing in the chamber of my bridegroom that had been forbidden me.

The living room was in chaos. It was quite obvious that no broom or duster had been laid upon it since Benedict had moved in there. The dust lay thick upon the floor, and cobwebs hung from the beamed ceiling in musty swags. I thought of bats—and stared about me in alarm, probing the recesses with the light of my lamp. To my utter relief, it revealed none of the little horrors hanging there with their hateful, leathery wings wrapped about them. Calmer now, I put the lamp on the table and turned the wick up full, so that its warm glow spread through the room, which was semi-circular and filled with an untidy clutter of furniture: a long table piled high with books and papers, a tall bookcase with a broken glass front, armchairs and a sofa littered with discarded clothes and dirty linen; and everywhere—standing on every vacant space, scattered about the floor, and filling the airless room with the stale smell of spirits—were empty bottles.

All around me was a monument to the secret existence that Benedict had carried on since our marriage; and, surely, it could not have been typical of the life he preferred. I had always—even since the far-off days of Roswithiel—regarded him as a fastidious, even dandified, kind of man. That he should have existed in this private pigsty as a matter of preference hardly fitted in with my estimate of his character and personal habits. It was pitifully clear—the evidence was all around me— that no servant had been allowed in to tend for him. And why was that, I wondered. Was it from choice—or had Benedict forbidden people from entering his apartment because he had something to hide?

I picked up a sheaf of dusty papers and let them slip through my fingers. They comprised a collection of bills for feedstuffs and farm equipment, lists of livestock and estimates of forgotten harvests, musty conveyances and indentures written in spiky writing by long-dead hands. Some of the paperwork was more recent: I saw Benedict's own characteristic handwriting here and there. But the whole impression was of such confusion that I remembered his mother's comment with wry wonder: how Benedict was so good at managing the estate. All around me was clear proof that he had let things slip to an alarming degree.

There was more confusion on a roll-top desk on which he had obviously done his work. An inkstand had been overturned and had stained a pile of papers and books. As I reached out to straighten the inkstand, my hand dislodged one of the books and it fell to the floor.

Bending to pick it up, I saw the pieces of screwed-up paper lying by the desk—and my heart suddenly turned over, as I saw my own name written there.

> *My dear Joanna,*
> *My mind is confused, and I scarcely know how to begin*
> *to explain* . . .

There was nothing else on the sheet. Hastily, I picked up another, straightened it out and read:

> My dear Joanna,
> The time has come when you must know the truth about . . .

Another piece of discarded paper revealed yet another attempt to begin a letter to me:

> My Dear Joanna,
> This is the most difficult letter I have ever been called upon to write in my whole life. What I have to tell you is so outrageous and totally unacceptable to a person in his or her right mind that you would not be blamed by anyone—and least of all by me—if, after reading it, you immediately left Mallion forever . . .

There was another crumpled-up sheet, but Benedict had made no further attempts to draft his letter to me; instead, this took the form of a series of random notes:

Why not tell J– the truth?

But—can I condemn her to share this horror with me?

(Should have made a clean breast of it before I asked her to marry me—too late for vain regrets!)

No! If there is to be further self-sacrifice, it must all be mine!

But she should be told about Mayana and the child.

I can't allow Mayana to go back to Jamaica. The risk is too great.

MAYANA IS AS STRONG AS ANY MAN!

I stared down at the last line of his notes, puzzled—yet with the beginnings of a dreadful suspicion that, even in its early and unformed stages, was causing my skin to prickle and my scalp to creep with sheer horror.

Another glance through the drafts left me no wiser. They were obviously attempts on his part to admit me to his dread secret; but he had decided, after all, to shut me away from it—in the form of the letter that I had actually received.

What, then, was his secret?

Clearly, it concerned Mayana, the deaf-mute mulatress who had long been his mistress and—there really seemed no further cause for me to doubt it—the mother of his child. Mayana, who was as strong as any man.

Alone, in that tower room, with the wild elements beating against the granite walls, and the sea thundering up on to the shore below, I reassembled in my mind all I knew or remembered of the beautiful deaf-mute . . .

Mayana at Roswithiel: the splendid figure in the black crinoline, capable, dominating, ruler of an army of servants who performed to her every nod and gesture; Mayana on the night of the Roswithiel Ball, when I saw her gaze directed to the blonde girl clasped in Benedict's arms within the cascading fountain—the look of primitive loathing that carried with it all the heartbreak of a jealous woman; Mayana and her child, like a she-leopard and her cub.

The blood of the savage forest—though diluted by generations of slavery and the addition of white blood—coursed through her veins. The passions that rule the human heart: love, jealousy, possessiveness, hatred, the lust for revenge—all these must be more real and intense for her than for us, tamed and thwarted as we are by the demands and customs of our artificial civilisation.

Mayana was primitive. Mayana was strong. Strong as any man—so Benedict had written, in his private notes to himself.

I thought back to the scene in the great hall that evening: of Benedict's change of attitude when it was all over and the hand of Nemesis had fallen upon him. I had put it down to relief at being free of the burden of deceit—but it had been relief of a very different kind.

It was the relief of a man who has successfully taken upon himself the blame for another. For a loved one.

"No!" (he had written) "If there is to be further self-sacrifice, it must all be mine!"

I had come to find answers, and they had been provided with a vengeance. In one stroke I knew the facts of Benedict's self-sacrifice, and his reason for it.

He had sacrificed himself for Mayana—for the best of all possible reasons—because he loved her.

Mayana—and not Benedict Trevallion—was the slayer of Feyella Mapollion; no matter what other misdeeds could be laid at the door of the poor, crazed master of Mallion, there was no other construction to be put upon his conduct. Feyella, coming to destroy the man who had rejected her so brutally, had herself fallen victim to the savagery of his jealous mistress and Benedict had taken the blame. Yes, that was it. That was how it had been.

Robert Vyner had said I was in danger every moment I stayed within the walls of Mallion. Danger from my poor, mad husband was what he had meant, but he could have been quite wrong . . .

And here was I, alone in the dead of the night, in a remote corner of the great castle, where no one ever trod. If anything happened to me, it could be days before anyone found out. I looked about me for a weapon, but there was nothing save my

246

brass oil lamp: I picked it up, lowered the wick and turned to quit the room and the northeast tower.

It was in that instant, above the distant moan of the wind, that I heard the sound of someone moving about overhead!

There was no mistaking it: light, catlike footfalls on the wooden floorboards immediately above my head. Someone crossing the room on tiptoe. Slowly, very slowly, a latch was lifted, and a door creaked painfully open.

A long pause—and then—the slow, click-click of heels on the spiral stairs. Descending.

Too late, now, for me to take refuge in flight; if I opened the door and rushed out on to the landing, I should only walk into the arms of—who?

Mayana? The footsteps sounded like a woman's, light and delicate, swift-moving. They had stopped now, on the landing outside. I waited, heart pounding, waiting for the blessed relief that would come when I heard them moving down the next flight.

Silence. Nothing but the drumming of a vein in my ear— so loud that it should surely have betrayed me to the listener beyond the door. I stood, breathless, convinced that I had not yet betrayed myself and that the intruder would pass. My own slippered feet could surely not have made enough sound to reach the room above. I was perfectly safe, provided I kept still and silent. If only there had been a lock or bolt on the inside of the door.

Time crawled past, and still no sound from the corridor outside. My limbs, fixed still in one position, began to tremble with fatigue, and the heavy lamp wavered in my hand. My breath began to be laboured, as if I had run for a long distance. There was a tickle in my throat that felt perilously like the beginning of a cough. And still no sound of movement beyond the door.

The absurdity of my position struck me then. Either the other had already continued on down the stairs, or was waiting, like me—probably shaking with fatigue and overwrought imagination—for the other party to make another move.

I had to do something, for it was impossible to stand frozen in one position any longer. The hand—my hand—that held the heavy oil lamp looked strong and capable. Not strong as any man, certainly—but I was capable of defending myself.

Without any further thought, I called out:

"Mayana! Is that you?"

No answer. She must, indeed, have continued on down the stairs. I breathed a sigh of relief and started towards the door.

And then—the latch of the door slowly began to turn!

I froze in my tracks, cried out in alarm.

"Mayana! Answer me!"

Then, the shattering remembrance of the obvious: that the mute do not answer, as the deaf do not either listen or hear. It was not, it could not be, Mayana.

The door began to open, showing the thin sliver of darkness beyond, gradually widening—till it revealed a solitary eye. Shaking from head to foot, now, with uncontrollable terror, I raised the lamp, the better to see the face that was slowly being revealed to me.

It was a dream, a waking nightmare—the last Figure in the strange Quadrille of Death that had haunted me ever since I came under the influence of the Trevallions. The revealing of a hidden face, and the growing certainty of horror to come. Only, this time, it was real.

I was already dropping the lamp—my fingers having lost all control in a spasm of total shock. It could not have taken more than an instant for the lamp to reach the floor at my feet, to shatter, and to be extinguished; but, in that brief moment of time, the image of the figure before me was imprinted on my mind in the greatest detail, and will so remain—haunting my sleep and my waking hours—till the day I die.

A cheese-white face. The head bald, save for a single hank of white hair that hung down over one ear.

A single, livid scar laid right across the bare skull, drawn in a jagged line down the face, splitting the left eye and cheekbone.

The left eye dead and sightless. The right eye blazing, red-rimmed, its centre as blue as the sea.

The figure, tall and well made; dressed in a hussar's tunic

248

that had once been blue, heavily frogged with unravelled fronds of what had once been gold lace.

I saw all this, and, before the darkness closed about me, I saw the mouth open as if to rend my throat, and hands reach out to seize my flesh.

My scream was cut off, and blind instinct made me turn and run into the centre of the room. I felt the edge of the table and swiftly edged my way around it. Almost immediately, my pursuer collided heavily with the table, bringing a pile of books and bottles crashing to the floor. By this time, I was halfway to the door, with the faintest possible sliver of light coming through an arrow slit in the corridor wall outside to guide me—and to guide the creature who was already on my heels again.

The choice between taking the stair up or the stair down was completely instinctive and never in any doubt: my whole mind rejected the notion of putting the creature above me, so that it could leap down upon my back. I took the steps leading up to the top of the tower—with no idea what lay ahead of me. All that mattered, in my panic, was to live each second, and then the second ahead.

I ran, three steps at a time, with my skirts raised high above my knees. The booted feet—dainty Hessian boots such as the light cavalry wear; I had seen them before the lamp shattered—clattered rapidly behind me. Close.

At the third floor, and by the thin moonlight, I caught a glimpse of the open door of the apartment from which my pursuer had come. Racing across the landing to the next flight of steps, I thought I felt the tips of taloned fingers rake down my back. And the creature gave an animal-like cry that could have been mistaken for a screech of triumph.

The next flight stretched to an eternity and my legs had lost all sensation of movement. I felt myself impeded by a tug on my flying skirts, and screamed when I realised that the creature actually had hold of the hem and was pulling me to a halt. The material ripped—and then I was through a half-opened door and reeling out into the moonlight and the freezing night air.

Before me lay the circular roof of the northeast tower, and all the towers and battlements of Mallion. There was not much farther for me to go. My life was running out. A few lurching steps brought me up against the waist-high granite wall—and that was where it would all end for me.

I turned round to face my killer.

At first, I thought that he had gone—but he was standing beside me.

Half the nightmare face was in shadow; the other half, with its lank strand of hair and the staring eye, was whitely lit by the high-riding moon. The lips parted in a hellish grin. With nowhere to go, my shrinking flesh could do nothing but receive the touch of a hand upon my shoulder and another upon my arm. A throaty chuckle broke from the pale lips. The blue eye burned even more brightly. Now the hands were questing towards my throat.

Useless to try and appeal to a creature from the dead, a thing risen from the deep. The single sabre slash had laid open the brain and removed every last vestige of humanity from the horror that had once been Piers Trevallion, the golden hussar. Useless—yet, knowing that it was useless, I tried to reach out across the gulf of time and madness.

"Piers!" I cried. "You don't know me, but I'm one of you now—a Trevallion. Married to Benedict, who must love you so dearly, to have cared for you so well . . . all these years . . .

"No one shall ever touch you, Piers! I'll match Benedict's sacrifice. He's my beloved husband and I love him. I've always loved him—I know that now. What he wants for you, that I want also. Don't you see, Piers? If you hurt me, you'll be hurting someone who loves Benedict . . ."

There was no comprehension in the red-rimmed eye, and the hands continued to move slowly, inexorably, to my throat.

I was pleading, half aloud and half to myself. Giving myself, in the short time left to me, the answers to all the questions.

"I thought he had sacrificed himself for a woman, Piers; but it was out of brotherly love and pride of family. He wanted to tell me about you, wanted me to share the secret—but he was afraid I might go away from here. That means he may love me after all . . ."

The hands—lean, strong hands of a horseman—were looping themselves loosely round my throat. I had the wild notion that, for so long as I continued to babble, so long would the creature allow me to live. Perhaps some spark of reason still glowed fitfully in that ruined brain—or perhaps it was only idly interested by the sounds coming from my lips, the way a cat may listen to the small shrieks of a mouse that it has impaled upon its claws.

"I don't want to die. Not now, of all times. Not without seeing him again. I must know what I can only guess. Please, Piers. Give me my life . . ."

The hands gave a convulsive jerk, choking off my words and silencing a scream before it was born in my throat. The white face wavered before me and a great rushing noise filled my ears. My hands clawed at the frogging of the military tunic; I felt it tearing under my grasp, then everything was soft and insubstantial to my touch. My senses were slipping away. I was dying.

The thunderclap of sudden sound was my release. Immediately after it happened, the hands relaxed their awful grip, and my whole being was concerned with the gulping in of a lungful of life-giving air.

My vision cleared. I was half-lying back against the ramparts and Piers Trevallion was slowly turning round to look across the roof, towards the dark figure silhouetted against the wintry sky.

It was Mayana. She had a pistol held at the full extent of her arm, and, when their gazes met and locked, she lowered it to her side and dropped it. The weapon clattered hollowly to the stone flags.

Piers Trevallion slowly began to crumple, a deep bellow of pain and fear issuing from his livid lips. This dreadful sound was matched by the animal cry of the mulatress as she darted forward, arms extended, to catch the uniformed figure before it fell.

She was strong: strong as any man. She held her to him

when his legs sagged away, nestling the ruined head against her shoulder, stroking the naked scalp and keening wildly. Still holding him, she moved towards a gap in the battlemented wall and was gone before I could raise a hand, or even comprehend what she was doing.

They went over very slowly, locked together in an embrace that would carry them both to death and beyond. I saw them turn over and over in their downward course; heard the unearthly voice of the deaf-mute as she cried out the first and last spoken sounds of her life: a wild paeon of the triumph of love over death.

I could not have wrenched my eyes away from them if I had tried; but, blessedly, they plunged into darkness below the walls.

The sound of the sea surging in the deep moat drowned all else.

CHAPTER 8

Towards the dead hours between night and day, the blizzard came down again, but the menservants of the castle kept up the search of the moat; I could see the lights of their torches down there, pinpoints of flame in the snowswept darkness.

I had raised the alarm immediately. No one had had the temerity to question the mistress of Mallion too deeply; as far as they knew or understood, Mayana and an unknown man had met their ends by falling from the ramparts of the north-east tower. There were murmurings among them about the northeast tower—murmurings that no one made any effort to conceal from me. Indeed it was as if they wanted me to know things—now that tragedy had struck—that I should have been told long before. As I stood on the ramparts with the women servants, looking down into the moat and the searchers, I heard them speak to one another in hushed tones about the northeast tower where no one but the Prendergasts had been allowed to set foot, where Mr Benedict had lived in untended rooms on the second floor, below the apartment on the third floor that had been padlocked for as long as anyone could remember . . .

It was nearly dawn, and I had retired to the solar, where Janey Maddern had urged me to drink some scalding hot coffee laced with brandy, when one of the grooms came in and reported that the search had been fruitless.

" 'Tis useless to look any further now, ma'am," he said. "Tide have gone out and taken 'em with it. Maybe tide will bring 'em back again somewhere along the coast, but like as not they'll be carried out to sea and never be laid eyes on again."

"Thank you," I said. "You've all done everything that could be done, I know."

" 'Tis a rum business, ma'am. A bad business," said the man. "We'll be having the police back again in no time."

I had already sent a groom, with orders to ride to Truro with all speed, with a note for Sergeant Menhenitt. I had hopes that the officer would be back at Mallion by the afternoon—and that he would not come alone.

"I hope so. I hope so indeed," I replied feelingly.

The groom would dearly have liked to have questioned. I guessed that the others would be waiting for him in the servants' hall, all agog for news.

"You can tell them . . ." I began.

"Yes, ma'am?" Eagerly.

"You can tell them all that tonight's happenings have changed . . . everything," I said. "You can tell them that I have every hope that the master will be returning to the castle today."

"That be the best thing I could have heard, ma'am," said the man, his homely face alight with pure pleasure. "And you may take it, ma'am, that there ain't a man or woman working in Mallion, nor on all the estates, as won't rejoice to hear it."

"Thank you," I said, mildly surprised on this, the latest facet of my husband's character of which I had had no knowledge: his capacity for earning the respect and affection of his servants.

"And happiness to you, ma'am," said the groom. " 'Twill be a great day for you, to have the master safely home again."

I bowed my head. "Yes," I whispered.

Would it, though? The master of Mallion would be returning, his name cleansed of all but the commendable fault of trying to shield the good name and honour of his family—and that would be happiness, indeed, for me. But my heart yearned for so much more.

It was at this moment—as I was sunk in the gloomiest of

doubts and fears about my future as the wife of Benedict Trevallion—that Robert Vyner's horse slithered to a clattering halt in the courtyard, and its rider hurled himself from the saddle.

* * *

Robert burst into the solar unannounced. He was unkempt and unshaven and looked as if he had been up all night. Despite everything, I could not but smile fondly at the relief in his face when he saw me standing there.

"Thank God!" he cried. "I never thought to see you alive again. My dear, you must sit down and compose yourself for what will be both a blessed relief and a terrible shock."

"I know about it, Robert," I said. "I stumbled upon it during the night, and now it's all over."

And then, quite calmly (and marvelling at my own calmness), I told him all that had happened. When I had finished, his face was drained of colour.

"I only just stumbled on the truth," he cried, "and I rode straight here to warn you. As soon as I returned home last night, I went back to old Trelawney's trunk, in the hope of finding out more about this dreadful business. The daybook told me nothing that I didn't know already, but, on emptying out all the books and papers, I came upon a false bottom to the trunk, and in it—this private diary." He held out a small, half-bound volume.

"It identifies Piers?" I breathed.

He nodded. "By name," he said. "Trelawney wasn't so specific in the daybook: he said that Saul Trevallion sent for him to attend his brother, whom I naturally took to be Benedict. It was only in the private diary that Trelawney reveals the truth about the eldest brother who was supposed to be dead."

I shivered. "It's a wonder that they managed to keep the secret all these years," I said. "Even Lord Cardigan and some of his officers must have been parties to the deception."

"According to Trelawney," said Robert, "it was all Benedict's idea. Cardigan had Piers delivered to the castle in conditions of secrecy, out of consideration for his mother, in view of his

255

terrible wound. It was Benedict who persuaded Cardigan to connive in the story of the burial at sea—a plan that would have met with his lordship's full approval, for a dead hero is greatly to be preferred than a mindless wreck of what was once a splendid young man. In any event, Cardigan must have thought Piers to be as good as done for. Yes, the deception was begun for the sake of the man's mother, and they all—the Trevallions and Cardigan—closed ranks to shield it from the world."

"In the beginning, it really was thought that he was quickly going to die?" I asked.

"Yes," said Robert. "But Piers possessed most extraordinary powers of physical recovery. By the time he had reached home, the terrible head wound had practically healed over, but the massive brain damage was past even the repairing hand of Nature; it soon became obvious to the two brothers that they were left with a hopeless—and dangerous—madman."

"Dr Trelawney knew all this?" I asked.

"It was Saul who sent for him, as we learned from the day-book," said Robert. "That was when Saul realised what a nightmare they had brought upon themselves. He took Trelawney into his confidence; as good as asked him quietly to put his brother to sleep, the way one would dispose of a sick animal. Naturally, old Trelawney refused—and earned the approval of Benedict."

I remembered a conversation I had had with Feyella—so long ago it seemed, now. "Saul never had any family pride," I said, half to myself. "Benedict was a Trevallion, through and through. He would have stood by his stricken brother to the grave and beyond—as a matter of honour. Saul was a bad Trevallion, with neither pride nor honour."

"Old Trelawney continued to attend Piers until his own death," said Robert. "This he did on the instructions of Benedict. There was little enough he could do save to administer soporifics of gradually increasing strengths. Some time before his own end, he was able to state quite firmly that Piers's agonies would only be terminated by natural death or old age. By then, the Prendergasts had taken over the task of guarding and caring for the patient. When I succeeded to the practice, there was no need to widen the conspiracy by taking me into their confidences," he concluded dryly.

It was now fully daylight. The wind had died taking the clouds with it. The faintest edge of wintry sunshine was casting shadows halfway across the courtyard, and every individual leaf of ivy was shaking off its mantle of snow. I wondered if my messenger had reached Truro yet.

"Feyella was wrong about Mayana and the child," I said. "We were all wrong. Jackie is Piers's son, I know it in my heart. Benedict was able to bring them both back here after Saul died, and I think that Mayana must quickly have made herself indispensable in caring for Piers. She was so strong, you see. Strong as any man. Possibly she was also good at calming him when he had these brainstorms. She would always be at hand to attend him . . ." My voice broke.

"Joanna, my dear. You're crying," said Robert, coming towards me, hands extended. "I should be horsewhipped for subjecting you to all this, after the night you've been through."

Once again, I availed myself of the comfort of my friend's broad shoulder.

"You don't understand," I said, trying to smile through my tears. "This time, I'm crying because of the faint ray of happiness that's come to me. I know now why Mayana went to the northeast tower in the dark hours of the night. It wasn't to be with my husband, but with Piers. I don't know if I dare build any hopes on that, but . . . it's beautiful to think about."

* * *

By midday, the sky was a high vault of dazzling blueness in which the white wings of seagulls slanted lazily. Pouring from every eave and from every grinning gargoyle's mouth at the castle roof, the melting snow told its own story. It was an end to the great storms, and the first thaw of spring was coming to the Western land. My heart was unaccountably lightened. At every hour, I found myself listening for the strokes of the clock tower above the stables. They seemed to say: the Master is coming home, the Master is coming home . . .

Robert kept me company, and we had a light luncheon together in the solar. I only toyed with mine, but he tucked in like a true trencherman and kept up a constant spate of comment and conjecture about the mystery of Piers Trevallion. I let a lot of it wash over me; the larger part of my mind was occupied with the thoughts of Benedict, whom I visualised as a tall figure on a tall horse, riding through the lanes towards Mallion, with the miracle of the first thaw taking place all round him and a newfound freedom in his heart . . .

"Of course," Robert was saying, "old Trelawney can't be entirely freed of all blame in the matter. As far as Benedict was concerned, his course of action had landed them with the responsibility of what, as a layman, he would have considered merely as a 'difficult patient.' Trelawney should have seen enough at the beginning to have diagnosed Piers as a dangerous and potentially homicidal lunatic who should have been put into an asylum. It really is quite remarkable that the deception was carried on so long without incident."

"There was the attack on the Pollitt girl," I supplied.

"That was the first occasion that Piers got free," he said. "The Prendergasts handled that matter, and with what we know of that pair of rogues, we can assume they handled it to their own advantage. I don't doubt at all that Benedict gave them very generous funds to pass over to the girl's parents by way of recompense."

Piece by piece, everything was suddenly becoming clear—and a new image of the man I had married was taking shape in my mind: an image that was not unlike the one I had had at the time of my marriage—before the horrors of my life at Mallion began to close in on me.

"The Pollitts only received a few florins," I said. "The Prendergasts must have pocketed the rest—which must have been quite a considerable amount. Why, when the Pollitts came here and asked for more, Benedict drove them from the door in fury."

"Mmm. He'd scarcely do that if it had really been a matter of florins," said Robert. "To revert to my theme, there was no further incident till your return from Jamaica. Tell me, by the way, why did the brothers go to Jamaica after the war?"

"The estates were suffering," I said. "Roswithiel was in a dreadful state of neglect. Saul was bored with Cornwall; the way of life in the West Indies provided more outlets for his pleasures. He went for the hunting and the rakehelly life, taking Benedict along to do all the work."

"Leaving the Prendergasts to look after the prisoner in the northeast tower!" said Robert. "What a pair! I suppose there's no doubt they deliberately freed Piers after you sent them packing?"

I shook my head. "They thought—or she thought—they were completely inviolable, here," I said. "They had the secret of the Trevallions and they believed the Trevallions would never dare get rid of them. Mrs Prendergast said I should have to take the consequences if I sent them away. I think she forced her will on him to unlock Piers's door; he would have been too frightened to do it himself."

"They should never go unpunished," he cried. "But I'm very much afraid they will. It was a deliberate attempt at murder. The intention was clearly there, but I'm afraid it could never be proved in a court of law. They will go free."

"Free to starve!" I said. "Two middle-aged working people without references, in this country, in this year of grace eighteen sixty-three, will suffer all the punishment you could wish on them, I assure you, Robert. I've seen something of it with my own eyes."

The stable clock struck the hour of two. My pulse quickened.

"But for Mayana," he said, "you would have met the same end as Feyella Mapollion—I'm sorry, Joanna, you won't want to be reminded of that again. We'll talk of something else."

My thoughts were far away. "It doesn't matter," I said. "It's all over. Only the future matters to me now."

"Mmm. I was going to say, I wonder how it was that Feyella came upon Piers that night—the night she came here to try to kill Benedict?"

Somewhere—surely not so very far away now—he was riding over last stretches of moorland that led to Mallion. From the crest of a high hill, he might even be able to see the seven towers against the line of the sea. I dearly hoped they had given

259

him a horse to ride, and that he would not be cooped up in one of those rattling vans . . .

Robert Vyner coughed politely. I turned to regard him.

"Benedict will know the answer to that, Robert," I said. "He'll be here soon. And when he arrives, he'll have the answers to—both our questions."

* * *

Waiting . . . waiting . . .

The tide was high, filling the rock pools and bringing the sea wrack up into the hissing surf on the shoreline. We walked together just above the edge of the sea, Robert Vyner and I, not talking much at first. The sky was still an untroubled blue dome surmounting all: the shifting waves, the sweep of sand, the cliffs, the walls and bannered towers of Mallion, and the wild Western land that faded, hill beyond hill, far into the aquamarine distance.

The white sail of a small fishing boat appeared round the edge of Wreckers' Isle. When it drew nearer, we could see two men gathering nets into their wildly pitching little craft, and when that task was completed, they turned towards the shore.

"Whatever you do, Joanna," said Robert, "whatever comes of your meeting with Benedict, I want you to remember that I am always at hand—always ready to help you, no matter what your need."

I squeezed his hand. "You're a real friend, Robert," I said. "And I'll never forget all you've done for me. But—if I leave Mallion for good, I shall want to take no memories with me, none at all. And you, my dear, have become very much part of the memories of Mallion, I'm afraid. No—if there's to be no life ahead for me here—no life with Benedict, I mean—I shall go and make my own way in London. One thing that's come out of all this is my own self-knowledge. I know, now, my own weaknesses and my strengths. There's no fear any more, not of the great big world outside the walls of Mallion. Nor of the people who inhabit it—I've met the best and the worst of the people I'm ever likely to meet in my life, and no one else in the world will ever hurt me more than I've already been hurt, nor bring me more joy than that I've already known."

"That sounds like a recipe for tranquillity," he said. "To accept that the best and the worst of life have already happened to you. Or is it? Isn't it, rather, like building round yourself the walls of a private convent, in which to eke out the sum of your days till death comes to call? I don't see you in this role, Joanna. I don't believe you can shed yourself of emotions. You say you don't fear the world any more, or its people. But you fear at least one thing."

"Do I now?" I demanded archly. "And what is that one thing I fear, Dr Vyner, sir?"

"You fear the prospect of life without Benedict Trevallion," he replied simply.

"Oh, Robert!"

"My dear . . ."

He took me readily to his arms, and laid my head against his shoulder. The hissing surf swirled about our feet, all unnoticed, and the wild gulls' cries seemed to mock at us.

"You're too cruelly perceptive for a man with such an open, kindly face," I cried. "You search me out and show me the things I don't want to see."

"I show you nothing you haven't seen—and seen very clearly —for yourself," he said. "When you say you'll make your own life in London, you're attempting to fool neither yourself nor me; you're simply whistling in the dark, like a frightened child who's been sent down into a cellar for more coal."

The fishing boat had nudged against the shingle some distance away from us. The two men leapt out into the shallows and pulled their craft up on to the shore, calling out to each other all the while.

"What am I going to do, Robert?" I said. "To be without him—never to see him again—will be a procession of dead, grey days reaching out of sight. I think I would sooner bear to carry on the way it's been. Wife in name only. Even that would mean that I could see him and say 'good morning' and 'how are you'; to bear his name and be invited out with him as the master and mistress of Mallion . . ."

We both looked round. The two fishermen by their boat were shouting—almost as if they were calling to us. But that was hardly likely.

"But it won't be like that," I said. "Not any longer. Now that Piers is dead at last, there's nothing to keep him at Mallion; nothing to tie him to a wife who, for whatever reasons he married her, had become an embarrassment and a burden almost as soon as they were wed. No—I think Benedict will cut his ties with Cornwall and go back to Jamaica . . . alone."

"They *are* calling to us!" cried Robert. And this was so. The two fishermen were waving and gesturing to us. It crossed my mind that, guessing us to be people from the castle, they were hoping to dispose of their catch in one good transaction. One of them was running towards us now; lumbering clumsily in his cumbersome thigh boots.

As soon as he came close, I knew that he was not selling fish; the expression on his face precluded all that. He touched his forelock to Robert, addressing him by name, and took him on one side. They walked off together towards the boat.

"What is it?" I cried. "What's happened?"

"I won't be a minute," said Robert. "Stay where you are, Joanna."

But I followed them, and neither turned his back to see me coming up behind. When they reached the boat, Robert's companion pointed inside it. I saw Robert's face stiffen, and then he slowly took off his cap.

I saw it all, framed between their shoulders.

The bodies of Mayana and Piers Trevallion were lying on a blue sailcloth in the bottom of the craft. The mulatress was as beautiful in death as she had been in life—and gentler and more feminine, because repose softened the arrogance that had often marred her classical features. Both her arms were wound around Piers, and his right arm held her slender waist. They could have been a hussar and his partner in a waltz.

Drying sand had mercifully covered the disfigured head of Piers Trevallion. His face, pressed against Mayana's dark flowing mane, that lay like a pillow beneath both their heads, was presented in profile. Pain and madness had not entirely obliterated, nor had death amended, the structural beauty of that profile. The eye of faith could clearly discern the golden hussar of the portraits.

"Found they caught up amongst the rocks off Wreckers' Isle," murmured one of the men. "'Twas a piece of good fortune, we did, or the next tide would have carried they off to sea, sure as fate."

"Strange how they both be together," said the other. "I never did see anything like it before."

Robert whispered to the fishermen to watch over the bodies, then he put his arm round me and urged me away. I went readily enough, with one last backward glance at the golden hussar and the magnolia beauty, clasped for eternity to the music of a soundless, endless valse.

*　*　*

In the late afternoon, I went up to the old garden, in the dying light, and with the threatening clouds swallowing up the last of the high blue sky.

It was there, after the long day of waiting and wondering, that my strength—like the strength of the dying, in the chill hour of dawn—fell to its lowest ebb.

The ivy-girt walls of Mallion, and five centuries of Trevallions, seemed to bear down upon me, to take judgement on me—and to find me wanting. And it was there, also, that the nameless panic seized me, so that I ran through the wilderness, till I came to the low wall that formed the far boundary of the old garden; and there I leaned, heart pounding, till the worst of the terror had passed and I was somewhere near to being in control of my faculties.

I must never, never again give way so completely to the pressures of my misery—for there, I told myself, lay madness. The laughter of the long-dead Trevallions was no more than the imaginings of my overwrought mind. To admit any other possibility was to give myself over to feelings that could soon destroy me.

It was growing dark. The shadow of Wreckers' Isle stretched darkly over the sea as far as the shore; the gulls circled and wove, forlorn and silent, reminding me of the souls of dead seamen that are supposed to inhabit them.

The light was going out of the sky, and it was time for Joanna Trevallion, née Goodacre, to find some other place than this to lay her head.

He isn't coming . . . he's never coming, I told myself. A day that you lived with the thin edge of hope and promise has ended in nothing. And his very absence gives you the answer to the only question you will ever need to ask in all the rest of your life.

Something moved; but I sensed his presence before my ears had picked up the faint sound and communicated it to my mind.

I turned. Benedict was standing a few paces behind me. His boots could have made scarcely any sound in the unkempt grass. His hat was in his hand and the night wind was ruffling his careless hair.

"I've just come from seeing them," he said. "My brother and Mayana, lying in the chapel. They'll be laid in the family crypt, below the altar, just as they are, and it will be sealed up, never to be opened again. They'll never be disturbed while Mallion stands."

"They'd want it that way," I whispered.

He moved beside me, resting his hands on the balustrade of the wall, looking out across the battlements and rooftops of the ancient castle.

"I would have given anything—my own life, anything—to have prevented Feyella's death," he said. "She burst into the room where we were trying to restrain Piers, and he was at her throat before we could prevent him. She had a pistol with her, which she dropped. I remember picking it up and holding it against . . . against my brother's side and pressing the trigger. But the priming was faulty and the gun misfired. She was . . . dead . . . when we dragged him away."

His hand was within my reach. I directed my own hand towards it, but fear made it falter and fall back to my side.

"I'm sorry, Benedict." There was nothing else to say.

"All these years," he said. "All these years since Balaklava,

I've envied my mother. God, how I've envied her in her cosy cocoon of memories and fantasies about the hero who died at sea in the arms of his commander and was buried there, in honour. The gentil, parfit knight. *Le chevalier sans peur et sans reproche.* And sometimes—often—I've resented her, and him also. That's been the worst part: the resentment I've felt against them both; he, for not conveniently dying a hero; she, for sharing in a fantasy of my own making. Poor Piers. Poor Mother."

"It's all over now," I said comfortingly. "Your mother need never know. She's old, infirm—the truth can be kept from her so easily. Her illusions about Piers can be kept alive—no matter what the reality. Does it matter that he wasn't all the things she believed him to have been?"

Benedict turned and stared at me in surprise, almost as if he had only just noticed me standing there. Then his mouth softened. He almost smiled.

"You didn't know," he said. "How could you? I've avoided speaking to you of Piers, and you could only have heard about him from Feyella, who always took a jaundiced view on anyone who didn't immediately respond to her blandishments." His sea-blue Trevallion eyes looked dreamily past me, towards the sable and white banner that fluttered over Mallion's tallest tower. "The truth is, Joanna, that my brother *was* the knight without fear and without reproach. He *was* the chevalier de Bayard, Galahad, and Lancelot; Bertrand de Guesclin, Richard Coeur de Lion: all the gentil, parfit knights of ancient chivalry embodied in one hero-figure. Even making due allowances for my own hero-worship, there was a brave splendour about him that far transcended the grubby ways of ordinary people. For instance, without being in the least priggish and pious, he was generous and unselfish to a most extraordinary degree. I'll give you an example: one day, when we were children playing up on the moors, I was threatened by an adder and would certainly have been bitten—only Piers kicked the snake away from me and took the bite on his own bare foot. He thought there was nothing very remarkable about his action: to Piers, it was simply the only way for a person to conduct himself. I never forgot that incident."

"I had no idea he was like that," I said. "My father—who must have known him quite well—scarcely spoke of him."

"Corporal Goodacre thought the world of him," said Benedict. "The whole regiment did. Goodacre—your father—was by his side all the way home, on Cardigan's yacht and after. He was a party to the deception we played on my mother and on the world."

"You repaid him well," I said, trying to reassemble some pleasant memories of my father, but only coming up with the recollection of his flushed, drunken face.

Benedict shrugged. "The corporal kept faith with his old comrade-in-arms. Never hinted a word of the secret to anyone. Like me, he seldom spoke of Piers at all. Better to forget. Remembrance only brought a vision of that horror we'd got locked away at the top of the northeast tower . . ."

"Oh, Benedict," I said. "How you must have suffered—loving your brother as you did."

"There was so little I could do to compensate him for the life he'd lost," said Benedict. "Being declared dead meant, of course, that Saul succeeded to his inheritance, but with Saul gone, I had the opportunity to bring Mayana and child back to Cornwall. You do realise, don't you, that Jackie is Piers's son, and, if he had been legitimate, would now be the master of Mallion instead of me?"

My mind went back to the long-gone night of the Roswithiel Ball. "I always thought," I said, as lightly as I could, "I always thought that Mayana was *your* mistress, Benedict. I seem to remember your scandalous behaviour on a certain night, when you leapt into a fountain with an extremely pretty blonde. Mayana wasn't very pleased about that—I saw the expression on her face."

He looked puzzled for a moment, then he said: "Oh, you mean Mary Hemmings. Why, yes, I'm not surprised she won a harsh look from Mayana, who was nothing if not basic in her reactions. Mary, her mother, and all her considerable relations, tried to snare Piers into marrying her before he went off to join his regiment in the Crimea—but Piers would have none of Mary. I think, indeed, he would have married Mayana, in spite of the prejudice, in the end. Jackie, of course, was born after he was . . . wounded. He never knew of the child's coming."

Day had died. Night clouds were shifting past a moon as round and bright as a freshly minted penny. All Mallion shimmered under a new coating of frost. Benedict was quite close to me, but he had never seemed so far away—not even when he had forsaken me, on my wedding night, and taken himself off to his own quarters in the northeast tower.

"I really am very, very sorry for the hurt I've caused you, Joanna," he said. "Words can never express . . ."

"You've already expressed yourself very well, Benedict," I swiftly replied. "Your letter put it very well. Your hasty decision to marry me was a ghastly mistake that can't be put right. I understand that perfectly, and I appreciate your position. It's been a great relief to me, to know that it wasn't for Mayana's sake that you put me aside—but it still leaves me in the situation of a woman who was won and wed by a man's whim, and who . . ."

"Joanna! You've . . ." he interjected. But I cut him short.

"No, you must listen to me," I said. "Whatever your reason for marrying me, I am perfectly willing to keep to my vows. I will honour and obey you in all things, the way a wife should. In return, all I ask is to be told what your intentions are towards me. Do you want me to go away? Does my presence sicken you? If so, go away I will—and not a penny piece will I accept from you, for I would far rather live by my own efforts . . ."

"Joanna!" he cried. "Will you please? . . ."

I waved him to silence; this was the new Joanna having her way at last. "On the other hand," I continued, "if you wish for me to remain here as your . . . official wife, I'll continue to do so. Or, if you want to go back to Jamaica and leave me here, here I will obediently remain. All I would ask is . . . that you write me from time to time and let me know how . . . how you are. Oh, drat you, Benedict Trevallion, now you've made me cry. Give me your handkerchief!"

The handkerchief was forthcoming. Turning my back on him, I dabbed my streaming eyes.

"You're quite mistaken in believing that I married you on a whim, Joanna," he said. "You'll not wish to hear this—hating me as you must, and as you're perfectly justified in doing—but my decision to ask you to marry me goes back a very long while."

"Please!" I whispered. "I think you're going to try to be kind to me now, and I couldn't bear that. Don't say any more. Go and leave me here—please, Benedict."

"Joanna . . ."

"No. I'm nothing to you, nor ever will be. I know that now, and I've learned to accept it."

I felt his hands close on my shoulders. Instinctively, I shrank forward, away from him, against the cold stone of the balustrade.

"Joanna, you're a very great deal to me. More than I could ever express. More than you would ever believe."

I turned to face him, uncaring of the appearance of my swollen eyes.

"Oh, yes," I said, as calmly as I was able to get the words out. "Oh, yes. The groom must think very much of his bride, who would leave her on her own, to cry herself to sleep on their wedding night."

Somewhere away in the trees beyond the castle wall, an owl hooted.

"But surely you understand all about that—now?" he cried.

"Understand?" I demanded. "What should I understand?" Men, I told myself, could sometimes be so bewilderingly stupid.

"Why, that I couldn't—we couldn't—compound the lie about the inheritance."

I shook my head. "I'm sorry, Benedict," I said. "You're forgetting I'm only a common soldier's daughter. Inheritance is something that concerns the landed gentry. It's a word that's almost meaningless to me, so how could I—as you say—compound it?"

His face was blanked out in deep shadow and I could only begin to imagine his expression. His voice was incredulous, urgent . . .

"But, surely, when you found out about Piers," he said,

"you realised that neither Saul nor I were ever truly masters of Mallion? That, while Piers still survived, we were both living a lie, one after the other?"

My heart stirred. Somewhere—like a light at the far end of a long tunnel—a ray of hope, unknown and unbidden, was beginning to take shape. I stared up into the dark oval of his face, drinking in his every word.

"What if I had been killed?" he said. "What if I had, say, broken my neck over a jump? A man must suffer the consequences of his own decisions, but what sort of legacy would it have been for me to leave a baby son as the false heir to Mallion? With the true master lying a prisoner in his own castle. No, Joanna—there could have been no children of our marriage while Piers still lived."

The owl hooted again. I could not have loved it more if it had been a nightingale.

"Tell me the rest, Benedict," I whispered.

"Piers might have made some sort of recovery," he went on. "No matter what that doddering old fool Trelawney said, doctors have been wrong before. He could have recovered sufficiently to come back into the world, marry Mayana and bear her another son. Why, he might even had declared young Jackie his legitimate heir—I for one wouldn't have contested the claim."

"I'm sure you wouldn't have," I said fondly. He was not listening.

"But all those are practical considerations," he said. "There's more to it than that. I concealed Piers's dreadful state for the sake of our mother's feelings—it would have killed her to have seen him—and not to steal his inheritance and falsely pass it on to my son. There's a principle involved, you see Joanna—and it goes further than a simple matter of right and wrong. You do understand?"

"Yes," I said. "It's a matter of pride. The pride of the Trevallions. It's the same for you as it was for Piers. The right way of doing things—even if it's the most painful and difficult—is simply, in your opinion, the only way for a person to conduct himself. You two must have been very alike."

"I'm no gentil, parfit knight," he growled.

"Not excessively gentle, sometimes," I said. "And perhaps a mite too perfect for ordinary mortals. But I expect I shall grow used to it."

He seized my hands. In doing so, he half turned and I saw the expression in his eyes. It was all that I could have hoped for; all I had dreamed of.

"You'll stay?" he said. "In spite of everything, you'll stay?"

Ignoring his question, I asked him: "What did you mean, just now, when you told me that your decision to marry me went back a very long while? How long ago was this?"

"Do you remember the ball at Roswithiel?"

"Do I not?" I cried. "But you don't really mean? . . ."

He nodded. "When I saw you for the first time and realised that you were no longer a child. Dressed in those ridiculous boy's clothes: frightened, but still half defiant. I told myself that I should marry you as soon as you were old enough—and I never swerved from that vow. Ever."

I looked hard at him. If only the light had been better.

"Benedict Trevallion!" I cried. "You're gulling me. You're being nice to me again to gain your own ends. I simply don't believe you."

"You could ask your father," he said, with a note of complacency. "If he were still alive, that is. He heard it from my own lips not long after."

"When was that?" I asked slowly—already guessing the answer.

"A couple of days after the ball," he said. "I had news that the gallant corporal, your father, was more than half inclined to be . . . er, obligingly complaisant, in the matter of my brother Saul's pursuing his acquaintance with you. I rode over to the yard and told him straight."

"Told him—what?" I asked, in delightful anticipation. The scene came back to me as clearly as if it were just happening.

"Told him to attend to his fatherly duties," said Benedict. "Told him to watch over you and protect you. Because I already regarded you as mine—spoken for by me. And that, in the fulness of time, I should be coming round to make you my wife. But, my darling Joanna—you grew up too quickly for me!"

Again the owl's cry, and, surely, this time it must have been a nightingale's song. Miraculously, I was nestling in Benedict's arms, my fingers questing the texture of the shoulders of his coat, half my mind marvelling at the difference from being held by my dear, faithful Robert Vyner.

"You were a very long time in coming round," I whispered. "It took my running away to make you do that."

He held me away from him, searching my face with his deeply shadowed eyes.

"I'm glad you ran away," he said. "But for that, I might never have had the determination and boldness. I might have waited—and God knows how long—for Piers to die, so that we could be man and wife in the complete sense."

I hid my face against his shoulder again. In a very small voice that sounded totally unlike my own, I said: "I'm glad you came after me. No matter what the pain and misunderstanding, I'm glad it happened the way it did. If you had waited, you might have waited forever. We could be old and never have known—this."

His lips found mine. I had never kissed or been kissed in passion, and had always wondered how it was done; I was agreeably surprised to find that Nature had provided for the answer to come all unbidden.

Down below, the stable clock chimed the hour of seven.

"Benedict," I said.

"Yes, my darling?"

"You are the rightful master of Mallion *now*?"

"Oh, yes, my darling."

"And our firstborn son—he will be master of Mallion one day?"

"Oh, emphatically, my darling."

CHAPTER 9

There was very little wind: not enough to make ghost noises in the chimney, but sufficient to draw flames from the beechwood logs in the fireplace and make them crackle merrily.

I bathed in front of the fire, and then put on the nightdress and matching *peignoir* of lilac silk. Janey brushed my hair one hundred times, while I stroked the bows of my *peignoir* and felt as pampered as a princess.

" 'Tis loverly you look, ma'am," she said.

"Thank you, Janey," I said.

" 'Tis the talk of the servants' hall, the way you were looking so pretty at supper with Mr Trevallion tonight," she said. "Begging your pardon, ma'am, but there was scarcely a soul—grooms, gardeners, and all—as didn't make an excuse to come and peep into the refectory through the serving door. They all wished both your healths and happinesses. 'Twas like having a new bride at Mallion all over again, they said."

I smiled at my reflection. "I do feel rather bride-like, I have to admit," I said.

"And Mr Trevallion," said Janey. "Never took his eyes off you all the meal, that he didn't. Lovely to see him, 'twas."

That struck a cord of memory . . .

"You told me the other day," I said. "And it was in this very room—that my husband was in the habit of looking at me in a certain sort of way. Now—what sort of look is this look that Mr Trevallion gives me, Janey. Tell me now."

The girl blushed crimson, then covered her face with her hands.

"Oh, come, child," I scolded mildly. "It can't be all that terrible. Out with it."

She lowered her hands and looked down at her shoe, tracing the pattern of the carpet. "Well, ma'am . . ."

"Yes?"

"Well, all the servants do say—and I have seen it myself—when that you're nigh, the master do follow you with his eyes, and with the sort of look that do warm a body's heart. As if—as if . . ."

"Yes?" I breathed.

"As if, begging your pardon, ma'am, as if you were the most precious and wonderful thing in his whole world. As if you were part of him, and when you went away and out of the room, that part of him went too. That's the way he do look at you, ma'am."

I blinked away tears. "And you've noticed this, Janey—ever since you first came?" I asked.

"Why, yes, ma'am," she cried. "And I've been here no time at all. The other servants, they say 'twas always thus. From the first day you and the master did come here from Jamaicy, there were never any doubt in anyone's mind but that the master would have you for his wife sooner or later. Pardon me for saying so, ma'am—but you did ask me."

"That's all right, Janey," I smiled. "I'm not offended, I assure you."

So that was it. Benedict had worn his feelings so openly that everyone had noticed and commented—everyone but me. If only I had known—the misery and heartache I could have spared us both. And how like Benedict, with his unbending code of honour, not to reveal his true feelings to me. If I had not run away and forced his hand, he would have loved me from afar till we were both old and grey and waiting for the bell and the sexton. The pride of the Trevallions!

"The warming pan's been in for over half an hour, ma'am,

and 'twill be as warm as a nest," said Janey, turning back the coverlet.

I slipped off my *peignoir* and crept between the lavender-scented sheets, while she drew out from the bottom of the bed the copper pan full of flowing charcoal. My bare feet were deliciously cosseted by the luxuriant warmth it left behind.

Janey tucked me in and smoothed the pillow around my head. "Will that be all, ma'am?" she asked.

"Yes, thank you, Janey," I assured her. "Good night."

"Good night, ma'am." The girl paused at the door. She looked very young and defenceless, and reminded me of my own self in those long-gone days at Roswithiel, before my life was changed. "I was to say from all in the servants' hall how glad we are that everything's turned out all right for you and master, ma'am. And how we wish you all the best, like."

"Thank you, Janey. Thank them all, please."

I sank back against my pillow and closed my eyes. Yes, everything had turned out all right. Janey and the servants were referring to the fact that news had come from Truro that there were to be no criminal proceedings against Benedict for attempting to conceal Feyella's death at the hands of his insane brother—an attempt that he had made, as I had guessed, further to shield me from the horror of the Trevallions' secret. There were other matters that had been happily settled between Benedict and me over supper. His mother, it was agreed, would continue to be kept in happy ignorance about Piers. Little Jackie was to be sent overland, in the care of a good nursemaid, to Switzerland, where the mountain air must surely arrest the course of his consumption and restore him to us as a sturdy young Trevallion who would grow up to play a proper part in the running of the vast estates that had once been his father's.

Everything was all right. We had settled everything and everyone to our mutual satisfaction. And yet, over that memorable and protracted supper, neither of us had mentioned the other, or both of us as a pair. I lie—the delicate subject was very lightly touched upon when Benedict, refusing a second glass of wine, had wryly alluded to his former heavy drinking, which, he said, had been his only consolation (and a poor one at that, he added) during a certain unhappy period of his life. We had both smiled at each other over that.

I nestled down lower in my beautiful carved pine bed and let my mind slip into a languorous daydream. I saw myself back in my little bedroom at Mr Albert's house in Ludgate Hill, where the chimes of St Paul's told every quarter of an hour. And now it was nearly eleven o'clock . . .

A clip-clop of a hansom cab in the street outside, and the sound of the cabbie calling his horse to a halt; the thud of the door knocker; voices in the hall . . .

As if prompted by my imaginings, the chimes of Castle Mallion rang out across the frosty night, over the towers and battlements, across the shore and the wild, wide sea and all the wonderful Western land.

Eleven chimes. I looked up, and Benedict was at the open door, with all Heaven in his sea-blue Trevallion eyes. And the earth stood still.

1